Praise for *The MisAdventures of Miss Lilly*

"[F]rothy, saucy chick-lit for fans of all things country, and Lilly Atkins is Erin Brockovich in boots, ensuring plenty of sass and Southern charm." – **Foreword Reviews** on *So Many Boots, So Little Time*

"Charming and heartfelt, this complicated love story delivers a well-developed journey of self-discovery and romance." – **Kirkus Reviews** on *So Many Boots, So Little Time*

"…full of sassy, gun-carrying, badass women. Lloyd checks off all the appropriate boxes — suspense, drama and humor — to keep readers turning the pages." – **Romance Times** on *So Many Boots, So Little Time*

"Prior fans will be delighted at the new twists and turns, while newcomers who have entered the roller coaster of her life will [find] themselves hanging on for the rollicking ride." -**Midwest Book Review** on *So Many Boots, So Little Time*

"[E]very ingredient has been perfectly measured, and it works… With sparkling wit, Southern charm, and a steady pace, Miss Lilly has hit her stride." – **Kirkus Review** on *These Boots Are Made for Butt-Kickin'*

"Lilly Atkins is the Stephanie Plum of the South." – **Amazon Readers**

"[P]art-charming chick lit romp, part cold-blooded murder mystery, and all parts girl power." – **Manhattan Book Review** on *These Boots Are Made for Butt-Kickin'*

"Delightfully fresh and original in its approach... returns surprises again and again - truly a standout." – ***Midwest Book Review* on *These Boots Are Made for Butt-Kickin'***

"Featuring a heroine worth accompanying home, [this punchy] debut begs for a sequel." – ***Kirkus Review* on *Home Is Where Your Boots Are***

"[A] 'chic lit' story with Southern spice...entertainment reading at its best." - ***Midwest Book Review* on *Home Is Where Your Boots Are***

"...perfect for beach and poolside." – ***Book Delight* on *Home Is Where Your Boots Are***

Other books by
Kalan Chapman Lloyd

The MisAdventures of Miss Lilly

Volume One: Home Is Where Your Boots Are

Volume Two: These Boots Are Made for Butt-Kickin'

The Prologues: Blame It All On My Boots (exclusive reader novella)

Mo(u)rning Joy: a memoir

So Many Boots, So Little Time

The MisAdventures of Miss Lilly
Volume Three

Kalan Chapman Lloyd

So Many Boots, So Little Time is a work of fiction. Names, characters, places and incidents are the products of the author's imagination or used fictitiously. Any resemblances to actual persons, alive or dead, businesses, events or a locale is entirely coincidental.

2016 Rebelle Press Trade Paperback Edition

Copyright © 2016 by Kalan Chapman Lloyd.
Excerpt from *When God-Fearing Women Put On Boots* by Kalan Chapman Lloyd copyright © 2016 by Rebelle Press.

All rights reserved.

Edited by Kara Beth Chapman
Published in the United States by Rebelle Press, distributed by CreateSpace

This book contains an excerpt from the forthcoming book, *When God-Fearing Women Put On Boots: The MisAdventures of Miss Lilly, Vol. 4*, by Kalan Chapman Lloyd. This excerpt has been released for this edition only and may not reflect the final content of the forthcoming edition.

ISBN 978-1523744978
eBook ISBN 1523744979

Cover Image: Catie Lawrence
Fonts: Euphorigenic and Honey Script

Printed in the United States of America

Rebelle Press Trade Paperback edition: October 2016

So Many Boots, So Little Time

Kalan Chapman Lloyd

For Rafe
And his Poppa

Chapter One

"Do you think they'll arrest me for running over someone?"

I looked up from a legal brief to glance at my typically overly dramatic sister as she entered my office. Tally doesn't walk into a room, she sashays. When the situation arises, she whips out a catwalk strut, which is ballsy and sharp, and appealingly mean if it suits her purpose of the moment. Tally, with her blue, blue eyes, is the stuff a country boy's fantasy is made of: six-foot tall with a body to rival any supermodel. She'd once been just that, until she'd allegedly decided eating was more fun than posing and had come home. Long, curly hair worn too long for convention is deep auburn that picks up sunny highlights in the Oklahoma summer sunshine.

Today, Tallulah Belle was dressed to the tens in turquoise pleather leggings, a black lace bustier, and red Indian blanket sweater. She'd shoehorned her extra-large feet into red leather cowboy boots with cream heart cutouts. Lips glossed, hair atumble, and eyes rimmed in lizard green, she looked like a sex-kittened Big Bird on diversity day at Sesame Street.

"What, exactly, are you talking about?" I took off the readers that were more to make me feel smart than to actually help my eyesight, and rubbed the bridge of my very nice nose. Nonnie, my grandma and legal secretary, had already gone home for the day, and I'd been finishing up some stuff before I headed for home myself.

"I clipped him," Tally informed me, not unproudly. "On Main Street. I'm thinking I probably just broke a leg or maybe a rib or two. It was just enough of a tap to bump him. It didn't feel like I actually ran *over* him. There were lots of witnesses."

My head was beginning to ache. Tally can never be rushed, prodded or shooed along. I picked up my sweaty tea glass and settled back into my newly reupholstered, navy leather office chair. If she wasn't finished with her story by the time a deputy might show up to arrest her, I'd take my cow money and bail her out.

"I'm assuming it wasn't an accident?" I asked mockingly. She narrowed her eyes and screwed up her otherwise beautiful face into a grimace.

"Hell, no. I've wanted to do that for a long time." I nodded plaintively, placating her.

"So which old boyfriend did you run over? Dan, Ethan, Todd? Who was it, sister dear? I'm on pins and needles as to who would cause you such consternation that you'd take it upon yourself to exact revenge in broad daylight on a Thursday afternoon."

She looked at me quizzically and her head tilted toward the right.

"Me? Sissy, I..."

A large, male silhouette filled my office doorway, and I glanced beyond Tally's grandeur. My jaw slipped, my heart skipped, and my palms started to sweat.

"Hello, darlin'."

Holy shit.

Chapter Two

"Hello, darlin'," he said again. I couldn't speak, seeing as how my heart was in my throat, and currently cutting off my words and the breath that hadn't already been knocked out of me.

"Well, well, well, if it isn't Mr. Lyin', cheatin' SOB," Tally said. He turned toward her, taking his eyes off me.

"You hit me with your car!" he exclaimed, pointing a long, tanned finger at Tally. She pointed a long, pale, Easter-egg-grass-green-tipped finger toward him.

"Allegedly. And I only tapped you, if anything." She shrugged nonchalantly, like she ran over guys every day, but her eyes were flashing and her chest was slightly splotchy.

"What'n the hell're you doing here?" Finally able to speak, my redneck vernacular and Southern drawl were enhanced by the stress of the situation. Two things happen when I get nervous: I puke and I start talking like I have marbles in my mouth.

"Just thought I'd come visit," he told me, his blue eyes flashing at an inside joke I was apparently not privy to. "It's been a while."

"Not long enough," I responded curtly, trying to quell the dizziness and the greasy slide of nausea. He ignored my response and sat down in the chair Tally hadn't chosen to occupy. Apparently unharmed by being run over on Main Street, he stretched his long legs out in front of him, crossing one super-slim ankle over the other.

When he'd entered the room, Tally had scurried to stand sentry beside me. I stood myself, in an effort to get some power and hide a deep breath.

"Miss me?" he asked smoothly, not even sarcastic. Van Payton Ehlers the Third has always been the biggest buyer of his own hype.

"Absolutely," I told him shortly, "Like I miss that boil you had removed from your ass." He blanched but didn't redden or ruffle.

"Now darlin'," he responded, wagging a buffed and polished index finger in my direction. Tally snorted beside me. It was a toss up as to who would shoot him first.

"I'll ask you again, Van. What the hell are you doing here?"

"I came to talk to you."

"Drop dead," I told the gutless wonder I once told I'd marry. I watched his dark blue eyes flash as he dusted a speck of invisible lint from his designer jeans. He had on a money-green shirt, custom, with sleeves rolled up to reveal purple paisley cuffs. The same purple was on the inside of the collar. He had on black tasseled loafers, soles scuffed from short walks on concrete and longer treks on expensive carpet and imported tile, and coordinated purple and green socks with boats on them. Big class rings rested on each hand, one from the University of Texas, one from the same law school I'd attended. His dark blonde hair was moussed, waxed, and perfectly tousled. And probably not the only thing waxed, I thought. He smelled like Ralph Lauren. He'd had enough sense to lose the pocket square before he'd hit the state line, I noticed.

I'd met Van at a charity poker event at Southern Methodist University Dedman School of Law. We'd started flirting after I'd cleaned him out. Van thought I was cute with my poker skills, my Oklahoma accent, and the package it all came in, I guess. That's what he said, mostly.

Van is tall. His eyes are an inky blue and his hair a golden, glistening, surfer-boy blonde. He's perfectly manicured; clipped and shorn, like a rather large, well-kept, expensive breed of dog. Like a Boykin Spaniel, I've heard those are fancy. One that was a few genes short of being able to compete. You know, the kind that you pay a lot of money for, only to find out they had some awful disease like alopecia. Van is also an idiot. You might be wondering why I agreed to marry him.

Van can be charming. A very charming asshole who had cheated on me with his secretary. It had taken me some time to discover that all of Van's supposed charm was just a jacked-up compilation of thin affectations.

I got that now. At the time, I'd needed to believe that two pretty packages could make a great life, but God, not so very gently, had shown me the error of my ways. Now, I was embarrassed that the rather large, alcohol-bloated, high-strung, highbred labradoodle had shown up in my town, in front of my people, to remind me and everyone else of my mistakes.

xxx

He had no real answer.

Tally and I sat again after he exited the office, and I tried to slow my racing heart. More perplexed and anxious than when she'd come in the first time, I watched Tally struggle for good words.

"He looked fat," she told me consolingly.

"He's six-seven. He'll never be fat."

"He's doughy. Too much drinking." I smiled at her conspiratorially.

"Thanks." I appreciated her trying to make me feel better.

"What's going on, Lil?" Tally asked me, her blue eyes locked on me with an air of a bulldog taking hold of a bone.

"I don't have any idea," I told her.

Tally shook her head, but her gaze remained unwavering.

"He hasn't called? You haven't emailed? He just showed up here out of the blue?"

I rolled my shoulders, feeling a familiar tightening as they rose toward my ears and stiffened. There was a stifling panic messing with me, making me want to run and hide.

"Nothing," I said. "I have no idea why he's here." And I didn't want to talk about it. I'd hightailed my ass out of Texas less than a year ago after finding Van cheating on me while the countdown to our wedding had clicked cheerily on my calendar. I'd put it all behind me, and as far as I was concerned, it was just a blip. Van was just a blip. A tiny, insignificant speck of jackass. I stopped chewing the inside of my mouth when I tasted blood. I avoided Tally's continually searching look and started running my tongue on the top of my mouth.

"Oh, sister," Tally said gently.

"What?" I bit out a little too harshly. She shook her head sadly.

"I'm sorry," she said sincerely, without a trace of comic. I turned my head and blinked my eyes, clamping my teeth together.

"I don't want to talk about it," I said shortly.

Tally nodded, "Want to cry?" she asked, a teasing tone, but serious.

I don't believe crying solves a whole lot of problems. It's a necessary evil, but as a rule, it doesn't always herald progressive results. So I generally avoid it.

"No," I said.

She gave me one last look and then finally nodded. "You let me know when you do," she said. I set my mouth mulishly.

Our moment was interrupted by Tally's phone jangling. She rolled her eyes and answered. Five seconds later, the caller had Tally's boots off my desk, a frown screwing up her perfect face, and she was gesturing toward me with agitation to get up off my butt and grab my stuff. She was halfway out the door before I caught up to her. On the street, she turned left without looking back for me. I jogged to catch up to her. She finally clicked off the phone and turned around.

"We need to go home."

"What's wrong?" I asked, stricken at the idea of a problem with my people.

"The FBI's there."

"What? Tally, stop!" I grabbed her long arm and spun her back around. She finally slowed down so I could catch up with her long stride. I somewhat trotted alongside her. "What's going on?" I asked.

"Something about the cattle," she said, digging in her purse.

"What about the cattle?" I asked, as I dug in my own for my keys.

"Someone freakin' stole them," she answered, pulling out a pair of pink rhinestone-studded sunglasses.

xxx

Once Tally had assured me the call was about the livestock and nothing to do with our family being hurt, I agreed to split up to go home. I didn't feel much better at the idea of harm coming to any of the animals on the farm, but I could calm down. I'm a terrible rancher's daughter. I love all the animals like pets. Yes, I eat meat. And yes, I most definitely damn well wear leather, but it's hard not to have a certain fondness for heifers that will follow you around like dogs. That's the juxtaposition of my life.

My name is Lilly Atkins. Lillian Katherine Atkins to be exact, a nod to my great-grandmothers. My Nonnie calls me Lilly Kay. I'm an attorney. And an unofficial private investigator. And God keeps rescuing me from bad decisions.

I'm tall, I have long legs, and my nose, never broken, is perfect. The rest of me is put together in a way that is best described as interesting. Probably because of the height and my sharp chin. I have hair currently the color of dark honey, which has been long and curly, bobbed and straightened, and cut short and crazy. In that order. My eyes are hazel, and mostly appear a weird yellow color. I once tried black eyeshadow in an attempt to look sexy. I ended up looking like a vampire. I'm *not* real sexy. And no one would ever accuse me of being an ingénue. But I'm smart and tough. And have a lot of character-building experiences under my belt. And I have been doing a lot of yoga, lately. I feel centered. I think. Although I often catch myself drifting from concentrating on my breathing to planning my next day's outfits or property disputes, which involves a lot of livestock.

Which brought me back around to Mama's summons... Apparently, that morning, Daddy and Poppa had discovered they were missing several head of cattle. The expensive ones. Which led them to call Sheriff Clay. Who supposedly called the FBI. And the Texas Rangers.

Meanwhile, back at the ranch, I wasn't sure what I was going to find.

Chapter Three

At my lipstick-red Jeep Wrangler (bought to replace the since-wrecked Jeep Cherokee I'd bought to replace the Jag I'd driven in Dallas), I hiked my red pencil skirt up and hauled my ass into it. I threw my bag into the backseat and pointed the Jeep in the direction of home, pulling out of the lot allocated to my office and taking a left at the first green light onto Main Street.

It was bricked sidewalks on both sides, most of the bricks bearing inscriptions from Brooks' oldest families, and some newer ones, mine included, done during a fundraising campaign for the new, shiny, black steel benches that now lined the street. Benches that all faced toward the storefronts, and not the street. This was a sore subject in Brooks, as, well, it looked stupid. There were newspaper articles, editorials, petitions, a general Facebook outcry, and a whole bunch of gossip carried on the wind. The crisis came to a head during the annual Christmas parade, when it was discovered that the new benches were, essentially, non-functional for that purpose. So someone had dug up the old wooden benches, which hadn't been destroyed, and hauled them from the armory building, to line the street so everyone's grandmamma could "freakin' have a place to sit." Because, seriously, "How in the hell is my mama gonna get to see Sissy Ann in her cheerleader uniform if she can't sit on the front row?"

Seriously.

After the parade was over and errant candy swept up and swept away by a howling wind the next day, the old benches stayed. Mostly because the city workers who had first moved them were incredibly lazy and kept allegedly "losing" the work order to move them back. Interim Deputy Mayor Janice Feldman, with almost a year under her belt, was enjoying her stint, and since no one had gotten real worked up to have an election, she was firmly in place and had no real strong feelings one way or the other. Except her middle son was crowned prince of the winter formal and her mother-in-law wasn't real steady on her feet. So the benches, both sets, stayed, end to end, the weathered wood bumping their fancier, expensive counterparts.

Downtown Brooks was like that, in some ways. All of Brooks was like that, in some way. None of the downtown buildings matched. Brooks is one of the oldest towns in Oklahoma, and because it was built before the idea of having a building code was invented, no two were the same. And each building, when built, had been done so by a different owner, and everyone wanted their own way, so… developers now probably would have died. But in some way, it worked, a patchwork kaleidoscope of old brick, newer wood, glass fronts, colored awnings, and always, for as long as I could remember, bright, friendly smiles.

A jewelry store that was actually internationally famous for their custom designs, a prom and pageant store that served all five surrounding counties (and currently boasted the current Miss Oklahoma), a shoe store that had survived the internet shopping influx, a Christmas ornament store, a bakery which, in my estimation, should have been world-famous, two beauty salons that didn't compete, and one women's store that served clientele mostly on a one on one basis. All this was peppered with various insurance, accounting, and law offices, including yours truly. The regional college where my mama had held court for my entire childhood lay due west of this sprawl. Banks anchored downtown, and there were various buildings that housed the Cherokee Indian Tribe and their projects.

    The street signs in Brooks are in both English and Cherokee, a nod to who had been there first. Something I'd taken for granted as ordinary until Van had pointed it out the first time I brought him home.

    I took a right at the last stoplight on the edge of town and hit the gas a little harder on the long stretch toward a dirt-road turnoff, anxious to find out what was going on at home. I rounded a curve topping the hill that led into the valley where most of the ranch lay. It was mid-March, and everything was stretching and growing, shaking the crackly brown and gray, shedding the huddled posture of winter. The creamy dogwood had come out in full force that very weekend, the baby-duck yellow jonquils had pushed through their waxy green bases, no threat of snow imminent. The robins were swooping, the cattle were lowing, and the blue heelers were paws-deep in the creeks. It was Spring for all of northeast Oklahoma to see.

    Our ranch sits deep in the valley of some of the rolling hills that occupy most of our part of Oklahoma. There are pockets of land on top of one of the hills, where the natural spring runs off down into the valley, for growing and grazing. We raise mostly Gelbviehs, an expensive brand that originated from Bavaria. Mama likes that because it sounds fancy. They're show cattle. But they taste good. There are also several cheaper breeds, but the proud sign on the main fence announces the fancy ones.

My great-grandfather, so the legend goes, was a sheep rancher. A rancher who lost all but a couple head in a drive from Louisiana back to his home state of Texas. This drive included his wife and two sons. After a breath and forming a plan to rebuild, they headed north to Oklahoma. Without the sheep.

With a rich Tex-Mex heritage influencing my great-grandma, and likely the fact that she was damn tired of running herself ragged, she crowned the green hills "Place of Peace" or "Lugar de la Paz." Grandpa bought cattle and built his wife a house. Grandma Lilly bought the pink couch Tally liked to dramatically throw herself on and announced, whether by fate, or her own force of will, that their luck had changed. So here they had stayed. And my Poppa after them. My daddy, who had inherited his own oil business, had also pitched in when he'd married Mama. His business savvy and Poppa's technical ingenuity had built "la Paz," as Tally likes to call it, to its current glory.

This year was the fiftieth anniversary of that fateful trek to Oklahoma. Mama and Nonnie were planning a Golden Jubilee celebration. We even had t-shirts. And now someone was rustling our cattle. Mama was going to be so pissed.

XXX

I pulled the Jeep beside Tally's T-bird, noticing she'd already gone inside. Mama's edict must have been emphatic. There was a big group of booted men right outside Nonnie's house, clustered around a tailgate. And Tally wasn't in the middle of them.

I got out and ignored my Nonnie's front porch and the potted plastic and wax flowers from Hobby Lobby, just yet exchanged for fake purple hydrangeas. I headed straight for my best friend's husband's tailgate. The grouping, from my initial standpoint, had consisted of an array of jeans, boots, chambray shirts, two suits, and several hats, ball cap and cowboy. On a more thorough inspection, I had to resist the urge to turn tail and track back to the flowers. My daddy stood, an aggravated and angry stance to his typical find-humor-in-all-situations demeanor. Today, he was more Sam Elliot than Jeff Foxworthy. His dark brown shirt was untucked in the back and his dark, creased jeans were splattered with the weird green special to money… and manure. His cognac brown, square-toe, Caiman alligator horseman's boots were covered in the same. Daddy's particular about his boots, which are all of the horseman's variety, because deep down, he's still a rich kid, no matter how often pretending to be a redneck hick might suit him.

My Poppa was thoughtful at the very edge of the group, dirty ball cap tilted, the back of his chambray shirt damp with sweat, gazing hard at the fields in the distance. His boots weren't covered in manure like Daddy's, but the nut brown, rubber-soled, cracked leather, steel toe, pull-on work boots were dusty instead, like he'd

So Many Boots, So Little Time

been in a different corral, or maybe one of the barns. Poppa's boots are custom, because as much as he doesn't care about frivolity, his extra-long, narrow feet can't pull off off-the-rack.

Scotty Wiseman, my best friend's husband, was there in serviceable light-brown, lace-up ropers. Sheriff Clay also stood seriously in dark gray traditional western boots. He stood with two unidentified men, one in worn Wranglers, expensive and serious chocolate ostrich-skin square toes with what looked like a python inlay, a dark navy wool suit jacket and a crisp white-grey felt cowboy hat. The other had on newer cowboy denim, an orange polo shirt, and equally loud and proud orange and black cowboy boots, into which his jeans had been tucked. He was wearing that same distinct green color as Daddy, and the smell that went with it. When I got closer, I saw the insignia of my alma mater on the left side of his chest. It seemed like the wrong time to offer the universal sign of my undergrad, two pistoled hands up in the air. There were so many of them, big and coiled with frustration, that it was almost overwhelming. All the boots stood in the gravel stomping and shifting… shuffling like angry feral horses.

The sheriff, the unidentified men, my Poppa's worried gaze, my Daddy's battle-ready stance weren't what gave me pause. The cause of my consternation and the bubble starting in my chest belonged to the fact that rounding out the men was Spencer Locke, in a suit he'd no doubt had on at the courthouse, and inappropriate, shined, amber colored, Cole Haan dress shoes, talking to the polo-shirted casual boot-wearer. Next to him was Cash Stetson, the recipient of my one gunshot and one punch. And also a little ole stomp on his injured-by-the-gunshot toe.

Just a little one.

Both Spencer and Cash looked helpful. And not out of place. I clenched my fists at my sides and picked my way through the grass toward them in my navy patent alligator stilettos. I keep a pair of shiny brown riding boots in the Jeep for occasions when investigations lead me out of office without time to change clothes. But I hadn't had time to change today.

I wasn't sure who I wanted to punch more: Spencer, for inserting himself into yet another situation that might be helped by his cool, calm, collected demeanor or Cash for simply being there, unafraid that I would kill him.

Spencer Locke is in the habit of rescuing me. He's the nephew of my legal mentor and had come to town to work for his uncle Charlie shortly before I'd arrived home with my tail between my legs. Spencer stood shoulders above the rest of the group of bulging testosterone. He has dark eyes, muscles for days, and a cocky grin, when he allows himself to grin. He's always perfectly put-together. His shoulders are Olympic-worthy, his hands are rough, and a harder jaw I've never wanted to smack. He's rescued me three times. We've kissed twice. He doesn't like me. Spencer is also a former FBI agent turned attorney, turned local lend-a-hand to the FBI. Which would explain his presence. Cash, however, required an explanation.

The two of them turned toward me. Spencer gave me a short nod of acknowledgment, but I caught the faint detection of an eye roll as he turned back. Cash sauntered over.

"Lilly…" he drawled, with a flashing smile and an obvious once-over directed toward me. I thought it was likely sexual. But he could have been checking me for weapons…

"Cash," I nodded, avoiding eye contact.

I used to make out with Cash. When I was young and dumb and convinced that I could get men to do my bidding with a bat of my eyelashes. I wasn't prone to doing that, but I held the theory. Since then, he'd become a doctor, gotten married, become involved in a black-market body smuggling ring, become an almost-divorced widower, gone to rehab for a gambling addiction, pretended to gain enlightenment, and gotten out.

Only to show up on my doorstep. Again. Oh, and had been physically assaulted by yours truly before and during rehab. There was that.

Today, he looked good. Dried out, buffed up, and turned out. His auburn hair still shone red through the shots of gray. His blue eyes were clear like Tally's, instead of watery and rundown. His muscles returned to glory. The paunch gone. The jowls erased. Sharp, clear-eyed. Dangerous.

If Spencer looked like everyone's idea of a savior, Cash, looked like an outlaw. Like a Tim McGraw music video, circa late '90s. A black baseball cap rested easily on his head. His blue eyes flashed underneath, highlighted by his dusty, heathered blue t-shirt. Cut just close enough to hint at a working set of abs. Dark jeans led to a set of black, exotic, pointed-toe, full-quill ostrich boots. It was my personal opinion that he should have been wearing snakeskin. To warn the rest of the world. The jeans were cut just close enough to show off a body that had once heralded the title of All-State Wide Receiver.

I can tell you all this objectively. I'm over Cash. Cash is Cash. And I'm Lilly, and there were some old habits I fell back into upon my return to Brooks, but habits were all they were. My trigger finger hasn't twitched in a while. I've been drinking green tea, listening to lots of Reba, and feeling Zen and centered. So I slapped the bubble back down, took a deep tantric breath, and gave Cash a sisterly pat on the shoulder, leaving him to walk toward my Poppa. I was satisfied to see he looked surprise. Good. I was Zen, but I was still me. And I liked it anytime I could catch anyone off-guard.

I caught Poppa Joe's attention with a tug on his shirtsleeve.

"What happened?"

He glanced down at me, distracted, then pulled me up under his armpit. His sweat mixed with the smell of grease and heavy-duty de-greasing machine-shop soap. He continued to gaze off in the distance.

"They took the twenty from the bottom pasture that we'd cut from the herd to sell to Joe Nakes. He was coming tomorrow to pick them up." I narrowed my eyes. I'd learned in my short stint as a small town lawyer in my hometown there were no such things as coincidences.

"Were they branded?"

He nodded. "Branded, ear tagged, registered."

"So what the heck are they going to do with them? They can't sell them without papers." He sighed.

"They can, quickly at one of the smaller sale barns, on the promise of papers. If they don't recognize our brand, no one will think to ask. They'll probably go across to Arkansas."

Hence the fact that the FBI was there.

"Any clues?"

He shook his head. "They backed up a trailer to the gate where the heifers were. It didn't look like they went all the way in the field, just stayed on the road. Snipped the gate lock with a pair of bolt cutters." He shook his head again. "Damn. This has never happened."

I'd never heard my grandfather curse. Ever. I squeezed his arm then left him to go check on my dad. He didn't appear to look as violated as Poppa Joe. He was ready to strike, angrily sketching a picture of our brand. It had been brought fifty years ago with Grandpa Cal, the circle on top and the cross below looking like the universal sign for girl power. Nothing indicated any such intention by my great-grandfather, but I'd always found it funny just the same.

Daddy finished his rough drawing and stepped back, handing it to the tall, Tommy Lee Jones character in the dark navy blazer and jeans. He had on a bolo tie and stiff starched shirt; a shiny gold star displayed proudly on the left side of his chest. All the other boots stepped in to examine it. I watched Cash go to stand by Poppa.

"You okay?" I eased in close to Daddy. I wasn't anything close to afraid, but I'm not dumb. Don't poke the bear. He glanced down as though he hadn't noticed I'd been there at all. He offered me a wry twist of his Magnum PI mouth, but was too distracted to meet my eyes.

"Fine." I nodded and let him lie to me. Everyone seemed to run out of steam at that moment, and they all collectively turned to form a circle. Hats were adjusted, belt buckles jostled, throats were cleared. Scotty pinched the bridge of his nose. Sheriff Clay repositioned his suspenders.

"Alright then. Round up the usual suspects," Sheriff Clay sighed, and nodded at Scotty, who moved to make a call.

Chapter Four

"Who are the usual suspects?" I asked Spencer, ignoring Cash, wondering what he was doing there, but not about to give him the satisfaction of asking in front of him. The two earlier unidentified men had left, after they'd been introduced as a Special Texas Ranger who lived in Oklahoma and was supposedly an expert in cattle rustling, and an FBI Agent with jurisdiction across the border in Arkansas. The Ranger had been the Tommy Lee in the blue blazer and white hat. The FBI Agent, who'd been more than friendly with Spencer before he'd gone, had been the one with the Oklahoma State shirt and farm boots.

Spencer looked at me with a shake of his head.

"Not your monkeys, not your circus. Stay away from this one." I put a hand on a hip and pointed a finger at him.

"Definitely my circus," I told spit-shined and spit-polished Spencer Locke with force. "This is MY family. This is OUR home. This is definitely MY circus," I reiterated. I could feel Cash's delight at my wrath being directed somewhere other than him. I whirled around to take in his smirk and tried real hard to channel my inner frustration into peace, but I hadn't mastered the chataranga pose. Or my mouth.

"What the hell are you doing here?" I asked him.

"I asked him to help."

They said it simultaneously, their shoulders coming together as they stepped in to unite, one set slightly above the other, but impressively intimidating just the same. I looked between Daddy and Spencer, confused.

"Help with what?"

"The ranch," Daddy said, stepping smoothly in front of Spencer. I noticed before he did that, Spencer had started to answer. And his answer wasn't the same as Daddy's. Spencer closed his mouth and stepped back. Cash had a wary look on his face. I'm not sure if he thought I was going to shoot him. Or yell at him. I eyed my father and his flagging allegiance, one that didn't always lie with Tally and me, but rather on the side of what he deemed most appropriate. And we all know Tally isn't that appropriate. I took a deep breath and fixed Daddy with an "I'll deal with you later look." I turned back to Spencer, breathing in through my nose and out through my mouth.

"I'll invite you to dinner if you'll tell me who the suspects are," I said sweetly, attempting to disarm him. He didn't get the chance to answer before my father, the traitor, sweetened the pot.

"You can both stay for dinner. Let's find the cattle."

My brain was scrambling, trying to figure out a way to calmly and serenely uninvite Cash to dinner. I didn't need my first crush and the hottest attorney on the planet eating my Nonnie's biscuits at the same damn time. Spencer just shrugged and Cash smiled his Cheshire cat smile. I was still flailing around when a powder blue BMW SUV with Texas plates pulled into my Nonnie's driveway, almost taking out the post marking the entrance.

"Sonuva.... Good grief." I muttered, bothered that I wasn't all that surprised.

"Who the hell's that?" Cash asked, eying the car suspiciously. Spencer said nothing. Daddy and I watched Van climb out of the car and sniff the air, looking around to spot us with a jaunty wave, shaking the gravel off his shiny black shoes. I could see my father's normally placid dark brown eyes squint in irritation.

"What the hell is he doing here?" he asked me, his eyes never leaving Van.

"Not exactly sure," I told him slowly.

I never knew if Rex Atkins liked Van. He'd never said one way or the other. He was kind enough to offer him the remote at Christmas, if not his chair, wrote checks for the wedding, and told me that as long as I was happy, he was happy. He'd offered to come to Dallas and kick his ass when I'd called to tell my parents I was coming home and why. But he'd never offered a bad word about Van, other than to accurately deem him an adulterating asshole. But that was just fact, so…

It must have been left over anger then, at the situation with the cattle, that caused him to do it. He'd already said two cuss words in my presence in the last fifteen minutes, which was a record. So it must have been frustration at the low-down, cowardly criminals that caused him to unholster the pistol he carried for shooting snakes and level it at Van.

Van stopped short, and his hands went up comically and quick. I felt Cash smile. Spencer sighed beside me.

"Get back in the car," Daddy instructed. My earlier pique at him over Cash dissolved with the quick raise of a .22. I hid a grin. I knew he wasn't going to shoot Van. Probably. Maybe.

"It's me, Mr. Atkins. Van," Van called, as though that were going to help.

"Yes, I know, son. Get back in the car."

Van looked confused and torn, looking to me and trying to take in Cash and Spencer. I was simply overwhelmed by all the tall testosterone and boots in combative stances around me. I took a minute to look at Spencer's inappropriate shoes and then back to Van's. Somehow, Spencer seemed to fit. Van, did not.

"Rex Atkins! You put that gun down this second! What if the neighbors drive by? Don't act like white-trash in my yard," Nonnie instructed my daddy with a yell. Nonnie, who regularly picked up road kill to place on the hoods of resident cheaters, and who had accidently tased my Poppa several months ago.

On accident.

We think.

But still.

Daddy lowered the gun and gave a nod of apology toward his mother-in-law. She harrumphed and adjusted the fake flowers in hot pink pots on her porch.

"Y'all get inside," she instructed, addressing everyone this time. My Nonnie, Margaret Lee Culvert, otherwise known as Miss Minnie, is all of 5'2" and weighs about a buck, soaking wet. She taught first grade miscreants for most of her life and has a firm belief that she can talk to anyone the same way she talked to her students and they'll mind. She hasn't been wrong. And is not the first woman I've encountered who thinks she can make things happen by her own sheer force of will. My sister inherited this notion too. I think it's a Southern lady thing.

The tone worked. Daddy, Spencer and Cash all filed in. Cash and Daddy were used to it. Spencer had had Nonnie's cooking once, so even if he wasn't scared of Nonnie, he wasn't an idiot.

After, I realized the gun's safety had been on the whole time. Rex Atkins is big, dark, and his pirate menace could rival Rhett Butler's. But he is a teddy bear underneath the exterior. He *is* sweet and likes to pretend he's dumb, but my father is brilliant and calculating. He had quickly put Van in his place and drawn the line in the sand. And Van didn't need to know that Daddy wasn't going to kill him. It was the sentiment that counted. Truly, it was what my daddy *didn't* say that was most important.

I remembered then that he'd never said he liked Van.

Nonnie blocked the door before Van, who'd mounted the front porch steps, could go into the house.

"Van," she said with a drawl, wiping her hands on her apron. Van smiled his charming smile: fifty thousand dollars worth of braces, yearly teeth bleach, and Kiehl's lip scrub. Nonnie wasn't impressed.

"Miss Minnie, it sure is nice to see you. I apologize for showing up like this. I was just hoping Lilly wouldn't mind me visiting."

"I mind," I said before Nonnie could answer. Nonnie hit me with a slow look and a slight raise of her eyebrows, and then a discreet wink.

"Of course Van, wipe your feet *darlin'*," she emphasized the word, chalking the field for me. "I'll fix you a glass of sweet tea."

"What the hell's he doing here?" she asked me with a whisper when he'd stepped through the door.

"No idea," I said with a sigh.

"No matter." She squeezed my hand before she followed him into the house.

Southern Belle Rule #498: Keep your friends close and your ex-fiancés closer.

I knew this, but there isn't enough yoga in the world to make me want to go into that house which currently housed my first boyfriend, my former fiancé, and the guy voted Most Likely to Always Be There When I Screwed Something Up.

In an uncharacteristic display of avoidance, I sat down in the swing on my Nonnie's front porch, the sweetly cloying smell of river water and new foliage bathing the chilly humid beginning of dusk. My grandparent's house exterior was an eclectic mish-mash of whitewashed brick, practical dusty-grey siding, and a special kind of river rock specific to our region of Oklahoma. The color of the rock runs from buttery yellow, to toasted almond and, unfortunately, Texas orange. The rocks are large and flat, and held together with a special, weird mix of mud and concrete. So the story goes, when they were first extracted from the river and used as construction materials, it was because they were cheap and easy. Years later, if rocks could be extinct, they were, thus making them historically significant, and in turn, expensive. The rocks were probably worth more than the rest of the house, in truth. They were part of the original building and the west wall of them was covered in rising honeysuckle, placed there by my great-grandmother. A similarly ensconced wall lay on the western-most side of my great-grandparent's house. My current bedroom shared that wall, and in the summer, I can open the windows to let the comforting smell of honeysuckle blanket my blankets.

"Sweetheart," my mama's voiced interrupted my thoughts. I looked up. She fixed me with a look. "Sweetheart," she said again, sitting down on the swing with me, crossing her ankles in a move that would have made the Queen Mother envious.

"I'm not going in there," I said. But it wasn't all that strongly stated.

"What the hell is he doing here?" she asked me calmly.

"Which one?" I asked crankily.

"Van."

"I am not wholly sure. Tally and I couldn't get a real answer out of him," I explained.

"He just showed up out of nowhere?" she said.

"Allegedly," I responded with despondent drama. There was a long pause.

"I put Metamucil in his tea," she told me, throwing her arm around my shoulders and leaning back. Her stack of bracelets dug into my shoulder as I held back a laugh.

My mama, Elizabeth (after the Queen Mother, of course) Nina Culvert come Atkins, is known as Lizzie. She holds a Master's in English, has written two college textbooks on Medieval Lit, and currently dabbles at interior design, which means she buys stuff, arranges it in a storefront, and spends a lot of time eating cookies and drinking tea with "clients." Her hair is a highlighted strawberry blonde, her eyes are true-blue like Tally's, and her features are pretty. Just pretty. I'd spent my whole life wanting to be pretty like my mama. I gave up a few years ago after trying on a ball-gown option for my wedding. I was no princess. I'd leave that to her.

"This is the twilight zone," I told her. "You realize that, right?" She nodded with a shrug.

"I do," she agreed. "But unfortunately, right now isn't about you. Your Daddy and your Poppa are both upset, in their own weird ways, and there's no time for you to freak out over those three that somehow got invited to dinner."

"I only invited Spencer," I told her.

"Hmmmm," she said.

"I get it," I told her. "I'll get over myself."

"Good girl," she said, following me off the bench.

"Why not Cash's?" I asked as we moved to go in the house. She shot me a look.

"Sweetheart, Cash may be everyone's favorite failure these days, but he's not an idiot. He fixed his own tea." I smiled.

Chapter Five

My grandmother's house had been built in pieces. The dining room, kitchen, and master bedroom were first. The screened-in back porch/mud room/laundry room combo next. Two bedrooms and another bathroom were then added when my mother was expected. The front room and living room with formal seating came once Nonnie decided they could afford for her to be fancy. The decorating scheme is early marriage "at-war," meaning that it housed Nonnie's very distinct, feminine, frilly taste as a first layer, and then my Poppa came in and tossed all his crap around. So the antique prints of birds and flowers, the family silver and china, and the heavily patterned window treatments and upholstered furniture are all accented with guns, gun magazines, tractor parts, tractor magazines and dirty hats and boots. As far as I knew, Nonnie has never complained. She just adds more crap in an effort to overwhelm Poppa's crap.

The way the house was laid out was a blessing, I guess, because each addition currently housed one tall, long-legged male, who all had me in common, allegedly. My father and grandfather had escaped to the back patio, both with cold bottles of beer; my Nonnie's effort to calm them down. Van sat in the formal dining room, flipping through an issue of *Southern Living*, the ice in his glass dwindling as he sucked the remnants of tea. I glimpsed Cash's profile in the living room, set up in a leather rocker recliner, flipping through channels on Poppa's big screen, going back and forth between a vintage baseball game and a black and white western. I wanted to run and hide. From them. Even from the safety of my people. Just away so I could hide the deeply flawed aspects of my choices that seemed to be ever so set on exposure.

With a deep breath, I dug my fingernails into my palms to focus on that pain in the vain hope it might distract me from being faced with the irony of the first love who'd broken my heart so many times and the last one who'd so easily broken my heart, being in the same place at the same time. I ignored Cash and Van and moved to go back to the kitchen. I was met with a low, terse voice coming from Nonnie's office right off the dining room. I stood in the doorway until Spencer turned around from studying a framed map of the ranch on the wall. His phone to his ear, he did offer me a small grimace before turning back around and continuing his phone call.

Undeterred, probably because it bothered me that he looked so perfectly at home in Nonnie's very feminine office, I stayed in the doorway to wait him out. He turned back around when he sensed that I hadn't left and ended his phone call shortly thereafter.

"Who was that?" I asked. He eyed me without humor.

"A friend."

"A friend you made in the FBI?" I knew Spencer had a hard time with the truth. Unlike Cash, he always told it.

"Maybe," he hedged.

"You know, don't you, that I'll eventually find out? Fae Lynn has her ways with Scotty, even if she is knocked up and bitchy." At this he smiled slightly.

"Okay," he offered by offering nothing.

"I'll withhold dessert," I told him. He moved to go around me.

"Nah. Your grandmother likes me. She won't let you. Who's *your* friend, by the way?" He said it casually, like any old answer would do. But it was too casual. I knew he knew my story before he'd ever met me. Even if we'd never discussed it. Brooks was a hotbed of gossip and anyone would have been easily relieved of the tale of Van's deceit. But I didn't see any reason in arguing with him about what he did and didn't know.

"That is my ex-fiancé," I told him.

"What's he doing here?" Spencer asked with the same nonchalant air.

"Making my life miserable, apparently. But truly, I don't know."

"And he's an attorney?" Spencer asked with an air of skepticism.

"Yes," I told him. Spencer nodded once with a thought in his eyes he didn't verbalize. He gave me a small ironic smile and eased around me out of the office. I allowed myself a strong whiff of him: spicy and not at all sweet. I refrained from trying to wrinkle something on him. I followed him into the kitchen and watched his retreat outside to join Poppa and Daddy, no doubt to discuss the rustling. I wanted to follow him out the door, but I was still my mama's daughter and I'd already gotten out of too much of the dinner prep already.

Spring, my grandma itched to go outside and light up the grill. Her freezer was filled with the best beef in the tri-State area, so as soon as she could, she started pulling it out to toss on the grill. Tally was currently massaging T-bone steaks with marinade, her pastel fingernails a whirl. She turned toward me as I walked over to help.

"Well, this is fun," she said, moving her eyebrows up and down with a smile. Like it was a positive thing that Spencer, Cash and Van were all joining us for dinner.

"Fun would not be my word choice," I retorted.

"It might as well be," she said diplomatically, "So many boots, so little time," she said with a wink, turning the phrase quippily.

"So many idiots, so little space," I shot back.

"Spencer's not an idiot," she pointed out.

"That's part of the problem," I said with a sigh. She only shot me with a look and then let that linger before moving on.

"Can you go make sure the grill's on? Daddy was supposed to, but he's a little distracted."

"I'll do it," Van offered, coming in the kitchen, filling the space awkwardly. He was carefully rolling up his sleeves more toward his elbows. Tally smiled sweetly, evilly toward him. I think it's pretty obvious, given the earlier events of the day, that Tally hates Van. On principle, I would assume. But maybe not on my behalf. I was currently very clearly seeing Van through my people's eyes. And it wasn't pretty.

"Make sure you be real careful. It hasn't been lit since last Fall," she told him. Van smiled right back.

"Of course," he said, "So glad you're looking out for my health and safety." Van had grown up at the country club, in pink and white striped wallpaper tearooms, and on wannabe yachts on Lake Travis. His tone wasn't even colored with sarcasm. We watched him head out of the back door.

"Do you remember…," Tally started with a heavily put-upon drawl, "when Poppa promised Nonnie he'd replace the fuse on the grill?"

"Vaguely," I responded, reaching around her to snag a mushroom bound for a kabob and the grill.

"And then Poppa asked Daddy to get him the fuse the next time he went to the parts store?"

"Okay…" I said, twisting off the cap from the mushroom stem and thumbing off a piece of dirt.

"Well…."

My eyes followed her finger, pointing loosely at a crystal bowl on the windowsill. It held various odd pieces: paperclips, a few loose keys, and a few small unidentifiable objects.

"AGHHHHHHHHHHHHHHHHHHHHHHHHH!"

Tally met my wide-eyed look with her own sly one as she slowly wiped off her hands and picked up the tray of steaks. Cash loped through the kitchen toward the commotion. Mama and Nonnie also followed him slowly, with Tally and I behind.

Spencer, Poppa, and Daddy all sat, light-colored Mexican beer in longneck bottles in mid-sip. Cash stood to the side, trying not to laugh, but I could see his medical training had him wanting to do something. The rest of us fanned out, watching the show.

Van danced from foot to foot, his long legs almost tangling.

Once upon a time, not quite a year ago, stone-cold sober, Tally had asked me candidly if there was any chance of me ever getting back together with Van, and I had very emphatically pledged that I wouldn't spit on him if his eyebrows were on fire. I want to laugh now, which was a small, sweet respite from wanting to cry. It was a God moment, really.

"What should we do?" Tally asked without making a move.

With the great sense of satire that had been drilled into me from the moment I could talk, I answered my sister, "I'm a girl of my word."

She smiled. "That is true," she replied. Tally sighed, moving between the long legs in chairs, grabbing Spencer's Corona on the way. She grabbed Van by the collar of his fancy shirt, and even though Van was abnormally tall, she yanked him down to head level, tilting his head back to aim the beer at his forehead. The foam sizzled on his eyebrows as it extinguished the already mostly dead flames. Tally released his shirt and patted him on the shoulder.

"Don't say I never did anything for ya, Vannie," Tally said.

xxx

Cash couldn't help himself. Once a doctor, always a doctor, I guess, even after your license has been revoked. He commandeered Nonnie's medicine cabinet and Poppa's livestock medical closet and commenced to making sure Van wasn't going to die. I'd never witnessed Cash's bedside manner before, but judging from the gritting of Van's teeth and his pained expression in contrast to Cash's whistling and happy eyes, Cash was probably not going to win any Florence Nightingale awards.

By the time Van had gauze and ointment on his eyebrows, the steaks were juicy and sizzling. I helped Mama and Nonnie carry the rest of dinner into the dining room. Nonnie had added the extra leaf and scooted up the extra chairs, making places for the three invited guests. The table swelled with what was best about my grandparent's house: thick, meaty mushrooms nestled next to sweet purple onions and waxy red peppers with black-charred edges on sticks. Caesar salad with anchovies and lemons under shaved Parmesan. Fat baked potatoes that had been basted with garlic and olive oil and sprinkled with sea salt before being wrapped and baked in foil. They sat in a heavy ocean blue bowl from New Mexico, next to smaller matching bowls that held butter, sour cream, green onions, chopped bacon, and three kinds of cheese. Tally brought in fresh garlic bread that Nonnie had doctored with more cheese and butter. I sighed and tugged down my red skirt. No wonder my former life of shopping at sample sales was a long distant memory. Luckily, being in the same room as Van had made my formerly restored appetite fairly non-existent.

They ate, and I picked at my food, Nonnie and Tally working to make sure no awkward silence inserted itself in the meal, not at all seemingly bothered by my first love, ex-fiancé, and last kiss being together at the table. My mama, trained hard at the marathon of

Southern belleing, knew how it all should go. But she was a sensitive, artistic type and couldn't hide her true feelings. So she kept the pace by adhering to the rule of not saying anything if nothing nice could be said. Although, she did complement Spencer's shirt and pants, eventually asking him if he used the same dry cleaners as she did.

Cash and Van finally left, Nonnie packing up servings of dessert for Cash's parents and unambiguously handing Van a card for the local B and B when he started to hint at needing a place to stay. I had ignored them both and rudely headed out back with my own dessert. Spencer followed me shortly with his second helping.

My grandparents' patio is heavy with slabs of the same rare rocks and oversized patio furniture that rings around a built-in fire pit. The night air was chilly, and the fire did a little to ward it off. I scooted a chair closer to the pit and settled in.

"What?" I asked him snidely when he sat down in the oversized outdoor chair beside me. He took a rather large swipe of pecan cobbler and ice cream and ignored me.

"Nothing," he responded after a slow and thoughtfully exasperating chew.

"Why are you still here?" I asked him, angrily spooning my own bite and chomping in irritation. Spencer usually hedged his bets with me, playing it cool and keeping it safe. He allegedly thought that our "need to know" basis was a good working relationship. I hated it. It surprised me then, when he offered an unusually frank explanation.

"To make sure you don't do anything stupid," he stated.

"Like what?" I asked, less irritated. Perhaps he could tell me what stupid things were a possible to-do in these types of investigations. He looked at me underneath dark slashes of thick eyebrows with a put-upon look.

"Like stupid," he said, back to the normal routine of PR bulldog. I sighed, trying hard to sweeten my tone. Which we all know, for me, is *hard* y'all.

"The last go-round you basically used me as bait because people told me stuff. Why not take advantage of that again?" I asked with a somewhat sarcastic bite. I meant it, but I wanted to point out the fallacy in all of it.

"I think I mentioned to you at one time that it would be better for me if you were alive," he said slowly, another gooey, chewy, smooth and melty bite making its way slowly into his large mouth and shark-white teeth. I shivered, not because I was cold. I ignored the goosebumps on my arms and stated the obvious.

"You don't like me," I told him succinctly.

"Who says that?" Spencer asked calmly without sparing me a glance.

"Me," I said, "You like to rescue me and we've made out twice, but you act like I get on your last nerve." Now, he looked at me with a sharp edge to his expression. I pulled back instinctively.

"We've never made out," he told me without humor. I frowned at him, confused. He must really not like me. I was dead sure I'd kissed him twice, although I was in the middle of a personal crisis the first time and high as a kite the second.

"Yes we have," I said argumentatively.

"No," he said matter-of-factly, dismissively. But then he looked at me, dead-on with a steamy haze, setting down his bowl and leaning toward me until I felt the warmth from his big body start to heat mine up. His voice crackled with electricity as he slowly spoke, his cool breath blowing toward me, "We've never made out. If we ever went beyond one kiss in a moment of crazy, you wouldn't leave standing." Spencer Locke, Esq. said this without one iota of sexual boast, as though it was fact and as though he had nothing to prove. I tried to hide a full on heat-flash and didn't respond to his statement, mainly because I wasn't sure how to respond.

Typically, if anyone was brave enough to say something like that to one Lilly Atkins, it was usually in an effort to see how I'd react, to provoke me. Spencer seemed to say it just because it was, well, true.

Without any good comeback, I tried to steer the direction back to the reason he was there in the first place.

"So who are the 'usual suspects'?" I asked him again, picking up where I'd left off an hour ago, setting down my half-eaten cobbler and leaning toward him. He let the heat linger between us as his gaze remained unflinching. I tried not to squirm. Then, with a short laugh, he pinched the bridge of his nose.

"You know that's a line from a movie, right?" he asked me, focusing again on his dessert in an effort to distract me. It was like he'd never even met me, bless his heart.

"I think it's a line from fiction literature," I told him, somewhat snobbily. He eyed me and didn't respond. "But Sheriff Clay wasn't being facetious," I said, throwing out a two-dollar word for good measure. "He's actually not that great at sarcasm, even though he grew up here. His mama's tetched in the head, if you know what I mean, so he's always had to be real literal. Sarcasm isn't his go-to," I informed Spencer unnecessarily. He wasn't the only one with distraction tactics up his sleeve. I mean, have you *met* my sister?

It didn't have much effect, however. He sighed. "If I tell you, will you leave it alone and leave it to the professionals?"

"Are you asking me to promise that?" I asked him. He blew out his breath.

"*If I tell you*, will you promise not to go off half-cocked with an agenda you fail to share with the people with badges?"

"That doesn't include you, right?"

He threw his spoon into the bowl with a pinging clatter. "Lilly," he growled dangerously, sounding annoyed… and deadly.

"See," I told him with slight triumph, pointing my finger in the air for emphasis, "That's how I know you don't like me." He just looked at me. I sighed, scraping my spoon along the soupy ice cream in my bowl.

"I promise not to do anything stupid," I hedged. His idea of stupid and mine and Fae Lynn's were obviously two very different animals. I could tell he wasn't buying my song and dance. "You know," I told him conversationally, "one of my very first cases when I got home was over livestock. It got resolved the day you ran into me on the sidewalk and ruined my dress." He smiled.

"You ran into me," he stated without malice, eyeing the rest of my cobbler and melted ice cream. I handed it to him.

"Allegedly," I said, with a noncommittal shrug, but not arguing with him.

"Allegedly," he acknowledged, finishing off my bowl. I could see my attempt at flirting had not swayed him from his previous stance on the matter. I decided a plea of honesty might be a better policy in this instance.

"Spencer," I said, "Do you have a grandpa?"

He looked at me suspiciously. "Everyone has a grandpa, Lilly, usually two."

I waved my hand dismissively. "Everyone has a grandfather, Spence. Not everyone has a *grandpa*," I emphasized the word. He nodded finally.

"Yes, then. I have one grandfather and one grandpa," he admitted. I nodded with him.

"I have one grandfather; nice guy, buys nice presents, hugs me when I see him, smells like Old Spice," I told him.

"Okay…" Spencer answered.

"I also have a *Poppa*," I said with force, "Who let me drive on his lap to check the cattle, starting when I was two years old. He picked out the nuts from his own ice cream because I didn't like them, he sends me out of town with five dollar bills, and he bought me a gun because I asked, without any questions. Even after I shot someone. He has always made sure I have the appropriate footwear because he went parts of his life with his feet hurting, and he shows his love in shoes. He smells like sweat, and truth, and loyalty, and manure."

"Okay," Spencer said again, looking at me intently.

"Did you see the look on his face this evening?" I asked him. He nodded slowly.

"Some sonuvabitch hurt my Poppa's feelings," I said, with feeling. "You wanna tell me this isn't my circus?"

xxx

Spencer looked heavenward for a beat, his teeth setting deliberately, intently, but not hard.

"Spencer," I started.

"Okay," he interrupted me quickly.

"Okay?" I asked.

"Okay," he said, the annoyance creeping back in. I shut up. "Usually," he started, "Cattle rustling attracts three types of people." I nodded. "*Usually*," he admonished, "Not always."

"That seems almost too easy," I said with a shake of my head. Spencer shrugged.

"Rustlers get caught eventually. It's just a matter of tracking them down. It may take a while, but enough evidence typically piles up to point the investigation in the right direction. In theory," he sighed here, "More often than not, convictions are rare, if not nonexistent."

"Okay," I said, noticing a little quirk of his mouth, "So what are the three types?" I could tell he didn't want to tell me. But I could also tell I'd struck a chord with my Poppa explanation. And it wasn't the least bit embellished. Nobody messes with my Poppa.

"Rodeo thugs and druggies, professional rustlers, and nearby breeders."

"That sounds obvious. And slightly clichéd."

"Would you like to talk about clichés?" Spencer poked calmly. I recoiled. Then regained my balance.

"Stop trying to distract me." He shrugged. "So rodeo people?" I asked, starting with what he'd said first.

He shrugged again. "That's probably a generalized statement. Not rodeo *people*," he emphasized, "Rodeo meth-heads is probably more accurate." I nodded. Good. I knew rodeo people. I liked them. They were mostly good, salt-of-the-earth, and revered the animals that were their livelihood.

"So the meth-heads steal because they're desperate for money?" I asked, not really a question. I hadn't been all that up close and personal with the drug scene, but I knew desperate times, in need of a fix, called for desperate measures. Spencer nodded like the conversation bothered him. I moved on, lest the effectiveness of my plea and Nonnie's dessert wore off, and he refused to talk to me.

"And there's really such thing as a professional cattle thief?"

Spencer laughed harshly. "They would be insulted to hear you say that," he said. "I think they prefer cattle rustler, as a rule," he told me.

"But, that's actually their chosen profession?" I asked, mostly disgusted, but somewhat intrigued. He nodded again.

"They're con men. They just happen to run cons in the agriculture arena. It's mostly accounting and sleights of hand, but they happen to deal in cattle instead of stocks and bonds most of the time."

"But that's not what happened here…" I trailed off. Spencer shrugged without a commitment.

"It doesn't seem to lean to that, but… you never know. The fact that they were marked for sale is kind of suspicious."

"So you're waiting to see what Joe Nakes' reaction is?" I asked quickly. He looked away and looked longingly at the two empty bowls. I kept going.

"And neighboring breeders?" I said.

"That's the most obvious. And sometimes accidental," Spencer answered. "Sometimes livestock wanders onto other property. And property is big and every square inch doesn't get surveyed every day. The problem with this area and your family's ranch isn't that it's so vast; it's that there's so much land attached to water, and weird pockets of it that are covered with brush." I nodded at that. Slowly. Spencer wasn't telling me much about the place I'd grown up on that I didn't already know. Which was weird. Why does a former Federal agent turned local attorney know so much about *my* land?

"I was debriefed," he told me sardonically, apparently noticing the perplexed look on my face.

"Hmmm," I said. I let it go. For now. "But this wasn't accidental," I said, "They cut the gate and drove in," I stated. Spencer nodded with a hooded expression.

I sensed he was done for the evening. I often got the sense that I was on a need to know basis because Spencer was afraid I'd hinder the process of the proper authorities. However, he'd somewhat alluded that he was concerned for my safety, so perhaps it was more for that reason that he wasn't all that keen on divulging details. Either way, I could tell I was done getting out of Spencer whatever nuggets I might get tonight. But there was one thing I just couldn't let go.

"One more," I said. He sighed, turning his head away and then back, fixing his eyes on me unwaveringly.

"One," he said without any expression.

"How do you know all this?" I asked. "You were in New Orleans when you were in the FBI, right? Last time I checked, they don't have a lot of cattle in the French Quarter."

"You'd be surprised at what wanders into the Quarter," he responded without answering the question.

"So what, you were an undercover cattle rustler?" I asked with a snort. At that, he smiled, liquid, smooth, a hint of sex oozing out.

"That, Lilly, is top-secret." I rolled my eyes.

"You'd tell me but you'd have to kill me?" I said with heavy sarcasm dripping.

"I'd never tell you," he replied, low and slow, "I'm better than that."

I wanted to ask him about Cash and what was going on, but I knew I'd probably already pushed my luck. Instead, I flashed him a bright-white smile. "Lucky me," I said.

He nodded without a smile, his dark eyes locked on my face, no trace of humor evident. "Lucky you," he agreed without mirth, leaving me feeling like I'd lost several pieces of clothing and needed a cigarette. And he hadn't even touched me.

Chapter Six

"Should we cancel the Jubilee?" I asked.

"Absolutely not," Nonnie stated emphatically. "This celebration marks a milestone in our family's history. It symbolizes perseverance, and hard work, and ingenuity. It's a celebration of overcoming and working with what you have, which is why we're using those Waterford tablecloths we bought for your wedding that wasn't."

Spencer had finally left, with a foil-wrapped plate of Nonnie's cobbler and another vague promise from me not to do anything stupid. Nonnie, Mama, Tally and I had gathered back in the kitchen, plotting and planning the nuances of the Jubilee, with random discussions about the cattle being stolen. My question was met with dismissive surprise. Catching the rustlers and retrieving the livestock was a process, according to the former FBI agent not so at my disposal. So, in theory, the best thing to do would be to trust the men in charge, trust the process, and go on about our business. But it unsettled me that someone was brazen enough to take bolt cutters to our gate. On land that has been in my family long before I was a thought. Land Rex Atkins had loved enough to take on even though he'd only married into it. Land that had essentially saved my family from ruin and had turned my Poppa into the Poppa he is today.

And we all know I have a problem trusting the process and letting the proper authorities "handle it."

"So we party," I said. Nonnie and Mama nodded.

"Of course," Mama said.

"Like it's 1999," Tally added with a smile.

xxx

"Why is Cash hanging around?" I poked a finger at my dad's big, burly shoulder as I came up behind him. He was on his iPad, running numbers underneath the yellow-green glow of a Tiffany floor lamp, no doubt doing his own investigative genius. While my father could fit into any situation, black tie or dirty boots, he was, above all else, a numbers man. And he held a firm belief that he knew better than most everyone. It was probably a damn shame for his humility, that generally, he did know better than most everyone. It didn't surprise me that he would think he could track down the culprits faster than the FBI. After all, I had to get it from someone.

He closed the King's Ranch leather cover over the iPad and took off the readers he was wearing. He blinked at me with tired eyes. Eyes that weren't sympathetic, or swayed.

"He's going to help out," he told me without any other explanation.

"Why? Why here? Is the cattle thing so bad you need security?"

"No," he told me. "Cash needs something to do with his hands." I grimaced.

"Why *here*?" I asked again, more emphatically this time. Daddy finally sighed. Rex Atkins is one tough hombre. But he'd also spent a lot of time in a house filled with estrogen. He knew when one of his women got hold of something, we weren't easily deterred.

"It's part of his sentence. Brooks doesn't have a halfway house. Working here is Cash's re-integration into society. He's still on probation. And house arrest. Kind of. So he's going to help here."

"Are you freakin' kidding me?!" I snarled at him. "What on God's green earth makes you think it's a good idea to have Cash hanging around here?"

Daddy snarled right back at me. "It wasn't my idea," he told me, shoving the readers into his shirt pocket and moving to stand, moving me out of the way.

"Then whose was it?" I asked crankily before he could retreat.

"Spencer Locke's," my father told me.

Sonuvabitch.

"Since when does he have more say than you do?"

"He doesn't."

"So....?"

"Spencer Locke is a stand-up guy, with good intentions and strong connections to law enforcement. He asked me and I said yes," Daddy explained, his dark eyes kind but unmovable. Tally is a Daddy's girl because more often than not it suits her purpose. And Daddy rarely tells her no. I'm a Daddy's girl because I'm fairly certain my father hangs the moon. And I've always known, no matter the distance, he always has my back. I sighed then.

"I'm sorry, Daddy," I said, meaning it. He smiled, softening, his hard features edged away in the soft spill of the warm light. "About the cattle, Spencer says it's only a matter of time, eventually rustlers get caught." Daddy sighed and rubbed his eyes.

"Usually not before the cattle are long gone," he said in response, tired.

"We'll get them back, Daddy," I said, my teeth slightly clenched.

His face was back to hard in Nonnie's living room.

"There's no 'we' in this Lilly. You need to stay out of it," he commanded me. My eyes narrowed and I adopted a stubborn look perfected by Tally when she was two.

"I can help, Daddy, in some capacity."

"They sent us a professional who knows everything there is to know about cattle rustlers, in addition to the FBI. You can go to town and be a lawyer this time. I'm not a client. And I don't need to be worried about you anymore than I already am."

"So you're going to sit back and let the professionals do their jobs?" I questioned him, already knowing the answer, and ignoring the part where he said he was worried about me. Just what that implied I wasn't sure. But I wasn't interested in delving into that conversation.

"Leave it, Lilly," he told me, not all that kindly, all but stomping his alligator boots. The boots were fancy and expensive. They were also scuffed and scratched, indicating Daddy's old money upbringing. The practiced carelessness with stuff had worked to my favor as a teenager when I'd run a farm truck through a fence and he'd shrugged off that the truck was a wreck once he'd ascertained I wasn't hurt.

I looked at him. We shared an expression. The Mexican standoff was just that. And could have lasted indefinitely. I sighed. Rex Atkins is the real deal. He seems affable and genuinely kind. He actually is those things. But he's also hard as nails and unrelenting when it comes to things he deems important. In some ways, he is his own manly version of a Southern belle, leading with fun, but ultimately ending with the impenetrable brick wall. Which could be frustrating when dealing with him. I'm sure he could relate. You've met my sister.

"You're not a client, Daddy. This is personal." I turned to leave before he could stop me.

xxx

"I want you to leave this alone, Lilly Kay," Poppa caught me before I was able to make it off the porch. He was sitting on the same swing I'd tried to glue myself to several hours before, his dusty, worn, extra-large boots stretch out long in front of him, the beam of the fluorescent light dancing greenly off his face, craggy and lined like leather.

"Isn't that why you got me a gun, Poppa? So I could right the wrongs of the world?" I teased him. He shook his head without humor.

"I got you a gun so you'd be safe. And because you asked me."

When I didn't answer he went on. "What's that Texas boy doing here?" he asked.

"He didn't say," I told Poppa.

He only nodded without any more comment then finally said, "Your daddy's right. You need to let the FBI and the Texas Rangers and Sheriff Clay and Scotty do their job." I noticed he hadn't named Spencer. I wonder if that was because he included him in the FBI, or because he was excluded.

Poppa's eyes were distant. I knew he wasn't trying to deter me because he didn't believe in my skills, but because the idea of me putting myself in danger was a distraction that he didn't need. It might seem unfeeling for him or Daddy to speak harshly to me on the subject, or for them to seemingly ignore the pain that Van had caused, but it wasn't. They were intent on keeping me safe, I knew, both mentally and physically. Poppa and Daddy's touch is always soft, even if it's callused. I was a lucky girl in that regard. Perhaps I'd chosen Cash and then Van because I knew there wasn't a man out there that could fill the boots of the real men in my life. So I picked the fake version, knowing that they'd always come up short. Poppa and I sighed together then. I put my thoughts aside for a minute and turned to him.

"They'll find them, Poppa," I said, reaching out to pat his hand. I wasn't talking about the rustlers this time. His shoulders drooped. There was no better life for a heifer than in the hands of Joe Culvert. They were spoiled, pampered, well fed, and well loved. I'm sure the idea of them in a trailer, shoved together with no thought to their well-being had him bothered. His big, warm hand covered mine and he patted me absently.

"Let them, Lilly. Let them."

Chapter Seven

"You sonuvabitch," I told Spencer Locke the next morning.

"What now, Lilly?" he asked, a patient exasperation in his tone coming through the phone. I'd caught him early at the office the next morning.

"Get Cash off the ranch," I told him. He sighed.

"That's between me and your dad...and Cash," he finally said with another sigh.

"Stop trying to save someone who doesn't want to be saved!" I told Spencer. He remained silent. I took the moment of silence to absorb what I'd just said. It was familiar to me. Because Fae Lynn had said the same thing to me the summer before I left for college in Stillwater. Her barb had been in reference to the same person I was currently referencing.

"I'm not in the business of saving lives," Spencer lied.

"Yes you are," I told him heatedly. "That's pretty much all you do around here."

"I'm an attorney, Lilly," he told me calmly. "I help people. But I'm not a savior."

"I don't want him there," I told Spencer, a slight edge of desperation creeping into my tone.

"Why?" he asked me softly. I tried to come up with something clever, and biting, and worthwhile. Something to convince Spencer that it was in *everyone*'s best interest to make Cash get as far away from me as possible. As it was, I could only come up with the truth.

"Because I'm tired of being reminded of my bad decisions," I told him finally.

He didn't speak for a beat, then said softly, carefully, "I understand," he said, "I do," he insisted when I started to protest. "I get it. But you'll just have to get over it."

xxx

"Mail call," Nonnie said, tossing a few envelopes on my desk. She rifled through the catalogs before she handed them over. I grabbed a bone-handled letter opener and started slicing the envelopes. A bill from an electronic legal search service, a solicitation for a new attorney a town over, letting me know he had all the fancy city qualifications for big-money estates and trust, and an invitation to donate to a benefit chili supper for Jack Dawson's son's medical expenses. Jack Jr. had been injured in a tractor accident back in December. Donations in a small town are kind of like the mob asking for their share. You just can't say no.

I handed the bill and the donation request back to Nonnie, depositing the letter from the fellow attorney in the trash. I picked up the last envelope and slid out the thick, crisply folder paper. It held no letterhead, only a watermark. It was addressed to me, but the inside wasn't typed or handwritten. On the expensive paper, from what appeared to be various magazines and newspapers, were cut out letters, pasted with careful precision.

The note was short and to the point. My first inclination was to laugh and call Fae, and start pointing my trigger finger at The Posse. My second reaction was to shiver. Like an old-fashioned kidnapper's ransom note, the letters shone, vividly disturbing.

I know what you did last summer

Nonnie, apparently noticing I'd gone white, pulled the paper from my fingers before I could stop her, shoved me into her chair and pulled my hair back as I emptied my breakfast into the trash can under her desk.

"You okay?" she asked when I was done. I nodded, lying. She let me and looked at the note and frowned.

"Must be a kid. They didn't even take the time to cut out punctuation," she said displeased and dismissive, which I suspected was somewhat put upon. I nodded, trying to stifle the feeling of an icy finger of something dangerous running down my neck.

"Must be," I said in the same fake tone she'd used. I picked up the envelope, which was typed with my name and office address. There was no return address on the envelope. The postmark was Marfa, Texas. I had been to Marfa once, a girl's weekend with some law school friends, on a Friday afternoon lark to visit the ironic fake fashion museum out in the middle of the desert. While there, we'd stayed in tiny cabins, biked our way around the extremely small town, sampled the strong coffee, and inhaled enough incense to knock over a goat. There had been nothing all that memorable about the trip, other than a souvenir was not to be found, and Van had been shocked that I'd arrived back in Dallas empty-handed. I didn't remember meeting anyone there. We'd had limited contact with all of our servers, and even the owner of the cabins wasn't on the scene. We'd deposited our keys in a drop box upon check out. That trip had been over five years ago.

"Any idea who would send that?" Nonnie asked, "Or what they're talking about?" I laughed.

"Nonnie, *you* know what I did last summer. The list is endless." She smiled with a shrug but it didn't quite meet her eyes.

"I'll get a plastic bag."

She brought me a Ziploc and we sealed the "letter" and envelope in it. I slid it into my purse and promised to take it over to Scotty so he could work his magic, if any. I touched my gun before I pulled my hand back out, tapping it thoughtfully.

"Are we going to talk about that Van Ehlers?" she asked when she moved to leave.

"No," I said emphatically, trying to tamp down the nausea again and brush away that cold feeling of dread, "We are not."

Chapter Eight

Later, I was sitting at the front of Tally's restaurant, an endeavor brought on by her boredom several months ago, nursing a glass of sweaty sweet tea, waiting for my best friend, Fae Lynn Wiseman. *Tally's Place* used to be an old department store on Main Street and the best tables sat in the big broad windows of the old storefront. I took a sip and watched Sam Williams steal a car on Main Street in broad daylight. Typically, my quivering sense of right and wrong would have hopped up with my new pistol and run outside to catch Sam and perform a citizen's arrest. But Sam was the resident repo agent, and this thievery was probably legal. Probably.

Fae Lynn waddled in, sweating and mean. Fae is either a certified or certifiable badass, depending on the assessing party and the time of day. She is also very pregnant and just getting over a broken arm, which was inadvertently my fault. Hence the noticeable pissiness.

Fae Lynn, used to be Robertson, now Wiseman, with her puppy dog brown eyes too big for her face and her skinny birdlike body, has been my best friend since kindergarten. She has minimum curves, bony shoulders and knees, and a major mouth on her. From cheerleading practices to car accidents to margaritas, from loves and loves lost, we'd been there for each other. Marriage and babies for her. Law school and a failed engagement for me. She was my ride or die.

She had on stretchy pants and one of Scotty's oversized work shirts. She'd given up on her own clothes at this late stage. But her makeup was flawless and her jewelry oversized. I knew she'd forced the local jeweler to trade her own wedding ring with a loaner when the swelling in her hands had outgrown it.

"What's up?" she asked me with a huff, planting herself in a chair.

"Sam's stealing a car," I told her, gesturing toward the window.

"Huh," she said without a glance toward a window, waving frantically at a waitress. She smiled shortly when Suze Penn came over.

"Coke. Cheese fries. Stat." Suze nodded at me with an eyebrow raise.

"I'll just eat hers."

"No you won't," Fae said. "Get your own."

I smiled affectionately. "Turkey burger." Suze nodded again.

"What's up with the cattle?" Fae asked. I'd called her that night and filled her in. I hadn't filled her in on Van. That wasn't over the phone material. It was more let's-hope-she's-had-enough-cheese fries-to-be-calm material. Like Tally, Fae Lynn wouldn't be happy to hear he was in town. You hurt one of us, you hurt us all.

"No leads," I said. "I think they have ideas but they're not sharing with Daddy. Or if they are, he's not sharing with me."

"Hmmm," she said, looking in the general direction of the kitchen, drumming her nails on the table.

"You okay?" I asked.

"Hungry," she said shortly.

"I'll get you a cracker," I offered, starting to get up.

"I don't want a damn cracker," she informed me.

"Whatever. By the way, I've been meaning to tell you…"

"Shit on a stick…?" Fae Lynn was sitting up straight and looking out the window with an intense expression. I nodded.

"I told you. Sam Williams is stealing a car. Although he could take some tips from you." She shook her head and spared me a short glance.

"Not Sam," she said, getting up from the table.

I caught sight of Van after she'd already pushed herself out the door.

The basketball wobbled on her skinny frame. She had her oversized purse in her hand.

He flashed her a smile when he spotted her. They'd met a few times. He opened his mouth to speak.

She whapped him upside the head with her purse. I think I've mentioned that Van is fairly tall. Luckily Fae Lynn's arms were long and her purse strap was strong. He went down hard, holding his right ear. Fae Lynn is left-handed. She whacked him again, in the face this time. And then a third time on top of the head. He was hunkered on the sidewalk, a growing crowd watching. Even Sam Williams had stopped his work for the show. I watched Fae shoulder her Coach, flick a speck of dust off the logoed front, and dust her hands. She turned and strode back into the restaurant and our table where Suze had deposited the cheese fries. She took a big gulping suck of her Coke through the straw and speared a French fry dripping with grease and cheddar. She dipped it in ranch dressing and waved the fork around.

"Did you know he was here?" she asked around a bite.

"Kind of," I hedged.

"Well, I guess you spared him a little time."

"Tally tried to run him over."

Fae Lynn smiled for the first time since she'd arrived. "Good girl. What the hell's he doing here?" she said.

"Embarrassing me," I said with gritted teeth, "for no apparent reason."

Fae frowned, "There has to be a reason. And why haven't you shot him?"

I tried to shrug nonchalantly. I was pretty sure it was unconvincing, what with the doubt and insecurity starting to crawl over me. "Not worth the bullet," I said, averting my eyes. Fae put down the forkful of fries very slowly and leaned in as close as she could with her belly.

"Lilly Kay," she said and waited until I finally looked her in the eye. "Your pain is totally worth a bullet," she told me fiercely.

I waved my fingers blithely while the tip of my tongue ran back and forth over the roof of my mouth. "I'm fine," I lied.

"You're lying," she said.

"I don't know what he wants, but I think if I just ignore him, he'll go away."

"He doesn't strike me as the type to observe the obvious," Fae said. I shrugged again and turned my head. Fae blew out her breath and started stabbing French fries. "You didn't do anything wrong," she said. I started to shrug again. "Stop shrugging your shoulders. You didn't do anything wrong," she reiterated harshly, "I don't know why you're hiding from him like you've got something to be ashamed of. You should be leading the parade of torches to tar and feather him on out of town."

I finally looked back at her with pleading eyes and a greasy pit in my stomach.

Fae Lynn noticed and held her tongue with a kind gaze. She paused.

"What else is it?" she asked.

I sighed heavily, "Cash is at the ranch," I admitted.

"What does that mean?"

"He's helping out," I said.

"What for?" Fae said, not shocked really, but thrown a little.

"His halfway-house re-integration program."

"Isn't he living with his parents?"

"Brooks doesn't have a half-way house."

"So your dad's decided he can halfway it over at the ranch?" Fae said sarcastically. "I didn't think your dad ever liked Cash." She wrinkled her nose.

"Did anyone ever like Cash?" I asked, not all that sarcastically.

"No," Fae Lynn said, like it was obvious.

"It wasn't Daddy's idea," I said.

"Whose was it?" she asked, shaking her head, and a light dawning in her eyes. "If you tell me it's Scotty, I'll kill him, I promise. He's on my last nerve right now anyway. I told him we needed a new van and he actually told me no."

"It wasn't Scotty," I told her. She looked disappointed. "It was Spencer Locke."

"Sonuvabitch," Fae said. "That's weird. Why would he do that?"

"I tried to ask him that myself this morning. He basically told me to get over myself." Fae Lynn jabbed another big bite of French fries, dragging them through the salad dressing and signaling to Suze that she needed topped off. The dressing, not her drink.

"Hmmmm," she said, "I'm confused. And you know that doesn't happen often," she told me emphatically. I nodded. It was true. And even if it wasn't, I wasn't about to poke the pregnant mama bear. "It's obvious Spencer's interested in you. Why would he set up your ex-boyfriend at *your* ranch?"

"You think he's interested in me?" I asked, getting to the most important part. She shot me a look.

"He's saved your life two and a half times," she told me, referencing three incidents. One, us being held at gunpoint, two, us falling into an abandoned well with a dead body, and three, you being held at knifepoint by a psycho mother.

"He did tell me he'd like me alive," I mused.

"He did?" Fae's eyes widened, "When was this?"

"A while ago," I said, waving my hands, "Before Mary Nelson tried to kill me." We paused over that, a shudder going through us both.

"So let me get this straight," Fae started, "Your ex-fiancé, who might as well have cheated on you at the altar, has shown up in town with no apparent agenda. The love of your adolescent life has the run of your family's property. And the former federal agent you like to make out with orchestrated a part of it?" she asked.

"That's the gist of it," I answered.

"And you're not curled up in a corner with a straw in a wine bottle *or* polishing your boots and your gun?"

"No," I said, "I'm fine. I'm doing yoga."

"Oh, Lilly," she said.

"What?" I asked caustically.

"Bless your heart," she said.

"I know what that means," I said crankily.

"I know," she said, then sighed and took a swig of Coke, "May I make a suggestion," Fae Lynn asked after a long pause, not really a question. I waited for her to go on. "Spencer's the real deal. You should stay alive to see what he wants," she said.

I rolled my eyes. "I'll do my best. Hey," I said, reaching into my purse and trying to leave the part of the conversation where we analyzed my pitiful predicament behind us. "Can you do me a favor and give this to Scotty? Ask him to see if he can find any fingerprints? Or if the postmark is legit?" I handed over the big plastic baggie with the more provoking than scary note in it. Last fall, someone had stalked me with the intent to do bodily harm, running me off the road, leaving dead bodies in my desk chair, intent on killing me with a knife. A stalker-like love note didn't set my teeth on as much edge as it probably should.

"What's this?" Fae asked, turning it over, and trying to separate the letter from the envelope inside the plastic. I shrugged.

"It showed up in today's mail," I said.

"Where the hell's Marfa, Texas?"

"Out in the middle of nowhere," I told her, "I've been there once, on a weekend trip with some girls from law school," I preempted her follow-up question. Fae Lynn frowned.

"Does anyone in Texas know what happened with Cash last summer?" I shook my head.

"Not that I know of. I didn't exactly broadcast it to anyone. And Ryan Nightly left our names out of the news coverage, as requested," I mentioned one of Nonnie's students, a reporter at the Brooks Gazette in charge of the crime beat, and the school beat, and the obituaries, and anything else no one wanted to cover.

"Should we be more concerned about this than you're acting?" Fae Lynn asked, slipping the baggie into her own purse, which was probably now considered a deadly weapon, what with the assault she'd just performed on Van.

"I don't think so," I responded by fudging my earlier fear.

"You know, it's probably a sign that your life is a little screwed up when you think this is normal. You should do something about that."

"It's probably a prank," I told her. "Some dumb kids itchy with spring-fever thinking they're cute. Or maybe one of Cash's newfound, many admirers."

"Cash has new admirers?" Fae asked, wrinkling her nose. "Hasn't he exhausted all the stock in this town? No offense," she said, "You were special," she tried to soften the blow. I gave her a short look.

"I would assume," I explained, "Don't criminals attract a certain sort of woman? And Cash isn't ugly." Fae Lynn pulled a long, stringy chunk of cheese off a fry, popping it in her mouth.

"He's not all that cute, either, Lilly Kay. Half of his good looks are his preceding reputation and quasi-charm."

"Hence the criminal groupies," I said, avoiding arguing with her. I brushed past any further discussion. "So you'll give that to Scotty?"

She nodded. "Are we sharing this with anyone else?" I shook my head.

"Nonnie was there, so she knows, but I don't see any reason to announce it."

"Gotcha," she said.

"Thanks," I told her. She smiled, then seemed to take me in. Her forehead furrowed as she took a pull from the Coke.

"What the hell are you wearing, by the way?"

I had on a grey and orange scarf tied jauntily around my neck, a black leather pencil skirt, extra tight, with a cream-colored top from some famous designer, fringed tassels and sequins strategically placed. It was low cut and long on drama. My shoes were black leather stilettos, a thick blank band around my ankle and cute little leather bows across the d'orsay toe. I had on chunky diamond earrings and a rose-gold rhinestone headband.

"I'm channeling Tally," I told her.

"Why?" Fae Lynn asked.

I shrugged, attempting to deflect, "Why not?"

Fae Lynn finally put down her fork. "Because your name is Lilly. And you look like you're in pain."

"I'm fine," I told her.

"Don't let either one of those pieces of shit send you into a spiral," she instructed me. "They're not worth it."

"I'm fine," I repeated, "Can't a girl try a new outfit?"

I could tell she didn't believe me, but Fae Lynn knew when to let things live so she could fight them another day. "How's the Jubilee coming?"

"Perfect," I said, "Mama and Nonnie are squaring off over napkins and music, so it's right on schedule."

"I will die if this kid keeps me from getting to come," Fae Lynn said, "It better get here before or after the Jubilee or I will hold a grudge for the next eighteen years. No one throws a party like your mama."

Chapter Nine

"Teddy Salz is here," Nonnie announced through the crackly rasp of an intercom we didn't need.

"Okay," I responded. "What about?" I asked, hoping she had me off the speakerphone. Teddy Salz had been on the opposing side of one of my first clients, Surly Clark. Salz was a livestock producer who owned two blue ribbon, three-state famous stud bulls in addition to a host of breeding show cattle. I'd represented Surly in a property dispute that Teddy Salz had filed not long after I'd come back to town. It hadn't involved real property. Several of Teddy's bred heifers had knocked down a neighboring fence in a dedicated effort to find some greener pastures. The neighbor, Mr. Surly, so the story goes, had been so fed up with the recurrent event that he'd essentially held the heifers hostage, allegedly. Teddy then sued to get the girls back. The heifers had been returned. Mr. Salz had pledged to return the fence to its original glory and to add a few rows of electric hotshot to ensure it didn't happen again. That was last July. This was March. I wasn't sure what Teddy wanted, unannounced, although the unannounced wasn't that outside the ordinary. In Brooks, it was likely someone coming in off the street either knew me or definitely knew my Nonnie. So while they may have been coming for legal advice, they likely considered it a social call as well, which required no appointment. I didn't complain; they usually brought baked goods. So it was all good.

"Livestock," she told me, cutting off the intercom before I could say anything else on the subject. I untied and pulled off the scarf, rubbing my hands on my neck to quell the itching. And while I was at it, I took off the headband too, running my fingers through my hair to rearrange it and rub out the pinching pain left over from the headband. I nodded at myself in the mirror, working on a vote of confidence, and opened the door.

"Mr. Teddy." He stood at Nonnie's desk, shooting the breeze and discussing the cattle rustling incident.

"How's the jubilee coming along?" he asked, "Annie's got herself a new dress and she's all excited."

"It's going to be perfect," I told him with a smile. "Or heads will roll," I said with a wink.

He laughed and shook his head. "No one throws a party like y'all. We'll be there with bells on come hell or high water."

"Good," I said, "What brings you in today?" I asked him.

"Well," he took off his dark gray Stetson and rubbed the pink band on his forehead, pushing back his white hair, "I've got a little… situation…, if you know what I mean." I nodded. Of course, I had no idea what he meant, but according to Nonnie, it was best to nod and go along with people's assumptions, until they at least got to what they were trying to tell you. Any other tactic just slowed down the process. Smile and nod, y'all, smile and nod.

"You want to come back to my office?" I asked him, gesturing toward the door. He nodded, the hat moving down by his side as he threw a smile and a nod back to Nonnie before he preceded me through the door.

xxx

"So tell me about the, er, situation...," I prompted him. Teddy had tossed his cowboy hat in one blue chair and rested himself in the other, one shined, expensive, grey-ostrich, stack-heeled boot crossed over a dark and starched Wrangler-clad knee. They were fancy boots. Ostentatious and in your face, just like Teddy Salz.

"Well, you know, after that last go-round we had, I thought I'd gotten all the fences fixed and there wouldn't be any issues."

"And there have been?" I asked, wondering. I had it on good authority from my Poppa that the Salz place had been outfitted with the most costly, state-of-the-art, electric fence that money could buy. And I hadn't heard of any more incidents since we'd resolved the last "situation."

"Not until now," he told me. "The fence worked great. That was the best idea you had. I kind of wish I'd thought of it." I ducked my head in faux-humility.
Damn right it was a good idea. That's the only kind I have. Mostly. Well, sometimes.

"But it stopped working?"

"Not really," he told me, his dark brown eyes settling on my coffee cup. I slapped back an internal sigh.

"Would you like a cup of coffee, Mr. Teddy?"

He smiled. "I would."

"I'll ask Nonnie." I popped up from my desk and leaned my head out the door, asking Nonnie for coffee. I closed the door back and sat back down at my desk.

"She'll bring it in," I told him. "So the fence worked, but…" I didn't fill in the blank, hoping he would. He nodded. "That's good…," I said. "That the fence worked…," I trailed off.

"It worked a little too well, if you know what I mean." Nope. I did not have any idea what he meant.

"Not really," I said with an embarrassed shrug, wondering if I should.

"Well," he drawled, "You see, it took quite a while and a pretty penny to build that fence. It was a pretty intricate process." I nodded. I did know that. It had been the topic of discussion in Brooks County for quite some time. "And while we were building it, I guess, some of Surly's livestock meandered on over," he explained with a wave of his hand, heavily adorned with turquoise and a rough, worn silver Rolex. I cringed, remembering one of my first clients.

"Okay…," I said, understanding this was an issue. Not really understanding my position on the issue.

"Well, see, you know I run a big outfit, Miss Lilly, it's hard to account for all the herd, and we've had some issues with all the ice storms this winter, and well, it just happened." I sighed. Southerners are storytellers by nature. I knew Mr. Teddy, like my Poppa, regularly held court over his coffee at the sale barn, making one anecdote last a whole cup. I resisted the urge to circle my hands around each other in a get-on-with-it gesture. I would get in trouble with my Nonnie. And I knew that for my whole life God has been trying to give me patience. It has never really taken, but He's been trying real hard. And He hasn't given up on me yet.

"What happened, Mr. Teddy?" I asked.

"Well, hell, Lilly, some of Surly's gals came across the downed fence, and you know, I usually keep my studs penned up, but I'd let them out, you know, give 'em a little breathing room." I fought down a smile with a nod.

"So your bulls hooked up with Surly's heifers?" I finally surmised. Mr. Teddy nodded with relief.

"Yep."

"So Surly's got pregnant heifers that are half pedigreed?"

"Nope," he told me, "*I* have pregnant heifers. They're on my land. We built the fence before they wandered back over."

"But the heifers belong to Surly," I told Teddy. "Have you told him? He'd come pick them up."

Mr. Teddy nodded, "That's where you come in. Those calves are half mine. And even if Surly's stock isn't all registered, some of it is, and they'll come with papers. And they're worth something." I sighed.

"So what do you need from me?" I asked.

"I need you to figure out who actually owns the calves. And broker a deal. Isn't that what you used to do when you were fancy? Broker deals?" I fought down a sigh and nodded.

"Yeah, Mr. Teddy, that's exactly what I used to do. Back when I was fancy."

Chapter Ten

"I'm going to see Charlie," I yelled at Nonnie as I grabbed my stuff and headed toward the door. I didn't mention that I intended to stop for a cookie at the bakery along the way. No doubt, it would require me doubling back with something for her. I'd get her a fruit bar, but I didn't want to be deterred from my mission. She'd be gone by the time I got done anyway. It was almost five. I knew Charlie rarely left the office before seven, and that was usually after a summons from Annabelle to get his butt home.

I wanted to catch Charlie and avoid Spencer. I wasn't sure about the office hours that Spencer kept, but I hoped that his well-honed body was due to a standing 5:00pm gym appointment, and not a 5:00am one. After a full day, which included hate mail, being a witness to an assault, and enough talk about the cattle in this county to make my head hurt, I wanted to run some hypotheticals by the greatest legal mind I'd ever known. But first, I needed a cookie. Charlie was easier to deal with when plied with baked goods.

I headed down Main Street, legal pad with my notes on it and pen in the red Firenze tote slung over my shoulder. My high-heels tapped assertively down the brick-paved sidewalk.

The fresh breeze sent a clean wave down the street as the sun beat down, warming the top of my head. I loved the way the crisp chill mixed with the heat of the winding-down day. It was almost enough to make me forget about my lack of a love life and how my bad decisions seemed to be closing in on me.

I sniffed overtly, the sweet smells of my childhood: cinnamon, fresh rubber, musty antiques, mixing with the new scents of lavender and thyme from the come-lately health food store and heavy oregano from Brook's latest installment, a gourmet cooking store that was surviving surprisingly well, given the population of Brooks and their allegiance to the local grocery store. I waved at Tad Jameson, who owns the Christmas store and looked to be locking up early. He sent a wave back my way. Right before I hit the bakery, I ran into Quint Jackson. Literally.

I bounced off Brooks' resident hard body. "Lilly Atkins. How goes it? You shoot anybody lately?" he teased.

I rolled my eyes. I think I've mentioned I'm not a huge fan of cute boys. Quint Jackson most definitely falls into that category. I think it must say something for the water in Brooks that there are so many good-looking, good-for-nothing guys in close proximity to each other.

The fact that they all gravitated toward each other and held court together made life growing up even more disconcerting. I should say here that Quint isn't one of the good-for-nothings. One of Quint's most redeeming qualities is that he loathed Cash. I'd hearted Quint quite a bit when I'd operated under the assumption that he'd hated Stetson on my behalf, and it'd only slightly diminished once I'd discovered he had his own reasons.

Quint is 6'1," bronzed from Indian ancestry and outdoor sports. His muscles are bulging and perfect, his arms and legs corded, his tush high and tight and his body fat practically non-existent. His teeth are an orthodontist's dream, his hair's close-cropped and dark, his eyes are darker and his sex appeal's darkest. He had on an expensive t-shirt that was made to look casual, a pair of jeans that were designer tight and a pair of urban boots that had never seen a hiking trail. He looked like he belonged in a Justin Timberlake video. It was edgy and sexy.

I must insert here that this is from a purely objective point of view. Quint was a childhood heartthrob, so by the time I was fifteen, his appeal was mostly just irritating. I like Quint, he's my friend, but trying to have a serious conversation in public is near impossible without some twit fawning over him. And him being the Southern "gentleman" his mama had raised, he feels it his duty to be polite (i.e. ask for her phone number).

Quint came back to Brooks after a college football career and stint in the arena leagues had left him craving home. He's now the Athletic Director at Brooks High School and was doing a bang-up job. Both the football and baseball teams had state championships last year and the new class was looking promising.

"Kiss it, Jackson. You're just jealous I did it before you." He smiled, unaffected, but nodded. I knew he would have loved to shoot Cash at one time. He'd probably grown out of the urge. Unlike me.

"Missed my chance, I guess. I would have aimed a little higher, though. You're the best shot in the county, save for me and Zach Charm. Why the heck you shot him in the toe is beyond me."

I shrugged. "My aim must have been off."

"Bullshit."

I jutted out my chin indignantly. "Don't cuss at me Quint Jackson, I will call your mother in a red-hot minute."

He held up his lineman's hands and backed away.

"Just sayin'."

"Well, "just say" this," I pointed a twitchy finger in his direction, "Bite me." He shot me a dirtily suggestive look and licked his lips.

"Oh, holy hell Quint! I am immune! Have been for at least ten years. Go down to the college to try that crap."

He laughed easily, his bright-white teeth glinting in the sunlight. His Popeye-d arm swung me into a headlock and he planted a wet smooch on my forehead.

"So you haven't shot anyone lately?"

I smiled, "No... but the day is young."

He frowned, "I heard the gutless wonder crossed the border. He still hanging around?" The gutless wonder was my own private label for Van. My eyes flashed slightly when I heard Quint refer to him as such.

"I am hoping he's been run out of town at this point. Fae Lynn had him whipped by noon. And Tally ran him over the minute he crossed the county line." He smiled at that.

"Leave it to Tally," he said, "She's nothing if not proactive." I noticed the way the crinkles next to his dark, liquid eyes deepened when he said my sister's name. Without much thought, I attempted to flesh out the look. And another theory that had been flitted around my mind for a while.

"How much do you know about Tally's proactive habits?" I asked him.

His eyes hazed and then went hard. "What are you talking about?"

"You know exactly what I'm talking about, Quinnie. I know you and Dawg and the other guys formed a secret society to protect my reputation and went back behind me putting out all my possible faux pas. I just figured you'd taken up with Tally's protection once I'd gotten engaged. We're kind of worried about her. She won't unseal her lips on why she left New York and has landed here with no apparent plans to leave."

"Lilly, I don't even know what a faux-pas is," he fibbed, "And it appears as though being engaged didn't do anything for your reputation or emotional safety." The hedging didn't slide past me.

"So you don't know anything about Tally?"

"Tally is a mystery, Lil. She likes it that way." I sighed dramatically.

"Would you even tell me if you knew something?"

"No," he offered absolutely and smiled his pirate's smile.

"Fine," I grumped, tiptoeing to plant my own cheek kiss on his high cheekbone and cuffing him on the ear. "Be that way. You coming to the Jubilee celebration?" I asked him.

"I wouldn't miss it for the world," he told me.

"Make sure your shirt's not too tight," I said, "I'd hate for you to split a seam. Or for anyone to faint," I said with sarcasm. He ignored my dig at his wardrobe choices and laid another wet smooch on my forehead.

"You want us to run that sumbitch out of town?" he asked me.

"No," I said, turning my head. He put his arm around me protectively. I tried to pull away. Quint just swung me toward him so I had to look at him.

"What's wrong?" he asked me.

"Nothing," I lied.

"You look like you're about to cry," he said.

"No I don't," I said, trying to wriggle out of his grasp.

"Yes, you do," he insisted.

"I'm fine," I told him. He squeezed me and I looked into his hot cocoa eyes.

"You say the word," he told me. I nodded and frowned. He frowned right back and nodded too, then swung me back out. "Stay out of trouble."

I turned and popped into the bakery, the smells wrapping me up warmly and the bell above me jangling a satisfying tinkle.

Baker's Bakery no longer belonged to the Bakers, although it still held the name. It was now in the hands of Laynie Francis, a former wild child a few years older than me. It had taken tooth and nail to get Mrs. Baker to sell her recipes; she had almost taken the famed cookies to the grave with her. And rumor went that she'd sworn to burn the place down before anyone got ahold of the bakery. She was in a nursing home with Alzheimer's when she said this, so it could have been made up or exaggerated, but it lingered. When Mr.

Baker died and Mrs. Baker stopped taking a shower, their kids had come home and stepped in, but it was never the same. Laynie had worked there in high school. Fresh out of college with an accounting degree, she had talked the Baker kids into selling to her, promising to bring it back to life. I knew from Mama that Laynie visited Mrs. Baker every day with a fresh something, which Mrs. Baker promptly critiqued and Laynie promptly took note and improved upon. Thankfully, the cookie recipe for the melt-in-your mouth Crisco concoctions wasn't damaged in the small kitchen fire of '01.

I stood in front of the smudged glass cases, the linoleum floor sticky under my feet. Since the day was almost over, the selection was slim pickings, but I spotted a butter sugar cookie, dressed with a colorful powdered sugar glaze.

"Can I help you?" The teenage girl wore a tie-dyed shirt, glasses and had her light brown hair pulled back in a ponytail. I nodded.

"I'll take one of those," I said, pointing at my first choice. She started to pull it out of the case. "And one of those," I said, pointing at Nonnie's favorite fig bar. "And one of those, and that one, and that one, and two of those," I finished while her eyes widened as she struggled to keep up. I'd almost cleaned them out, but I needed an offering for Charlie, and I grabbed a pecan tart or two for Spencer, remembering his appetite at Nonnie's just in case his trainer had cancelled. My mama's cookies are far and wide famous, but if my people knew I'd been to the bakery and didn't come home bearing gifts, I'd be in trouble. She finally sacked it all up.

I swung out the door and continued down the street. The day was fading, and while the sun was still bright, the shadows of the buildings started to override it, no longer hot on my head.

"Hey," I said as I pushed through the glass door, nodding at Loretta, Charlie's secretary, who was currently shutting down and packing up her stuff.

"Hey girl," she smiled at me.

"He here?" I asked.

"Which one," she said suggestively, raising an eyebrow. I rolled my own eyes.

"The grey-headed one," I said, shutting down Loretta's suggestion. The town of Brooks used to talk about how cute I was. Then, they talked about how smart I was. Then, they worried about me with Cash. They all breathed a sigh of relief when I'd left town for good and news of my engagement floated back. Upon my arrival back, the town worried about Cash again. Until I'd shot him. Then they'd applauded. Now, it seemed, the latest option was to speculate about me and the one guy in this town who actually didn't like me.

Loretta nodded and locked me in after sliding out the door.

"Whadya want?" a gruff voice had me turning around with a saucy smile. I raised the white paper bag.

"I have cookies," I told him, walking toward the door of his personal office. He barely moved and I skirted his girth into the room without much protest from him.

Charlie Locke is the best attorney in Brooks, Oklahoma. Just ask him. He has a thick shock of silver hair, brown eyes that always laugh, even when the situation is no laughing matter, and likes his cookies, if you know what I mean. He wears custom suits, that no matter how well fitted, always seemed to be a bit off, and has worn suspenders since the seventies, and not because they were in style.

Charlie caught me at the courthouse when I was ten, listening to closing arguments, and had taken me back to Daddy's office with instructions to get with Loretta so I could hear the best cases. I'd worked for him during college summers, and it had been a sore subject when I took internships with high-profile firms in Dallas during my summers off from law school. Charlie is sweet as pie and sexually inappropriate as all get out. Tally loves this about him. I tolerate it because I know he's full of crap.

Charlie tossed me a Diet Coke from the mini-fridge under the credenza. I handed over the sack, and he pilfered through it, pausing at the pecan tarts with a knowing gleam in his eyes, but ultimately pulling out a cream horn, as predicted. I popped the top on the Coke and ignored my mother's voice telling me to get a glass, taking a pull. I grabbed my own cookie as Charlie rolled his eyes and reached behind him to hand me a crystal tumbler. I scooted a coaster closer toward me and poured the Coke into the more appropriate glass.

"Your daddy 'bout to kill your mama over the budget for the Jubilee?" he asked.

"Ironically, no," I told him, "But he hasn't seen the final bill yet."

"Heard that Dallas attorney you used to spend time with made his way up here," he said. "What the hell's he doing here?"

I shrugged, "If I knew, I might be able to get him to leave," I said, without a more expansive explanation.

"I never knew you to leave something alone," Charlie commented.

"I'm ignoring him. And he'll go away," I said.

"That's uncharacteristic of you," Charlie responded with a frown. I shrugged and didn't meet his piercing gaze. "You avoiding him because you're hiding from the pain of a great betrayal," he started sarcastically, "or because you're guilty of something too?" he asked.

"I didn't do anything," I said defensively, looking at him hotly.

Charlie smiled then, "I know that," he said, "just make sure you do."

He let that hang between us and it went on until he smiled kindly at me. "So what do you want?" he asked finally, his thick, silver mustache hanging onto a glob of cream for dear life. I ignored it.

"I have a hypothetical," I told him, breaking my cookie into more manageable pieces and popping one in my mouth.

"So talk," he said around a mouthful.

"Cattle," I said. He shook his head before I could go on.

"I thought you'd been instructed to stay away from the cattle-rustling?" he asked, not really a question.

"Different cattle," I said by way of explanation. He looked skeptical. I went on. "So hypothetically, if some heifers made their way across a downed fence and the other side had a prize bull and then the poor girls got themselves knocked up, who would the babies belong to?" Charlie frowned at me. Charlie knows everything. Just ask him. And he's usually quick on the draw. I could see I had him at a loss for an answer.

"Downed fence?" I nodded, "And heifers go across it to someone else's land," I nodded again. "Put out and the bull impregnates them?" I ate another bite.

"Yep."

"And now the owner of the heifers has pregnant livestock and doesn't know how they got that way?"

I shook my head and took a bubbly sip. "Not exactly," I said.

"What exactly, then?" he asked impatiently.

"They're still on the other side of the fence."

"The broken one?"

"It's fixed."

"With the cows on the wrong side?"

"Yep."

"And Teddy Salz is holding Surly's cows hostage, claiming rights?"

"Yep," I smiled.

"Where do you come in?"

"He wants me to broker a deal."

Charlie shook his head. "I thought Surly only dealt in rough stock."

"He did. Until last summer, when Daddy sold him a couple of fancy girls cheap."

"What do you know about livestock rights?" Charlie asked me rhetorically.

"That's why I'm here," I told him, not above flattery.

"I thought I told you to stay away from the cattle-rustling."

Spencer's deep, dark voice invaded Charlie's office. I had to resist the urge to throw a tart at his head and dodge around him out the door. I was still smarting from the issue of Cash and my own admission to Spencer about why it bothered me. Not that Spencer hasn't already seen me at more than my worst, but that wasn't by choice.

I didn't look at him as he came to sit in the chair beside me. Charlie handed him the white paper sack.

"These are different cattle," I said again, watching as he pilfered the sack and came away with the mini pecan pies I'd purchased with him in mind.

"Whose?" he asked, his kissable mouth closing over one tart in one bite. I blinked.

"That's confidential," I said uncomfortably. He shot me a look.

"I'm an attorney too," he said. "What's the hypo?"

I shook my head. "I came to talk to Charlie." His eyes narrowed, and they almost took on a disappointed shade.

"You don't want to talk to me?" he asked.

"No," I said, remembering our earlier phone conversation. He pursed his lips and rolled the sack back up, wrapping up the leftover tart to take with him.

"Okay, then," he said, picking himself up and heading toward the door without a goodbye to his uncle or me.

"What's that about?" Charlie asked after he'd shut the door behind him.

"Nothing," I said, breaking my cookie again without eating it.

"You mad at him?" Charlie asked crustily.

"No," I said shortly, pulling on my Diet Coke.

"He's a good attorney," Charlie told me, still looking at me intently. I continued to avoid his gaze.

"I know," I said defensively.

"Hmmm," he said.

"What do you think?" I asked him, redirecting the conversation back to my earlier purpose. His eyes never left mine as he shrugged.

"I don't know," he said.

"You don't know?!" I said with shock.

"Don't know," he confirmed. I was slightly dumbfounded. "I don't do much livestock law," he continued. "But it seems like Surly and Teddy are going to have to share custody. Or you're going to have to get someone to sign away their rights," he winked at me. I knew that this wasn't like a child custody case Charlie was taking great pleasure in comparing it to. But he was probably right.

"What should I do?" I asked. Charlie looked disappointed.

"Research," he said plainly, "And someone probably needs to tell Surly he's going to be a grandpa."

Charlie was done with me. I'd gotten what I came for. But I didn't move.

I really shouldn't ask. Maybe because I really didn't want to know the answer. But I almost needed to. It had been a question that had been burning since the moment he ruined my dress. A burn that had smoldered and flamed when I found out about his former career, and almost singed me each time he rescued me.

"Why is he really here in Brooks?" I asked succinctly. Charlie sighed, spinning his expensive pen, his thick fingers bumping into another expensive paperweight. He didn't look at me, only gazed toward the door and the distance beyond it.

"He killed someone."

xxx

Charlie refused to give me any more details, even after a threat to tell Annabelle about the cream horn. He'd simply shooed me out of his office. I left reluctantly. The light in Spencer's office was off, his door slightly ajar. I gathered my stuff and started the short walk back to my Jeep, bound for home and the delivery of baked goods.

Chapter Eleven

It was Saturday morning. The sun was rising hot and pink against a blue and grey fog, and steam puffed from horse and heifer nostrils, mixing with the moisture coming off the clover, green dotted with white. I was up with the chickens, not on purpose, and hadn't been able to reverse breathe myself back to sleep. So I'd slipped on some sweats, scraped my hair into a ponytail, and shucked on a pair of gardening clogs my mama had left on the porch of my great-grandma's and slipped out of the house without waking Tally. Not necessarily a hard feat.

I'd headed a quarter mile down the dirt road, winding up at my mama's doorstep. She'd met me at the door with a mug of hot tea, wisps coming up out of the mug in dancing slivers, a half-read magazine dangling from her hand, and baby-blue giraffe print glasses perched on her perky button nose. She had on a red Chinese-print mu-mu and matching slippers, her hair pulled back in a silk headband.

"What's a girl got to do to get a muffin around here?" I asked.

"Are those my shoes?" she responded with a nod toward my feet. I nodded. "Get in here," she said, adding a kiss on my cheek and a smack on my backside with the magazine. I scooted inside, lest a long-distance neighbor see me begging so early in the morning.

While I skimmed mama's newly purchased cookbook on the "Best Cakes in the South," she threw together a pan of blueberry muffins, heavy on the fresh blueberries.

Once the muffins were in the oven, I made my own mug of Earl Grey with milk and lemon, and then another for my mother, sans milk, while she started coffee for my father. Daddy wasn't an early riser unless he had to be, and can be a bear in the morning. Mama attempts to alleviate this by having his coffee on the ready and refusing to speak to him before he's one cup in. It's a good method, generally.

"Why are you up so early?" Mama asked, pointing at a picture and recipe of a fresh strawberry cake. I nodded and studied the ingredients.

"Couldn't sleep," I replied. "It has fresh lemon curd in it," I said, "I always ruin curd."

"You can buy curd," my mother said.

"That's sacrilege," I replied with a pretend-shocked expression. She shrugged.

"Sometimes your Nonnie buys Mrs. Smith," she informed me, which was not a shock. I smiled.

"She's a working lady, you know. And Mrs. Smith does make a mean peach pie."

"True," Mama said, turning the page and tapping a picture of a chocolate cake with what looked to be a big mess of gobby pralines on top, indicating I should inspect that recipe. "Have you gotten rid of Van yet?" she asked me, hitting the nail on the head.

Since I hadn't had success, as far as I knew, even with two alleged assaults against his person, I demurred.

"Has Daddy gotten rid of Cash yet?" I responded instead of answering her question.

"That's between him and Spencer Locke," she told me, turning to grab Daddy a camo mug and pouring in a mellow morning blend of coffee, black.

"Mama," I started, watching her as she set the mug down and started pulling out faded yellow, starched breakfast napkins from a drawer lined with lavender scented paper, "Did Daddy *like* Van?"

"No," my father said emphatically, entering the kitchen with a case of dark, kinky bed head, scratching his broad chest over his white sleeping shirt, a pair of green camo pajama pants tied tight. On his feet were the fancy leather slippers he was constantly wearing outside and ruining, causing my mom to have to replace them about once every six months. I turned to him with not so wide eyes.

"Daddy! Why didn't you ever say anything?"

He shrugged, finding his mug and breathing in the aroma like a really bad coffee commercial at Christmastime. He took a sip and an arm found my mom's shoulders, pulling her close in a sweet, awkward gesture.

"You never asked," he said matter-of-factly.

"I shouldn't have had to," I said, a little hurt. He set his mug down after another few sips and a hard eye at me.

"Since when has it ever occurred to you to ask me about the boys you date?" he asked, a rhetorical question. True enough. But no one in my family has ever lacked for an opinion. I just always assumed that no news was good news.

"Did you like Cash?" I asked now, before I went anywhere further down the rabbit hole of Van.

"No," my sister answered, the storm door popping behind her, her bed head matching my dad's, although hers was more red in color. "I smelled muffins," she told my mom, sniffing the air. Mama pointed at the oven and pushed Tally toward the fridge. Tally started pulling out butter and a variety of jams, including a jar of the offending lemon curd. I cut my eyes at Mama. She turned away with a smirk.

"What do you mean, 'no'?" I said to Tally's back.

"No," Tally said, turning around and stealing Daddy's coffee mug, stealing a sip. "No one ever liked Cash."

I turned to my mom. "You did," I said, somewhat accusingly, "The first time we got together." Her mouth thinned.

"Meh," she responded with a slight lift of her slight shoulders.

"You love Cash," I said, turning back to Tally, who'd moved to get her own mug. "Like a brother."

"Meh," she said, with a similar shrug to Mama's.

"Are you serious?" I said to Tally.

"Like and love are two different things," Tally explained. "Cash is like a brother. I love him as such. But like is such a strong word."

"Are you kidding me?" I said in consternation. I blew out a frustrated sigh and turned back to my father.

"You don't like Cash, either?"

"Cash comes from good people, Lilly. His dad and I are old friends. There's good in him, his genetics can vouch for that." He didn't answer the question.

"But you didn't approve of him?" I probed, "For me?" Daddy hot-potatoed one of the muffins that Mama had pulled from the oven and placed on a plate. He grabbed the butter.

"Of course not."

"And why have all of you stayed silent on these issues all this time?" I asked, somewhat indignantly. They all looked surprised and annoyed.

"We didn't," Tally pointed out, "None of us have ever led the parade for Cash or Van. But you're not all that easily deterred once you make up your mind."

"You knew Cash was Cash," Mama said, "The same way you know that Van's not just here for a friendly visit. What's going on with that?"

Feathers ruffled, I avoided her gaze and fiddled with a banana. "I'm not sure," I said.

"Probably best you find out," Daddy said without much emotion, which said a lot.

"You know," Mama started, "Hiding from a problem usually doesn't fix it."

"Yes," I admitted, trying to hide my feelings of unrest with a sardonic tone, "apparently it rises from the dead and follows you to Oklahoma."

No one laughed. I was only rewarded with another round of looks that said they weren't buying my bullshit. And the looks were tinged with pity this time.

xxx

"Well, of course, I buy frozen pies. I buy frozen ice cream, don't I?" my grandmother sniffed, not the least bit chagrined, or really that offended. Nonnie had made her way down to Mama and Daddy's to discuss the Jubilee, helping herself to a cup of Daddy's coffee. Daddy had escaped the kitchen and all the women for the shower. We're bright and loud. Daddy and Poppa spend much of their time escaping from the women they love.

"But not the cobbler?" I said, remembering Spencer's enthusiasm for that particular dessert a few nights ago. She shook her head and stirred cream into her mug.

"Nope. That's all me. You can't replicate that one," she responded with a smile. I smiled back. Our moment was interrupted by several sharp raps on the storm door. The jarring sound had Nonnie jumping, the coffee dribbling a little as the spoon fell onto the granite countertop. She frowned and grabbed a rag from Mama's sink.

It was Saturday, it was early, and none of us were really dressed to answer the door to company. Nonnie had on real clothes but her face wasn't done. I took the bullet and pushed myself out of my chair and tightened my ponytail, wiping underneath my eyes. I made my way to the front door through the wide, long, never-ending foyer, stepping over Daddy's boots and a gun as I went. I opened the door with a smile, it dimming somewhat when I saw who it was. I hastily pasted it back on.

Angus Spade stood on my parent's wraparound porch, a shotgun resting, butt-down on the toe of his mud-caked, black work boot. Angus is a neighbor. The ranch is big, but it was all kind of spread out in pockets, and we had several neighbors that we claimed. Angus, as far as I know, is a nice guy. His outfit isn't as big as ours, and his land sits up on the hill, so he wasn't a neighbor we saw often. I don't dislike him, never had a reason to. But his first appearance, initially, would cause anyone to take a step back.

He wasn't tall, with a medium, wiry build, and a constant heavy layer of scruff. Most men grew out a beard through winter, starting around hunting season. They then shave it off come spring, to rid themselves of any lingering critters and because it was hot. Angus did not. Nor did he get real excited to cut his hair, either. It had originally been red. It was now shot through with gray and grizzled in the way that gray hair does. His age wasn't immediately identifiable through the mane of hair, but I knew he was older than my Daddy and younger than my Poppa. He had on brown Carhartt hunting pants and a thin camo t-shirt. He didn't speak when I opened the door, only nodding shortly, his green eyes hooded under the low bill of his greasy brown hat.

"Mr. Angus," I said, widening my smile again, because when I felt awkward and uncomfortable, I usually resorted to the training of my youth, and all its trappings.

"Lilly," he nodded again. "Your daddy home?" he asked me. I took immediate umbrage at the insinuation that I needed to be dismissed and pushed aside for my father. But I tamped it back down, because I didn't know what Angus wanted, and I wasn't dressed to do anything real manly. Nor did I really want to.

I nodded at him with another smile. "I'll go get him," I promised, opening the door wider and offering with a gesture for him to come in to wait. He shook his head shortly, and I left him on the porch. I moved through the house toward the back wing and my parents' master suite.

"Daddy," I knocked on the door to the bedroom. He popped his head out, droplets still on his hair from the shower. He didn't have a shirt on yet. "Angus Spade is here," I told him. He nodded his head and grabbed a t-shirt, throwing it on as we walked. My job done, I left him when the wall diverged, and made my way back to the kitchen.

"Who was it?" Mama asked.

"Angus Spade," I said, grabbing another muffin. Nonnie wrinkled her nose.

"Did he smell like roadkill?" she asked.

"Mother," Mama said with distaste in her voice. Nonnie ignored her and remained focused on me.

I shrugged, "Kind of," I said, buttering my muffin. Tally ignored us all, munching on bacon she'd apparently unearthed from the fridge. I snitched a piece from her plate. She swatted my hand.

"What did he want?" Mama asked, ignored her mother.

"Daddy," I said.

"For what?" Mama asked. I shrugged again.

"Didn't say. I wasn't brave enough to ask." Mama wrinkled her nose. Daddy chose that moment to pop his head in the kitchen.

"I'll be back," he said, grabbing his pistol from the shelf above the refrigerator. Which in other parts of the country would be odd. Here in Brooks, totally normal. Most everyone keeps a gun in the kitchen.

"What's wrong?" Mama asked. *Now* do you see where I get it?

"Nothing?" Daddy replied, shoving the pistol into the back of his pants and shoving his feet into his fancy and scratched horsemen's boots.

"Where are you going?" she asked.

"Up to the Spade place," he said busily, looking around and grabbing a light gray felt cowboy hat.

"Why?" Mama pressed, not giving up. Daddy finally looked at her and sighed.

"Someone broke into one of the barns. Busted it up and ruined a bunch of stuff."

"Kids?" Nonnie asked with a frown. Daddy shrugged.

"Not sure," he said, "We'll see." Mama looked bothered.

"Be careful," she admonished Daddy. He looked at her.

"I don't think they're still there," he said, "especially this early on a Saturday morning. It probably was some drunk kids," he nodded back at Nonnie, "and they're long gone, sleeping it off by now."

"Be careful," Mama said again. He responded by kissing her on the top of her head and slipping on his sunglasses, flashing a hint of teeth beneath his black mustache. The easy gesture and mild countenance, to an outsider, would indicate it was just another day at the office. But I would not, under any circumstances, want to encounter Rex Atkins when he'd only had one cup of coffee and had to holster his kitchen pistol before nine in the morning. I shivered as I watched his long legs eat up the ground toward his truck with efficiency disguised as ease.

Chapter Twelve

"Daddy's been gone a long time," I said, not wading into the fray that consisted of Nonnie and Mama arguing over the music selection. Neither one of them answered or acknowledged me. "I think I'll go check on him," I said, not all that loudly. Tally shot me a knowing look.

"Why don't you just text him?" she suggested.

I shrugged. "He might not have his phone," I said.

"Why don't you find out?" Tally said.

"Because I need some fresh air," I said defensively.

"Where are you going?" Nonnie asked, "To the Sonic? Get me a Coke."

"Me too," Mama said, "But I want a peach iced tea. Extra peaches."

"Yeah," Tally said with a seemingly charming smile, "I'll take a grape slushie."

I nodded affirmation at them all and ignored Tally's eyes boring into me as I grabbed a set of keys.

I climbed into Mama's Lexus and instead of pointing toward town I turned onto the dirt road in the opposite direction. I turned up the radio, palming off the feeling that my daddy was going to be irritated with me showing up to check on him, and would likely recognize it for the ruse it was.

I pulled up to the wrought-iron fence marking the entrance to Angus and Missy Spade's house and cattle operation. Daddy was standing with Angus near his truck and two more vehicles, both men had their hands on their hips. Angus was nodding.

Daddy's head turned when I switched off the engine and opened the door. An aggravated look crossed his face and he didn't greet me as I walked up. Neither did Angus.

"Call me if you think of anything else," Daddy told Angus, who finally nodded at me as I stepped up next to Daddy. I smiled at him as Daddy took me by the arm and pulled me back to Mama's car.

"What happened?" I asked, trying to free my arm. He looked incensed underneath the easy façade and quick smile, his t-shirt damp and sticky, a band of sweat on his forehead.

"Kids," he said, opening my driver's side door and shoving me in. "Busted up some stuff in his barn and threw some red paint around." I frowned.

"Did they take anything?" I asked. Daddy shook his head.

"Nope. Someone was either ticked off at Angus, or high, or just stupid," he answered with slightly less irritation.

"You don't think it could have anything to do with the cattle, do you?" I asked him delicately.

"Go home Lilly," Daddy said sharply. "It was just someone being an idiot. I'm sure the word will make its way off the hill at some point and we'll figure out who it was. I have some suspects, but it's not worth trying to prove it."

"Who do you think it was?" I asked him, complying with the order to get in, but stopping him from closing the door on me.

"Leave it alone, Lilly," he all but growled. At that, I worked real hard to look offended.

"Daddy," I said, trying to seem indignant.

"Leave it alone, Lilly," he said again, shutting my door and turning hard to go back to his truck.

xxx

Sunday afternoon after church I was at a loss. If my hands are idle, so is my brain, and that's not the best state for me to be in. Mama had a pot of chili on to try to drag out the cool weather the warming temps were sneaking up on. I'd promised dessert, but I had a few hours to kill. Laundry wasn't high on my list. I'd just finished a trashy romance novel and had no good recommendations to start something else. I could eat my way through the afternoon, but I was looking forward to the chili. The Real Housewives were all on hiatus, and I'd just finished a Netflix marathon of Gilmore Girls. I needed something to do. Something besides wonder if my ex-fiancé was still in town or worry if Cash was wandering around outside my window.

Work was my last resort, but it wouldn't hurt to get a jump-start on the week. I set up at my great-grandmother's writing desk, an inexpensive-at-the-time piece, but more than serviceable. It had held up for over fifty years, was solid wood, and had inkblots on it in the most interesting of places. Laptop in place, one leg curled under the other, and yellow legal pad at the ready, I opened the easiest search tool first. I perused the Internet for livestock rights and got an interesting array of sights dedicated to paternity, maternity, artificial insemination, and breeding methods.

Beyond the re-opened wound that was Van, and the sore in my mouth that was Cash, and the edgy feeling that Spencer created whenever he was near me, I was overwhelmed. And avoiding the obvious. I needed most of all to tell Surly what had happened. Teddy Salz and Surly Clark weren't exactly the presidents of each other's fan clubs. Abutting land tends to bring out the best and worst in people. They were currently operating under a gentleman's agreement and their respective wives admonitions, and to my knowledge had been rather pleasant to each other after the fence incident. But this latest fiasco would likely send Surly through the roof. And at the very least give him another reason to bad-mouth Mr. Teddy, which was why Teddy Salz had appointed me to go deal with Surly. I was no dummy. It wasn't so much that Mr. Teddy thought I was a legal genius as he thought I was going to be able to sweet talk Surly into calming down before he got to Teddy.

After an hour of searching, I was at a dead end. It was possible I was going down the wrong paths, since I didn't really know what I was looking for. Story of my life, but it tended to serve me well for the most part. I sighed and checked the time. I had just enough time to go do my due diligence and slide into Mama's in time to throw together the dump cake I'd volunteered for.

But I needed reinforcements. No way was I going alone to tell Surly Clark that Teddy Salz was holding his pregnant heifers hostage on the Salz side of the very fancy fence he'd just erected. I needed a wingman.

xxx

"Poppa?" I called into the barn where all the cattle got run through the chutes and were doctored, tagged and branded before released to greener pastures. Nonnie had said he was down taking stock of antibiotics in the big refrigerator at the back of the well-organized operation.

"Back here," I heard him call. I made my way to the back of the barn. I'd changed from my church finery into jeans and a button up when I'd gotten home. I'd added a new pair of fancy red muck boots and a ball cap before I'd headed out. The boots were built to withstand cold, wet, and shit.

I found him with the industrial-size, clear-glass refrigerator door open, a clipboard and pen handy beside him, his reliable and understated boots in the dust.

"What you need, sweetheart?" he asked me without looking up from his task. I took up the clipboard to help him and hurry him along, nodding as he picked up a vial of something in a dark brown bottle. He unscrewed the cap and inspected the depth of the contents and told me the name of the drug, noting how much he needed to order.

"You have anything else to do after this?" I asked. He didn't look at me.

"I always have things to do, Lilly Kay. What is it you need?" I started to hem and haw, but that was a dumb option with my Poppa. He lived with Nonnie, had raised Mama, and had never been fooled by Tally or me.

"I was wondering if you wouldn't mind going with me to visit Surly Clark?"

At that, he paused and looked at me.

"Do what, now?" he asked distractedly.

"I've got a client, and I've got to go break some news to Surly. I thought it might help soften the blow if you were there with me."

"You worried about Surly?" Poppa asked.

I shrugged. "Not really, but if you're there you can probably calm him down better than me."

He nodded. "Maybe. I thought Surly was your client?" he asked.

"He was. Last summer."

"But now you're on the other side of a case?" he asked, not all that approvingly.

"It's not really a *case*, Poppa. I'm hoping it doesn't turn into that."

"You gonna tell me what all this is about?" he asked, uncapping another drug and noting it for me to write down.

"On the way," I drew out hopefully. He nodded again.

"I'm in."

xxx

I filled Poppa Joe in on the somewhat short ride to Surly's. I could tell he wasn't too impressed with Teddy Salz and the way he was handling it. In Poppa's succinctly stated opinion, Teddy should have returned the heifers as soon as he found them. I sort of agreed with him, but I'd been a little too perplexed with the complexities of the true ownership of the soon to be born calves to really get excited about Mr. Teddy's less than ethical standpoint.

"That boy still in town?" he asked me.

"Not sure," I answered, then was saved from any more lectures or comments on my bad choices when we rolled up to the Clark ranch in Poppa's heavy truck, and I hopped out. Susan Clark met us at the porch steps.

"Little Miss Lilly. Just how are you?" she asked sweetly, not at all bothered by our Sunday afternoon intrusion. "And Joe, good to see you," she greeted Poppa warmly. He slipped off his cap and shook her hand with a kind grin. "Y'all come in. I just slipped some cookies out of the oven and brewed a fresh pot of tea. It's that new-fangled cold brew kind, but it's actually really good." Susan Clark was of medium build and height with frosted hair and big brown eyes. She liked Eileen Fisher and Vanelli. Farm life or not.

"I'd love some tea," I told her, "But we were hoping to speak to you and Mr. Surly too, if he's around." She paused but didn't frown and nodded.

"He's down in the fields, but I'll call his cell."

Poppa ignored us while Susan and I discussed the color scheme for the jubilee. "Nobody throws a party like your family,"

Susan told me, "I met Surly at one of the ranch parties," she said with a smile.

We were three cookies deep and half a glass down when Surly walked in with a quick smile for Poppa and a sweet wink for me, wiping his expensive charcoal boots on the rag rug at the door. His wife handed him the big glass of tea she'd had waiting on him, and he snitched a cookie and sat at the kitchen table with us.

"Something going on?" he asked easily, not that worried. Poppa didn't speak, just accepted a refill from Susan. I brushed the crumbs from my hands.

"Kind of," I told the Clarks.

Surly smiled at me, "I don't speak that swanky language you had to go all the way down to Texas to learn, Miss Lilly, why don't you just come out with it." I laughed and nodded.

"Well, you know last year, when we had the issue with Teddy Salz and his fence?" I started. Surly nodded.

"I do, you did a good job handling it," he told me with a nod toward Poppa, who nodded back as if to say, 'of course.'

"Well," I told him, "It seems like it worked a little too well," I said. Susan was frowning, confused. I went on, "When's the last time you counted your herd?" I asked. Poppa shook his head. Surly got red and started to look belligerent. I'd just insulted his person like no other, but I didn't know a better way to ask. Surly looked at me long and hard, and finding me, the little girl who'd grown up eating pie at the sale barn and solving his problems of last summer, relented.

"I lost a few," he admitted, finally, "over the winter, with the ice storms. It was a damn shame. We counted them all as loss," he finished. I nodded.

"They're not gone," I said slowly. He frowned. Poppa ate another cookie. He really was no help. He hadn't spoken a word since Surly walked in.

"Where are they?" Miss Susan asked. I grimaced and tried real hard not to play with a cookie. I finally met Surly's gaze.

"At the Salz place," I admitted, setting my teeth. Surly didn't respond real quickly. He finally nodded. "And they're pregnant," I said in a rush, ripping off the Band-Aid.

xxx

Surly didn't get as worked up as I thought he might have. He stayed silent through my explanation and finally nodded when I told him what Mr. Teddy wanted. He didn't agree, but he did agree to think about it. And then very pointedly told me he'd be going down to see Charlie Locke the next morning. Poppa and I had taken that as our cue to exit, so we left, thanking them for their hospitality.

Chapter Thirteen

"Hey," I said into the phone when he picked up.

"Yes...," he drew out dryly without much question. He didn't really sound all that excited to hear from me early on a Monday morning. But he didn't sound overly upset, so there was that.

"I need a favor," I said, because any attempt to try to butter him up would fall hard and heavy on deaf ears. After years of friendship, I had discovered it was best just to bite the bullet and hit him hard, no punches pulled.

"Yes...," he said again in that same unhurried, detached tone. I smiled. On other days, I sometimes wanted to punch Jason North and his lack of excitement, so unlike me and mine. But I was all Zen and shit and could take any amount of slow teasing he could send my way. Pretty much.

"How much do you know about the accounting side of cattle rustling?" I asked. I heard him slowly set something down on his desk and barely repress a sigh.

"Enough," he said without elaboration.

"How does it work?" I asked. He sighed deeply this time, not even trying to hide it.

"Haven't you been told to stay away from this?" he asked. I rolled my eyes.

"Because I always do what I'm told," I responded sarcastically.

"I respect your daddy more than I like you," he told me, unapologetically.

"Ouch," I said, unhurt.

"Hey, that's life," he said.

"You still like me better than Cash, though, right?" I asked, not all that concerned about his answer. Everyone liked me better than Cash. I always had that going for me, no matter where I was in my life. Even his best friend. Jason North is incredibly good-looking, incredibly competent, and incredibly frustrating at times. Everyone likes Jason, namely because he'd led both the football and baseball teams to State when we were in high school. Jason is an accountant trained by the Oklahoma State Bureau of Investigation in forensic accounting. He hadn't gone into the Bureau after the training. He'd come home to Brooks with his new wife, and they'd settled into a slightly calmer lifestyle. Allegedly. Jase in Brooks works well for me. He'd helped me out the last time I'd had questions I didn't know how to answer, and then double-crossed me by teaming up with Spencer Locke. They had saved my life, but still.

"Pleading the fifth," he said. I smiled into the phone.

"So how does it work?" I repeated. He sighed again.

"It's nothing complicated," he said finally, "The livestock industry goes around on a handshake and a reputation. Sometimes a reputation isn't forthcoming and all you have to go on is a handshake. Sometimes a producer gets duped with a handshake."

"Spencer said it was an accounting con," I responded.

"Yeah, kind of. It's a banking thing. They promise wire transfers at the same time they take possession of the cattle. By the time the local bank figures out there's no money to transfer, the rustlers are long gone." I was confused.

"But they know who took them, surely they can't get far before they find them? If they know who they pretend-sold them to, they can just go to wherever they're from."

"In theory," Jase said, "But it's a little more sophisticated than to just load and run. They either have a fairly elaborate plan to disburse on different land with different ranchers. Or they have another buyer already lined up. Or they sell them that day at a sale barn across state lines. And whoever you think they are is usually just a cover."

"Those cattle were earmarked to sell to Joe Nakes," I said.

"I know," he told me, "But he hadn't paid yet."

"But he knew they'd been pulled off from the rest of the herd. It would have been easy for him to take them before he paid for them," I mused out loud.

"Joe Nakes didn't steal the cattle," Dawg shut me down rather quickly. I sighed.

"Any ideas who did?" I probed.

"Nope," he said. I assumed he was lying. Jason North always has ideas.

"Did you ever deal with something like this?" I asked, wondering where his knowledge came from, other than the fact that Jason North usually knows everything. To a maddening degree.

"Nope," he said again.

"Are you lying?" I asked.

"Are you calling me a liar?" he asked, nothing offended in his tone, not answering the question.

"Bah," I said, "Are you and Susie coming to the Jubilee?"

"Of course," he said.

"Good," I said, "I'll see you there."

"If not before," he responded. I started to hang up. "Hey," he said.

"What?" I asked.

"Are you okay?"

"I'm fine," I told him.

"I heard an overbred lap dog was up here sniffing around."

"What is your point?" I asked.

"I'm asking if you're okay," he said with uncharacteristic feeling.

"I told you I was fine," I said.

"I'm not sure I believe you."

"Are you calling me a liar?" I asked.

"Yes," he responded.

"Are you willing to shoot him for me?" I teased to deflect, knowing the answer was 'no'.

"You bet your ass," he responded quickly, stunning me into silence.

"Thanks Jase," I finally told him.

"Pretending like it doesn't hurt isn't going to help, Lilly. And you've run out of places to run. I'm willing to shoot, but you have to be willing to face why the trigger needs to be pulled," he said succinctly, then hung up on me. I set the buzzing phone down and buried my head in my hands, trying to think of something to do to feel better.

xxx

I started with the newspapers.

I was looking for bits about rustling in Oklahoma, Arkansas, and Texas. I knew it wouldn't herald all the results, but it was a start. I found multiple articles on the methods, confirming Spencer's list of possible suspects. The write-ups in Texas were especially detailed and lengthy… and interesting. It seemed like you could write a whole book on cattle rustling.

Apparently, when everyone decided that fencing in the livestock was better than open range grazing, cattle rustling kind of died off. Then it revived when rustlers got sophisticated. The articles called it suburban rustling. Rustlers sneak in during the night, drug the livestock, and sweep them directly to auction, rustling and getting rid of them in quick succession. They allegedly targeted bigger outfits because it generally took longer for the loss to be noticed. The most successful culprits were usually professional con men.

I turned to a fresh sheet on my yellow legal pad and sharpened my pencil. I took note of the dates and locations of the thefts, noting especially if a rustler had been apprehended in each instance, highlighting names. Several popped up multiple times.

Spencer had said that most rustlers were serial thieves, making it their life's work.

I exhausted most of my research source options and had a long list and an interesting background to color my dealings with and for Surly Clark and Teddy Salz. I tapped my pencil and stole a sip of cooled coffee, grimacing and pushing it away.

My pencil moved in rapidly grating thwacks as I thought. I finally called out loudly, "Nonnie, can you get me a map?"

Nonnie's head popped in. "What for?" she asked. I hedged.

"I just need to see something," I told her. She frowned at me.

"How big?" she asked. I looked down at my list.

"Fairly big," I said. "With Arkansas and Texas on it, too," I added. The rest of Nonnie's cute little body popped into my office.

"Your Poppa told you to leave the cattle alone," she told me.

"Poppa's cattle aren't the only ones in the country," I told her with a defensive tone.

"Lilly...," she started.

"Can I just have the map, please?" I said. She shook her head.

"No." And with that, she went back out to her desk without another word. I stuck my tongue out at her general direction. "I heard that," she called. I rolled my eyes and brought up a map website, creating my own request, which I probably should have done in the first place. Once I had the three states and the Kansas outline I'd added, I printed it off on legal paper. It wouldn't help me with Nonnie's attitude to tack it up on my wall and fill it with pushpins. I used dots and different colored pens instead, color coding by rustler, suspected and convicted. I looked down at my crisscrossing art and frowned. It needed to be analyzed, but I also wanted more background.

I dug into Oklahoma's prison system website, finding mugshots and backgrounds on each rustler, printing off the info. Then I went back to the Oklahoma court system, plugging their names in to get a more expansive background, other crimes, traffic tickets, and marital and parenting history, if any. One rustler, interestingly enough, had an arm's-length list of cases with his name on them. As the attorney. Apparently, livestock theft was more lucrative than the law.

I did the same procedure for Texas and Arkansas, leaving Kansas for last. I was in deep reading and jotting notes on all the rustlers when Nonnie's wobbly voice crackled through the very unnecessary intercom.

"Charlie's on the phone," she told me. I set down my highlighter, still looking intently at the map and the mug shot of one old rustler, blue-eyed, white-haired and quite pleasant looking.

"Yes sir?" I answered. I heard him smile into the phone.

"Surly Clark came to see me this morning," he said by way of greeting. I put down the mug shot.

"And...?" I said.

"And we need to work out a deal," Charlie said.

"Me and you? Or us and them?" I asked him.

"Doesn't it usually work better if it's me and you and then we involve them?" he said.

"Usually," I said.

"So let's you and I figure this out and then inform our clients," he instructed me.

"Okay," I agreed.

"What'd you find?" he asked me. Embarrassed, I paused. I didn't want to tell him that my day's research had consisted of compiling a list of possible suspects for my family's livestock and not figuring out what to do with the pregnant heifers on the wrong side of the fence. I'd finally realized how rude it was of Teddy to even come talk to me without trying to work it out with Surly. That, and the fact that he'd approached me first and was probably trying to use me, had bothered me enough that I hadn't wanted to pick up the very flimsy case file.

"Nothing yet," I finally confessed.

"Have you looked yet?" he poked me.

"I called Auggie," I said peevishly, referring to Charlie's former associate, an attorney with flair a county over, whom I knew had a large animal vet sister.

"Auggie's on tour," Charlie said shortly. Auggie, in addition to being a lawyer with little to no fashion sense, driving a red old lady Miata and besting most attorneys in rural Oklahoma, was the front man for a garage rock band.

"I know that *now*," I told Charlie. Charlie sighed. I could tell he was disappointed in me. And was at a crossroads. Charlie would want this tidied up quickly and a bright red, shiny bow put on it. But he would always want me to learn something. So, he could either do it himself, therefore slightly enabling me, or he could wait and let me flounder while I figured it out.

"I'll give you two weeks. The next Thursday at 3:00. Call Salz. You be here at 2:00," he instructed me, and then hung up before I could agree. I sighed and gritted my teeth, putting the pencil down and putting the appointment on the office calendar.

Chapter Fourteen

After a full work week with no real productivity on my important cases, I was avoiding the issue of Surly and Teddy Salz. I hadn't done much research as Charlie had suggested and then instructed and had decided that my Saturday was family time. Livestock was at the forefront of my mind and not the slutty heifers who'd wandered away for a midnight snack. I needed to find our missing livestock, the livestock that had been taken off our property like someone steals gum from the convenience store.

I wasn't sure what else to do, other than to start at the top of Spencer's list and work my way down, in the vain hope that I might bump into something on the way, as was typical of my bumbling investigatory skills. So I'd decided to start with the neighbors first. Allegedly, the FBI agent from Arkansas and the white-hatted, blue-blazered, cowboy-booted Texas Ranger had pretty much done so, but, well, you just never know what someone might tell you when they've known you your whole life. I wanted to see if anyone had seen anything suspicious that they hadn't, at first blush, considered. And I wanted to see if anyone acted suspicious. I do have a psychology degree, as well as a host of lying, cheating turds in my wake.

I was in the barn, looking at my ATV options, when a long shadow fell across me. I saw slick black boots first and looked up.

"What the hell are you wearing?" he asked, looking me over, up and down.

Cash, because he was an asshole or because he was insecure, always wanted the upper hand. In adolescence, and early adulthood, Cash had perfected finding some small minute detail of your person and basically exploiting it. It had taken me ten years to figure out he did it on purpose, and the question or comment was done to throw me off guard and distract me, all the while giving him the upper hand while I was left spinning, wondering if my hair *needed* to be highlighted.

"You don't look like you," he said when I didn't answer, pushing his black cowboy hat back, his thick auburn eyebrows pinching together over his dusty blue eyes.

"What are you talking about?" I asked him.

"This," he said, gesturing, waving his hands at my chest.

I had on an army green polo shirt, a tan cardigan, and capris in the same color as the polo and fancy trekking shoes. "Why are you dressing like a cross between Brandy and a zookeeper?" I rolled my eyes.

"Why are you here on a Saturday? Can't you be on house arrest at your own house?" I asked him, heavy on the snark.

"I don't have a house, remember?" he said, a shadow crossing his face, referring to the one that had been burned down. With his estranged wife in it. But I'd known Cash since I was sixteen, it was all in an effort to make me feel sorry for him.

"I meant your mother's," I said without any feeling. He shrugged.

"She's having a tea party or something," he said. I frowned at him.

"It's not a good idea for you to be here, Cash," I said honestly. He perked up.

"Why? It bothers you?" he asked, a smirk twisting on his mouth, his eyes flashing happily.

I turned away, breathing in calming breaths, my thumb and forefingers pressed together so hard that my thumbnail dug a deep crescent into my finger. I turned back around.

"Not at all," I lied. He smiled then, a slow, satisfied one without teeth, his sharp blue eyes clear and assessing.

"What are you doing down here?" he asked, changing the subject, on purpose. I knew Cash did nothing without intention. I think.

"Looking for a vehicle," I said without explanation.

"Why?" he asked, stepping in front of me.

"I need to go talk to the neighbors," I finally said, choosing a dark green Mule and reaching in to feel for the keys.

"Why?" he asked, moving in front of the ATV to ensure I couldn't move it without running him over, which was ever so tempting. But I'd assaulted Cash enough in the last year to last us a lifetime. Probably.

"I just do," I said, not interested in giving him any ammunition to help him further integrate himself into a supposed conspiracy with my father.

"I'm pretty sure you've been told not to," he responded without any heat or glee, knowing exactly what I planned to do. I climbed into the front seat.

"Move," I told him.

"I'll go with you," he said, moving to sit with me in the front seat.

"No," I told him. "Get out."

"You told me to move," he pointed out, one auburn eyebrow arching.

"And now I'm telling you to get out," I said just as evenly, the keys cutting into my palm. He responded by settling down deeper in the seat, propping a booted foot on the dash and grabbing hold of the roll bar with a long corded arm, his shirtsleeve flashing a slight farmer's tan. When I didn't say anything, he turned his head and offered me a smooth wink and a nod, then started to lean toward me.

I was saved from punching him by a cloud of dust rolling into the driveway of my parents' house. Before I could debate the sanity of kicking Cash out and running over him, Jason North opened the driver's door to his big black pickup and stretched his long legs out, his old trusty brown work boots landing lazily on my parents' drive. He moved slowly around the truck, an easy smile, idle nod, and languid wave directed toward us as I suspected he calculated the distance between the house and the barn, and debated whether it was worth it or necessary to start toward us.

While he contemplated without any hurry, the passenger side opened up. Spencer Locke slid out in a movement of contained efficiency. When his head turned toward us, he pulled his ball cap lower, a short, sharp move. He started his long stride toward the barn. Dawg sighed, shrugged, and started an amble this way. I got out, Cash following.

As previously mentioned, Dawg is Cash's best friend. This not-all-that-unlikely friendship was forged early due to the fact that in a small town, they were big, athletic, and their daddies were friends. Cash is smart. Dawg is a genius. Cash is athletic. Dawg could have played in the NFL. Cash is cute. Dawg looks like Ben Affleck. Cash is allegedly charming. Dawg is just straight cool. Their friendship has survived all this, along with an ill-timed and badly fated trip to Vegas that Cash took with one of Dawg's ex-girlfriends, when the ex-factor wasn't exactly clear.

This bright Saturday, Jase had on a Willie Nelson concert tee, old, ripped jeans, worn work boots and an old Brooks High School zip up hoodie. He wore it well, and indolently. A cover for the keen interior.

Spencer, in his grey cargo shorts, expensive, ocean blue, odor-absorbing hiking shirt, and St. Louis Cardinals baseball cap, should have looked out of place. Somehow, he didn't. The well-worn hiking boots highlighted tanned calves lightly dusted with dark hair. Dawg cleared his throat, and I realized I'd been staring at Spencer's legs. I looked up.

Spencer was looking at me. Cash was looking at Spencer. Dawg was looking longingly toward my mama's porch.

Jase turned back to our little circle.

"How y'all doing?" he asked with a slow drawl that was ever so clearly fake. I shook my head at him so he would more than understand that I hadn't been in the front seat of the all-terrain vehicle with Cash on purpose or of my own free will. He sent a short head raise my way, almost undetectably, before turning his eyes on Cash, his expression unwavering and unreadable.

"Lilly thinks she's going to go investigate the cattle rustling by interviewing the neighbors," Cash tattled on me to Spencer, not Dawg, which was interesting. I took umbrage with the way he pronounced "investigate." Like I was just some silly little girl. Had he known I had my red-etched pistol in the back pocket of my pants, he might have taken me more seriously.

Dawg grinned slowly. "That so?"

Spencer's eyes were on my face. I sighed. And took a play from Tally's book.

"What's it to you?" I said defensively.

"I thought I asked you not to," Spencer replied, managing to inject a hurt tone into the statement. "In addition to your father. And your grandfather. And Charlie. And Scotty. And Sheriff Clay. And the FBI. And the Texas Rangers," he finished without a trace of irony. Dawg was still smiling.

I sighed. "People tell me things, remember?" I said. "Maybe they'll tell me something."

"It's a great idea," Dawg interjected before Spencer could answer. I turned to look at him sharply, a little confused. Cash looked at him with the same expression I had. Dawg nodded at Spencer, whose eyes were hooded under the navy brim of the hat. I watched his jaw set and release as he worked a sharp grind with his teeth. Dawg nodded at Spencer again, "You go," he suggested. "I know we told Rex and Joe we'd help with the new load of heifers, but Cash and I can handle it." I looked up slowly toward the house and thought I saw the curtains twitch in the kitchen window. Spencer looked at Dawg. And then at Cash.

"I'll go," he said, turning back to me, a concession. Cash looked irritated. Dawg looked amused. Spencer looked impatient. I sent a half-smile Dawg's way. I didn't want to go riding around the countryside with Spencer. Except I did. And I definitely hadn't wanted to be up close and personal with Cash. Jason's maneuverings (much like those he'd displayed on the football field once upon a time) had more than worked in my favor, even if it wasn't as I'd originally planned.

Cash and Jason walked toward the porch as I started the engine. Spencer got in the seat that Cash had occupied without a protest about me driving. I appreciated that. I waved as we drove past them. I headed down the dirt road, our land on both sides of us.

"You were going to wear *that* to work cattle?" I asked by way of conversation starter.

"I'm not a cowboy, Lilly," he told me. Not crankily, really. But not all that pleasant either. "I can't really pretend to be something I'm not."

"Didn't you used to work undercover?" I pointed out gently.

"I'm not in the business of pretending anymore," he said curtly, a slight shadow passing across his face. And then gone just as quickly. I wiped the dew off the seat, and then wiped it on my pant leg.

"Where first?" Spencer asked, closing the door to his past. I sighed. Somehow it didn't seem fair that my shortcomings and failures were on public display for all to judge while Spencer got to hide whatever he chose. I couldn't even hide the embarrassment of my bad choices, and I also couldn't get my sea legs back, feeling like I was the ball in a pinball machine and the theme was pain and betrayal.

I took a deep breath and discreetly blew out like a lion. It was Saturday, the sun was shining, the birds were singing, allergy season hadn't started yet, and I was sitting next to the hottest guy in Brooks County. I was going to ignore the fact that he was constantly, consistently annoyed with me and do my best to make the best out of the situation. Because it wasn't about me, it was about Poppa. And Daddy. And truth.

"The Morgan's," I told him, giving juice to the gas pedal, the green and brown of the trees whizzing by, the chill crisp from the wind and speed. Droplets of sunlight peeked in through the overhang of the trees. I swerved to seemingly avoid a puddle, tackling it instead and soaking Spencer's calves and hiking boots in the process. I shrugged innocently when I thought he might cut his eyes at me. But he didn't react.

"This is all your family's?" he asked, raising his voice when I slowed down, gesturing to the barbed wire fences on both sides of the rode, orange posts marking each increment. I nodded.

"This was the original part," I pointed to my right, "That my great-grandparents bought when they got here," I explained. I pointed left, "Poppa added this. He won this part in a poker game, so the legend goes." Spencer looked at me doubtfully.

"That sounds like something out of a bad western," he said. I nodded.

"That too. Poppa doesn't play poker. But he wanted this, and the person who owned it before was a gambler and that was going to be the only way to convince him to sell. So Poppa learned. And he tends to best anything he sets his mind to," I said, almost as an afterthought, just then realizing how true it was.

"Sounds like someone else I know," Spencer said with the hint of a smile. I cut my eyes at him suspiciously. "So you all are planning a party?" he asked me blandly, ignoring my look.

"A Golden Jubilee," I corrected him.

"Of course," he said, "Excuse me. Because it has to have a dramatic name."

I rolled my eyes with a smile and patted his big shoulder, "You're learning."

xxx

We pulled up to the Morgan's house. They had a small farm that mostly consisted of wheat and goats. Lindsay Morgan was a real estate agent and her husband worked at one of the banks in town. They'd had delusions of being country people and escaping it all when they'd moved out here. Mr. Morgan was what one might call a gentleman redneck, which meant he played at it on the weekends.

Their front porch was screened and big, their shutters green and their trim a rust red.

"Should we have called first?" Spencer asked when I moved to knock on the door. I shot him a look, which he didn't return.

"You can knock on your neighbors' door on a Saturday morning without calling first, Spence," I told him, adding the shortened version of his name to needle him, which had never ruffled him, but you can't blame a girl for trying. "Maybe not in Yankee land, but here in Oklahoma, it's okay. If they don't want to answer, they won't." He didn't respond.

Lindsay Morgan answered the door with a smile, her dark auburn hair still wet and curling into a frizz at the temple.

"Come in, come in," she said, opening the door wider and waving us in. "The boys are gone, but I just made muffins. Come in and have one." Spencer started to protest and I elbowed him in the gut when I stepped ahead of him past the threshold. I offered her my own smile.

"That sounds amazing," I said, "I'm starving," I lied, not mentioning the homemade donuts I'd scarfed as soon as they'd come out of Mama's fryer. I don't believe in lying. I do believe in having manners. And manners always win. Spencer snorted and I turned my head back to shush him. For someone who'd apparently spent a lot of time undercover, I wasn't all that impressed with his skills.

"John's gone?" I asked her as she handed me a cloth napkin and gestured to the basket in the middle of the table. She nodded.

"He took the boys to feed," she explained. "We just inherited some pot-bellied pigs, and the little guys are in love," she shook her head with an indulgent smile. I remembered then that the Morgan's had two grade school age boys.

"What grade are the boys in now?" I asked, watching as Spencer discreetly but enthusiastically polished off two cranberry orange streusel muffins before Lindsay Morgan could bring the butter.

"First and second," she told me with a tired smile.

"Oh my," I said, "I didn't realize they were so close together."

She smiled again. "Yep."

"Bless your heart," I said, meaning it.

"Thanks," she nodded, "We need all the blessings we can get. So, what can I help you with?" Lindsay asked. "You working on a new case? Or you need a new place to live?" she nodded at me, "There's a new set of condos going up by the college that would just be darling for you. Of course, if you need something bigger…," she trailed off, looking between me and Spencer, who'd started on his third muffin. I shook my head at her.

"No, I'm good for now. Although I'll keep that in mind. Tally can be hard to live with some days," I said with a grin.

"So you've got a case, then? I heard you took down Tim Nelson through real estate records. Who do you need to take down now? I can't really pull any of the confidential stuff, but I could maybe hint at some stuff, if you know what I mean?" Lindsay Morgan was eager to help. That was good. Although the fact that my preceding reputation revolved around 'taking people down' probably meant that the sweet little girl everyone remembered was apparently long gone.

"I just wondered if you'd noticed anything out of the ordinary around your place?" I asked her, "I know Sheriff Clay brought out the FBI Agent and the Ranger to talk to you, but I thought maybe you might have remembered something else. Anything weird or out of place?"

A looked dawned on her face. "This about the cattle?" she asked, "They still haven't caught the rustlers?"

I shook my head. "No. I just thought maybe I'd see if you had seen something lately. Even if you thought it didn't mean anything." She sat for a second, a thoughtful look on her face. She finally slowly shook her head.

"I can't think of anything," she said apologetically. I tried to hide my disappointment. I decided to try another approach.

"Did you hear about the vandalism at the Spade place?" I asked her, hoping maybe that tidbit might jog her memory about something, a strange truck, a misplaced set of bolt cutters, something. She nodded, her eyes distant as she moved up to pour another cup of coffee for herself. She turned back to us.

"I heard from Missy," she said, "But it doesn't surprise me."

"Why?" I asked, my head cocked. Spencer sat still beside me, done with the muffins.

"Angus Spade's as mean as a snake," she said. "I'm sure he's ticked enough people off for there to be a long list of suspects."

"I think they think it was just kids messing around," I told her. I didn't really experience Angus as mean, per se. Cranky, smelly, yes. Mean, not necessarily. She shrugged.

"Maybe. Hopefully." But her tone wasn't all that hopeful. It spelled out clear as day that whatever happened to Angus Spade was more than deserved.

"But y'all haven't had anything like that happen here?" I asked her. "Ever?"

She shook her head with a surprised look, "No, this is the best place we've ever lived. There's no place like this in the world." I agreed with her, and begged off a to-go muffin, stepping out onto the porch with a wave good-bye.

"See you at the Jubilee," I called back.

"Wouldn't miss it," she said, "I hear y'all throw the best parties."

"Well, that was fruitless," Spencer said as we made our way back to the Ranger.

"Why weren't you talking? How come you didn't ask her any questions?" I asked him as I moved behind the steering wheel again. He propped his foot on the running board and leaned in ever so slightly.

"First of all, because I don't approve of this mission. I'd like to leave it to the professionals. And second of all, because I'm not an idiot. These are your people. They're comfortable with you. They'll tell you things they may not tell me. I'm not above sitting down and shutting up," he explained shortly. It made sense, although he was at odds with himself I'm sure. If he didn't think I should be questioning everyone, I'm sure it pained him to accompany me.

"You must not think it's a totally worthless endeavor," I said, "Or else you wouldn't have come," I pointed out without any gloat. We were only one neighbor in; I didn't need him to call the audible of "interference of an investigation" and have me arrested again. That simply wouldn't do.

He shrugged. "Those were excellent muffins."

xxx

Next on the list was Jane Watkins. Miss Jane was in her late seventies, 4'9," skin and bones, and addicted to sugar. What little hair that hadn't been shorn off was dyed Tahitian Red, according to the box. She had once been an acrobat with Barnum and Bailey, but had married her husband before she'd broken anything. When he died he'd left the family place to her. Miss Jane now owned a traveling petting zoo, the base of the operations being the old family place, which, coincidentally, used to be a goat ranch.

"What's that smell?" Spencer asked, sniffing the air as we pulled up to the chain link fence encircling the light pink A-frame house. Two white rockers sat on the porch, rocking in the wind. It looked like a spring tornado had picked up the house from the beaches of inland Florida and deposited it in the middle of nowhere Oklahoma.

"Goat shit," I said, walking up to the swinging gate.

Miss Jane was on the porch before I could open the gate.

"Lillian Kate," she said with a welcoming wave, somewhat butchering the usage of my double name. I ignored it and Spencer's look and waved back, doing my best to avoid stepping in any errant piles of animal crap.

"What's shaking Miss Jane?" I asked. Jane Watkins has known me all my life. She's a free spirit, of somewhat kindred sorts, and has always been entertained by my more flavorful language. She wouldn't be put off by me being less than formal.

"At my age, Lilly dear, it *all* shakes. I've got a coffee cake cooling on the table. Who's your cutie patootie friend?" We followed her into the house, the smell of cinnamon wafting out to greet us, warm and spicy. Spencer followed behind me, sniffing heartily.

"You might want to pace yourself, Locke," I told him.

I introduced Spencer to Miss Jane and watched her twitter around him. To his credit, he flirted right back, which meant the Southern gentleman lessons from his Aunt Annabelle were paying off. We settled in Miss Jane's living room. She refused to let us in her kitchen, a nod to old school proprieties. Spencer looked more than out of place on the tiny orange sofa, his knees near his ears. Miss Jane came back with thick slices on a delicate Havilland pattern, the blue around the edge winking in the sunshine filtering through the grass green sheers on the windows in the front room. Spencer accepted his and the petite gold-plated fork and stiffly starched blue napkin graciously, balancing the napkin on his knee and taking a hearty bite. Miss Jane took one look at him and brought him an icy Mason jar filled with milk.

After three slices of cake between us, we'd garnered nothing except for the fact that Miss Jane thought the Spade vandals had probably gotten their paint from her stash and would I please tell Nonnie to make sure the dance floor at the Jubilee celebration was smooth enough for her to actually dance. Miss Jane had a plethora of spray paint housed in her shed. She used the paint to make signs for the petting zoo. And rustic chic craft projects. She had told us that she generally kept the shed locked, but a few weeks ago, the lock had been missing.

"Did someone cut it off?" I asked, wanting to know if this someone had been using bolt cutters like they used on our gate. She only shook her head.

"The lock was just gone. I thought maybe I was getting old and going crazy. But in hindsight, someone had to have cut it off."

xxx

"Where next?" Spencer asked. I sighed, riled that my search wasn't heralding any good results.

"The Judds."

We were making our way up the hill, slowly but surely. The Judd's place lay on the very bottom of the road which started the winding, steep climb toward our hilltop land.

Tate Judd met us at the road on his four-wheeler. He waved us in and we followed him up to the red-brick house. Aimee Judd had on a ruffled cherry-print apron and was carrying what looked to be a pan of biscuits when she opened the side door under the carport to let us in. We stepped in after her and her husband brought up the rear. The Judds were fourth generation Oklahomans. Their land had been in their family before mine got here. Tate Judd was Cherokee and his great, great grandfather had settled a large patch of land. They'd survived harsh Oklahoma winters, scorching summers, threats of tornados, and news of all Depressions. It had unmoved them all. I would assume, if your people were the kind that survived The Trail of Tears, you were made of fairly hardy stock.

"We're so sorry, Lillian," Aimee told me, and she gestured for us to sit at her side table in the airy kitchen. I shook my head, confused.

"It is a hard thing," I told her, "But we're doing our best to find them." She and Tate exchanged a glance.

"That FBI man didn't tell you?" Tate Judd asked. Spencer stopped buttering his biscuit ever so slowly. I shook my head.

"Tell us what?"

"It was probably our guy. We didn't know when we hired him that he'd been in jail. We don't run background checks around here. And he seemed like a nice enough fellow."

"Who?" I said, confused. Kind of.

"Jack Thomas," Miss Aimee said, handing Spencer the orange marmalade, which he took quickly. Whatever pause he'd given had quickly passed as he dug into his second biscuit. I hadn't touched anything Miss Aimee had offered. That name sounded familiar to me. I mulled it around while she went on.

"We hired him to help out. Mend some fences, work some steers," her husband went on. "We didn't know about his background until that fella with the star came to talk to us."

"Out of curiosity," I asked her, "What does he look like?"

She blushed just a bit. "Handsome," she said honestly and her husband just smiled, "White, white hair and blue eyes. Quintessential cowboy, you know?"

I nodded, remembering the mug shot that had stood out the other day. And the name that went with it.

"We really are sorry, Lilly," Tate said.

Spencer still hadn't said anything other than 'thank you,' which I thought was telling.

"Not y'all's fault," I said, waving at them. "Did he take anything from you?" I asked. They both shook their head.

"We're not missing anything to speak of. But I'm sure they arrested him before he could wring something out of us."

xxx

"Where is he?" I asked Spencer once we'd discussed the Jubilee, the weather and Teddy Salz's new fence with the Judds.

"Who?" he asked pleasantly, not even looking green around the gills like he should be after all the carbs he'd been loading that morning.

"Jack Thomas," I said with heat. I hadn't inquired further with Tate and Aimee, because I knew Spencer knew more than they did and I didn't see the point in upsetting them any further.

"Gone," Spencer said without elaboration.

"Gone where?" I said caustically. "Did they arrest him? If he's the guy, where are the cattle?"

Spencer sighed. "He's not the guy," he told me. "He had an iron-tight alibi. But he wasn't going to stick around after he got picked up and the word got out."

"Are you sure he didn't facilitate it? That he wasn't working with someone?" Spencer looked off into the distance.

"No. I don't think the Ranger working the case is sure of that. He's been tailed." He didn't offer any more after that.

I was tired. I wanted to go home. I wanted to get rid of Spencer, avoid Cash, and put on yoga pants and eat chocolate cake. This seemed like a stupid idea the further we went on the path to nowhere. And the further down the road we went, the more it seemed Spencer knew. I suspected, heavily, that he was baby-sitting me. Placating me. Indulging me. I swerved again, mud splashing up all the way onto his Ray Bans. He pulled them off slowly and started to clean them on his shirttail. I was rewarded only with a shrewd look.

We pulled up to Farley Nelson's. Mr. Farley was an art professor at the local college. He'd been famous for a hot minute when one of his mixed media oil on oils had sold for over three million dollars. He'd been a one hit wonder. Most of his work hung in the gallery in downtown Brooks and had for over twenty years. Given the state of his house, car, and person, I had always been curious where the money had gone. He hadn't spent it on himself. Critics had called him a miser, but rumors as to where the money went abounded. I thought he was nice. Weird, but nice. I would describe his art the same way.

"Who's this?" Spencer asked when I pulled up to the dilapidated house that served as Farley Nelson's abode and art studio.

"Farley Nelson," I told him, rolling to a slow stop.

"*The* Farley Nelson?" Spencer asked, looking around.

"The one and only, as far as I know," I told him. "How do *you* know about Farley Nelson?"

He shrugged, "I took some art classes in college." I studied him for a minute, wondering who he was, really. An FBI agent, an attorney, a former movie star? An art aficionado? A Yankee in dyed sheep's wool? I wondered further about what Charlie had hinted at. I searched Spencer Locke's face for something telltale that whispered he'd taken someone else's life. In the pursuit of right, I was sure. I could relate. Kind of. I'd never killed anyone, but I did have a problem being hell-bent on truth and justice.

"What?" he said grumpily when I realized I'd been staring several beats longer than was polite. I started to answer when Farley opened the wooden screen door.

"Lillian Katherine," he called, crooking a long, crooked finger my way. I walked past Spencer to the local starving artist.

"Mr. Farley, how are you?" I simpered. Mr. Farley, while his house belied the fact, was kind of fancy. He'd sent champagne in lieu of money for each of my graduation announcements, from kindergarten to law school. He believed in a proper celebration.

"Just fine, Lillian. Do come in. I have some scones," he pronounced it funny like the proper Brit he was not, "They're a day old, but they'll do on a moment's notice," he explained. "Jane Watkins said you're asking about suspicious goings on?" he said. Spencer was wide-eyed, taking it all in. Farley Nelson's porch was covered in crap, eclectically collected. It was also dotted and swabbed with thick globs of paint. All over. It looked like we'd stepped onto one of his canvases, I'm sure. It made me dizzy. Spencer looked enthralled. I shoved him, not so discreetly, toward Farley, who shook his hand firmly. Spencer all but gushed, and Farley was kind enough to allow him that before he shut him down and moved on. Farley left us on the porch to go plate the scones on brown glazed Frankhoma pottery and came back with strong black tea in a matching tea pot and mugs. I demurred to the milk and sugar he offered, taking it black and nibbling on a blueberry scone. Spencer dashed off his tea with a hearty dollop of milk and several sugar cubes.

Once Farley had gotten settled, I started the routine again, asking if he'd seen anything, even if he didn't think it was that out of the ordinary. He couldn't think of anything missing, although it would have been hard to identify, given his hoarding tendencies. He mentioned that he'd met 'that Jack Thomas' but that he didn't remind him of someone suspicious. When I mentioned the vandalism at the Spade's, he rolled his eyes and suggested that the paint job wasn't surprising. Or that inventive. Before we left he told me to tell Mama that he'd be up to supervise the twinkle light placement for the Jubilee. I nodded.

We left him on the porch, a paper sack of scones beside us, and I started down the road, our land on the right, the scrub cattle munching happily.

"I've never seen so many people so excited about a party," Spencer told me.

"We throw a good party," I told him.

"Yes, I heard. What about that one?" Spencer asked, pointing as I whizzed by a wrought-iron entrance with an elaborate and heavy gate.

"That's where Angus and Miss Spade live," I told him.

"You don't want to stop there?" he asked.

"Not particularly," I told him, "Angus is cranky and Daddy already talked to him. I doubt we'd get anything else out of him. And his wife can't really cook," I finished, patting him sisterly on his big, buff shoulder as I continued down the road, the clean air rushing past us.

xxx

"You have interesting neighbors," Spencer said as I headed off the road onto a trail tucked into the woods. It led back to the main portion of the ranch and came out behind Nonnie's house. We'd gone in a big circle and were coming back around to close it off. Spencer wasn't wrong. They were interesting. And not a one of them leaned toward being a suspect.

"The land of misfits," I said with a smile.

"The island of misfit toys," he corrected me.

"We're not on an island," I said with an eye roll.

"It's a Christmas special," he told me unnecessarily, "From the seventies, I think."

I sighed, "I know Spence. I get it. But it doesn't have to be literal."

He looked at me. "The world tends to work better if people mean what they say and say what they mean."

"I would agree with that wholeheartedly," I told him with a nod, "But without creative license, the world would be a mighty dull place."

Chapter Fifteen

"Hey," Tally said, throwing her feather and fringe too-late-in-the-season-to-be-appropriate suede bag on one peacock-colored upholstered chair, and then throwing herself in the other. It was Friday at noon, Tally's busiest time at the restaurant, so it must be important.

I'd spent the last hour going back over my cattle raiding research, confirming that the name and face of Jack Thomas matched. Knowing that the hired hand who'd been out at the Judd place had a record a mile long did me little good without good evidence to implicate him, but it seemed worthwhile to look again. It hadn't merited much, and I was more than happy for a break, even if it was Tally in a tizzy.

Tally had on red and pink patterned Lululemon running tights that looked like they were splattered with blood and guts, and an oversized bubblegum pink cashmere cardigan over a loose red tank top. She wore neon yellow Frye Campus boots that would probably hit a normal sized person at knee level. They hit Tallulah Belle below her calf. Her hair was scraped into a genie-style ponytail, and she had on two red crystal headbands and one peach-colored one. Her nails were the same color neon as her boots. Her lipstick was purple and her eyeshadow copper. She looked weirdly gorgeous. I took a minute to be jealous.

"Hey you," I said. "What's up?" I asked. I watched her gnaw her plum-stained bottom lip.

"Where's Nonnie?" she asked with a nose wrinkle. Nonnie had left her post reluctantly to run to the post office. Not reluctant because she had work to do, but reluctant because my whole family kind of took issue with the fact that *this* office was still *my* office.

Several months ago, back in the Fall, a very sad, desperate, deranged mother had, in a very public effort at secret keeping, left a dead body in my desk chair. She'd done so to scare me off my effort of trying to find justice for another of her victims. I'd wrongly fingered everyone but her, but we all know in matters of family and crazy mamas, reality rarely matters.

After I'd found the body of the man I'd thought was the killer of my former client in my office, my father had swiftly moved me to Charlie Locke's office. This was done under the guise of my office being a crime scene. The real reason was that they wanted Spencer to babysit me. I wasn't sure whether it was flattering or bothersome that my people thought I needed a former federal agent to protect me.

Once the case was cleaned up and the perpetrators in jail, I'd quickly started the campaign to move myself back to my own office. No one had been enthusiastic. Not even Nonnie, who has a love/hate relationship with Charlie's office manager, Loretta, and has been at war with her organizational methods since we'd taken up space at Charlie's. I'd had to arrange for fumigation, a new chair (the dead guy had been placed in it and there was really no saving) delivered and new locks installed. And then everyone had been suspiciously busy when I asked for help in moving my stuff back. These were the same people who had moved me into Charlie's in the span of half an hour.

But I needed my own space, and didn't need to be under the watchful eye of Spencer or Charlie's critical one. So I'd packed my crap and hauled it the five blocks all by myself.

I hadn't completely redecorated when I'd moved back in, but I had needed to make sure that nothing reminded me of the bloodstains. So I'd spent a weekend repainting the blood red accent wall and its surrounding friends an ocean blue. I'd traded out all the Rorschach-inspired black and white graphic sketches for blue-shaded botanicals and added a few green plants. It was all meant to be soothing and distract from the idea of death. I still didn't feel completely comfortable there, but I figured the further the idea of dead bodies in the space moved away, the better I'd feel. I'd also bought economy-sized gardenia candles from a hotel supply website. They were burned round-the-clock. If anything could drown out the smell of death, gardenia would do it.

"Post office," I told her shortly, minimizing the search I was conducting on the history of cattle brands. "What's up?" I asked again. Tally looked bothered. And pained. Like she was worried about upsetting me. Tally lived to rock worlds, so I started to get a little nervous. "What?" I said, irritated. She sighed.

"You remember that theory we came up with about Van being here because he wanted you back?"

"Yeah," I said slowly. Tally bit her lip again. Not so long ago, that look would have whipped a photographer and the

Victoria's Secret marketing department into a frenzy. Now, it had my stomach on the upswing of knots.

"I don't think that theory holds water anymore," Tally told me. I nodded.

"Okay," I was mostly relieved. I didn't want Van. I wanted Van gone. But I wanted to be wanted, always. And if Van wasn't in Brooks to win me back, then why was he here? "How do you know?"

She bit her lip again.

"This," she laid a piece of paper on my desk, softly, without any aplomb, rare for Tally. I picked it up. It was a printed version of an engagement announcement from the Dallas Morning News. Van's. And I wasn't in the picture.

Mr. and Mrs. Thomas Aaron Gilligan are pleased to announce the engagement of their daughter, Valerie Marie, to Mr. Van Payton Ehlers the Third, son of Mr. and Mrs. Van Payton Ehlers the Second...

The announcement went on to lay out Van's professional and educational achievements and the fact that Valerie Marie was a former Miss Texas currently employed in the PR department for the Dallas Cowboys. She was dark-haired, toothy, and beautiful. I sighed, trying to show Tally I didn't care. But deep down, I wanted to hide in the kitchen with a box of baked goods. I didn't want Van, but the piercing sting of finding someone who'd promised to promise to love, honor and cherish you all your life in bed with his secretary doesn't go away all that easily. And being shown that you could so easily be replaced, in black and white for all of Dallas to see, was like re-opening the flesh wound and dumping finely ground salt in it.

"And this too," Tally said, cringing as she laid a second piece of paper on my desk. Another announcement from the same paper. It was a bit about Van's run for a senate bid come next Fall. Apparently, all his mother's dreams were coming true, bless her heart. And yes, I meant that in the most Southern way possible.

"Okay…," I said slowly, laying the paper down on top of the other, noticing Tally's eyes were looking at me worriedly. "I'm fine," I told her, lying. "Really," I said more emphatically, then blinking my eyes. Covering up pain with a blasé attitude and dry wit is the Oklahoma way. I wasn't sure how much longer I could carry it off, but Tally was kind enough to let me keep trying, at least for now.

After an appropriate interval for me to get my blinking under control she spoke. "You know what this means, right?" she said.

"No," I shook my head, "What?"

"If he doesn't want you, he wants something from you," she surmised. Probably very true. But weird. But what….?

Oh shit.

"Oh shit," I told Tally.

"What?" her eyes widened.

"I might have told one little bitty lie before I left Dallas," I said.

"Oh sister," Tally sighed with a shake of her head.

xxx

"What is it?" Tally asked with a frown.

"I might have told Van, in an email, that I had a copy of a sex tape. With him in it."

Tally was agape, a new thing for her. She still looked pretty.

"Ewwwwww. *You* made a *sex* tape?! I thought…," her eyes were wide with confusion.

I waved my hand with a shake of my head. "No! Don't be gross!"

"You filmed him having sex with someone else?!" Tally looked shocked and disgusted.

"NO! That's even more gross!" I said.

"You found a sex tape? I thought you'd walked in on him?"

"I did."

"So you found it after?" Tally was obviously confused, and I was too embarrassed to do anything but just let her flounder.

"Well, no, I kind of lied." She looked at me quizzically. "I never had a tape. I just told him that, so he'd leave me alone permanently. To make him go away for good."

"You *blackmailed* him?" Tally looked more disturbed than proud.

"Kind of," I hedged.

"You're going to hell," she told me in no uncertain terms. I shot her a look.

"Don't be dramatic." She shook her head, with an expression that told me she'd revisit it later.

"So there is no tape?" Tally said.

"Right," I answered.

"But Van thinks there is?"

"I guess," I responded. Tally pursed her lips, looking thoughtful.

"Oh sister," she said finally, "You know what this means, don't you?" I shook my head.

"There *must* actually be a tape. And given his latest list of to-dos," she gestured toward the Dallas paper write-ups, "he wants it back."

It took a minute for it all to sink in. And then I grimaced.

Tally went on, "And if it's not you, and you never made one of him with that slut of a secretary, then one that HE made must exist. Otherwise he wouldn't be up here looking for it."

"Shit," I finally said. Tally eyed me with a thoughtful look.

"What the hell are you wearing, by the way?" I frowned, running my hands down the front of the black tulle skirt and straightening the lapels of my denim jacket.

"I've been watching Sex and the City reruns."

"You look like a cracked out fairy princess in cowgirl boots," she told me shortly.

"Have you met a mirror today?" I asked her defensively.

"Have you?" she retorted, "I wear stuff like this all the time."

"I thought I'd try a Carrie Bradshaw outfit," I told her.

"Untry it," Tally said.

XXX

"Find anything?" Tally asked.

"No," I responded with a frustrated sigh. I had a sheen of sweat on me, and the t-shirt I'd changed into upon my arrival home was smelling a little musty at the armpits. I wiped my forehead on my shirtsleeve, the faded black of one of my mama's Cher concert tees coming away with a thin layer of makeup.

When I'd run home from Dallas, away from Van and the fallout of my failed engagement, I had come with only a trailer-hitched U-Haul and what it could carry. When I'd pulled into my great-grandparents' driveway after the long haul home, I'd pulled out my clothes, some other essentials, and two boxes of books. The rest, Tally and I had hastily shoved into the shed adjoining the house, and it had remained there since last Summer, mostly untouched.

Now, we were neck deep in stale, somewhat moldy boxes, digging through the remnants of a life I could hardly remember, looking for the last thing I wanted to lay eyes on. The thing is, there are two problems with this scenario. One, Van had maybe made a sex tape before he met me. A viable option, given what I knew about his legacy-inspired fraternity career in college. But if so, and this was the problem, that meant he'd kept it through the duration of our relationship. Why this bothered me, in light of the fact that I'd, in fact, caught him in the act of *doing it* with his secretary, was probably surprising. But a betrayal, is a betrayal, is a betrayal. And one shock does not necessarily soften the blow of another. I'd been working real hard to move on with the devastation that Van had created with his indiscretion, and now it had followed me across the Red River. My chest tightened, and I felt my fingers clenching.

The other option was that Van had made it *while* we were together, which meant that he'd either lied to me or cheated on me more than once, given that he had sworn at the time that the secretary was a one-time thing. Again, I think we can all agree here, that it is all up front and out in the open that Van is both an admitted liar and cheater, but the idea of evidence, other than the scene that I would like to permanently blot from my brain, made that unsettled, queasy feeling bubble up in my chest.

Tally tossed a pack of unopened playing cards at me. "You really should have gone through this crap before now," she told me. I threw the cards in a nearby trashcan that we'd commandeered from the house.

"I really should have just set a match to it," I told her. She pulled out a law school graduation program.

"This was your life, sister. Granted, parts of it didn't suit you. And being home looks a lot better on you, but this was your life." I shrugged.

"It seems like such a long time ago," I said, trying to adopt a nonchalance that was fake. "A lifetime ago."

"Maybe," she was looking at me intently. "But it's still *you*. You think you'd be the lawyer you are if you hadn't gone to SMU? You were a badass attorney in Dallas. You're a badass attorney now. Where you are doesn't change where you came from, and Dallas is a part of your journey. *Van* is a part of your journey, whether you want to admit that or not."

"I don't want to admit that," I said with a dismissive smile. What I didn't want to admit is how much it freakin' hurt. How before I'd packed my bags and called my Mama to tell her I was coming home, I hadn't been able to get out of bed for three days. How I'd drunk a bottle of wine alone and then spent the next hour puking it up. How I'd toyed with the idea of going out to have a one-night stand to feel better about myself. How Lilly "Take Charge" Atkins had straight lost her shit before she came running home.

"Sis, if you can't reconcile yourself with *all* of yourself, you'll probably find yourself at the crossroads of an identity crisis. Judging by your clothes lately, you're kind of coasting into that intersection."

"Are you done, Dr. Phil?" I asked her sarcastically.

"For now," she said, "Can I have this?" she waved a Waterford vase. I nodded and stuck my head back in a box.

"Shit," I said.

"Find something?" she asked, scurrying over.

"No," I said, "but maybe." I grimaced. The box was filled with DVDs, and recordable CDs. The CDs were labeled and seemed to contain law school outlines and class notes. And engagement pictures and bridal portraits for reprint. Allegedly.

"Shit," Tally said. "You know what this means, right?" I didn't say anything for a long time.

"I can't," I told her finally, turning to her with consternation, the bubble rising and the lack of yogic breath threatening to turn into something ugly right there in my grandparents' shed. Tally took one look at my face and apparently sensing that I damn sure wasn't kidding, took pity on me.

"Me neither," she said, with a thoughtful set to her mouth, turning back to follow my gaze back to the box.

"Char," we both said at the same time.

xxx

"You are going to owe me for this," Char told me frankly as we loaded the box into the back of her black Audi SUV that Friday night. She dusted her hands on her jeans, designer, cuffed and ripped in all the right places. She had on a bright, off the shoulder, sequined Aztec print top, an extended array of serape print bracelets, and a pair of red converse tennis shoes. Turquoise feathers dangled from her ears, and a chunky piece of real turquoise was on the opposite hand from her wedding band and engagement ring set. Her long dark hair, straight, thick and a true testament to Moroccan oil, was high in a ponytail. Her nails were painted black and her lips were a shiny nude. The rest of her face was impeccably turned out, but you couldn't tell where the natural beauty stopped and the makeup picked up.

"Of course," I said, somewhat wearily. "Name your price," I told her.

"Your mama's cookies," she told me.

"I will have her whip up a batch," I agreed, moving out of eyeshot of the box that may or may not hold a video ensuring Van's run for state senate would be short-lived.

"And get me out of having to hot-glue shit for your mom for the Jubilee."

"Done," I promised, which was one I couldn't likely keep.

"Are you okay?" Char asked, getting into her car.

"Yes," I replied automatically. "No," I said after a beat. "I don't know," I finally said with a sigh. "Is it that obvious?" I asked.

"You have on a ratty Cher t-shirt, what appear to be *cargo* pants," she sniffed, "and ugly tennis shoes." I looked down at my feet, which I'd shoved into a pair of grey New Balance tennis shoes I'd pulled out of my closet in distracted haste when Tally and I had gotten home with the plan to search my stuff for Van's tape. I narrowed my eyes at Char.

"Didn't you used to be nice?" I asked her.

"Nope," she told me. "But really? Why don't you just let us run him out of town? So you can stop dressing like a bag lady."

"Just see if you can find some incriminating evidence," I told her, "and that will more than likely do the trick." She shrugged and shut the door, waving. I waved back and started to head toward the house.

"Burn those shoes," she yelled from her open window, waving again and blasting old school Nelly as she pulled out and spun gravel.

Chapter Sixteen

Having passed the buck to someone more qualified, I wanted to do something productive. The list of usual suspects was burning a hole in my pocket. A thought occurred to me, and I stole across the gravel road to my Nonnie's house. She met me at the door.

"What are you wearing?" she asked, her pert nose wrinkling and the few escaped salt and pepper curls bobbing. She had one of Poppa's work shirts over her clothes, purple rain boots, and one of Poppa's bandanas covered most of her hair. I gave her a once over in return.

"I was looking for something," I told her. "I just threw something on."

"Why do you even have that available to throw on?" she asked me. I sighed.

"Do you have a paper?" I said without responding to the question.

"Of course," she said, eyeing me skeptically, her eyes resting, bothered, on my shoes. I slipped them off and left them on the porch, moving to go into the house. When I didn't sense my Nonnie behind me, I turned around. She had the tennis shoes by the laces and was heading around the house, out back, in the general direction of the burn pile. I squared my shoulders and let her go.

I found the paper on the leather footstool next to Poppa's recliner, in pieces. I grabbed the so-called *Scene* section and sat in the chair.

Nonnie came back when I was two pages in and just when I'd found what I was looking for.

"What are you looking for?" she asked, not saying one word about the fact that I was going to have to walk barefoot back across the yard. I hesitated.

"Just seeing what's going on this weekend," I said. She looked at me. Nonnie had taught first grade for over thirty-five years, while keeping my grandfather in line. She can spot a fib from a mile away.

"There's a motorcycle rally," she told me slowly, waving her hand at the paper, her eyes never leaving my face.

"Hmmmm," I said, noncommittally.

"And the Unitarian church is putting on *The Vagina Monologues*,"

"Oh, yeah?" I said, not interested, and not meeting her gaze.

"And there's a rodeo," she finally said.

"Huh," I responded.

"Lilly...," she drawled out.

"Ma'am?" I finally looked at her. She shook a bent, arthritic finger at me.

"Do I need to remind you what both your daddy and your grandfather told you *not* to do? And what you promised Spencer Locke you wouldn't do?" she said, referencing a conversation I hadn't known she'd been privy to.

"I don't know what you're talking about," I lied to her.

"Don't lie to me, Lilly Kay," she said smartly. I popped up from the chair, pecking her on the cheek and starting toward the door, paper in hand, slipping off my socks as I went.

"Love you Nonnie," I said, avoiding her eyes and avoiding her words. I was out the door before she could grab me and shake me.

I picked my way back across the road and grabbed my phone from my appointed bedroom. I threw the paper on the bed and stood in front of the windows, the scraggily honeysuckle vine blocking most of the view of the ranch.

"Hello," Fae Lynn answered, out of breath and sounding exhausted. I immediately felt bad.

"Never mind," I told her. My best friend was a good sneeze from going into labor, and because I was a selfish jerk I thought it would be a good idea to invite her along for the ride on one of my least thought out ideas.

"What is it?" she asked me, interest piqued. I heard her yell at Scotty to help Hazzard with his pudding and then the screen door slammed. I could picture her slipping outside to sit on the wicker bench on her porch.

"Nothing. I meant to call Tally."

"Liar," she shot back. "What do you want?"

I sighed. "You wanna go to the rodeo?"

"You buying snacks?" she asked me.

"Yes…," I drawled out slowly. "But I know it might get cold, and I know you're pregnant, and it's really not that big a deal…"

"You calling me fat?" she said sarcastically.

"No."

"This about the cattle?" Fae Lynn asked. I hesitated.

"Yes."

"Pick me up. I'll see if I can shoe horn my fat ass into some Rockies."

xxx

"I'll go," Tally told me once she figured out why I was laying on the bed trying to zip up my tightest jeans.

"No. You're too loud," I told her, referring not to her voice, but to her appearance.

"Haven't you been instructed to leave this alone?" she said, her voice a faux-threatening taunt.

"Tallulah Belle, I'm hoping to slip in unnoticed, do some discreet surveillance, pretend we're there to see Jacque and slip back home to dissect what we find. Not create a scene with a world-famous supermodel."

"Sister, you realize that you and Fae Lynn aren't that covert yourselves, even when Fae's not pregnant?" I took a pause from the zipper and sat up, giving Tally a slow, deliberate once over, landing on the internationally renowned cleavage.

"We're slightly less obvious than you," I told her, squatting down in a yoga pose to try to loosen the denim and shimmy the jeans up a little higher. Tally blew out her breath with exasperation.

"Sis, for someone so smart, sometimes you can really be an idiot," Tally told me with a consoling smile. I narrowed my eyes without comment. She rolled her own back my way. "I'll be the distraction. With my boots, my boobs, and my brilliant personality, no one will ever remember you and Fae were there."

I took in the boots, boobs, and million-dollar smile. 'Nough said.

Chapter Seventeen

My parents had limited my exposure to the rodeo circuit. I'd been exposed to it, of course, but intentionally and not without great care and diligent watchfulness. I was a junior rodeo princess, which meant I dabbled at barrel racing and rode around the arena with a flag and a tiara stuck on my cowgirl hat. I liked the bling. I loved my horses. But I never went all in.

Yes, it's bulls and blood and clowns and mud, but it's also so much more. There's a showmanship and a spectacle of bravery that you can't find anywhere else. It's like WWF, but *real*. The toughest show on dirt, if you will.

The world of rodeo is also a breeding ground for drugs. It's hard living, easy money some days; with the constant near-death experience waiting around the corner, it's a haven for adrenaline junkies. It has a lot in common with a drug high. Drugs were closely monitored, after the cool availability of coke in the 80s, and wasn't the reputation most cowboys wanted to follow them around, but the lingering possibility was still there just the same. To me, it made sense. I wouldn't want to get on a bull either and hold on for eight seconds without a hit of something that made me feel invincible.

I hadn't been to a hometown rodeo in years. I'd gone a few times in high school because it was a good meeting place for my friends and something to do on a Saturday night, but it stopped being my thing. Jacque's family had rodeo stock, but even Jacque liked to wear her leather pants and sit high up in the bleachers to avoid horseshit.

"So what's the plan?" Fae Lynn asked, a corndog in one hand, a Dr. Pepper in the other. We hadn't made it to the county fairgrounds before a stop at the Sonic. Tally took a loud slurp from her grape slushie.

We were sitting in the dusty dirt and grass parking lot behind the rodeo arena. My red Jeep Wrangler was parked in between a gold minivan and a navy Mercedes convertible. To the far left, further toward the stretch of woods that marked the end of the county allotment, stood horse and stock trailers, big diesel trucks, and some front cabs of semi-trucks, waiting to hook up and haul the livestock home. I slid my sunglasses up on my head, taking a long look around at our surroundings.

"I just kind of want to walk around and look for suspicious druggies," I told them, my words dying off at the moment I realized how dumb that sounded. Fae cut her eyes at me, and I heard Tally laugh from the back seat.

"Jacque's here, right?" Fae asked.

I nodded. "I texted her."

"So we can walk around by the chutes and pens and tell anyone who asks that we're looking for Jac," Fae said.

"I doubt if anyone asks," Tally responded. I was growing to the better idea.

"And we can just kind of ask around about the cattle. See if someone says anything weird, or knows any gossip," I said.

"I'll just flirt with cowboys," Tally piped in from the back. "I'm good at that. I'll leave the nosy crap to y'all."

"Since when have you not wanted to be in the great big middle of something?" Fae turned back to Tally, her big belly in the way. Tally shrugged.

"Daddy promised me a new car if I kept an eye on Lilly. I'm sure he meant stopping her, but apples and oranges," she shrugged. "At least I can say I didn't participate."

"He really offered you a car?" I asked with some heat, turning to look at her. She smiled.

"A Mustang." I rolled my eyes.

"I'll keep your secret if you keep mine," I told her.

"Done," she said. "Although this isn't likely to be secret for long. We're at the Brooks County Fairgrounds. Nonnie will be calling me about five seconds after our feet hit dirt."

"She already knows," I told Tally.

"And she let you come?" Tally said with surprise.

"What was she going to do? Sit on me?" I said with a confidence I didn't necessarily feel.

"Uh, yeah," Tally replied.

"Well, she didn't," I responded. "And here we are."

"Hmmm," Tally said.

"Let's go," Fae interrupted. "I'm out of corn dog. I want you to buy me a funnel cake and a pineapple whip."

We left the Jeep. Tally, true to her word, had done her best to outshine us and the rest of the free world. I was fairly certain her designer cowgirl jeans had never seen a speck of manure, but the rhinestone horseshoes on the back pockets highlighted an ass once bound for Hollywood. On top was a turquoise ribbed sweater. It laced up like tennis shoes at the chest. It was untied as though Tally's feet hurt. Her boots were chocolate fringe, as were the matching bracelets at her wrists. Her hair had enough hairspray to cause a firebomb, and her mascara was enough to weigh down the strongest of eyelids. She looked like sex on the hoof. It was perfect.

I'd finally given up and wriggled into my second tightest pair of jeans, a dark wash Levi pair that I'd had since college. They were worn in all the right places. I'd put on my red boots, a red tank top and a jean jacket with a sheepskin collar reminiscent of a motorcycle jacket. For the first time since Van had come to town, I finally felt comfortable in myself. Kind of. I hadn't had time for much makeup and my hair was flyaway, but somehow it felt appropriate for the setting. I used to wear rhinestones at rodeos. They seemed unsuitable tonight.

Fae had on maternity jeggings, a pair of black and pink Fat Baby cowgirl boots and a pink hoodie. Her makeup was heavy and seemed the further her pregnancy progressed, the bigger her diamonds became. Her hair, short and dark, was jacked up with spray wax. The higher the hair, the closer to Heaven, y'all.

"Where did you tell Scotty we were going?" I asked her.

"To get ice cream," she replied. "Don't forget to get me ice cream on the way home so I don't have to lie to him." I linked arms with her and pointed us all toward the steel and wood stadium.

The Brooks County Fairgrounds are on the west edge of town. The open-air arena has been there since the sixties, as evidenced by the sagging and splintered wood, rusted fence and corrals, and fairly dilapidated concession stand. Weathered and faded tin signs announce local rodeo heroes, dead or alive, who had made it big. Newer vinyl banners boast the rodeo stock owners. I saw a large sign for Jacque's family, and a smaller one for Jensen Smith, Fae's cousin. Rodeos in Brooks, much like parades, are like homecoming each time. Everyone knows everyone, and they are a tight, loyal group. I knew we'd be greeted with enthusiastic aplomb.

I waved up to the grandstand at Jacque and watched her pull off her red felt hat, waving it in our direction with a grin. I took in the red leather blazer and tan English riding pants with her Tory Burch boots and laughed. She was a fashion statement. I wondered if Tory knew her boots had made their way to the rodeo grounds in Oklahoma. I hope she'd be flattered.

"Let's go back by the chutes," I said, repeating my earlier idea. My cohorts both gave a discreet nod, and we turned to head that way, sidestepping the lines for the porta-potties.

"And… that's my cue," Tally said, with a jiggling adjustment to her breasts and a quick fluff of her hair. I watched her head toward Matt James and his much taller friend, Sam Conn. Matt was a high school friend who had turned into a client. He was short, cute, and could've been the cowboy Scott Eastwood had played had he been slightly more ambitious.

I waved at Matt as Tally shimmied up next to Sam, invading his space and draping herself on the high fence, a fringed boot propped on the lowest rung, not as casually done as it might appear.

But Tally was a model by trade. It was her job to make weird look normal.

Fae Lynn and I went on, eyes peeled and ears open, hoping to catch a tidbit of something floating on the wind. These were the people who could know something, more so than our neighbors. These people took livestock very seriously, and might have information they didn't know was important.

Before we could get that deep into the chutes and corral pens, a dark figure shot out and stopped us. He had on a dusty gray V-neck t-shirt, long, dark Wranglers, his dangerous, just-shined black boots and a black felt hat pulled down as low as it could go.

"Go home," he told me.

"Get out of my way," I shot back.

"Now, Lil."

"Move." I moved to go around him while Fae Lynn looked on with tired indifference.

"Lilly."

"Cash."

"You're causing a scene, you dumbasses," Fae Lynn finally spoke, no hurry in her tone. Cash ducked his head and jerked his chin toward a corner of the corral, his light blue eyes sparking granite under his hat. I moved slightly, in no way indicating I was going to acquiesce to anything he wanted.

"Aren't you under house arrest?" I asked him with barely concealed frustration. He sighed his own frustrated sigh, crossing his arms over his renewed chest.

"If you want to come to the rodeo, you need to go sit in the stands and look pretty. It's not safe back here," he told me without answering my question, nodding toward the men and the oversized animals. He jutted out his pointed chin with an authority he didn't have and fixed his eyes on me.

"Screw you," I said. A slow smile eased into place, replacing the frown, the blue eyes relenting, always more comfortable with games.

"Oh, Lil," he said with barely concealed pleasure, all but licking his lips as he looked me up and down. I looked back at Fae, who was studying her manicure. My habit with Cash was to get sucked in. He had the skill to get me worked up enough to distract me and then leave me standing trying to figure out what I'd been intent on doing in the first place. But I was older, wiser, slightly more flexible, and had no claim to stake on Cash Stetson. I wasn't interested in playing.

"We're just here to see Jacque."

"She's in the press box," he told me, smile still in place, still not making a move to get the hell out of my way. I decided to try a different tactic, one I rarely had the head to use with Cash.

"What have you heard?" I asked him, knowing he was here for the same reason we were. "Anything?" His black hat dipped as he glanced behind him, the light in his eyes dimming. He shook his head. But the answer was a beat too slow. I took a deep breath, rolled my neck slowly and stepped up to him, under his hat, watching his eyes widen slightly and his mouth part.

"Fae Lynn and I are going to take a walk back here. We're going to do one lap and see if anyone decides to tell us something because they think she and I are too dumb to understand. You may trail along behind us, far enough back so no one suspects you're actually following me, if that makes you feel better. Now move out of my way, and I won't call your probation officer and tell him you're not at home watching Hee Haw with your mama."

Fae Lynn had edged up beside me, a deceptively docile look on her face.

"I would suspect, Lilly Kay, that his probation officer knows right where he is," Fae Lynn said. I frowned. She and Cash weren't exactly squaring off, but there wasn't a whole lot of lost love there. Fae Lynn had tolerated Cash because he'd been my choice, and this town's too small to be real mean. And while she'd never really said "I told you so," she'd also been the first to call shotgun when it was decided Cash needed to be taught a lesson. Cash would never utter a bad word against Fae Lynn, because, well, it was Fae Lynn, but he knew what her opinion was of him and that she wasn't hesitant to voice it.

"Who's your probation officer?" I asked him. He shrugged, his eyes not meeting mine, the slashes of his eyebrows raising slightly.

"I don't have to tell you that," he answered. I turned to Fae Lynn.

"Is it Scotty?" She shrugged. "Are you here on your own accord, or because someone sent you?" I asked Cash. He pulled the hat down lower over his eyes. I sighed huffily. I could see Tally out of the corner of my eyes. She was surrounded by cowboys of all shapes and sizes over near the entrance to the back pens. She was doing her job, but I could see that she recognized Cash and looked pained, a frown marring her otherwise perfectly symmetrical features.

"Cash," I finally spoke. "Just move. This is important to me."

Cash has been enabled all his life. It had been easier to give in to Cash than to try to buck his dynamic personality. So his family generally caved. It was Cash's example. So I couldn't really fault him for it when he stepped aside with a pop of his jaw, but a part of me was disappointed. Spencer Locke wouldn't have moved. Spencer Locke was immovable. I smiled quickly at him and stepped past him. Fae Lynn took a long minute to grind her boot heel into the square-toe of Cash's boot before she followed. I didn't look back.

xxx

We found nothing. Nothing notable anyway. I thought that identifying tweekers would be easy enough, but the rough adrenaline that coursed through the back pens had the whole lot of them so high I wouldn't have been able to tell if it was chemical or natural unless I had a drug dog with me.

Matt James had conveniently started a conversation about the cattle, inquiring about Poppa Joe, who I knew Matt saw once a week at the sale barn. I'd taken note of the crowd of cowboys and their reactions, but nothing had really tripped any triggers.

I'd finally given up and given the nod to Tally and Fae that we should move on. They went up to sit with Jacque, and I made my way over to the concession stand to fill their orders. I requested popcorn, two funnel cakes, and three frozen lemonades and was fumbling with cash when a cloud of sweet perfume tickled my nose and a sneeze sent the bills flying. I squatted down to catch them and a perfectly pink-polished hand handed me a wad of ones. I looked up as I stood.

Missy Spade stood up with me. Her smooth, light-brown hair had a few highlights, her clear brown eyes were kind and her pink lipstick parted with a smile. She had on a pink plaid button-up, starched jeans and light brown snip-toed boots. Missy, as I knew her, was sweet, well put together, and always appropriate. She was married to Angus, the rough mountain man who'd needed Daddy. I smiled back.

"Miss Missy, how are you?" I asked, perfectly at ease with her brand of manners, unlike her husband, who was short on Southern niceties.

"Just fine, Lilly, you?"

"Good," I nodded, "Just thought we'd come out and support Jacque," I told her, repeating my story, even though she hadn't appeared to wonder. She nodded back with a smile.

"How's the Jubilee coming along?" she asked.

"Great," I said, "Custom rustic-chic picnic tables being built as we speak."

"No one throws a party like the women in your family," she said. I smiled and nodded my agreement.

"Y'all had anything else happen up there?" I asked her, referring to the vandalism on their property.

She shook her head, "No. It was a one-time thing. I think it was probably drunk kids. Angus went ahead and set up the game cameras," she said, referring to video equipment typically used to track deer for hunting or predatory animals that needed to be eliminated, "But we haven't seen anything suspicious."

"That's good," I said with a smile.

"It is," she said, nodding at the cashier, who had our food and drinks ready. I paid and gathered it all up, stealing a load of napkins too. "You need help?" she asked me. I shook my head.

"I'm good. Thanks though. Nice to see you Miss Missy," I told her, moving toward the arena stands. The soft wrinkles around her eyes crinkled with a smile.

"You too, Lilly. Stay good."

There wasn't any hint of sarcasm in her tone, which was funny enough in and of itself. I nodded and smiled my way to Fae Lynn and Tally, the drink holder wobbling precariously.

I turned the corner to start the climb up the rickety bleachers and spotted a shock of white hair. My eyes widened, and I took in the chambray dress shirt and boots, the wide grin and the generally unconcerned countenance.

"Damn it," I cursed softly to myself, looking around. Jack Thomas was planted in the bleachers, flanked on all sides by a few other good ol' boys, telling stories. My hands were full and I didn't know what I could do anyway, save for walking up to him and accusing him of theft, which didn't seem like a great idea. I ground my teeth as his head came up and met my eyes. He smiled wide at the pretty girl in the crowd and then turned back to his audience. Left with no good options, I went about my climb.

"'Bout damn time," Fae Lynn grumped when I reached them. I handed her a funnel cake without comment, plopping myself next to Tally and reaching for the popcorn. I took a deep breath and inhaled the heady scent of money, shit, and smoke; one eye on the confirmed felon a few rows away.

Chapter Eighteen

"Do you want me to shoot him?" Nonnie asked, putting her head in and pistoling her right hand. Deadly serious.

"Who?" I asked, already knowing the answer judging by the way the hair on the back of my neck was at attention and an unpleasant feeling was making its way through my body.

"Me," he popped his coiffed head in with a greasy smile, edging his large body past my grandma. Undeterred, she stepped in front of him, as though she were going to stop him.

My office is small. As said, it sits on Main Street in Brooks. It has a bathroom, leaden with pink potpourri and expensive hand soap, a reception area that takes up the whole front half of my rental space. That half holds Nonnie and her very heavy antique desk, a dark coffee table, two matching end tables, and a comfy couch and two uncomfortable chairs, all three in muted shades of mauve, the chairs coordinating with the tables. There's an electric blue rug underneath the seating area, with slashes of pink and orange to bring it all together. Nonnie painted all the dark paneling Sweet Mimosa after she decided the walls depressed her and washed her out. She and Mama then decorated the rest without my permission or a request for my opinion. It works. As does Nonnie. She's a fantastic receptionist/legal secretary/intake counselor. Crazy as she may be, no one is ever brave enough to cross her. She's good for business, mostly, except for the potential divorce clients she usually sends home with a lecture, a copy of *The Five Love Languages,* and a brochure for a marriage retreat. Which never really bothers me. I hate doing divorces. They're depressing. She's saved several marriages by the sheer fact that no one, and I mean no one, doesn't do exactly what Miss Minnie Culvert tells them to do.

Van, allegedly, hadn't gotten the message.

"What do you want?" I said grumpily, knowing the answer, even if I hadn't told anyone but Tally as such. It was mid-morning on a Tuesday and even though he'd called, sent two bouquets of flowers that I'd immediately trashed, and three emails to generally harass me, a part of me thought maybe he'd gone back to Texas since I hadn't actually seen him.

No such luck.

"Now Lilly," he smiled charmingly at me, "Do be sweet."

The sweet train, in case you aren't keeping up, left the station a long time ago. Back when I'd first been done wrong by Van. Likely back when I'd been done wrong by Cash that first time so very long ago. There isn't a sweet bone in my body, y'all.

"Can we talk?" he asked, "Privately?" he nodded at Nonnie with another high-wattage smile. Nonnie's small chin set, and I could see her wheels turning, wondering where in the hell she'd hidden that Taser after she'd juiced my grandpa. I tried to hide a grimace. It was probably best to get this over with.

"Yes," I answered him, watching Nonnie start her indignant quiver, a flash-forward to my elder years. I nodded at her that it was okay and ignored her gestures that indicated she was going to get a gun and closed the door behind her.

I smiled *sweetly* at Van and moved to sit behind my desk.

"I hear y'all are having a party," he said.

"That's none of your business," I told him.

He sighed and put on a fake smile then looked me up and down. "What *are* you wearing, Lilly dear?"

Van had on what appeared to be polyester pleated pants with a somewhat large black and white houndstooth check, black loafers with no socks, and a rather shiny black golf shirt. He was wearing houndstooth only because it was too early for seersucker. I'm sure it was all very designer and had cost his mother a pretty penny. His hair was slicked back with the same texturizer spray I also had a bottle of back at my great-grandmother's house. There was a fine white line where his sunglasses had lay on his head, a contrast to his otherwise ruddy face. His eyes were almost a grape color against the white. An old, smushed, moldy grape, I thought. He looked like a used car salesman. With a trust fund. And had the nerve to hint that I looked out of place. I looked down. I had on black slacks, a pair of black cowboy boots stitched in orange, an orange button up, and a crisp black hoodie, all severely ironed, which had taken me forever, and it was only after a can of spray starch did the crease in the hood of the hoodie stay put. I'd also jacked a whole bunch of orange beaded bracelets from Tally before I'd left, and stolen one of Nonnie's diamond necklaces from her neck that morning. It was all very FBI agent meets Fae Lynn the college years. I bristled. I looked okay, I thought. I didn't answer him and he took that as a signal to go on.

"I barely recognize you in those clothes... Is that a sweatshirt?"

I played with a sparkly bead on my wrist. "I think I know why you're here, Van," I told him in an effort to be done with this and send him the hell back to Texas so I could resume pretending that he hadn't hurt me. He looked surprised, and relieved.

"Well, Lilly, that makes things a little easier," he said, a faintly sheepish tone coloring his words.

I didn't respond.

"It just sort of happened, you know. She's in mother's Trim and Tone class, and Mom thought we'd hit it off. So we met up in our box at Cowboy Stadium during the season opener. You know, the one where Tony injured his finger?" I nodded, even though I'd long since cared less about Tony and all his supposed injuries.

"So you're engaged," I said, wondering why he was leading with this. Wouldn't it just be easier to ask me for the tape and move on down the line?

He nodded.

"And running for State Senate," I told him, too eager to be done with him to care if he thought I was keeping tabs on him. He nodded at that too with another surprised look.

"Yes," he responded.

"And you think I have something that might derail those two things," I went on. His face colored and his jaw started to move to the side. He tugged on an ear.

"Well.... yes," he said slowly. I waved a hand.

"Let's not even get into it," I said. He looked relieved again. "I don't have it," I said. Surprise came back to flood his pink face. His mouth came open.

"Are you sure?" he asked me. I was sure, because up until a few days ago I hadn't even known it had actually existed. And the down and dirty rifling of all my crap from Dallas had confirmed that *it* wasn't in my possession. Char had later corroborated that the next morning, along with the declaration that she was keeping all my Die Hard DVDs. And the demand for a stiff drink.

"I'm sure," I told him, deciding then not to tell him that I'd lied to him. His eyes narrowed and the country club demeanor cleared way for the litigiously unpleasant lawyer.

"I don't believe you," he said, leaning forward, the ankle that had been resting on his knee sweeping down to the floor.

"I don't care," I told him, leaning forward myself, face over my desk.

Van and I had never argued. We just didn't. Mostly because he placated me on certain issues, and I went along with what he wanted on others. There just hadn't been anything to argue about. I'd once wanted to wear red to a children's hospital gala, and he'd balked at the idea of a red bow tie and cummerbund. The tussle was short-lived and the disagreement decided by his passive-aggressive purchase of a purple sequined number from Neiman's. Matching evening accoutrements for himself, of course. I am now well aware of how superficial our relationship was, and I've almost come to terms with it so you can hold off on your desire to slap me upside the head.

"Lilly, I don't want to make a stink over this. But you don't seem to understand what's at stake here. The future of Texas rests on your compliance."

"Please tell me you're kidding," I said with a shake and a real laugh. Van didn't waver. Fae Lynn says that the biggest favor you can do for yourself is not believe your own hype, good or bad. As previously mentioned, Van had more than bought into the ego his parents had bestowed upon him. "Van, let me review for you the events that have brought us to the place where we are today. You cheated on me. You lied to me. You made all sorts of promises and then you just wrecked it," I said, trying to mask the pain of those truths with a clipped, sardonic tone.

"Now Lilly, I've never lied to you," he told me with a straight face.

"I found you having sex with your secretary!" I exploded, losing whatever faux aura of cool I was trying to maintain and anger winning out over sadness. I'd been doing yoga, but I was my Nonnie's granddaughter. I wanted to punch the shit out of him, I wanted to tase him. I wanted to shoot him. And not stop until I was out of bullets. I could feel my hand itching for the rough etching on the handle of my gun, the weight of it a slight more calming than a headstand at a time like this.

"But I didn't lie about it," he defended.

"Van, you went to the same law school I did. A lie of omission is still a lie."

"Allegedly," he responded. I blew my breath out heavy.

"GET OUT!" I yelled, standing up and pointing toward the door.

"Calm down, Lilly," he instructed me without so much as a flinch. I pulled my bag out from under my desk and started digging in it, finally pulling out my pistol and leveling it at his head. Shooting him was something I'd been trying to pretend I wasn't interested in doing since he'd shown up on my doorstep.

Nonnie's head popped in, and she nodded approvingly when she saw the gun.

"Finally," she said without any facetiousness to her tone.

"Get. Out," I said coldly, adding another hand to the gun to quell my shaking arm. "And keep heading south once you hit the streets. And don't come back across the Red River. Ever." I was trying to play it cool, but I kept feeling a tight itchiness in my muscles.

"Now, Lilly," he said.

"Stop saying 'Now, Lilly'," I told him with force. "Or I will shoot you."

He looked at me like I was nuts. I could see where he was coming from. The way he knew me, I wasn't one to be ruffled or ruffle any feathers, no matter who might spill champagne on my silk evening dress. But I'd been home for some time, God had handed me some clarity and some tools, and Van was ruining my attempt at Zen. I wasn't interested in revisiting my relationship with Van. I wanted to pretend like it never happened. I settled for pretending like his presence didn't ruffle me that much.

"You wouldn't be the first ex I shot, Van," I told him. He sighed and looked put-upon. He waved his long fingers, blasé, in my general direction.

"This Carrie Underwood-after-a-few-drinks persona you've adopted isn't all that becoming, Lillian," he told me. I happen to think Carrie's a lot cooler when she's a few drinks in and she's got a baseball bat in her hands, but hey, that's just me.

"Van, I don't have what you think you need," I told him, putting a bullet in the chair next to him. My mother would die when she found a bullet hole in the new upholstery on Queen Anne's chairs. But this wasn't my mama's broken heart. "Go home," I said, adding another shot closer to his nether regions this time. He finally scrambled to stand but his eyes took on a hard cast.

"I don't believe you, Lilly. And I'm not leaving until I have what I came here to get."

Chapter Nineteen

"We need to do something before Fae Lynn pops and is elbows deep in poop and boobs." My phone buzzed with the start of a group text, initiated by Jacque.

"Word," Char responded.

"What?" Tally asked.

"I'm in. After 4, though. I've got a volunteer meeting," Brandy offered.

I sat watching the live byplay pop up on my phone. My friends are hilarious, sweet, mean, loyal, tough, pretty, and awesome. My Daddy calls us the Posse on the sly, because he knows the kinds of things we do in our free time, after dark. Dressed in black. With the aforementioned road kill.

"I expect y'all to be bringing me muffins and Mt. Dew while I'm knee deep in all this shit. But yes, celebrate me. I like foot rubs," Fae Lynn answered while I was trying to come up with a cute response.

"Let's do yoga," I texted. "A private prenatal yoga session. I can set up," I finally answered last.

"Stop smoking crack," Char responded.

"I do have some new pants I ordered off the Internet," Jacque texted back.

"That sounds like work," Tally pointed out.

"Hell, no," Fae Lynn came through.

Brandy didn't answer, probably because she couldn't think of anything nice to say.

"Come on," I sent, "It'll be fun. Girl's day out."

"Let's drink instead," Char said.

"I like day-drinking," Tally agreed.

"Outside? There's a great new Mexican place with a patio," Jacque said.

"Bitches? I can't do either of those things," Fae Lynn sent.

"Those both sound like fun," Brandy finally responded.

"Drinks it is. Virgins for Fae," I relented. "Saturday?"

"One last hurrah," Tally responded.

"Fine," Fae Lynn said. "But y'all still have to bring me donuts at home."

"Done," I sent, "Saturday."

"After 11, okay? I've got to deliver flowers at the hospital," Brandy told us.

xxx

I gathered my stuff together at 1:30, waved goodbye to Nonnie after fending off her offer to come take notes "because that Loretta couldn't manage shorthand if her life depended on it," and headed out the door.

I walked into Charlie's office at a quarter 'til, bearing my briefcase and a big white paper sack. Charlie had bested me in the early arrival game and was sitting in his conference room with a shit ton of unnecessary papers spread out in front of him. I would guess the bottom portion of the stacks were probably blank copy paper. I know this because he'd taught me how to stack them just so. I slid Loretta a fried cherry pie before I went into the conference room.

"You got a plan?" Charlie asked me without looking up.

"Kind of," I said, sitting the sack in the middle of the table, "That's part of it." I moved my hand at the sack. Charlie sighed.

"I'd like to be mad at you, but I didn't find anything real good either, other than some stuff about dog breeding." I sat in one of the chairs Charlie's wife Annabelle had upholstered in a weird English hunting pattern back in the nineties.

"Charlie, it's like my Gigi says: if you can't dazzle them with brilliance, baffle them with bullshit."

Charlie eyed me without humor, "I've met your grandmother Gwen, there doesn't seem to be much brilliance there." I shrugged.

"She has her moments," I defended the woman who would probably do the same for me. Probably. "She can be quite dazzling," I added with a smirk.

"Big diamonds don't mean a whole lot in this town," Charlie, the man who wore Burberry scarves and raincoats, pointed out.

"Don't I know it," I said with sarcasm.

"He still here?" Charlie asked, pulling out a chocolate chip cookie from the sack.

"Who?" Spencer asked, easing himself into the room. I nodded and shook my head at Charlie, who was sweet enough to let it die between us. I didn't want to discuss Van in front of Spencer. Cash was enough. Charlie changed the subject quickly as Spencer started to dig into the bakery bag, pulling out two wrapped pralines with a sly smile. I frowned at him.

"What are you doing here?" Charlie asked Spencer, "I thought you had a hearing?"

Spencer shrugged. "Got done early. Thought I'd come watch the show," he said, stretching out his long legs in front of him. I didn't like the idea of Spencer being a spectator to my legal wrangling, but to argue with him would be to admit he perturbed me, which I was not going to do. Not today anyway.

"We don't really have a show," Charlie said. "We're still trying to work out a deal." Spencer shrugged again.

"You're making it too hard," he said. Charlie pierced him with a sharp look. No one, and I mean, no one, tells Charlie how to lawyer. He must be getting soft in his old age, though, because he relented.

"How so, Socrates?" Charlie asked him sarcastically. Spencer pointed a long, elegant finger, better suited for Carnegie Hall, at Charlie.

"It's like you always tell me, an equitable result is good, but it's better when the clients get what they want. What do the clients want?" Charlie paused.

I spoke, "Teddy wants the calves. He thinks the registered ones will bring something and since they've got his bull stock in them…" I trailed off, not all that excited to talk about bull sperm in front of Spencer.

"I think Surly just wants his heifers back," Charlie mused, "And for Teddy to stop dicking him around." My surprised look amused Charlie, "Teddy Salz is the worst sort of neighbor," Charlie said, "I wouldn't be surprised if this wasn't as accidental as Teddy claims."

It wasn't the first time I wanted to sock and fire one of my clients. There was the one that had assaulted me with a brick. And the one who'd almost gotten me killed. And Cash Stetson.

"So Teddy needs to pay," I said, "Literally." Charlie nodded. I thought a little harder.

"Charlie," I started, "That baffling thing… would you mind if I handled it?" I asked him, not wanting to step on his toes as the director of this shit show. Charlie smiled, catching on that two old ranchers who were contemporaries of my Poppa and had watched me grow up at the sale barn, were coming in to argue over cattle, and that the best method might be to let me hit them with a Southern belle's brand of bullshit: steely insistence masked with sweetness. His smile widened underneath his silver mustache, and he made a grand gesture with his hand.

"By all means."

xxx

I could tell Spencer was confused and trying to act like he wasn't, but he didn't move from his chair. When Teddy walked in, I offered him coffee, along with a honey-sweet piece of baklava from the paper sack. I'd slapped on another layer of lipstick after the planning session with Charlie and had pushed my hair back from my face, pouring myself another glass of tea. When Surly Clark came in,

I popped up to greet him with Loretta, and got him a strong cup of coffee and handed him a lemon bar before ushering him into a seat at Charlie's conference table. Once they were settled at the table, snacks in hand, I smiled ever so sweetly, popped up, slapped my hands on the table and looked each of them in the eye.

"This is how it's going to be, gentlemen."

xxx

Bullshit, as a legal maneuver, is a very effective tool when used appropriately. Thirty minutes after they'd walked in, Teddy and Surly had walked out together. Teddy was several, several thousand dollars poorer, and Surly would be picking up his girls that Saturday to ensure the rest of their pregnancy went to his liking then returning the weaned calves back to Teddy. Once I'd detailed the agreement that neither of them had agreed to, I had pulled a page out of my Nonnie's book, lecturing them on the art of good neighboring. Charlie had taken over before I'd gotten in too far. When Teddy started to balk, Spencer had eased in with his practical explanation of what Teddy really wanted, as though we'd hired him to mediate the damn thing. I was too happy with the outcome to be too pissed.

I think they'd been so shocked that little miss Lilly Atkins was lecturing them that they forgot to be offended. There had been nods, and handshakes and kisses on my cheeks. And most importantly, they did what I told them to.

Chapter Twenty

"How's Fae?" Amber asked me through the phone, as I heard her simultaneously hush one of her twin boys. Amber was another of my best friends from high school. Redheaded, sassy and artistic, she'd moved to San Francisco quickly after graduation. And unlike me, she hadn't come home with her life in shambles. We tried to manage quick phone calls. This one was a short Saturday morning check-in.

"She's good," I said, "Really hateful."

Amber laughed, "She is very pregnant. That makes sense."

"True," I agreed.

"How are you?" she asked, finally getting around to it.

"Fine," I said quickly.

"I hear you've been using that line on everyone, including yourself," she responded kindly.

I sighed, "I wish you could be here for the Jubilee," I said, changing the subject.

"Me too. No one throws a party like your mama. But I'll be there for Christmas."

"Speak of the devil," I told Amber when Mama's head appeared in the doorway, "Give kisses to the twins. See you at Christmas. Love you."

"Will do. Love ya."

We clicked off, and I opened the door for her.

"What are you wearing?" my mother asked.

"Yoga clothes," I told her.

"Interesting..." she drawled, looking me up and down from head to toe.

"Interesting" is the kiss of death in the South. She might as well have told me that I looked like shit on a stick, bless my heart. I looked down. I had on brown and purple tie-dyed, cropped yoga pants, and a matching flowy top with a dark purple bra attached. On my feet were a version of orthopedic Birkenstocks. It was all very expensive. And much the rage, according to the *Yoga Journal*. I sighed.

"Did you need something, Mother?" She pursed her lips, still looking at my workout attire. She shook herself with a shudder but didn't say anything else about it.

"Yes, Emma Sue called and said she was finished with the centerpiece mock-ups for the Jubilee. Can you run and grab them and bring them home?"

"What time does she close?" I asked.

"Noon," Mama said, straightening the pillows on the sofa.

"I'm meeting the girls for lunch," I told her. She looked at me with a keen smile.

"Well, then you should leave now, put them in the fridge at your office, and get them before you head back out of town." There was no room for discussion or argument. "Go quick, so Emma Sue can close early. She said she was going to Tulsa to do a wedding." I smiled back just as keenly, and stole a move from Tally, sending a salute Mama's way.

"Yes ma'am," I said.

"Don't sass me," she said with a smile.

"Yes ma'am," I sassed, moving toward the door and away from her swatting hand.

xxx

The girls were all already there when I arrived at Ruby's, Brooks' one Tex-Mex restaurant. Fae Lynn was surrounded by pink packages, and I deposited mine in the stack. The Southern rule is that you only get one baby shower, and all babies thereafter were relegated to Sip and Sees. But the rules flew out the window when your friends wanted to day-drink and fête you, and the rules would *always* be damned when the Posse was involved.

Everyone had a thick, pale-green slush except for Fae. Her's was pink. I knew it was a virgin daiquiri. I grabbed my seat next to Tally, who'd chosen the head of the table. I was scooping sweet salsa onto a hot, salty chip when the white-shirted, black-aproned waiter came to take my drink order.

"Corona with a lime," I said, offering him a smile. He nodded and turned on his heel, nodding again at Fae's calling for more queso.

"You're drinking beer?" Char asked with a shocked look. The rest of my friends' heads turned to inspect me.

"What's wrong?" Brandy asked me, laying a hand on my arm.

"Van's still in town," Fae Lynn said with a snort.

"Van? That tall, pudgy guy you were going to marry?" Jacque asked.

"Yep," Tally answered before I could, flagging down a waitress for more chips.

"And he's still here?" Jacque asked.

"Yep," I said.

"Why?" Brandy asked with shock.

"What's he doing here?" Jacque asked.

I shook my head with glances at Tally and Char, "No idea." Char looked pissed. Tally looked pained.

"You think he's trying to win you back?" Brandy asked with an anxious look on her face.

"No," I promised, "He's engaged to someone else."

"What?" Brandy asked.

"Well, let's get rid of him," Jacque proposed quickly. There were enthusiastic nods all around before I could get a word out. I shook my own head.

"I want to ignore him until he goes away," I told her. Tally snorted and Fae Lynn looked pissed as she wiped sweat from her upper lip.

"Why?" Jacque asked, confused and peering intently at me.

"Because I don't want to deal with it," I said.

"Sometimes you don't exactly have a choice," Jacque argued. I frowned at her. She frowned right back. "Why are you acting like you're responsible for anything? He deserves to get shot and then some."

I shrugged, which was my new habit when I wanted to avoid something uncomfortable.

"We should run him out of town," Char said again. Even Brandy nodded this time.

"No," I said, squeezing a lime into the bottle the waiter had deposited in front of me.

"We don't exactly need your permission," Char said saucily, "Sometimes you don't know what's good for you. You're lucky to have friends like us." I laughed.

"I am lucky you're not my enemies," I agreed. "Y'all scare the shit out of me sometimes. And I'm one of you," I admitted.

"Damn straight," Fae Lynn said with a raise of her glass. We all leaned in to clink drinks.

"Damn straight," I echoed with a small smile.

xxx

I was halfway out of town before I realized I needed to turn around and go back to the office to pick up Mama's damn flowers.

I fumbled with the keys to my office, huffing out my breath, a bead of sweat forming on my forehead. I was a little buzzed from the one beer. I'd made the short walk back to pick up Mama's flower arrangements and my Jeep, but now I was having trouble getting in the office. I am a lightweight, but damn.

I finally managed to push in the key and turn the lock with force, the bells that served as an announcement system knocking me in the head. I swatted them away and stepped in, moving to turn on a light. The sole of my fancy yoga shoe scraped against something. There was a stack of mail on the floor. We have a P.O. box, but we also have a physical address, obviously. Usually the mail that came in through the slot of the front door was cleaned up and deposited by Nonnie before I had a chance, but the Saturday run lay in the floor. I picked it up and started to absentmindedly thumb through it, laying a magazine subscription bill and office supply catalog on Nonnie's desk. I took a copy of the *Oklahoma Bar Journal* for myself and was left with a thick business envelope, expensive heavyweight paper. I slid it open without the help of a letter opener, a tiny drop of blood appearing out of nowhere. I sucked my ring finger. I didn't hurt now, but it would probably sting later. I unfolded the thick, white paper.

Without anyone there, on a chilly Saturday, the office was weird. I was rarely there on a weekend, and didn't make a habit to be there alone, given the prior events. I worked some, but mostly I took it home with me. I only ventured into town if I really needed dead quiet. But usually I appreciated the distraction of Tally's chatter and the easy access to fresh baked goods. Today, with only half the lights on, it made me uncomfortable, even with the sun shining a backdrop into the front room. The refrigerator buzzed from the back and tiny pings and dull scratches made their way to my ears. It smelled like musty potpourri, stale coffee and dead gardenias. I pulled my tie-dyed sweater closer.

I still know what you did last summer…

Nonnie would be happy to know they'd taken the time to procure appropriate punctuation this time. I turned the envelope over. It had, allegedly, been mailed from Fayetteville, Arkansas.

Fayetteville and its quaint surrounding suburb-like neighboring towns weren't that far away from Brooks. The University of Arkansas lay in Fayetteville, as did excellent shopping. Fae's brother had gotten his undergrad at the U of A, where they "called the hogs," boasted a pig on every single inanimate object, and had beer with a higher alcohol content than we did here in Oklahoma. Fae and I had taken advantage of J.W. and his student tickets when we were in high school, driving back and forth to football games in the Fall and baseball outings in the Spring. Even though it wasn't that much farther east than our small town, it was ever so *Suthen*, honey, and I'd always felt at ease there, given my family and their incessant preaching on rules. Somehow, it didn't seem like such a burden to curl your hair when you were going over there. Fayetteville made you want to slap on the perfect shade of red lipstick, wear a dress to a football game, and make sure your boots were polished.

J.W. was now in Massachusetts getting his PhD in something like brain chemistry. I didn't know anyone in Fayetteville, that I knew of. I'd gone back for an SMU/Arkansas football game a few years ago; a meet-up with Fae and Char that had included blueberry beer and ended with Char on top of a bar on Dickson Street.

XXX

"You busy?" I asked when Fae Lynn answered the phone. I'd dug through the kitchen to find the box of freezer bags and had put the new note in it, securing the seal. The offending piece of mail was now dangling between my fingers.

"Yes," Fae Lynn answered, "You exhausted me and now I'm real bitchy. Scotty took Hazzard to the driving range and sent me to get a pedicure because he couldn't stand me. He told me not to come back until I was pleasant. I'm never going home."

"So Scotty's at the golf course?" I asked. I heard her take a drag of what I suspected was the diet Mt. Dew her obstetrician frowned upon.

"Why?" she asked. I sighed. Fae Lynn didn't need any extra stress. I didn't need to be the one to give it her. But I was still attempting to operate under the assumption that the letters were cruel jokes. So I decided to nonchalantly mention why I needed her husband.

"I was wondering if Scotty had found anything on that letter I gave you," I told her.

"I just saw you thirty minutes ago. You couldn't mention this then?" Fae Lynn's discernment was her best and most aggravating quality. I sighed.

"I got another one," I told her.

"You shitting me?" she asked with a heavy breath.

"No," I said.

"Where are you?" she asked.

"The office. It was in today's mail," I explained.

"I'm down the street at that fake spa place. Bring your ass down here."

xxx

Fae Lynn looked like a beached whale plopped and propped up in the fancy massage chair of the nail salon. The short, dark-haired woman working on her feet looked anxious. The rest of them hovered nearby, diet Mt. Dew at the ready. One was giving her a hand massage. It wasn't because they were so very afraid of her. It was because they loved her so. Fae Lynn was a good tipper, magnanimous with her gossip, and I didn't know anyone who didn't want to be around Fae, grumpy or not.

"Tell me again why you're wearing that," she said by way of greeting.

"These are yoga clothes," I told her, a tad defensive. "Very expensive yoga clothes, I might add," I said a little ruefully. Fae Lynn snorted.

"You wasted your money," she said. I slipped off my sandals and slid into a chair, scooting the seat back to accommodate my legs, nodding at another pedicurist when she made a questioning motion at my feet.

"You wear diamonds to mow the yard," I told her. "Leave me alone."

She took a sip of what looked like sparkling apple juice, a Mt. Dew nowhere in sight. "You know, Lil, that God knows you, no matter how hard you try to hide. You're you, no matter the bad ideas, poor fashion choices, or skeletons that have come out of your closet."

"I can't believe I was ever going to marry him."

"You were young and dumb," she said.

"It was less than a year ago!"

She shrugged. "Comme ci, comme ca," she butchered the French expression.

"I want him gone," I told her.

"Say the word," she said with another shrug. I shook my head.

"Tally has run him over, his eyebrows have been set on fire, you've assaulted him and he's still here. Not sure what else anyone could do to convince him to leave."

"We have our ways," she said with another delicate sip.

"I'm working on it," I told her. "He wants something I don't have. It's a little sticky."

"Char told me. She also says you have my copy of *The Mexican*. I want it back."

"Fine," I said, distractedly.

Fae decided to let Van die. "Where's the note?" I wriggled to get my purse, shooting an apologetic look at the pedicurist as I splashed water. I handed the note to Fae Lynn and stole her *US Weekly* while she inspected it.

"This is stupid," she said. "When's the last time you were in Fayetteville?"

"That last time I drove up and met you and Char."

She smiled at the memory. "I have never seen someone lose so many sequins in one night."

"Lord love her."

"You know anyone living over there?" she asked.

"Not that I can think of off the top of my head."

"Jake Newsmith got recruited there out of high school," she said. "You went out with him a few times, right?" Jake was a soccer star who was now a photographer in South Dakota, according to Facebook.

"Twice," I responded, leaning back and relaxing in the chair, giving a thumbs up to the little girl who'd brought me my own juice. "But he moved after college. I don't have any ties to Northwest Arkansas, other than it's a great place to shop."

"We should plan a trip after this kid gets here," Fae suggested, patting her belly.

"Agreed," I nodded. Fae deposited the alleged hate mail in her purse, promising to hand it off to Scotty. She asked for a Twinkie before we fell into a comfortable silence, the whir of the massage chairs, and the chirp of the travel channel on the oversized TVs attempting to drown out our thoughts.

I made Fae Lynn drive me back to the office and stand sentry while I got the flowers out of the kitchen and loaded, waving at her once I had locked the door and was on the last trip to my Jeep. I climbed in, kicking off the ugly shoes once I was behind the wheel. The radio blasted full-force as I headed for home, Billy Currington crooning, "Don't," as the town passed by in a blur.

Chapter Twenty-One

"Ommmm. Hahahahahahaha. Ommmm."

"What'n the hell are you doing?" Tally announced, throwing her rose-gold metallic, spiked purse in the general direction of our great-grandmother's hot pink couch. Startled, I tipped over toward our great-grandmother's china cabinet, narrowly missing it and possible disaster. And a broken toe.

"Yoga," I told her, pointing out the obvious.

"You look like an idiot." She informed me.

"Thanks," I said sarcastically, rubbing my hip.

I had taken to standing on my head. Every day. Religiously. Because Cash was out of rehab, my clients were still crazy, and I was getting fat. It had been a week since my last run-in with Van and either he was gone or laying low. So yoga it was.

"Why," Tally drawled gratingly, "pray tell, all the yoga? Surely not Van."

"Van. Cash. The missing heifers. Mama's chocolate chip cookies."

"Damn. That's a long list of stress." Tally winked. "What about Cash?" she asked, "I thought we were done with him?"

I nodded in exasperation, "I thought we were too. Until he showed up here at the ranch."

"Who cares?" Tally said with a limp toss of her wrist. "Just avoid him."

I sighed. "It's just…," I trailed off, biting the inside of my cheek.

"It's just what?" Tally said impatiently.

"I thought I'd be able to look Cash in the eyes and see that he's repentant. I can't," I said, irritated with myself that I was dwelling on Cash. Tally looked thoughtful.

"That's kind of between him and God, don't you think?" she asked with a pointed look at me, "And does it matter?"

"What's that supposed to mean?" I said to her testily. She eyed me knowingly.

"Oh sister."

"What?" I snapped.

"You're pretty," Tally told me sweetly, not at all trying to disguise that she thought I was being dumb.

"Pretty is as pretty does," I murmured Nonnie's favorite saying out of habit. Tally nodded emphatically.

"Yep," she said with another smile. "So stop being dumb." She sighed when I didn't answer. "Are you ready to cry yet?"

I rolled my eyes her way while I pointed and flexed my toes in front of me. "Stop," I told her.

"You know what you need?" she asked me seriously.

"What?" I asked shortly, anticipating where she was going as I stood up to roll up my mat. She smiled evilly.

"Not that. Good grief, get your mind out of the gutter. Although that might help," she drew out in put-on thoughtfulness.

"Tally," I said with a warning tone.

She sat up quickly. "There is only one thing to do at a time like this," she said.

"A time like what, exactly?" I said skeptically.

She puffed out her breath and rolled her eyes. "A Saturday night when I am so obviously having the best hair day I've had in weeks." I laughed then as she stood up resolutely and struck a million dollar pose. "Besides, if you won't cry about it, we might as well dance."

xxx

We were looking for trouble. The kind you get into or egg on; it really didn't matter. So after a few calls to the girls, we'd headed toward town, jamming to the Eagles in Tally's T-bird. Tally had gotten impatient with the intense perusal of my closet, stomped her foot and told me to just "pick something, damnit." I'd grabbed without thinking much, which might have been the best method. I was casual in a pair of tight Levis and my favorite silver-studded red cowboy boots with a white tank top. I'd scraped my crazy hair into a ponytail, thrown on a red leather motorcycle jacket, forgotten earrings and slid a thick black calfskin cuff on my wrist. I felt a little like myself, whatever that really meant.

Tally had avoided anything close to casual, donning a cheery yellow tutu dress and lace-up green gladiator sandals, lining her arms with silver bangles and slashing pink lip gloss across her lips, earrings made out of feathers. I'd long since stopped giving her any grief or even rolling my eyes. If she could get away with it, why not?

Avoiding Chester's and Sticks and Balls, we'd decided to check out the new honkytonk on the outskirts of Brooks. Tuxey's Two Sippin' advertised steaks, a hardwood dance floor and dollar long necks. No doubt there would be a plethora of boots lined up against the wall, sipping from bottles. Hopefully a few of them would be safe enough to allow to push me across the floor.

We pulled into the parking lot, the glare from the multiple neon signs temporarily blinding Tally, causing her to take up two spots instead of her one allotted. She oozed out and slammed the door, checking out her parking job. She shrugged her shoulders and fished her purse out of the back seat, waving her hand nonchalantly at the idea of someone being offended or put out by her lack of societal niceties. Here, I did offer an eye roll. I did, however, forego the lecture. Hey, I shoot people in public; I am no one to talk about being a menace to society.

We waltzed through the swinging doors and surveyed the scene. I could see Tally licking her lips at the boys posed along the dance floor. Without pause, she sashayed to the closest four-top with the most men gathered around.

The club pumped and pulsed with the beat of a Timbaland song. He was accompanied by Nelly. The disco ball bounced twinkling sprays of light as it met with the colored strobe lights. The younger set was working hard to grind each other down to a nub as the synth-heavy song pounded out. I felt my teeth rattle as I waved to my girlfriends and their significant others. I pointed to indicate I was going to get a drink, turning to walk around the dance floor, dotted with seats made out of saddles and faux hay. Before I could get there, the song changed abrubtly to a classic Brooks and Dunn, and the co-eds scurried for a barstool while real dancers, with fancy moves and quick feet, moved in. Most were my parents' age and older, and man could they give a two-step a run for its money. I stopped at a saddle and watched Brandy's parents execute several ballroom-worthy three-sixties, tucked tight together, cheek to cheek, their form never wavering. I smiled.

Tuxey's was a nod to the country bars of the 90s, when being "country" all of a sudden became cool, and everyone went out and bought boots for fashion's sake. Bars with a cowboy theme popped up all over the Southern U.S., catering to the generation of wannabe cowboys and girls who got their information about farm life from people like Tim McGraw. The bar owners had to mix the classic country with the younger bump and grind in order to really satisfy the crowd. There were line dances aplenty. I could probably count down the next line dance from the DJ if I stayed long enough.

The exterior had looked like a very clean barn, neon lights proclaiming cold beer and hot music. The inside was rough plank wood, punched tin walls, and swinging doors. It smelled like sawdust, and there were peanut shells on the floor, unused ropes on the walls, and slick boots sliding across the floor. The lights were low, and the strobe lights danced across the room. It screamed good time. It also most definitely required a drink to make it all believable.

I made a beeline for the bar and asked for a So-Co and lime. The drink, not the shot. I know I'm a lady, and ladies shouldn't drink hard liquor in public, but I felt like Southern Comfort whisky with splashes of lime flirted on the edge. It was smoother than a mint julep and not as potentially messy as something fruity. Plus, I like it, and liking any sort of alcohol was tough for me. I could sip it all night while it watered itself down and still look like a badass.

I paid the bartender, Tommy Johns, and settled myself on a tall swiveling stool, facing the dance floor and all that it encompassed. Some of Brooks' finest were out strutting their stuff. I flip-flopped between being jealous and amused with their dancing skills.

A long, well-built shadow fell across my body, and I turned toward none other than Spencer Locke. My insides started to quiver just a little and I tried my best to tamp down the urge to pretend I was drunk and throw myself in his arms and at his lips. Been there, done that, got the t-shirt, wasn't pretty. Spencer was a by-the-rulebook kind of guy, who waffled between keeping me at arm's length and toying with my emotions.

He flashed a shark-white grin down my way, and I blinked away the blindness, wishing I had on one of Tally's get-ups so I could pretend my self-confidence came from being outrageous. The neon lights bounced off his Michael Phelps-esque shoulders and the highball glass dangling from his extra-long piano-suited fingers. I did my best to ignore the amusement settling on his face, trying to calm myself with surveying how out of place he looked. In a dancehall filled with buffed boots, hefty hats and shiny dinner plate buckles; he was the sorest thumb, in designer jeans, Cole Haan loafers and a dress shirt with the sleeves rolled up. I hated how hot he looked. It should have made me feel better that he didn't have the right wardrobe to fit in with a town full of good ole boys and rednecks, but judging from the waves, nods, and simpers, he was fitting in just fine.

I sighed dramatically and took a gulp of liquid courage.

"So," I started antagonistically, "are we going to dance or not?"

For not the first time since I'd met him, Spencer looked slightly caught off-guard. I eyed him carefully. Could he not dance? Or did he just not want to be seen dancing with me? I was Lilly Atkins, damnit! He'd be lucky to polish my hand-tooled cowgirl boots.

Then, as swiftly as it had appeared, the look was fleetingly gone. Back in place was the perfect smile and perfected charm of a man used to being in control, getting what he wanted, and playing it safe. After setting down his bottle, he offered his arm to me and we started toward the dance floor.

"Shall we?"

No sooner than we'd stepped out onto the sawdust, the song changed from a perfect quick two-stepper requiring some skill to a slow song to which anyone could dance. I eyed the DJ suspiciously.

Spencer had on a smile when he took me into his arms. Alabama crooned as we shuffled slowly around the circular floor ringed with tables. I tried not to be too overwrought with lust at the apparently dangerous combination of Spencer's soap, dry cleaning fluid, and wholesome goodness.

"How's the Jubilee coming?" he asked. I frowned up at him. He shrugged. "When in Rome," he said. I didn't respond. "I didn't know you could be quiet," he said, looking down at me.

"What's your game, Spencer?" I asked suddenly.

"No game," he said with a slight shake of his head and the hint of a frown.

"Isn't it? Isn't that what cute boys do? Play games?"

"You think I'm cute," he said conversationally.

At that, I truly bristled. I narrowed my eyes and not so accidentally stomped on his designer shoe. He grimaced slightly and calmly held me out at arm's length.

"You know you're not ugly," I said crankily.

"That's true," he agreed pleasantly without elaboration. I couldn't say anything else outside the cloud of my moody countenance. "Monopoly," he said finally.

"What?" I asked, irritated.

"I'm good at Monopoly," he told me seriously. "And basketball. Those are the games I play." He said it blandly, but his dark eyes were locked on my face, boring through my expression, the one I was using to try to mask my thoughts. "You?" he went on as though the double entrendre didn't really exist and I was imagining the conversation we were having in an alternate universe. I eyed him suspiciously.

"Checkers," I said finally, giving in. "I play a mean game of checkers."

He nodded, "Not chess?"

I shook my head, my eyebrows coming together over my eyes, "Not chess," I confirmed with some reluctance.

He nodded again, his eyes never leaving my face. I couldn't quite look into his.

"I figured as such."

I took in a sharp breath, sure I should be offended, but too lulled by the feel and smell of him to know why. I tried to disentangle myself from his embrace to no avail; he only used those rope-iron arms to pull me closer.

We lapsed into a silence, uneasy on my part, easy on his, I suspected. He twirled me once more as the song wound down, depositing me on the same barstool where he'd found me, and much like his larger-than-life uncle, appeared to tip his invisible hat my way, before grabbing his drink and melting into the crowd.

"Damn, girl. Break yourself off a piece of that."

Tommy Johns had reappeared. I smiled and accepted the second drink he'd poured.

"Can't. Something about him burns my cookies."

He rolled his eyes and smiled knowingly. "You might need your cookies burnt," he said inappropriately. "Burnt cookies might be just the thing you need," he nodded past me.

"Let's dance." Quint Jackson took the drink from my hand and sat it back down on the bar, grabbing my hand in a proprietary way. I didn't balk, even though a small part of me chafed at the hint that I didn't have a choice or a say in the matter.

The DJ had taken pity on the old folks, a slow spinning of a newer Sam Hunt song. The rapping, and the promises, and the word play gave Conway Twitty a run for his money, but it definitely was an acquired taste.

"Did you know he used to play football?" Quint asked after he'd led me to the dance floor, pulled me close and started pushing me around the floor.

"What?" I said, "Who?"

"This guy," he pointed skyward, indicating the singer, "Tried out for the Chiefs, I think," he said in thought.

"Is that why you like his music?" I asked. Quint shrugged.

"Guy has to be a little worthy, you know, to be able to get that far." Quint had played in the arena leagues and likely would have made it to the equivalent of a Kansas City combine, but for an injury to his Achilles. An injury that had caused an about-face and brought him home to run the Athletic Department at Brooks Senior High. As far as I knew, Quint had never complained about this, but I knew it had to grind some gears, the idea that a dream had been shattered without any say or control.

"You would have made it, Quint," I told him, wanting to comfort him. He shrugged.

"I'd like to think that I wouldn't have," he said with a wink, but I could tell it still stung some. "No shoulda, coulda, wouda's, you know. I am where I am because I need to be here." I looked at his face, the strong profile, the full lips, the soft, dark eyes that wouldn't quite meet mine. I squeezed his bicep flirtatiously.

"For what it's worth, I hear you're doing wonders at the high school," I said. "First bid at State since we graduated," I continued, "That's huge." He smiled.

"So which one?" he asked, changing the subject without any force, or any subtlety.

"Which one what?" I asked, confused. I must be off my game. On a bad day, I could usually follow a free-associative, half-sentence, insinuated conversation with Quint.

"Which guy," he asked, "Should I point you toward? There are so many options," he said. I laughed, throwing my head back, not an attempt at attention but in real mirth. Quint felt it was his job in life to make my paramours jealous, namely Cash Stetson. I suspected he liked kissing me in front of Cash because he knew it irritated him, made me uneasy, and was ironic. Quint had nothing but brotherly love for me, and we'd had our relationship set since sixth grade. But it never hurt to give them something to talk about.

"I'm good," I told him, "But thank you." He took a second to look disappointed.

"If I remember correctly," he started, "it worked pretty well," he told me. I nodded.

"Yes, your memory is pretty accurate. But I don't think I'm in need of your services."

"You sure?" he asked again, his eyes above me, scanning the room.

"I'm sure," I told him as the song wound down and he shuffled me back toward the bar. I saw his gaze gleam a little. The sparkle was hard, even though the bright white grin never faltered or became anything less than pleasant. Before he planted me back on my barstool, he leaned down and planted a soft, seemingly sensuous, but somehow chaste, kiss smack dab on my mouth. After a breath, but before I could protest, he winked and walked away.

Right then, Cash showed up, plopped himself down next to me, and ordered a bottled Bud Light. I eyed him without words. Pretending as though he'd just spotted me, he tipped the bottle Tommy had set in front of him toward me.

"It looks good on you," he told me.

"What?" I asked caustically, without thinking not to. He smiled.

"This," he gestured to my outfit, my hair, and my boots. "Home. Brooks. You."

"Do you remember what happened the last time you tried to pretend to befriend me?" I asked him. He rolled his eyes.

"I don't need a reminder. I'm just stating facts," he told me, bringing the bottle up to sip and turning away from me. Another day, another me, I'd be bothered he'd been the one to end the conversation. This day, this me, I really didn't care. I pushed myself up off the stool to go find my friends and ran smack dab into my former fiancé, the gutless wonder.

Chapter Twenty-Two

"Agh! Are you *still* here?" I felt someone come up to stand beside me and glanced up to find the hard profile of Cash, blue eyes flashing and icy, his fingers curled readily around the neck of his beer bottle, the whites of his knuckles standing in contrast to his tanned hand. I frowned.

I looked around Van to see my people on point, coiled in anticipation of a butt-whooping they had no doubt determined Van more than had coming to him. I sighed. I didn't really want him to die. Not yet. Not in front of everyone.

"Darlin' You're a hard woman to nail down. Thought we might step outside and have a little chat." Van said all this as though it was a good idea. As though it was normal for an ex-fiancé to follow his former almost-bride to her hometown, track her down at the local honkytonk, and want to *talk*.

"I don't think she needs to go outside with you," Cash informed him, stepping around me protectively in an irritating move most typically reserved for say, Jason North or Quint Jackson. Van, while an asshole and a wimp, wasn't an idiot. He eyed Cash warily for the second time and took a tiny step back. But Van had had a few inches on Cash and had also survived law school. And a plane crash in a private jet when he was seven so…

"I don't think that's any of your business. Last I checked you weren't responsible for her decisions," Van told Cash while my eyes widened. True, but still.

Char was beside me in a flash, a couple inches on me in her heels and never one for subtlety. She had a lot in common with Tally. Except Tally was nice.

"What are *you* still doing here?" she asked Van. I watched him take in Cash and Char, trying to decide which one was a more dangerous proposition.

Char. Definitely Char.

I ground my teeth in thought.

"I could whip him. You want me to whip him?" Char asked, interrupting my debate about whether to go outside with Van and save my mama a call in the morning or to let him die on the dance floor. "I don't mind doing that. Here, hold my earrings." She started to pull off shiny, expensive, trashy-sized silver hoops while her husband Aaron sat across the room with an eye on her, cringing. I didn't answer immediately. Not because I was actually contemplating letting her... but because I wanted Van to *think* I was contemplating letting her. I took the earrings she shoved my way, the weight of them heavy in my hand. She was rolling up the sleeves of her Double D pearl snap shirt, black and brightly stitched with an array of flowers. She took a minute to check her black shellac manicure, which I knew was recent, and then looked back at me and shrugged, balling up her fists and stepping toward Van.

Cash and I stepped in front of her at the same time.

"I'll do it," Cash said out of the side of his mouth, his eyes never leaving Van's face. Van had several inches on Cash, but it was rumored that Cash had been doing yoga and had mastered the crow's pose in rehab. Allegedly. I shook my head.

"That would be a definite violation of your parole," I told him, watching Van's eyes narrow at that. Van didn't have a well-honed sense of sarcasm, so he wouldn't know if I was kidding or not. Cash shrugged without looking at me.

"Worth it," he said, cracking his knuckles and rolling his sinewy shoulders.

I saw Spencer start the slow walk toward us, and I started to move Van out the door. I wanted to alleviate any more embarrassment that Van might cause me. The music stopped then, with a screech and a crackle, and I heard my sister's voice, loud and obnoxious.

"Ladies and gentlemen," Tally started, "I just wanted to take a minute and introduce you to the one and only sack of shit who was responsible for installing those Main Street benches the wrong way. He's the city planning consultant we hired and then ran out of town," she said, blatantly making stuff up. "He's the big tall guy who looks like he's an interior designer who drinks his feelings," there was a pause, "Fellas," I heard Tally whisper, "Could you…"

The spotlight shone on us hotly, the glint from the mirrored ball above twinkling.

"Tally out," my sister said with ghetto flair, dropping the mic. I was going to kill her slowly.

"Outside," I said tersely, grabbing the front of Van's strategically untucked shirt. He stumbled as I pulled him toward the exit door. I was not all that worried about saving him, but instead trying desperately to save myself the extra shame of my personal business being conducted on Brooks' newest dance floor.

"Now, Lilly," he sputtered a little, trying to right his stumbling feet.

"Outside, Van," I repeated with more force this time. "Unless you want your ass handed to you." He perked up at that, turning a little to catch glimpses of Char and Cash, still on point like a couple of my Daddy's most expensive bird dogs, watching us with intensity. He kept up with me.

I pushed the heavy metal door under the EXIT sign open, the cool air hitting my face, the smell of exhaust and sweet springtime night air swirling. I wanted to be back inside, dancing with Spencer Locke, wondering why he never blundered when he looked so out of place. Not outside a bar with my ex-fiance who wouldn't get gone, while my best friends and first love itched to send him on his way. By force.

I spun on Van, my back to a pick-up truck, the bugs twitching at the soft fade of an outside light that bathed the spot where we stood.

"WHY are you still here?!" I yelled at him, waving my arms, the stretch of the red leather pulling as they came up. I grabbed the hem and shoved my jacket back down. Van looked at me like I'd gone crazy.

"I told you," he said, between clenched teeth, "And if you would only admit that you have it and hand it over, I will more than leave this godforsaken place in my rearview mirror." He had me at "godforsaken." I closed the short space between us quickly, glimpsing the door swing open out of the corner of my eye, not caring or pausing when people started to pile out. Cash, Char, Tally, Quint, a very large Fae Lynn. Scotty. The rest of the girls. And finally, Spencer Locke, who stood at the back of the pack with a wary expression on his face. Van looked over his shoulder with nervous apprehension. I wasn't sure what he was more afraid of: what they might do, or what they might find out in the process.

I pointed an index finger at him and reached up to stab him in the chest.

"I told you, I don't have it," I said emphatically, punctuating each word with another stab of my finger into his weak chest. He flinched but didn't back down.

"And as previously discussed," he dropped his voice and looked around. Everyone was looking on with interest, the door to the club propped open, a gathering crowd of random patrons bulging out of the door. It appeared as though the music had been turned down. So much for my mama not knowing about this. "I don't believe you," he finished.

I figured this was as good a time as any to confess, what with all the witnesses and everything. I crossed my arms over my chest and rocked back on my boot heels.

"I lied," I told him neatly, without any guilt. Van pulled back, as did the rest of the crowd.

"You don't lie," he said with a incredulous shake of his head. I could see some more head shakes in my peripheral.

"I did to you," I replied, not moving my hands from across my chest.

"You don't lie," he repeated. I rolled my eyes.

"I wanted to make sure you were good and gone," I said. "I didn't want you to think there was any chance of you having a chance. So... I lied," I finished by way of an explanation.

"So you lied to me?" he asked redundantly, actually having the nerve to look hurt.

"I believe that's what she said, shithead," Fae Lynn called out. I cut my eyes to her. Half the town was waiting with a bated breathlessness, waiting to see how this would play out.

"But, but, I... It," Van looked for words. I nodded.

"Exactly," I said.

He finally got enough composure to work it through.

"You blackmailed me!" he yelled, gesturing with his fist, a move which caused the crowd to swell toward us, a buzz beginning. I stepped forward and poked Van again.

"Are you freaking kidding me? You cheated on me! With your secretary!"

He knocked my shoulder. "You lied and tried to blackmail me!" The push caused me to step back a few steps. I fell into someone. I didn't pause to see who it was.

"So you'd stay away from me for good!" I said, going back toward him aggressively. I'm not scrappy by nature. Okay, not physically anyway. But I wanted to slug Van. I needed a chair so I could reach his Botoxed forehead. Someone caught me before I could scale Van and beat the crap out of him. I looked up to see Dawg, who had me by the middle in a football hold, my legs kicking the air. My breathing was heavy as I hung there, futilely swinging at Van as I wondered who in the hell had called Dawg. There was nothing more embarrassing than throwing a hissy fit in front of the guy who made it his life's goal to never participate in a hissy fit. Although he'd seen me throw a few. And had held my hair when one such fit had started with the kind of ice tea that originated on Long Island and ended with the room spinning and me hanging off a deck, relieving myself of my dinner. I twisted my head up.

"Let me go," I said, swinging aggressively and trying to wriggle loose.

"No," he said, holding me aloft and still without much effort.

"Come on, Jase, let me at him." I felt like Scout Finch, mulish and petulant. A light dawned in Van's dark blue eyes.

"Jase, huh? You must be the infamous 'Dawg'," he drew out the word almost nastily. I stopped punching the air and got real still. "I've heard so much about you," Van went on, a sarcastic bent to his tone. "Maybe I should have been listening a little better. Seems like our Lilly actually does have a propensity for lying. So maybe all that flowery talk about how wonderful you are meant something a little more."

The crowd sucked in a collective gasp, and I could see people removing hats and jewelry around the circle. Tally was shoving her way through the crowd, throwing off people like they were bugs. Van was just straight wrong. Of course I'd told Van how wonderful

Jase was. He *is* wonderful. Sometimes a turd when he didn't bend to my will. But a most wonderful turd. But the very idea of a) accusing me of cheating, and b) accusing me of doing something wrong with Dawg, who did no wrong was just. Not. Done.

Jase dropped me, and I quickly moved to get my legs back under me. His eyes, mild and still as the green lakes of Northeast Oklahoma, had a hard edge to them. I'd seen the edge before. When an opposing pitcher had beaned Cash in the head on purpose, Dawg had retaliated without comment during the next half-inning. Only his eyes had given him away. Just barely.

Jase hadn't taken his eyes off Van.

I watched Cash step forward, realizing the insult extended beyond me and Jase, but to Cash as well. Even if the statement Van had made was so very outlandish and so very untrue, the idea of a betrayal by me and Jase to Van would also mean that we would have betrayed Cash, in a weird, convoluted way. And Van had just insulted his best friend. And Cash owed Dawg.

So Van, with his folly, had managed to insult me, Brooks' favorite bad boy, and the town athletic legend, all in one fell swoop. In front of a crowd that was probably a few drinks in and several loads shy of giveashit. Tally stood in front with a Wonderwoman pose.

"You take that back, you asshat," she directed at Van. His eyes were a little wild, taking in how heavily the deck was stacked against him, but the waver only lasted so long before his stupid, Southern bravado slid back into place. His gaze swept over me,

Dawg and Cash before he looked right back at Fae and squared off with her, a stubborn set to his otherwise weak chin.

"No."

Dawg sighed beside me and Cash stepped over to flank me.

"You want first?" Jase asked over the top of my head.

"Yep," Cash answered, licking his lips. I glanced up quickly and was privy to the look they probably used to share on the football field, right before Dawg deposited a bomb into Cash's hands in the end zone. I shivered. But I wasn't on the sidelines now, and didn't have any pom-poms to get in my way.

"No," I said strongly, "I get first." They both took a second to look down at me with slight incredulity.

"I don't think you can reach him," Cash said, a smile on his sharp lips.

"Then lift me up," I said, pointing out the obvious. They both grinned then, the easy smiles of two boys used to winning, as though a touchdown was a foregone conclusion.

"You get first," Dawg nodded, uncharacteristically agreeing to contribute to my delinquency.

"And then you get out of the way," Cash said. I nodded in agreement, my eyes moving toward Spencer Locke across the parking lot. He looked resolute, but I couldn't see the full play of emotions on his face, if there were any.

"Agreed," I told them.

"Me too," Tally said, squeezing in between me and Jase. "I don't need a boost." She straightened her rings, cracked her knuckles and rolled the apparent kinks out of her neck.

It was then, right there in the parking lot of Brooks' newest, shiniest establishment, with half the town packed in a crush in front of the door, under the neon lights, with Willie Nelson declaring allegiance to an illegal substance, that all hell broke loose.

I got in my one good punch to Van's nose, and then was quickly deposited next to Spencer Locke on the edge of the fray. The pain in my hand was the best I'd ever felt, although the glee was short-lived and didn't seem to do much to deter Van, other than knock him back a few steps. I flexed my fist and moved to get a better vantage point. I could feel Spencer easing toward me. I ignored him, and the embarrassment of my bad choices coming to this.

All I could see was a kaleidoscope of blurred, colorful figures under the neon lights. Then the figures parted, and I could see Char straddling Van, whaling the tar out of him, blows coming from both fists while Tally stood sentry over them to make sure no one interfered. A redundant post.

Out of the corner of my eye, I saw Quint Jackson make a run for Cash, who took it square on the jaw without much protest. Brandy looked contemplative on the sidelines as she watched Char. She flinched every time Char made contact, but her eyes were unwavering. I couldn't find Jacque.

The rest of them, I didn't really know, but apparently peanuts make one bloodthirsty and a free for all caused by a Yuppie out-of-towner at a bar meant free licks for anyone who thought they were deserved. It was a good time to right a lot of wrongs, it seemed. Jake and Levi Austin, brothers, twins, and former All-State Academics, were whaling the tar out of each other. It looked like a couple of long-held grudges. Perhaps over a missed basket. Or ACT score.

Rhonda and Bill Givens, twice divorced and thrice remarried, all three times to each other, were yelling and clawing. I saw blood on Bill's face. Charlie would probably have a retainer in his trust account by Monday morning.

Jenny Sue Hunt and Andrea Rand were pulling each other's hair, going around and around while they screamed obscenities at each other and cried in unison. Jenny and Andrea had been best friends since third grade. Andrea had also married Jenny Sue's brother recently, which maybe could explain a lot.

Spencer and Scotty stayed on the fringes together. I stood on one side of Spencer, and on the other side Scotty had his hand clamped on the back of Fae Lynn's neck, as she stood with an exasperated look on her face, arms laced over her belly. I watched Spencer's jaw work overtime and his right fist clench and loosen repetitively. It looked like Spencer probably wanted to grab a hold of my neck too.

In high school, there were inevitable fights. Boys with too much testosterone and not enough places for the energy to go. The fisticuffs occurred right before the bell signaled the hour when most of them went off to athletic endeavors, woodshop, or FFA. Girls with hormones, mad over a guy, or a hairdo, or a hateful word. These tussles happened at lunch, usually. I had always noted how interestingly slow the teachers moved to interrupt them. When I'd mentioned this to my mom, she'd laughed and explained the twofold reasons for the method of moving like molasses toward breaking up a fight. One, sometimes a bully needed a beatdown. So if an underdog was getting in a stray punch or two without taking a beating and they needed to get their aggressions out, sometimes it was best to let nature run its course. Two, no one really wanted to fight. It was painful. And exhausting. And sometimes the best lessons are learned when you figure out that what you thought you wanted, or what you thought was important, actually isn't all that worth it. Smart people, the educators of Brooks' finest.

I kind of wanted to wade into the fray and get another lick in on Van before law and order broke it up, but I was fascinated by Char's work, which seemed to be very inspired. Sure, she was on my side and sure, Van totally deserved it, but it was almost like she'd taken Van and all his transgressions personal. Before I could make a move, Scotty finally released Fae Lynn and started a slow amble toward the dust cloud encircling the fight. I was somewhat surprised my parent's hadn't rolled up yet, seeing as how it seemed someone had taken it upon themselves to call Jase as soon as I stepped outside with Van.

"Stop. Police," Scotty said lazily and not loudly. Dawg smiled and moved to stand beside him, his eyes darting slowly, contemplating who to pick up first. Spencer was still looking itchy at all the mayhem; I'm sure more than bothered by all the lawbreaking and irony unfolding right in front of him.

Two sets of blue lights pulled up in haste, parking haphazardly outside the circle of pickup trucks. I wasn't sure if Scotty had radioed it in or if the redneck grapevine had done the job of reporting the small-town throw-down. The deputies scrambled out of the cars, their black police uniforms crisp, no guns drawn, as they took in the pandemonium. They exchanged looks with Scotty and Spencer, and after a sigh, the men waded in. Cash transferred his allegiance to violence once it looked like the party was over, moving in tandem with Dawg to pull people off of each other. Spencer carefully and deliberately handed Char back to her husband, Aaron, and pulled Van up off the ground, handling him with disdain and in deference to his bloody nose, what appeared to be two soon to be black eyes, and deep fingernail scratches on the left side of his face. Quint and Cash exchanged nods, if not a handshake. Before long, the rest of the crowd was sorted and order was returned, most of them making their way back inside, with a pat on Scotty's back. After it was all over, only one set of cuffs had been used. Only one person had made it to the back of a squad car. After all, there was only one person to blame.

xxx

Char had a pack of ice on her left hand, courtesy of Tommy Johns. She was sipping on a bottle of Corona, nary a hair out of place or a chip in her manicure.

"How'd you take him down?" I asked, grabbing a tall stool and stealing Brandy's cherry sour. Char held up the bottle with a nod and slight smile. I grimaced. I hope Van's plastic surgeon was on call. She handed me the ice pack, and I stuck it on my right hand.

"Feel better?" she asked me, nodding at my hand.

"Some," I said.

"You should have let us come down to Dallas before you left," Char said after another slow slug from the bottle and a wince when she moved her other hand.

"Maybe," I agreed with a shrug.

"Maybe, my ass," Jacque spoke shortly. "Surely this will get rid of the piece of shit?"

"Maybe," I said again. Surely, I thought. Surely after finding out he'd been lied to and then getting the crap beat out of him, Van would run for the border.

"If not, we will gladly tie him up and dump his ass in the Red River," Fae Lynn said. Brandy looked on, wide-eyed.

"Hopefully that's not necessary. I just want him to leave quietly into the night," I said. Fae Lynn looked hungry. And irritated.

"Can you take a break from all that yoga and find your inner badass again? You should have shot him just now," she snapped at me.

"I like being calm," I told her, pretending to be calm, but feeling nothing of the sort. I felt more like I needed to go underground for an indefinite period of time. There were knots even yoga couldn't unkink. Fae snorted with an eye roll that almost took off her head.

"You're not a calm person. And pretending you are is like trying to hold a beach ball under water. Eventually it will pop up and sock you."

"I can be calm," I told her resolutely, with a slightly argumentative tone, "It just doesn't come naturally."

I felt Tally sigh beside me. "Sissy, you can do all the yoga you want, but sometimes life smacks you in the face and you gotta deal with it." Fae and all the girls nodded in unison. I noticed Brandy's pitying, worried face.

"Van is shit you need to deal with," Char said strongly.

"I punched him in the face!" I said defensively.

"And what if that's not enough to make him go away?" Jacque asked. I wasn't sure if she was talking about him leaving town or me being able to get over it. Again. I didn't want to dwell on it.

"I'm ignoring him until he goes away. Eventually he'll go away," I said, trying to convince myself. Fae Lynn raised a puffy finger and aimed it at my face.

"I didn't get to know Van all that well, mainly because I didn't like him, and mainly because I think you were embarrassed of him and that's why you didn't bring him home," I narrowed my eyes at her and started to retort. But Fae Lynn was sweaty, pregnant, and unable to wear really expensive jewelry. I wasn't brave enough or dumb enough to really cross her. She didn't give enough of a pause long enough to really let me. "But I know this about him. If he wants something, he's probably going to stay around long enough to get it."

"And what if that something's you?" Brandy interjected softly.

"Not an option," I responded quickly with a soft nod toward Tally.

"You sure?" Jacque asked before anyone else could.

"I'm sure," I said, my eyes locking on Fae's before I could keep them from avoiding hers.

"See that you are," Jacque said with a shake of her party-girl hair and a flash of her grey eyes toward the bar's exit. "What was all that about anyway? Him accusing you of lying?"

I shrugged my shoulders, "Not sure," I lied, determinedly not looking at Char or anyone else who knew what was really going on. The less involved, the better.

I avoided Jacque's strange look and turned toward the bar. My eyes landed on none other than Jack Thomas. I'd studied the mug shot just long enough to be able to recognize the shock of white hair and bright blue eyes. He was fairly drunk, judging by the happy expression and glaze of his eyes.

I swear on a solemn oath, my boots made me do it. They walked me right across the floor and were the sole reason I pointed my shaky finger in his drunken face and started accusing him of rustling our livestock and livelihood, an idea I'd had and discarded for its utter stupidity.

"Whoa, whoa, whoa," he said jovially, holding up his hands and laughing, rolling his eyes toward his partners in crime, who appeared to be as drunk as skunks too. "What's all this?"

"You stole our cattle, you thief! You broke into our field and took our heifers, you low-down coward." I was on a roll, waving my hands, pointing fingers, the beach ball that was Van having popped right up in the cowhand's face.

"You don't know what you're talking about, little lady. Best you get back to your girlfriends and stop causing trouble for tonight," he told me levelly, adding another "women-are-crazy" look at the guys around him.

I launched myself at him, not sure what I planned to do, other than pull him down and sit on him and wait to be congratulated on my citizen's arrest. I had him knocked off the chair rather quickly and moved to find his loose-jointed wrists so I could pull them together.

Spencer and Scotty were on me quicker than goose grease, pulling me off. Scotty shoved me toward Spencer as he turned to Jack. Spencer pushed me back out the door where the earlier fight had occurred. No one had lingered outside, and we were alone.

"What is wrong with you?" Spencer all but spat.

"That's him!" I told him, mad and spitting myself.

"No shit," he told me without any excitement to his tone.

"So do something," I told him, moving to stalk back inside. He clotheslined me gently and shoved me back away from the door.

"I am," Spencer informed me. "Why else would I be here?" His voice was even and calm, even with the slight exertion.

I paused and looked him up and down.

"You don't like to dance?" I asked him in an attempt to be cute and distract him. It didn't take.

"Depends on the type of dancing," Spencer said darkly, never taking his eyes away from my darting ones. I just looked at him, a shiver running down my spine.

"Why do I annoy you?" I asked Spencer without any sort of sweet tone in my voice. He took a second to look surprised. It quickly passed.

"You don't annoy me," he told me, almost a little defensively. I gave him a strongly skeptical look.

"Bull," I said shortly. He looked around warily and took a deep sigh.

"You scare the shit out of me," he told me finally. I frowned.

"Thanks?" I said, shoving my hands deep in the pockets of my red leather jacket, squeezing the satiny liner tight, running my tongue over the roof of my mouth in an effort not to cry. I don't cry in public. No way, Jose. And then, because I just couldn't help myself, I dug my hole deeper.

"What are you waiting on?" I asked him. "You claim you haven't made a move on me, but I'd beg to differ."

There was a long moment of silence. I finally looked at him when it went on long enough to get awkward. His sharp jaw was working hard, and his brown eyes were sparking.

"You," he finally said definitively, his voice sharp but not harsh, "I'm waiting on you."

I frowned.

"That's not exactly how that works around here. I wasn't raised that way," I told him, the appropriate response, according to my raising and Southern belle standards. He rolled his eyes.

"I'm not expecting you to throw yourself at me," he said sardonically, a somewhat irritated tone coloring the statement.

There was another long pause. I blew out my breath and started to speak, not sure exactly what to say. It seemed I didn't have the tools to keep step with Spencer Locke.

"You're worth waiting on," he said, interrupting my attempt to speak. His voice was deep and dark and matched his tall, dark and handsome self. I wasn't so far gone into my suicide mission that I didn't notice he didn't exactly answer the question.

"What does that mean?" I was so surprised at the alleged compliment I couldn't even muster a simper and a flippant response.

His fists were clenched. He looked like he wanted to punch something. "*You*," he said tersely, piercing the air with his long finger, pointing it at me, "are not easy," he said, moving his hands around to reference the fight he was apparently blaming on me. "Loving you? Not easy. You are exhausting. *Exhausting*," he pointed again at the air toward me, a sharp look accompanying it so I'd understand just how *exhausting* I really was. "But worth it. Those two boys you messed around with? They choose easy. They choose the path of least resistance. I doubt they've ever picked the hard way in their life. Ever. I'm a man who chooses hard. I don't pick easy. Because I'm a man who knows that if it's hard, that usually means that it's worth it. You're exhausting. And a diva. And totally worth it."

I was nodding slowly, focused on his upper lip, where it looked like sweat was threatening to appear.

"Okay," I said, not sure what else to say. He looked at me sharply, exasperated again. He moved in real close, inching me to the same truck bed I'd encountered when I'd gone outside with Van. He moved deliberately, a coiled rattler, ready to strike at a moment's notice. He shifted his weight and the breeze blew his sweet, spicy scent my way, like a waft from an open oven. Spencer smelled like my mama's world famous chocolate chip cookies, and dry cleaner fluid, and hand soap, and truth, and kindness. My knees loosened. He leaned down and my eyes came up to meet his. Eye to eye, he narrowed his as mine widened.

"I want you," he said, poking a long index finger at my head. No cuteness, no guile, no flirting. Just a statement. I wasn't used to statements. I was used to questions. And promises. And games. I wasn't sure what to do with Spencer Locke.

"I kind of want you too," I said in an attempt at flirty, sexy, silly, remembering a long, long time ago when I'd said the same thing, again in an effort to deflect my lack of sexual prowess and fear at appearing unworthy. I watched him grit his teeth and purse his lips, an annoyed sigh finally puffing out like a deflating balloon.

"Kind of isn't good enough," he told me, in no uncertain terms, moving closer still, moving his knee between my thighs and his hand on the truck by my head, his face down to mine, eye to eye, nose to nose, mouth to mouth. Not aggressive, not possessive. Just, decided. Close enough for me to feel his hot breath on my face and smell the grown-up taste of subtle sips of expensive liquor.

"I want you," he said again slowly, "But not 'kind of.' I want you to want all of me with all of your being. I'm not settling for less than all of you. And I'm not interested in kind of. We're not doing this until you're so burning up for me you can't stand yourself. I want you to want me enough that just the *idea* of me makes those two boys seem like a couple of distant memories. I want you to want me so hard you can't think, can't eat, can't sleep."

Cash had *hurt* me. I'd felt such breath-stealing, heart-squeezing pain that I'd thought, surely, that must be love. I'd *chosen* to love Van, because I thought I'd be safe from hurt. And that had blown up in my face. Spencer was real. And wanted me. And didn't appear interested in playing games.

I couldn't breathe.

He was breathing hard and steady. I wanted to say something right. Some good truth. Something brave.

But for all my growth, I was still just some silly girl used to playing with silly boys.

"Is that how you feel about me?" I asked, needy for reassurance, not plucky enough to be woman enough to tell him that I wanted desperately for him to like me, to want me, to love me.

"Yeah," he said shortly, frustration coloring his tone. He pushed himself away from me and walked away. Leaving me there. Waiting under the beams of a neon moon.

Chapter Twenty-Three

"What?" I answered the phone with a pounding head and cottonmouth. I hadn't even glanced to see who was calling at this ungodly hour. Mama had been waiting on the porch when Tally and I had come home. Tally had managed to slink away by pointing the blame at me and I'd been left with Mama's probing questions and special brand of pity. I was short on sleep and mostly hungover.

"Lilly?"

"Van?! Are you freaking kidding me? Go away," I told him grumpily.

"I need you to come get me," he told me calmly, like this was a rational thing.

"What?"

I wasn't sure why I answered the phone. Maybe because it was early, and I'd gotten to the point in my life where, given my people and their predilection for shenanigans, I was always on point. And a missed phone call could spell trouble. So I almost always answered and rarely screened calls these days. I most definitely should have turned off the ringer, snuggled back into my fur throw, and thrown a pillow over my head and ignored it.

"I need you to come get me," he said.

"No," I told him. He sighed, and I could picture his blue eyes narrowing and his narrow lips pursing.

"I'm still in jail."

xxx

I'm not sure why I went to get him. I should have left him there to rot. Jail… hell… two places too good for Van Payton Ehlers the Third. But, Van was in Brooks because of me, and all of Brooks knew it, and so far, as far as I could see, it not only reflected very poorly on me, but also magnified my poor choices in between my raising and my return to my hometown.

I was embarrassed. Embarrassed of my choices. Embarrassed that Van was one of them. Embarrassed that he'd followed me home to parade around for the whole town to see that I'd almost married a guy who was an official cheater and wore purple paisley on a regular basis. So, in an effort to alleviate my embarrassment, I'd thrown on a blue and purple Lilly Pulitzer workout ensemble, an unmonogrammed baseball hat low on my head, and a pair of dark sunglasses. I'd foregone boots with the get-up and laced up my running shoes. Not so inconspicuous, but an attempt at that would have been futile anyway.

The mist was rolling off the highway when I pulled onto it, the bright white sun burning off the morning and the crisp blue sky staking its claim, save for a few defiant whisps of cloud. I took two lefts and headed into town, cranky without coffee and irritable regardless of that.

Another time, another frame of mind, I might have laughed. It was funny. I would know, Spencer Locke had me arrested awhile back, for posterity's sake, and on a challenge from me. I had erroneously thought it was because I assaulted our good friend Cash Stetson. Again. But, alas, it was because Spencer had the nerve to be offended because Fae Lynn and I stole his car. Mind you, Fae Lynn never saw the inside of a jail cell, and she'd been the one doing the driving.

But now, today, with Cash at the ranch, the memory of Spencer's heavy breathing heavy in my mind, and everyone in Brooks wondering what Lilly Atkins' ex-fiancé was doing in town, I couldn't really cough up a laugh. I knew everyone was wondering what I'd ever seen in Van. I grimaced.

I'd seen superficial success. And black tie galas. And the Junior League. And trying to hide from my pain in a brand new world.

For the love.

I pulled into the lot across from the shared city/county building that housed every municipality function one could need in Brooks, including the jail. It was an early Sunday morning, but the exterior doors swooshed open, and I managed to make my way downstairs via the seldom-used flight of stairs next to the elevators without running into anyone. My luck ran out when I opened the door from the stairwell and saw Scotty manning the desk.

"What are you doing here?" I asked him without a nicer, more tempered greeting. "Aren't you a fancy detective? Why are you working the front desk?"

He shrugged, his eyes tired but clear, unlike mine. "It's Sunday. We're understaffed. And I get overtime. And Fae wants a new car." I moved my mouth around without an answer.

He frowned at me. The bullpen of the police station was glaringly bright, Sunday morning or not. The light oak paneling, cheap and quickly done, covered the bottom half of the walls. Mint-colored paint, sickly and green, covered the top half. The layout was battered desks, a few offices on the perimeter, and a whole lot of Naugahyde left over from the 60s. It was mostly a mottled shade of forest green. Scotty was behind the tall desk that resembled a cashier's stand, balanced on a high-top stool, a toothpick in hand and a stack of paperwork beside him. Bad coffee cooled in a Styrofoam cup nearby.

"What are *you* doing here?" he asked. I sighed and ground my teeth.

"I was Van's one phone call." Scotty frowned again.

"That sonuvabitch called *you*?" he asked, provoked.

"Apparently," I said, with a gesture of my arm, indicating the obvious reason I was there. He frowned harder.

"Sonuvabitch," he said. I sighed. "So what the hell are you doing here, then?" he asked, not all that conversationally. I set my teeth, fighting a burbling rise of anxiety, trying to covertly relax the tightness in my neck and upper back. I squeezed my right hand in an effort to get the tingling in it to stop.

"I came to bail him out. And hopefully get him gone, back to the hell from whence he came," I informed Scotty, trying to adopt a dispassion I hadn't honestly felt since Van had shown up in my office. My best friend's husband wasn't impressed with my attempt at flippancy.

"No," he said, dropping his gaze back down to the files he'd been perusing, indicating he was done with the train of conversation. I set my keys on the desk beside him noisily.

"What do you mean, 'no'?" I asked, still trying to shove down that bubble in my chest moving to my throat.

"I mean 'no'," he said without any other expansion on the word, and without looking up. Irritated and uneasy, I waved my hand across the files in front of his face, and then when he didn't look up, laid both my nail-bitten hands across them. With a sigh, he raised his head.

"Scotty, you have to let me get him out. The whole town's going to be talking about me and him!"

"So? The whole town's been talking about you as long as I can remember. Since when has that ever stopped you from doing the right thing? Even on the wrong side of the law," he finished deliberately.

"I just want him gone," I told Scotty. He pinched the end of his pencil and slowly took a sip from a miniscule Styrofoam cup.

"Do you remember when Fae and I got married?" he asked.

"What?" I bit out crankily, not sure where he was going with this crap. Only aware that the clock was ticking, and Brooks proper would be stepping out their front doors to church soon. Last night's events were probably already on everyone's lips, and I didn't need to add any other fuel to that wildfire of gossip.

"At the rehearsal dinner," he went on, "You came right up to me and told me you were so happy that Fae had found such a good man."

I nodded. I remembered it fuzzily.

"And then you told me if I ever hurt her, you'd hunt me down and shoot me like a rabid dog." I smiled then at the clearer memory coming back.

"Yes," I told him. "What is your point?"

The lines in his face deepened a little. "I told Fae about it. She wasn't all that surprised. Told me that you were the kind of friend who'd take a bullet for her. And that she'd do the same for you. And if I was going to survive our marriage, I'd probably better have the same sentiment." A slow, creeping understanding crawled over me.

"Shit. Scotty. Come on. Please." I would not cry. It would have no effect on Scott Wiseman.

"This," he gestured at me roughly, "is toxic. That piece of crap down there," he jerked a thumb toward the door that led toward the drunk tank, "is toxic. What I saw last night, toxic."

"Scotty," I interrupted him.

He held up a hand, "I'm not done." I shut up and waited. "Now I only had two psychology classes," he drawled thoughtfully. "And they were light. But this bullshit co-dependent, enabling relationship you seem to have going on with that Texan seems to me to be enough to cause a personality disorder."

"I don't have a relationship with him anymore," I said defensively. My psychology degree was heavy, but I wasn't up to arguing with Scotty. Mainly because he was more than likely right.

"Then what the hell are you doing here?" he asked again. My shoulders dropped and my whole body deflated. My tongue was stuck tight to the top of my mouth. I sighed then. He was right, but that didn't stop me from wanting to shroud my ex-fiancé on out of town before anyone else saw the lingering source of my shame. I wasn't interested in exploring my toxic non-relationship with Van Peyton Ehlers the Third.

"Can I at least see him?" I asked finally. Scotty shook his head, disgusted, then picked up the keys and preceded me to the door.

xxx

"Hey," I said sharply to Van, peering into the cell where he was currently situated with Bobby Don Henley. Bobby Don, former baseball stud and current Little League coach, was passed out cold on the lower bunk of two cots attached to the wall. The basement jail was more of a holding tank. Brooks didn't really have any hardened criminals and the bad stuff got passed on to a higher security facility an hour away. The few cells were a dark, bluish grey, reminiscent of the inside of an old submarine I'd toured once, grounded since its last run up the Arkansas River. The cells had gotten a new coat of paint since the last time I'd been here to visit a client, one that had attacked me with a brick on the front steps of the courthouse while he held it hostage with dynamite. Over the custody of a dog.

The bars shown with a high gloss, glaring defiantly against the fluorescent lights, our tax dollars hard at work.

Bobby Don stirred and opened one red, blood-shot eye and offered me a crooked half-smile before he closed it back.

"Hey Bobby Don," I acknowledged.

"Thank God," Van said with a sniff. "Get me out of this place," he instructed me. I sighed. Scotty's words about toxicity and dysfunction were ringing in my ears. I was so frustrated with the whole ordeal that was Van. Why couldn't he have stayed gone and let me pretend he'd never happened? I stretched out my fingers, wondering if the bruising on his face was all attributed to Char, or if I'd gotten in a good enough lick to leave a mark. Either way, it hadn't gone far enough toward making me feel better.

"I can't," I told him, somewhat sadly. He put his hands on his love handles, the buttons on his shirt stretching taut.

"What do you mean, you can't?" he asked me with a narrow of his almost purple eyes.

"It's Sunday, Van," I told him, leaving out Scotty's refusal to allow me the indulgence of another delve into the co-dependency that was me and Van. "There are no judges on call, no matter who my daddy is," I offered a sardonic smile. He wasn't amused.

"I will own this town by the time I'm done with a lawsuit for assault and battery and false imprisonment," he told me with a courtroom toughness that didn't intimidate me all that much. My back muscles clenched at his tone. I nodded and then relaxed as

Bobby Don sat up slowly and put his hands on his knees, getting his bearings.

"So you agree the charges are bogus?" he said with bite, acknowledging my nod as agreement. I nodded again slowly as Bobby Don walked over to the lone urinal and unzipped his pants. I closed my eyes quickly and turned around, wincing slightly at the sound of pee hitting stainless steel.

"They didn't tell me what the charges were," I said, still turned around with my back to him.

"Me either!" he exploded. "Which was their first mistake! And would you believe the only doctor I've seen is that backwoods one that you dated in high school?! I'm pretty sure that idiot set my nose crooked." At that, I spun around, not even waiting for the sound of Bobby Don's zipper.

I wanted Van out of jail. I wanted him gone. I wanted to forget I'd ever thought I'd loved him. I was embarrassed that he was here. I wanted to stop feeling like I was going to cry. I wanted the ghost of my past to stop chasing me. I wanted to move on with my life.

"Why'd you call me, Van?"

"Who else was I going to call?" he asked me churlishly. I shrugged, my shoulders tense.

"Your mama? Grant Fowler? Jason Denny?" I named two law school classmates, one I knew was in Tulsa, and the other whose hometown had been one of the suburbs of Oklahoma City. "Why call me?"

"You're here," he told me, not the least bit repentant.

"The question is," I said, "Why are you here?"

He danced away from a stream of tobacco juice Bobby Don had expectorated. It had landed near Van's heel, perhaps on purpose, given the sly grin Bobby Don was subtly sending my way. I hid a smile.

"We've discussed this," he told me, his shoulder coming toward me as he lowered his voice and attempted to block Bobby Don's earshot.

"Yes," I told him slowly, "And I told you, I don't have it. And as I told you last night, I lied to you the first time."

"And I told you, I don't believe you."

I sighed. "And yet, here you sit, in jail. You have some nerve," I finally said, going back to my earlier point, "calling me to come bail you out. You do realize that you cheated on me... after you gave me a very expensive family diamond and told me that I was the missing link to your future?"

"Allegedly," he said with complete seriousness. I looked at him in shock.

"What do you mean, *allegedly*?" I asked, the air quotes bringing sparks from my fingers.

"I think you might have been in shock, Lilly. You may not have known what you saw." This was all said with a straight face, as though *I* might be the crazy one.

I had mistaken all of Van's supposed manners for just that. All the while he was acting as though everything was okay it really just meant that the man wasn't sorry. I pointed a finger at him and gave a slight nod to Bobby Don as he raised his eyebrows at me and worked up a good amount of chaw.

"I don't think you ever cared that you hurt me, Van. I don't think you care that you cheated on me. I don't think you ever even loved me at all. I think you only love yourself." I told him, the end of my accusation dropping off when I realized how much that hurt, how much I'd been pretending that it didn't. And then the almost crushing realization that maybe *I* hadn't loved *him* like I should have. It probably hadn't been all that fair to love him and make promises when one part of my heart was still back in Brooks. I didn't pause long enough to examine that. I watched him try to arrange his features into a mask of care. I was sad and nauseous, embarrassed mostly. A melancholy mourning of what never should have been.

"You should leave, Van," I told him, "Pack your bags and run for the border. I've told you I don't have what you want, and you've been beat up enough to last a lifetime. It's only a matter of time before someone kills you." He looked more resigned than scared.

There was a reason Van was a trial attorney. His closing arguments were legendary. And unfortunately, he wasn't quite the buffoon he appeared to be on first blush. He was mostly all boots and no cows. But sometimes he wasn't. I didn't intend to find out how far he was willing to pursue this. I turned to haul myself out of there.

"Lilly," he called out, attempting to dodge another stream of spit. I ignored him.

Scotty's back was to me as I emerged, on the phone with a hunched posture.

"Yes, pepperoni," he told the caller. I smiled, reaching him. I started to grab the phone from him and then stopped. On the off chance that maybe Scotty hadn't informed Fae Lynn that I'd shown up to bail Van out of jail, it wouldn't behoove me to confess that to her. I stepped back, and he finished and hung up.

"Did you call her?" I asked. He sighed and moved to pour himself another cup of crappy coffee.

"I didn't tell Fae," he said, with a tone of cryptic. I nodded.

"And you won't tell her?" I asked for reassurance.

"I won't tell Fae," he told me, the same weird edge to his voice.

xxx

I walked out to the glare of the sun, shielding my eyes and pulling my hat down lower. The bright sun was shocking enough to bring about a hiccup, and before I knew it, I'd propped myself up against the brick of the courthouse and was trying to squelch the tears that seemed so freakin' intent on coming to the surface.

A long shadow fell across me, and I slumped against the sharp edges digging into my hunched back. Quickly, I swiped my hands across my eyes and pasted on a smile. It wilted when I saw who it was.

He was looking at me with a strange mixture of curiosity and hurt, his eyes deadlocked on my face. I held up a hand and shook my head, moving to push myself away and move around him. He didn't move to stop me.

"You never cried over me," he said before I could get away. I spun around, wondering when he'd shown up and how much he'd seen.

"I'm not crying," I said bitterly, not even able to slap back how selfish he was. He didn't answer, only nodded, his blue eyes disbelieving. It hit me then, what I'd been avoiding addressing for so long. The real source of my shame was not the fact that Van was here, reminding people that I'd been dumped ceremoniously by a man who wore brighter patterns than I did. The breath came out of me in a gasp. I watched Cash frown.

I'd run away from Cash after being let down one too many times. Run all the way to another state. I'd run hard and fast, thinking that would fix it. And me.

But I'd run smack dab into a different version of Cash, maybe a much worse version if I squinted enough. I'd found a poor man's Cash with enough money and faint pedigree that I'd unconsciously hoped I could parade in front of Cash and make him feel some of the pain I'd felt when he didn't choose me.

I looked at Cash, sorry and heartsore, blind and stupid in a love triangle that I'd created in my head. I didn't owe Cash anything, I think. But I couldn't think of anything to say then, other than the truth.

"I cried over you," I told him, tears miraculously dried up. "Plenty. You just never stuck around long enough to see them." He nodded slowly and stuck his hands in his pockets, his shirt stretching across his chest and his blue eyes calculating.

Cash's lips, which could be cruel, or sensual, or both at the same time, didn't smile.

"Or maybe you just ran away before I could see them," he told me, driving the stake home.

"I don't owe you anything," I told him stonily, again not sure if that was really the truth. He smiled then, disarmingly, as was his strong suit, his lips parting to flash bright white teeth, his blue eyes twinkling.

"You shot me," he said, not seeming to care all that much.

"I apologized!"

He shrugged.

I heard a car motor distantly. Other than that, the morning was still and chilly, a fine misty fog clinging to the edges. I bit down on both sides of my cheeks. Not quite meeting his eyes, which were still studying me, I asked a question I'd asked before, and only gotten a prevaricated answer.

"Did you *ever* really cheat on me?" I narrowed my eyes at him then, locking them with his, daring him to lie to me, daring him to tell me the truth. His sharp mouth flattened into a thin line. He looked off past my left shoulder and then finally blew out a breath, a faint steam puffing out.

"No," he answered, shoving his hands deeper in his pockets and rocking back on his heels, "Not really." I blinked back a fresh set of hot tears, the painful robbing of an old grave bothering me more than it probably should have.

"What does 'not really' mean?" I asked him deliberately, so very tired of the two-step Cash couldn't decide if he wanted to lead. I wanted to tear up my dance card and set fire to it. I watched him grit his teeth.

"Why him?" he asked without answering me. "Why that guy?" he pointed toward the courthouse. I couldn't tell if he was hurt or disgusted or just surprised. I pointed my finger and started waving my hands around, all of a sudden not giving a shit or two that I was in the middle of my hometown, and I'd only come to town to try to hide my embarrassment.

"Him?" I started, "Because *you*," I said, pointing sharply. "I've spent almost half my life thinking that I wasn't good enough for you. Thinking that I was somehow unworthy. So sure you didn't pick me because I didn't measure up to the weird standards of Cash David Stetson. And you *let* me," I finished, somewhat tortured. It probably wasn't fair to take out on Cash what Van had coming to him, but Cash was in front of me, and it seemed it had all started with him. I heard a car door slam but didn't look around. I was breathing huffily, and Cash and I were in a standoff.

"How y'all doin'?"

Jase said it casually as he strolled up to us, like it wasn't weird that we were all in front of the courthouse on a Sunday morning and that Cash and I were obviously into it, something I'd sworn I was done with.

"Fine," Cash said hastily, not quite meeting the eyes of his best friend. I shook my head, but didn't say anything. Dawg surveyed us both with a sigh and then nodded slowly.

"Aren't you supposed to be helping your mom haul some crap to church this morning?" he asked Cash, who looked at him levelly for a long beat, then nodded and turned his eyes on me.

"Always a pleasure, Lil," he said sarcastically, shooting a short nod my way. I shook my head and Jase and I stood and watched him. I heard Jase sigh beside me.

"I don't want to hear it," I told him before he could chastise me.

"I don't want to have to say it," he said with much more excitement and a harsher tone than he typically displayed.

"What are you doing here?" I asked him, avoiding the subject of Cash, hoping to diffuse the situation with Dawg. He shot me a pointed look and didn't offer any verbal explanation. Realization dawned, crisp and clear.

"Scotty called you?" I asked. He responded by picking up my keys, which had fallen to the grass while I was trying not to cry over Cash, and Van and myself. Irritated, I grabbed them out of his hand. "I don't need saving. And what were you going to do?" I said peevishly, knowing that I shouldn't be cranky with Jase or Scotty, but at a loss to really rein myself in.

Dawg shrugged, "Not sure. Sit on you maybe?" he diffused the situation and my attitude and forgave me with the calm reference to another incidence. I looked at him then.

"I'm okay, Jase," I told him softly. "Really," I said when he didn't answer me. Dawg isn't much for talking. He generally avoids analysis, or comments on the human condition, either reserving or hiding his judgment. He always appears, for all intents and purposes, to be a neutral party to any calamity. He didn't ever tell me I was wrong or right. I suspected he did the same with Cash, which I didn't like, but acknowledged. He surprised me then, with the rare addressing of my mental state.

"Why do you look like a hungover Florida sorority girl who's lost her cell phone, then?"

I sighed, "Because I'm an idiot," I told him. His face never changed, no expression even to read.

"Go home, Lilly," he instructed me gently. I nodded and turned toward my Jeep, hoping then to be showered and dressed for church before Tally woke up. At the very least, before my mama laid eyes on me. I wanted a shower to get rid of the stench and stickiness of the jail. And to rid myself of the look I knew I was wearing. The one that said I didn't know which way to go, what to wear, who I was, or how to get rid of Van.

Chapter Twenty-Four

I was still undone the next morning. I'd gotten up early in an effort to avoid my family. The same reason I'd spent the Sunday afternoon at my office.

It seemed like the tenuous grip I'd gotten on my life in the past nine months was slipping out of my fingers. What I'd thought was major growth seemed to be nothing but a molehill. I couldn't seem to get rid of the discomfiture that was my ex-fiancé, and my male people didn't want my help with the problems at the ranch and seemed to be making an all-out effort to thwart me. Everywhere I turned, there was some big pair of testosterone-filled boots trying to get me under control. I couldn't get the yoga breath to calm down the overwhelming issues of Cash on our north forty, Van in my town, and Spencer acting like there might be a maybe. Not to mention my Daddy and my Poppa and my Charlie.

Whatever.

Screw it, I thought, straightening my shoulders and pushing my hair back.

I'm Lilly Atkins. I'm an attorney, I'm bendy, and can rock a mean pair of Old Gringos with a pencil skirt. I'm not going to let this slow my roll. I have clients to represent and I needed to get my ass to work.

Before I could get real far into that endeavor, I spotted Jack Thomas' shock of white hair at a four-way stop. His eyes weren't focused on me and when they glanced off the Jeep I moved my gaze down to my lap, hoping he didn't recognize me. Then, when he turned away from my office, I followed, staying what I hoped was a discreet distance behind him. The black truck looked familiar, but that didn't necessarily mean jack. Black trucks are plentiful in Oklahoma.

Keeping the truck in my sights, I dug in the mess that was my front seat, finally unearthing the ball cap I'd worn to the jail the day before, jamming it low on my head, and adding sunglasses in an effort to muffle my usually loud presence.

Several turns through town later, we finally came to a stoplight and there were no blessed cars between us. I gritted my teeth and slowly slid to a stop behind him, more carefully away than was normal. I was focused on the license plate, memorizing the combination of numbers and letters, repeating them over and over in an effort to burn them into my brain. Why I thought this was important, I wasn't sure. It wasn't like knowing the confirmed felon's license plate number was going to change anything. But in times like these, I always reverted to what little investigative experience I had, which mostly came from *NYPD Blue* re-runs and Mary Higgins Clark novels.

I was so focused on the maroon and blue letters, I didn't notice the shadow that came across my driver's side window until there was a sharp rap on the glass.

Startled, I jumped and looked out into the face of Jack Thomas, Saturday night drunk joviality replaced with Monday morning hard callousness. He was peering at me through the window, the bright sun glinting off the shiny barrel of what looked like a large antique revolver, which was currently, very decidedly, pointed at my head.

I cussed out loud and started frantically feeling around through the mess to try to find my purse and *my* gun, trying not to show him exactly what I was doing. He pounded on the window with the gun butt again and gestured for me to roll down the window. I stopped my furtive search for my own gun and pasted a wide smile on my face. I slowly punched the button and felt the sharp breeze blow in as the window came down.

"Hello," I said brightly, as though it were totally normal to be stopped at a stoplight and held at gunpoint before the workday had begun. My eyes were darting around, praying for someone else to roll up.

"Why you following me? Do I need to add stalking to the assault charge I'm still thinking of filing?" he spit out. Again, any trace of festive cordiality was erased. There was nothing else to do, y'all. I consider myself a strong Southern gal and want to be rewarded on my merit, but I was about to pee in my designer drawers, if I hadn't already, and my hands were slick with sweat.

I widened my eyes and blinked them furiously, trying to work up some surprise and just a touch of ladylike indignation.

"Following you? Why, I? Following you? I'm just trying to get to work," I responded in fake confusion, praying he wouldn't wonder at why the hell I had on a sharply cut Victoria Beckham (don't judge, she makes a mean sheath) dress with a rumpled ball cap. He ran his eyes over me and the front seat. I still wasn't sure if he recognized me, what with the ball cap still pulled down over most of my face. His hard blue eyes peered in the Jeep. He leveled the gun at my temple again, cocking the trigger. The sweat turned cold as the icy finger of fear ran up my spine, and I swallowed hard, squelching the urge to puke. I might need to do that later.

He shoved the gun in the window further. "I'm going to get back in my truck," he told me. "And you're going to go in the opposite direction."

I nodded at the instruction, the overdone smile frozen manically on my face. He smiled then, not one dulled by spirits and low lights, but a scary smile, disturbing because it changed his face so quickly, and he looked to be enjoying himself.

He uncocked the hammer. "Best mind yourself, Miss Atkins. Hate to have to use it next time."

He flashed the creepy smile again, tipped his hat to me, and turned to make his way back to the black truck. I found my breath, dug out my gun to lay on my lap and turned myself around, heading, as he had so kindly suggested, in the opposite direction.

xxx

"What's wrong?" Nonnie asked as soon as I walked through the door, tucking my gun in my purse. I had sat in the Jeep with the door locked and my gun on my lap in the parking lot behind the office for twenty minutes in an effort to get my bearings. After finally feeling like I wasn't going to lose control of any of my bodily functions and that I looked semi-normal, I'd made my way into the office. Apparently, I should have given myself another ten minutes.

"Nothing," I told her, "I'm fine." It wouldn't do to tell Nonnie what had just happened. She wasn't at all supportive of my need to help with the cattle rustling investigation, and I didn't see any point in worrying her unnecessarily.

She frowned though. "Are you lying?" she asked me.

I frowned and waved my hand, not quite meeting her eye. "Of course not," I said.

She nodded like she didn't believe me but had decided not to hit me head on.

"I think we might have a problem," she told me, changing the subject, for which I was relieved. She had a white envelope in her hand and was tapping it on her palm. It was open, the flap waving as she slapped it hard each time.

"Is it a bill?" I asked, reaching out for it. "We've been doing fairly well. There should be plenty, unless it's something crazy we didn't plan for."

"It's not a bill," she said as I slid the thick, white tri-folded piece of stationery out. I unfolded it.

I'll always know what you did last summer...

"You've got to be kidding me," I said, shaking my head. I looked at Nonnie, fighting irritation, exasperation, anxiety and an uncommon fear. Nonnie looked upset and I could see her thin, slight fingers shaking just ever so slightly. My first instinct was to throw it in the trash, step outside and flip the bird to Main Street in hopes that the sender was watching and then go about my day with a fiery zeal, burying myself in work and ultimately sticking my head in the sand. But I'd had enough. And now my Nonnie was upset. Someone was going to pay.

xxx

"Well, at least we know it's local," Scotty said, tapping the clear plastic bag that currently housed the offending letter on the side of his thigh. There was no postmark on the envelope. It had been hand-delivered.

"In theory," I pointed out to Scotty. "Someone had to get those other two dropped in the mail in two different states. Who's to say they didn't mail it and pay someone to drop it," I thought out loud. It was enough to give Scotty pause.

"That's not really a Brooks thing to do," Scotty said. I snorted.

"Neither is sending hate mail," I retorted. "If someone has a problem with someone, they just go find them and confront them. Like Jan Stetson came to my office last Fall," I pointed out.

"Like you visited Cash at rehab," Scotty threw right back. I rolled my eyes but refused to take the bait.

"Yes. Exactly like that."

Scotty smiled. "Well, unfortunately, that leaves us with a lot of options," he paused. "Did you do anything else last summer I need to know about? Besides shooting Cash?" I thought fleetingly of the email I'd sent to Van before I'd left Dallas, but no one who knew about that would think to threaten me on paper, so I didn't see the point in making Scotty's stomach turn. My mind walked thru last summer, step by step. I remembered the bad decision to accept Cash's retainer when he'd asked me to help him get divorced, the way his not quite ex-wife had accosted me at the hair salon, the even worse idea to make out with Cash on top of the hill. I looked at Scotty slowly while a slow creep of angst made its way down. I didn't want to confess to Scotty. There weren't many that probably knew. The parties involved hadn't told. I thought.

"I kissed Cash last summer," I said with apology. Scotty's eyes widened ever so slightly, and then they turned skyward.

"Damnit, Lilly," he said. I cringed. I'd more than dealt with the guilt from that and knew that God had forgiven me, but Scotty being disappointed in me wasn't something I was interested in.

"It was a one-time thing. It was just... bad habits," I explained. He waved his hand, brushing me off.

"I don't care that you kissed Cash. Who else knows about this?" he asked. I shook my head.

"Tally, and Fae, and you... and Cash," I said. Scotty frowned.

"Would he have told anyone else?" Scotty asked. I shrugged and shook my head.

"I doubt it," I said.

"Was this before or after we found his wife dead?" Scotty asked. I paused. The events of my return to Brooks were somewhat burned in my mind, but I wanted to make sure the facts I was giving Scotty were straight.

"Before," I finally said. Scotty's lips pursed.

"What?" I said finally, "You think he told one of Tina's people? And now they're jacking with me?" Scotty shrugged and didn't say anything, but I could see that was what he was thinking. Tina Stetson's people weren't into subtle. There would be no cleverly pasted notes dropped in the mail. If they thought I'd done Tina wrong, they'd have been on my doorstep way before now. From what I'd heard, they were even on good terms with Cash. And I don't think Cash was one to kiss and tell about me. He'd tried that once. It had heralded no good results.

I shook my head, "Not them," I told Scotty.

"Then who?" he said shortly. I opened my mouth wide to stretch my jaw then sent an apologetic look toward Scotty.

"I don't know. There are probably more options than I could care to acknowledge."

Scotty looked at me hard; a discerning, unrelenting look tinged with pity. I squirmed. "Do you need an intervention?" he asked me.

"No," I said, just as Nonnie said, "Yes."

He didn't respond.

Chapter Twenty-Five

"Get your gun ready," Fae Lynn barked into the phone. I loved my best friend. Truly. Loved her. Would shoot, trespass and vandalize for her. But her being pregnant was making me want to clock her.

"What now?" I asked, one eye on my email, another straying to my yoga mat.

"Target practice," she said shortly. "We're all going. I'll pick you up."

"Why?" I asked, knowing the answer was irrelevant.

"Because. We've got problems, right here in River City. And there's no problem that can't be solved with an extra layer of blush and a round of target practice. Screw yoga."

"Are you still at work?" I asked, not in the mood to argue with her, especially after the morning I'd had.

"Yes, and I spoke to my husband. Why'd you call him instead of me?"

"That was Nonnie. You can be mad at her."

Fae Lynn snorted. "Why do you want to know where I am?"

"I need you to run a plate for me," I told her slowly.

"What is it?" she asked. I rattled off the plate I'd memorized. "You wanna tell me why?" she went on after she'd typed it into the system.

"Will you promise not to tell Scotty?"

"No," she promised. I sighed and relayed the incident with Jack Thomas.

"Well that makes for an interesting morning," she said finally, "I hope you'd already had your coffee."

The blessing of having a best friend like Fae Lynn is that they know when you need to be coddled. And when you need a straight shot of sarcasm to get your sea legs back under you.

"Just barely," I told her. "Anything come up yet?" I asked.

"Yeah, white Chevy Yukon, 2013 model, registered to Missy Spade." I was shaking my head.

"No, it was a black truck," I said. Fae waited a beat.

"Are you sure you have the number right?" she asked.

"Please remember who you're talking to," I told her.

"You were being held at gunpoint," she pointed out, "That might make even your abilities waver."

"That's the number," I told her, confident and sure. Of that, at least.

"So he switched the plates?" she said.

"He'd been working at the Judd place, that's just as close to the Spades as it is us."

"So Missy's Yukon has a plate registered to Jack Thomas?" Fae reasoned.

"I would assume," I said, confused.

"But why?" Fae Lynn said aloud what I'd been thinking.

"No idea. But I intend to find out," I said strongly.

Fae Lynn, like the good best friend that she was, didn't argue, "All the more reason to get your ass to the gun range. We need to straighten you out before the Jubilee. See you in five."

She hung up before I could respond. My eyes left my email and landed squarely and longingly on the yoga mat. And then, remembering who I was and where I'd come from, I squared my shoulders, traded my pumps for a pair of Lucchesse cockroach killers (money green and bronze), grabbed my lollipop colored Kate Spade shoulder bag with my gun, and headed out to the street to catch a ride to the range in my pregnant best friend's minivan. I kissed my Nonnie on the way and asked her to lock up. She promised that and biscuits in the morning.

Fae Lynn was idling at the curb when I stepped out, the minivan freshly washed and gleaming white. Britney Spears reverberated throughout, causing the vehicle to shudder. Fae Lynn had a magazine in her lap and was mouthing the words to some auto-tuned song, her head bobbing along. I opened the passenger door to the front seat.

"That kid is going to come out a stripper if you play her this music in the womb," I told her. She turned it down and shook her head.

"Nope. I played classical music to my other little shit all through my very long pregnancy. Even slapped headphones on my belly at night. And he's dead intent on being a juvenile delinquent."

I laughed. "All you can do is try," I said, snapping my seatbelt in place. She shrugged, and we motored off. "Tell me again why I need to go shoot guns in the middle of the afternoon?" I asked her, not necessarily in dire want of the answer.

"Consider this your intervention," she told me with a glance as she stopped at a four way stop, waving to Miriam Frank. I waved too.

"And why, pray tell, do you think I need an intervention?"

Fae Lynn rolled through the next stop with a minor tap on the brakes. She took a right and pulled onto another major street in Brooks, which intersected with the Main one and led out of town to the west, turning into highway at the county's edge.

"Dude. Beyond the obvious of someone threatening you this morning, you won't run off your ex-fiancé, even though he's causing you to have an identity crisis because you're embarrassed that you were with him in the first place." I felt like I'd been slapped.

"That stings," I said. "Have y'all been talking about me?"

"Duh," she responded without further elaboration.

"And you think I'm having an identity crisis because…?" I want to note here, that I got it. And I didn't necessarily disagree with her. But I also wanted to make sure I wasn't missing anything. She rolled her eyes my way.

"Have you looked in a mirror?" she asked.

"What?" I said defensively, running my hands across thighs.

"You have on sequins," she told me.

"So?" I said. "I used to wear sequins."

"In the rodeo ring," she said without sympathy. "Not as an attorney."

She had a point. The t-shirt with the sequined pineapple applique was covered up with a blazer and I had on a pencil skirt for professionalism, but still.

"I was channeling Char," I told her.

"I know," she said. "Start channeling Lilly. She's not so bad. We all like her, whether she ran away and decided to marry an oversized wiener dog from Dallas or not."

I didn't say anything else.

Fae Lynn pulled off the highway and onto a well-maintained set of dirt road ruts, the sign and mailbox announcing that we'd made it to Trigger's Tactics, the place in Brooks to buy guns, sight them in, shoot them, and blow off any and all amount of steam you might be carrying. It wouldn't have been the logical choice for an intervention, but this was Brooks, where logic didn't always align with purpose. The minivan bounced over the road, trees and overgrowth lining both sides. We emerged to a large, closely cropped patch of grass. Fae pulled up to a yellow metal outbuilding with a white tin roof. No rust shown through the paint, another small sign with the same logo as the one by the highway was perched carefully in front of the steps and wheelchair ramp, which were side-by-side, front and center toward the door.

Tally'd had a small kitchen fire at the restaurant to deal with, but Char, Jacque and Brandy were waiting on us when we stepped in. Jacque waved bright pink slips of paper.

"I got you covered," she said, as we stepped over, indicating that she'd paid our way onto the range. I smiled. Jacque loved her guns. I suspected this was her idea.

"I need bullets," I said, moving to the glass counter.

Jess Clark leaned on the counter, a toothpick in her mouth, in between teeth so white they were blue, and heavy red lip-gloss. She had on a cream silk blouse, which looked quite custom, black cropped tuxedo pants, and black and gold leather booties. Her jewelry was thick and gold. Her bright red hair was bobbed and sleek. I wanted to be her when I grew up. She might be the only person on earth who could make a toothpick look classy. I don't know how old Jess is. She might be thirty. She might be sixty. She wasn't telling. And no one was willing to get shot finding out. She slid the toothpick out from between her teeth and flicked it behind her to an unknown trashcan.

"Whatcha packin'?" she asked with a nod. I pulled out the .38 pistol Poppa had procured for me on request. Bigger than Tally's, the handle was dark gray and had a red argyle pattern etched into it. It wasn't enough to take down a bear, but it had a kick and let's just say that if I'd had it when I shot Cash, he wouldn't have kept the toe. Jess nodded and pulled out a box of bullets from behind her, ringing me up and taking my credit card without any conversation. I smiled and nodded when she handed me the receipt, her long, square, red-lacquered nails scraping me ever so slightly. She locked eyes with me. I turned to follow the girls out the back door to the range, which was manned by military veterans and serious business.

"Lilly," she said at the back of my head. I turned around.

"Yes?"

"See that you keep your gun pointed at the target," she instructed me with a secret smile, one that hinted she was one of the legions who approved of me pointing Tally's pistol at Cash Stetson. I nodded.

"Absolutely."

xxx

"Should you be out here?" I asked Fae Lynn, watching her breathe heavy and rub her lower back.

"No," Jacque and Char said in unison, not moving their eyes from their guns and the bullets they were loading. Brandy bit her lip and looked uncomfortable.

"I've been trying to get her to sit down," she whispered to me, eyes on Fae. I frowned.

"Do they allow pregnant women at a gun range?" I asked.

"No," Char and Jacque said again. Fae Lynn fixed them with a hateful glare. I squared off with her.

"Seriously?" I said. She didn't back down or look all that intimidated, gun in my hand or not.

"You need to shoot stuff," she said by way of explanation. "So you'll get your head straight, and maybe aim the gun toward that Van Ehlers."

Jacque nodded. "You should really shoot him," she said.

"You should at least let us run him out of town," Char said, rubbing her gun with a silver chamois cloth.

"Haven't you all been trying?" I asked.

Char shrugged, "Not that hard."

"Since he's been here, he's been run over, assaulted with the deadly weapon that is Fae's Coach purse, had his eyebrows set on fire, been given laxative, assaulted by you, and thrown in jail," I pointed at Char, "How is that 'not that hard'?" I said, heavy on the sarcasm. Jacque stepped up. Brandy was still looking worriedly at Fae Lynn.

"No one's shot him," Jacque said.

"Yet," Fae Lynn said with a grin that looked like it took too much effort.

"But even after all that, he's still here," Char said in a musing tone. "Even after the other night and your confession," she said.

"Yeah, what was that all about?" Jacque asked. Jacque and Brandy, out of the loop, looked confused.

"Van thinks she has something," Char said before I could protest.

"What does he think you have?" Brandy asked, taking her eyes off Fae Lynn for the moment.

"A sex tape," Fae inserted.

"*You* made a sex tape?" Jacque said. Jacque was typically shockproof, but I noticed her voice rose up and the gun slipped a little at her side.

"No!" I yelled, wrinkling my nose in disgust. I saw a big, burly set of fatigues start our way.

"Van made a sex tape," Char filled in the blanks. "And thinks Lilly has it."

"Why does he think you have it?" Brandy said with a quizzical expression.

"Because she lied and told him she did to get him to go away and leave her alone forever," Fae Lynn supplied.

"That's what he meant about blackmail," Jacque said with a nod and purse of her plumped up orange lips, "Impressive." She offered me a fist to bump. I resisted the urge to roll my eyes, and reached out my own fist to knock knuckles with her.

"But you don't have it?" Brandy asked, still unsure of where we stood with the puzzle.

"No," I said with a shake of my head.

"Are you sure?" Jacque asked.

"Yep," Char said definitively and quickly. Jacque eyed her.

"How do you know?" Jacque asked.

"I reviewed all the possible evidence," Char said, "and there wasn't anything incriminating that Lilly needs to turn over."

Jacque frowned. "But he's still here," she said, her eyes on Char.

"He doesn't believe me, even after the other night," I told her.

Jacque thought for a second. "Let's go hog-tie him and drop him in the Red River," she suggested.

Char dropped her gun, "Genius. Yes. Let's," she said. Brandy looked pained.

"No," I said, "He'll go away eventually. Once he figures out that I'm not lying. This time." Char looked thoughtful. Fae Lynn, who'd been abnormally silent, rolled her eyes.

"See, this is why you need to shoot something. Get your freakin' badass back. Sometimes even Ghandi could approve of ridding yourself of toxicity. Van is toxic waste. Let's dump him," Fae said.

"No," I said again, facing her, noticing the pale cast to her face and the sheen of sweat across her forehead. "Are you okay?" I asked her, stepping closer. Brandy stepped in closer toward her too. I could hear the pops and bangs of guns from other shooters beside us, the echoes bouncing off the hills in front of the long range, muffled by all the trees. Jacque and Char laid their guns on the table and moved around it with some speed. The poster boy for Army recruiting had reached our tableau.

"Everything okay?" he asked, his handsome face etched with concern. Fae Lynn rolled her eyes and gritted her teeth, jumping at the blast of the ricocheted sound of another round shot off by someone. Her eyes widened and then her face took on a pissed off expression.

"Sonuvabitch, mother trucker, and shit on a stick," she said. The army vet literally scratched his head and wrinkled his nose, as a new odor besides gunpowder infiltrated the air. Jacque looked determined, her eyes darting calmly as she assessed the situation. Char's shoulders were shaking with barely disguised laughter. Fae Lynn glared at her as she shook off Brandy's arm and her pats of concern.

"Can I get you something, ma'am?" he asked Fae Lynn. She snapped at him, but it was done so sweetly that he never knew what hit him.

"Hell yes, you can get me a frickin' ambulance. Or a tank. I need to get to the hospital. My damn water just broke," she pointed her finger at him and cringed as what appeared to be a contraction came on. I could see him scrambling. I patted him.

"We'll get her there," I told him, taking Fae Lynn by the elbow and leading her toward the out building.

"But get me a damn Mountain Dew," she bossed him before we could leave. "A real one. Not that diet crap." I smiled at him apologetically and led her through Jess Clark's redneck sanctuary, leaving a slimy trail. Char and Jacque followed, guns gathered and in hand. Brandy tried valiantly to clean up our mess with the wet wipes from her purse.

As it was, when it was all said and done, we made it to the hospital in record time, what with the police escort and all. Fae Lynn had managed to down an entire can of Mountain Dew before Jacque rushed up to a screeching halt in front of Scotty at the emergency room bay of Brooks Regional. Fae Lynn barked orders at us to take her van home without a scratch, bring Scotty a *People* magazine, and not to come visit her until she'd told us we were welcome. I grabbed a kiss before turning her over to Scotty, and we headed back out to the range so we could follow orders.

Chapter Twenty-Six

"She's perfect," I said, cuddling close the sweet-smelling, dark-haired, smushed combination of Fae Lynn and Scotty. She scrunched her eyes and wrinkled her nose, her pink, pink face peaceful and calm.

"Duh," Fae Lynn answered with a slurp of a Dr. Pepper frostee and a chomp of a salty French-fry. I rolled my eyes at her. Scotty had taken a break from bedside to grab a shower and make sure five year old Hazzard hadn't tied up his grandparents. I'd come bearing gifts. Lots of pink crap and junk food for the second-time parents.

I looked back down at perfection and shivered. She was perfect. And I'm sure perfectly sweet, but knowing Fae Lynn… well, Heaven help us all, this little girl was going to be a hell-raiser, no matter how much her mama and daddy might try to deter her. And as honorary aunt, I was planning on taking great pleasure in spoiling her rotten.

"Give her back," Fae said, "Everyone that comes in wants to cuddle the little brat, and I haven't had enough time to do it myself." I handed her back to my best friend and sat on the edge of the hospital bed, snitching a French fry.

"Stats?" I asked. Scotty had sent out the all call when the baby had arrived, but of course, just like a man, he hadn't given the pertinent details. Just a pic and that everyone was good.

"Eight pounds even. Twenty-one inches long. Textbook."

"Perfect," I said with a nod and a smile, feeling sentimental. "Good work."

"Thanks," Fae Lynn said, looking down at her daughter with a look of pure mush in her eyes.

"Name?" I said, sitting up a little straighter. I should have asked that right away.

"Dixie." I frowned, not wanting to poke the hormonal one.

"Dude. You realize your first child is named Hazzard, right?"

She eyed me testily. "Dixie was my great-grandmother's name."

"Oh, well then it's perfect. Was she a hell-raiser? That's a hell-raiser name."

"Her middle name was Lynn."

"Gotcha," I said with a short, ironic laugh. "So what's this little shit's middle name?"

"Kay." I blinked twice and looked Fae Lynn in her dark eyes. Hers were misty. Mine were glimmering.

"As in short for Katherine? As in Lilly Kay?"

"As in she's named for her Auntie Lilly, crazy-ass do-gooder, righter of wrongs, maker of good and bad decisions. Boot-wearer." I shook my head.

"I'm not worthy," I tried to quip and inject some levity, trying not to cry. Apparently, Fae Lynn, was hormonal enough to want to make a *moment*. She didn't let me get away with a joke.

"No, you're not. I hope one day she gets that. It's my hope that she learns lessons the hard way, just like you."

"I'm not sure whether to be flattered or hurt," I told her, only half-joking.

"Be flattered. I love your ass." I laughed at that.

"So Dixie Kay it is," I took a slurp from my own Cherry Coke and tipped the straw toward her dark, little pointed head. "Hold on to your ass."

"I've already started praying," Fae said with a contented sigh. "So, what's going on with everything? Van's left town, finally, I assume? Cash still hanging around? Anything new with the cattle? I feel like I've missed a week, even though it was only twenty-four hours."

"Van's gone, as far as I know," I said with a sigh.

"Girl, you need to shake that shithead loose," she said with a wrinkle of her forehead.

"I'm fairly sure he's crossed the border," I said drolly.

"That's not what I meant," she said.

"I know," I said without sarcasm.

"You seem all uptight," she told me astutely, punctuating the statement with the stirring of her drink.

"I have a crick in my neck. From yoga."

"Girl."

"Don't start," I told her.

"When are you planning on giving it up?" she asked me.

"What? Yoga?"

She rolled her eyes, "No. Although, I think yoga's dumb too. The idea that you need to be calm."

"What are you talking about?" I felt off-balance again. And guilty. I hadn't been here when Hazzard had been born. I'd sent a big blue care package and had headed home to hold him when my schedule opened up. But he'd been six months old the first time I'd met him. In retrospect, I should have hauled my ass back home when he'd been born, but I'd been in Dallas with my own first-world problems. So I was more than glad I'd made it to the hospital twelve hours after my namesake had arrived. But now the visit had turned back to me, myself and I. I was so selfish and self-centered I couldn't even make my best friend's birth solely about her.

"Lil, you're kind of a hot mess. And there's nothing wrong with that. That's just you."

"You're not like that," I said, waving my hand with its chipped nail polish toward her. Fae, with her perfectly arranged and sprayed hair, full face of expertly applied makeup, and clearly unchipped and smoothly manicured fingernails. "You're always put together. Your hair's always in place. And your house is clean. And you're ironed. And your life has turned out exactly like you planned."

She sighed, looking down at Dixie. "Your Auntie's an idiot."

"Thanks," I said, wanting to redirect the conversation, but again, too selfish and needy. I wanted her to reassure me.

"Lilly," she started, "Do you know that every time you take a curling iron to try to straighten your hair you have little fuzzy curls that pop up around your temple?" she asked me.

"What?" I said, wondering just how much happy juice they'd pumped into her spine.

"Seriously, Lil. You really would feel a whole lot better about yourself if you'd just embrace the chaos. I'm like that because that's me. It makes me feel good to clean. It makes me feel good to iron. Having known you as long as I have, those things do not make you happy. And you've always cared less about your hair and makeup. You just started to give a shit because you thought you should. Although I am pro the mascara. It helps." She smiled to soften the blow. "But you know, I'm not perfect. That's kind of insulting for you to say that. I've made bad choices in boys, even if they were early on. I've smoked, I've drank. I stole some gum one time, just to see if I'd get caught. I'm not perfect. That's kind of the point. But, I have learned this lesson… one that you seem to be having trouble learning…. I'm a hell of a whole lot better off when I'm *me*. Not trying to be you, or Char, or my mama. Just me. As perfect or imperfect as that looks."

"You're perfect," I assured her.

She nodded. "Duh," she smiled, but then went on. "It's okay to admit that Cash was part of your past, Lil. And Van. Stop trying to be someone you're not. Bad choices and good."

"Okay," I said.

"Spencer too," she added.

"What about Spencer?" I asked.

Fae Lynn sighed. "What's the point of being enlightened if you're not willing to have your cake and eat it too?" Fae Lynn said. I was more confused.

"I annoy him," I told her, "I don't think there's a cake there to eat."

"Maybe what you think is annoyance is actually impatience," she surmised.

"What?" I asked, confused, "What's the difference? And what are you talking about?"

"He wants you, Lilly Kay. But you have to admit that the state you showed up in when you got back wasn't the best foundation to start a relationship. And in the time that he's known you, he's met both the men in your life that came before him."

I just looked at her.

"You think he wants me?" I asked, tagging on one thing. She rolled her eyes.

"He wants you," she said kindly. "And I think he has the patience of Job. But at a certain point, for a guy like Spencer, waiting for you to get a clue about yourself could get old."

With a heavy sigh, I told her about the exchange outside the bar the other night.

"So he told you he wants you… and you're asking *me* if he wants you."

"Yes," I said morosely.

"Bless your heart," she told me with a shake of her head. "You are an idiot."

"I'm a shitty friend," I said with a sigh.

"Sometimes," Fae Lynn said with a nod, a shrug, and a tilt of her head. "But why today?"

"I came and made it all about me. I didn't come to whine and complain. I came to see Little Miss and make sure you had real food. Not so you could solve my problems."

"Well you saw her. And I'm more than grateful for the caffeine. Come back tomorrow with the same thing for breakfast and I'll forgive you." I smiled.

"I love you."

"Duh," she said with a smile. We both looked at Dixie Kay in the moment as she stretched and mewed like a cat. "Don't be sorry," Fae Lynn said, looking up again to catch my eye, "I'm fat, puffy, and it burns when I pee. Hearing about your problems makes me feel better."

"I love you," I said again.

"Duh," she said, "But one more thing," she went on as I stood to leave.

"What?"

"We need to stop cussing," she told me, looking down at Dixie Kay. I was fairly certain she might still be high, given that Fae Lynn was a dirty word aficionado, but I didn't argue with her. "She needs to be a lady," Fae explained without prompting. "So we need to stop cussing around her. Tell the rest of them."

"Will do," I promised, not believing her one iota. She smiled again and shooed me out the door so she and the newest member of the Posse could rest. I slipped out with a smile, making a note to swing by the Sonic to do a drop off at the hospital on my way to the office in the morning.

I knew Fae Lynn was right. God loves me as I am. He can see me for the good, bad, and oh so ugly, no matter how far I try to run and hide. Spencer… I wasn't so sure about him.

Chapter Twenty-Seven

"What is he doing?" I asked Daddy as we looked out the kitchen window to watch Spencer Locke pace back and forth around the equipment barn.

It was later that evening, after a full day's work, a dinner with my family, and a general sense of unrest and unproductivity. I squinted out at Spencer.

"Hell if I know," Daddy said, snapping a tortilla chip covered in homemade guac between his teeth. An after dinner snack. Daddy and I weren't necessarily at odds, but we also hadn't had a candid conversation about any of the things we'd squared off over a few weeks ago. I hadn't mentioned the cattle rustling again to him, and he'd left a copy of Cash's work schedule in our front door and hadn't asked me again about Van. There wasn't a need for more words between us. I knew where he stood. He knew where I stood. Neither one of us liked the other's stance, but we were too much alike to relent. And too smart to try to bring the other to our side.

"Didn't you ask him?" I asked peevishly, rolling my eyes. My father has a very strict policy against running off guys. Much like the Southern belle rule of keeping one's enemies close, Daddy has always thought it prudent to befriend my male friends, romantic and otherwise. Then, if their allegiance lay with him, they'd be too afraid to hurt me. It was likely why Cash had never been brave enough to openly burn me and hid his transgressions instead. It might be a fatherly display of love, but with my limited scope of right and wrong, it was rankling.

"Said he needed to get a feel of the place," Daddy told me with a shrug. I stared out the window at the tall set of shoulders, striding around and around my parents' yard. I took pity on him. Or perhaps I was itching for a fight. I snatched my dad's red handkerchief and dropped a couple of my mother's ever-present cookies in it, tying it up with a flourish and grabbing a bottle of Coke from the fridge.

"That's dirty," he said without turning, his gaze still directed out the window. At Spencer, I wasn't sure.

"I know," I told him, heading outside.

In the fading dusk, as I got closer to Spencer, I was struck by how very attractive he was. He should've been in pictures. Hot was the word everyone used in town. Hot he was.

"Hey," I told him, not unkindly, as he watched me approach, on guard. Forever on guard.

"Hey," he responded back. I handed him the Coke and the bag of cookies.

"What's this?"

"Cookies. Coke. Thought you might need sustenance for your stakeout." He set his shoulders and looked around at all the land spreading out around us.

"It's not a stakeout. I'm just trying to get a feel."

"That's what Daddy said. You're doing it wrong."

"Excuse me?"

"You're doing it wrong," I repeated, slower this time.

"I think I know how to conduct an investigation. The FBI badge on my dresser says so."

"You still keep your badge on your dresser? I thought you'd retired?"

"I did," he sighed. "And then I got here, which was supposed to be a break. Not so much." The abnormal admission of personal information gave me pause.

"Come on," I told him, tugging on his arm.

"What?" he asked, too quickly to have it colored with the normal irritation.

"I'll show you where you need to go."

I practically shoved him into one of Daddy's all-terrain vehicles. I grabbed the keys from their velcroed spot under the dash and started it up. We had apparently decided we weren't going to talk about the other night. I wasn't all that okay with ignoring what lay between us and what hadn't transpired in the parking lot of the honkytonk but I also didn't quite know how to bring it up without appearing desperate. And I wasn't sure what there was to talk about.

I headed toward the hay barn, pulling up to the front. The hay was stacked high in all its glory with round bales, rich and gold. I got out and waited for him.

"What?" he said again.

"You have to sit up here to really get the full effect," I told him, beginning the climb.

I reached the top of the pile, three bales high, and waited for him. More intent with "the job" than appearing dumb, he climbed.

He settled beside me. The sun was setting off to our left, in the west. It was that odd Saturn-red, indigenous and special to certain parts of Oklahoma. So special our sunsets were mentioned in several country songs. My great-grandparents house sat under the burning ball going down, the gray glazed with light, turning it a sweet pink. Nonnie and Poppa's was far across the road, almost directly in front of us. The dimming light highlighting the Longhorn orange of the stones. Her fake flowers blew in the evening breeze, the redundant wind chimes singing rows of chorus over and over. I shivered in the sweater I'd grabbed walking out the door. I looked down. It was mama's. Expensive, cashmere, blue. I grimaced. I'd just take it straight to the dry cleaner and avoid her.

The house I'd grown up in was a rising roof on the horizon. The double chimneys like two beacons, the sinking sun blinking off them like glitter. It had been warm in the sun. The shadows brought out the chill. The heat coming off Spencer helped. He sat beside me, surveying. I wondered if he even knew what he was looking for. It wasn't that I didn't respect his training, but well, this was my place. These were my people. Suspend your disbelief for a minute and ignore that I've yet to have any success in scrounging up a suspect other than Jack Thomas, either, but still.

Spencer had attended Tulane in New Orleans for law school, a very distinctively Southern choice, which Spencer was not. It didn't make sense that he'd gone to Tulane. But not much about Spencer made much sense to me.

"Why'd you decide on law school?" I started conversationally, not sure what else to start with.

He weighed and measured his words, thinking about how much he should share. "Come on," I jabbed him. "I won't tell any of your secrets." The annoyed look came over him again.

"I don't have secrets," he said shortly. "I didn't love being an agent. It was too loose. Especially undercover. Too creative. In the courtroom the law is the law." I furrowed my brow skeptically.

"Not in Brooks. Have you met Judge Morrison?" He smiled slightly.

"The law is the law. The judgments are sometimes creatively suitable. But right is right and wrong is wrong. It's not always like that undercover."

"What's it like?"

"Blurry," he said. I remembered he'd used that word before.

"You weren't into blurring the lines?" I asked. He shook his head, his eyes still on the horizon.

"I wasn't that kind of agent. I respected the protocol. All of it. I never went rogue," he told me, not really all that proudly. I couldn't ever really see him going rogue, anyway. Unlike me, who was a great big heap of rogue waiting to happen.

"How did you get in?" I asked. "Something you always wanted to do?"

He shook his head. "Not really," he said ruefully. "They recruited me out of high school." My eyes widened.

"What? Why?"

"I'm a genius," he told me matter-of-factly. I shrugged, but didn't say anything. I also knew that when the FBI started recruiting you and not the other way around, it was because you fit a profile.

And that profile generally, allegedly, included being somewhat without family. I knew he was Charlie's nephew, and since they shared a last name, Spencer's father was Charlie's brother. Obviously, allegedly. I wasn't sure whether to pry right then and there or to hold my thoughts and go pester Charlie to see what he'd confess. And *then* do a cross-examination on the uncrossable Spencer Locke. I didn't say anything else.

"You were wrong, you know," he told me with a smile.

"I doubt it," I responded. "About what?"

"The quote 'the usual suspects' *is* from a movie." I looked at him.

"Are you sure? Which one?"

"*Casablanca*," he replied, his eyes turning back to scan the horizon.

"Well," I said, a little defensively, "Isn't that based on a book?"

He shook his head. "A stage play." I sat silently, not sure how to contend with being wrong. So obviously wrong.

"You know this how?" I asked, "Because you're a genius?" I teased to deflect.

"A genius who knows how to use the Internet," he replied without any bragging.

"Huh," I said, for lack of a better response. I paused, waffling, a confession on the tip of my tongue. I sighed finally.

"I know, Spencer," I told him.

"Know what?" he asked distractedly, looking off into the distance.

"Charlie told me," I told him, trying not to say it out loud. His head turned slowly toward me with intention, a sharp look in his eye.

"Told you what," he tortured me. I bit my lip at the look in his eye.

"Why you're here," I said softly, not leaving his face.

"I told them I'd help," he said with a gesture of 'duh.' I shook my head.

"In Brooks," I said. His jaw set like stone.

"And why exactly did Charlie say I was in Brooks?" he asked. I hesitated. Maybe I'd bitten off more than I could chew. I wasn't wholly apprised of the uncle/nephew dynamic. Maybe Charlie had shared a confidence with me, and I was too dumb to realize it was just that.

"Nevermind," I told him. The sharp look hadn't wavered.

"*Why* did Charlie tell you I was here?"

"He said you killed someone."

The air changed between us. More crackling, more electric. I didn't think it had anything to do with chemistry. Spencer's eyes grew distant, and I regretted saying it, regretted asking Charlie in the first place. Spencer's secrets were his to keep. Just because mine kept showing up to get assaulted didn't mean it was fair to spread Spencer's on Main Street, too.

"I'm sorry," I started.

"It's true," he said, before I could ever get the apology all the way out. I reactively leaned toward him. I didn't say anything else. It would have been the easy thing to do to fill the silence and wave it away, but that didn't seem to be the right thing to do. "St. Louis, in certain parts of the city, is a hotbed for drugs," he went on, "I'd worked undercover before I decided to go to law school. They were willing to pay for me to go to school, so they let me take a quasi-sabbatical," he shook his head. "Which is as ridiculous as it sounds." He hadn't looked at me.

"Spencer, you don't have to…," I interjected. I could see how much it bothered him, the way the bitterness crept into his otherwise normally even tone. I hated the way Spencer, who I didn't really know to appreciate irony, was biting out words in the most ironic tone of voice. He waved his hand at me, his eyes on the red and blue horizon.

"I picked Tulane because it seemed like another world. And New Orleans is a good place to hide, kind of."

I'd been to New Orleans once when Char was in undergrad in Atlanta, and we'd met her there for a Spring Break. It had seemed dark, and seedy, with an almost oppressive humidity that blanketed the city, the gaiety and heavy opulence not fully covering up the eeriness. Of course, I'd been reading a lot of New Orleans history books and that could be what had colored my impression. But I sort of agreed with Spencer on the hiding. It seemed likely you could probably turn down a corner in the French Quarter and never be heard from again.

He went on, "Drugs are just as rampant in New Orleans. They asked me to head a task force while I was in law school. I should have said no. I could have said no. But I agreed to anyway. I was pulled in two directions and wasn't doing a great job at either. I was about to graduate when it happened. One of my informants was a crack whore," his wry, twisted smile didn't diffuse the term. "Literally. Not like you and your friends say around here." I nodded without speaking. "She'd asked me to come get her, said her man was out of prison again and back to taking it out on her. I went over there one night thinking I was going to rescue her, take her out of the ghetto and find her something better." He shook his head again and stopped. His normally golden complexion had gone pasty. I thought it was probably best for him to get it out and get it over with. If he thought he needed to tell me and purge himself of that, then it was best to do it quickly, in my opinion. I tapped a finger on his knee.

"What happened?" I asked.

"Her pusher was there. Who also happened to be her pimp. Who also happened to be the father of her youngest child. Who was also there. She was high. He was high." I wanted to cry. For Spencer. For the kid who probably never had a chance. For an impossible situation that had nothing to do with me. Spencer went on, "He had a gun on her when I walked in the door. I pulled mine but I was too late."

"He killed her?" I said softly. Spencer shook his head.

"He killed his son," he said, "Because it seemed like a better fucking statement." I felt sick, my fingers clenched in my lap. I'm a puker. It just comes naturally. I swallowed vomit for Spencer's sake, shaking my head. Spencer, the man of few words, and none of them curse-worthy, had just dropped the world's biggest bomb on me, and I didn't know what to do with it.

"So you killed him," I said, a statement, not a question.

"I killed him," he agreed.

"And your informant? She's better off today?" Spencer turned to me then, his brown eyes dark, the slightest flecks of blue-grey glittering hard.

"She killed herself the next day."

I could see, in his eyes, on his face, the way his broad shoulders were set, with a slight hunch against the weight of the world, how very, very sorry he was. The regret, the wish for one more chance, the repentance. I remembered something that someone very wise had said to me one time.

Slowly, I put my hand on top of his, just like my Poppa is wont to put his on mine to soothe my feelings and fears. Spencer's hand twitched, but he didn't pull it away. I pressed my palm on top of the back of his hand, but didn't pat like Poppa might have done, only let my hand rest there.

"You couldn't have saved her," I told him softly but strongly. "You can't save someone who doesn't want to be saved." He shook his head. I could see the distance starting to build up in his eyes. I dug in deeper. "And you said yourself you're not a savior. God is the only one who can ever save any of us from ourselves."

He let out a short, sharp laugh. "I believe that," he told me, "but easier said than done."

"Easier said than done," I agreed. "But you have to try," I urged. He looked at me then, a dark, hooded look, one that didn't erase the pain he seemed to work real hard at covering up. I could relate.

Spencer was sexy. Hot. Oh so very mysterious. But not. He was a person. With pain. Like the rest of us. Something dawned on me.

"You ran away too," I said. He frowned, a short shake of his head. "To Brooks. You ran away. To heal?"

"I didn't run away," he told me. "I walked away. I passed the bar, went to work as a desk jockey, found out it wasn't for me, left the Bureau, and asked Charlie for advice. His was to take the Oklahoma Bar. So I did. And came here to help him."

"Charlie doesn't need any help," I told Spencer pointedly. He didn't spit at me, but his expression said he wanted to. "Running isn't always a bad thing," I told him in defense. His eyes locked on mine.

"Unless you can't outrun what you left," he said directly. I didn't back down or look away.

"Yes," I agreed, "Exactly that." I wasn't thinking about Van, although I agreed with Spencer on that. I was thinking about the haunted look in Spencer's eyes when he talked about what he'd witnessed.

He kissed me then. To shut me up, because he couldn't help himself, for distraction's sake, I wasn't sure. It was just as messy as the other times before it, but it had a ringing taste of desperation. It didn't stop me from kissing him right back, the hay itchy and uncomfortable, his stubble prickly. His big nose jabbed me, his long fingers dug into my back, hard. I snaked an arm around his neck and pressed myself into him. Because I couldn't get enough. It would never be enough. And just as quickly as it began, it was over. He pulled back and pushed me away, shaking his head and wiping his mouth, a dot of blood smearing where I'd apparently bitten his lip.

"I can't, Lilly," he said. I shook my head and straightened my shirt, not looking at him, confused as hell by the change in direction. This, I thought, was the very man who'd pressed me up against a pickup truck and told me in no uncertain terms how much he wanted me to want him. Allegedly.

"Okay," I said.

"It's just..." he started.

"Oh-kay," I said again, definitively, starting the climb down from our perch. I wasn't interested in the ways and means of why someone who *wanted* me was turning me down so efficiently. He followed me down slowly, and we got back in the Ranger. I started the engine and pointed it in the direction of my parents' house and Spencer's black Mercedes. I pulled up next to his car, rolling to a stop. The sky was dark now. The air was cool. He started to hand me back the cookies.

"Keep them," I said, waving him off, willing him to get away from me. He nodded. I sighed and remembered my manners, pulling myself up, squaring my shoulders, and putting on the dog of fake cheer.

"You're coming to the Jubilee, right?" I asked. His eyes narrowed.

"I'm invited?" he said, with a teasing tone that was just as put upon as mine.

"The whole town is invited," I told him defensively, then reconsidered. "I'm personally inviting you," I told him, trying to find some kindness. He nodded.

"I'll see you there."

I left him with a wave and a smile, heading back to return Daddy's farm toy and get a ride back to my own place.

My emotional trauma at the hands of two tall, blue-eyed idiots had been coloring my world for quite some time. I knew Spencer, with his dark eyes and strong sense of right and wrong, wasn't like them. But after all the mistreatment, I just didn't know how to find myself again.

I refused to hang my head, instead gathering all the gumption and grit of my days of racing around a dusty arena in rhinestones and adopting an erect posture. I put my tongue on the top of my mouth. I couldn't cry now. If I started, I might not stop.

Chapter Twenty-Eight

"Tally!" I hollered as I slammed through the door to the living room I shared with her. Her large, curly head popped out from the kitchen with a frown.

"What?" she asked, a bowl and spatula in hand, a smear of brownie batter on her cheek.

"How do you feel about a stakeout?" I asked her.

"There's donuts, right?" she said seriously.

"Usually," I said with a shrug.

"I'm in," she said, "But you gotta wait for my timer to ding."

"Deal. Find your black," I said to the back of her head. She only offered me a short wave as she went back to the kitchen.

I headed to my bedroom and pulled out a pair of tight black jeans and a black turtleneck sweater. It was no fashion statement, but it was warm and covert. I hadn't informed Tally that this little endeavor was taking place outside. I searched through my great-grandmother's hall closet until I found an old camo jacket. Having belonged to one of the large men in my family, it was too big, lined and functional. I was pulling on a pair of black muck boots when Tally bounded back in the room, a black lace jumpsuit on. I resisted the urge to roll my eyes.

"Is that something you care about getting cow shit on?" I asked. She took a half beat to look slightly surprised then shrugged.

"Not really. Some magazine gave it to me," she said.

"Did it come with a sweatshirt?" I asked, going around her to look for a flashlight, and tucking my phone in the zippered pocket of the jacket.

"Why," she drew out suspiciously, "would I need a sweatshirt? And be concerned about poop? And why are you wearing camo?"

"We're going outside," I said.

"Where, exactly?" Tally asked.

"The upper bottom field," I told her, referring to a portion of our land with no better geographic description. She knew immediately what I was talking about.

She sighed, "You wanna tell me what's going on?"

"Nonnie's going to be late in the morning because they're selling about thirty head of cattle. They're cut from the rest of the herd and I'm guessing in that field. We're going to go hang out and see if anyone comes to inspect them early," I said, warming to the idea as I said it out loud. I wasn't going to admit that it had been inspired by Spencer Locke's lack of stakeout. And perhaps driven by my need to prove I was on par with him.

Tally wrinkled her nose, "I'm not getting a Mustang, am I?" she asked sadly.

"You can afford your own Mustang. Get your coat," I told her.

xxx

It was pitch black when we stepped onto the porch, the red sunset Spencer and I had shared long gone, replaced with a weak slice of moon. Tally and I were faced with a problem. The field I had referenced was about two miles away. Both my grandparents' and parents' houses lay in between. If we drove one of our cars, the noise would cause either of those two households to look out the window and wonder what we were doing going down the road. We could borrow the same vehicle I'd squired Spencer around in earlier, but we'd have the same issue. On rural roads where neighbors were few, it was a habit of country people to keep hard tabs and what and who went past their house. The rumble of an engine sent everyone on point to a door or window. I, myself, was guilty of this, but it posed a dilemma for me and my sister in that moment.

"We have to walk," I told her finally.

She grimaced in the glow of the porch light. "Are you freaking kidding me?"

"Someone will hear us otherwise," I told her. I could see the well-greased wheels turning as she thought, her lips pursed.

"We can go around the back way," she suggested.

"Nonnie and Poppa might still hear the car start up," I pointed out, "And then they'll be calling one of us wondering where the other one is going at ten o'clock on a school night." Tally blew out her breath, exasperated, but she knew I was right.

"Shit," she said, "Let's go."

We headed the same direction I'd gone with Spencer when I'd taken him to talk to all the neighbors, staying in the shadows away from all the floodlights of the barns. We were careful to avoid the obvious security cameras Daddy had installed several years back. I tried not to dwell on the fact that there were probably quite a few we couldn't see. But no one came out guns blazing to stop us, so either Daddy wasn't watching, or we'd been successful. Mama and Daddy's house was farther from the road, but we didn't dare turn on a flashlight or phone, making our way silently by memory instead.

Once we'd cleared the house and were almost a mile in, Tally spoke.

"I feel like it's my duty to point out that this is a bad idea," she told me.

"And yet, here you are," I said back without any malice, wanting to turn on my flashlight, but worried it might still be seen from the house. Our feet crunched in the rock and dirt of the road, but the sound wasn't enough to cover up all the other little creaks and groans of the woods and the river bend we were approaching. The dark was disconcerting and the faint outlines of the gnarled tree branches only contributed to the eeriness.

This was my home, this was our land, but I wasn't a fan of the dark, and even the boogeyman can come find you on your own turf. Van was proof of that.

"This wouldn't happen to have anything to do with the little time you spent with Spencer Locke this evening, would it?" Tally asked, clicking on her flashlight and sweeping it across the road. I wished she'd turn it off; it only upped the creep factor.

"No," I said defensively, but didn't elaborate.

She sighed, "You at least brought a gun, right?"

"Of course," I answered, patting my other pocket, "Didn't you?"

"Yeah. And a Taser. Just in case."

I don't consider myself brave, contrary to what the town of Brooks might think. But my daddy has always maintained that facing your fears will make them disappear, so I generally try to fake a bravery I never feel. But this night and the woods and all the letters I'd been getting and the being held at gunpoint before I could get in a second cup of coffee was giving me the heebie jeebies.

Tally's flashlight glinted off the shiny metal of a lock on a swinging corral-panel gate. We'd arrived. "After you," she said, gesturing sweetly. I shot her a look and started to climb over the gate, swinging softly over to the other side and climbing back down. I waited on Tally do to the same. "You're sure the right livestock are here?" she asked me. I clicked on my own flashlight and guided the beam of light out toward a clearing where clumps of what looked like black boulders huddled. She nodded grimly.

"Let's go back further into the trees, closer to the river," I suggested. A branch of the river cut through this section of the fields, some days still and peaceful, others swift and loud. It was noisy tonight, the water rushing, quickly carrying what flowed into the bend out further into the wider swath.

It was loud enough that we almost didn't hear the car engine, and might not have if the headlights hadn't swept over us. We immediately scrambled back toward the water, under better cover of the trees, crouching down in the rocks and dirt and moss. Flashlights turned off, we watched from afar as a vehicle parked at the gate. It was bigger and set up high and could have been a truck or a soccer-mom SUV, but the glare of the headlights and the way it was parked prevented me from seeing for sure. I thought it might have been silver or cream in color, but I couldn't tell that either.

Car doors slammed and two figures got out, ghosts dancing in the mist and glare of the lights. One of them made their way to the side of the gate with the lock and stood, then both of them barked at each other. The one by the gate kicked it, and they both climbed back in. But not before I caught a glimpse of the glint of a large pistol in one of their hands.

"Daddy put on new locks," Tally whispered, "Bolt cutters aren't big enough to do it in one try." I turned to look at her.

"That's genius," I said.

"That's Daddy," she answered with a shrug. We watched the big vehicle start to back up and I was intent on catching the make and color when the body of it turned one way or the other. So intent that I didn't realize I'd been unconsciously scooching back while I crouched. Peering into the darkness at the light through the trees, I didn't notice when my feet started to slide out from underneath me. I still wasn't sure what was going on even after I took my eyes off the car at just the wrong time and started to try to scramble for a handhold. Having been in silent mode, I couldn't make my mouth work to yell for Tally or grab at her.

I didn't realize what had happened until she was calling out for me and saw her long-fingered hand reach out to snatch me back. When the icy blast of the water hit me, it was too late. I went under once and then again and started frantically treading water, reaching out for anything in a panic to try to get back to solid ground. The current was strong, and the freezing water made all my movements seem sluggish. I twisted and turned and thrashed, and then common sense prevailed and I worked myself around so my back was facing the current, tucked my knees and rode it out, praying I'd land on a gravel bar and not something harder. The moon picked up objects around the water, coming sharply into focus and then just as quickly, flashing by. I tried hard to quell my panic and my natural urge to want to try to fight the current again.

Finally, the river turned and the flow ebbed. I untucked myself and started the long swim toward a swatch of shore the moon lit up, sputtering and shivering. I dragged myself to the rocks and sat, with trembling limbs and chattering teeth, surveying the situation. I had no idea where the hell I was, in the dark. My phone, zipped safely in my pocket, was worthless. I'd lost my flashlight somewhere in the water. I was freezing and wet and I'd left my sister to fend off cattle rustlers armed with a gun, a Taser, and her good looks. I pulled out my own gun, worthless now too, wet and cold, and with shaking hands hugged it close.

Shit. And damn it all to hell.

Rocking back and forth, I wrapped my arms around my knees and waited.

xxx

That's where they found me, two hours later, in the same position, frozen to the bone, icy tears I didn't know I'd cried on my cheeks mixed with the river water.

"You must have a death wish," Spencer Locke said, frustration and annoyance ringing in his otherwise gravelly-smooth voice, as he wrapped a silver blanket around me and scooped me up easily off the rocks. I'd faintly heard the airboat, but I hadn't been in tune enough to recognize what it was. I was too tired to answer him, too frozen to form a retort. I saw the hard frown of a River Ranger and Tally's stricken expression when Spencer deposited me back in the boat.

Tally moved toward me, but Spencer waved her off and sat me down on his lap, wrapping his big arms around me. I knew he wasn't comforting me, only trying to keep me from dying. I wasn't strong enough in that moment to resist, my mind and body dulled by the cold. I found myself sinking into the warmth of his body.

I was startled when he picked me up again and carried me to a waiting ambulance, crowded with my family and Scotty.

"Take her to the hospital," he told the EMT, "Make sure she doesn't have hypothermia." He hesitated, looking at me with a hard look. "I need to call in what you told me," he said, redirecting his gaze back to Tally. She nodded and then was shooed out of the way when the EMTs started to load the stretcher in. Mama climbed up in the ambulance with me and laid her cool, dry hand on my forehead.

"Mama," I started.

She waved her hand and fixed me with pretty blue eyes. "You'd better hope you die on the way to the hospital, sweetheart," she said, "Because if not, I'm going to kill you myself for scaring the hell out of us."

I didn't respond, turning my head instead when they started checking my blood pressure.

Chapter Twenty-Nine

I survived. After my foray into the river, I'd managed to escape hypothermia. I'd spent three days in bed with the sniffles, hot tea and soup at the ready. I wasn't sure if I was nursing my body or my pride. As far as I knew, what little Tally and I had seen hadn't moved the investigation forward. Spencer hadn't called to yell at me, Cash had silently dropped off a new flashlight, and I was fairly sure Van was gone.

But I was at my wit's end on this bright sunny Friday morning. With Spencer. With Van. With the cattle. With Cash still hanging around. But mostly, with myself for being more bumbling and badass these days. After I found my gutless wonder in bed with his secretary and subsequently called off my engagement, I'd come home to find myself. I'd dusted off my magic cowgirl boots and slid them back on to a perfect fit. I'd gotten some balance, some clues, a sense of purpose and place. But when Van had rolled into my town, it seemed Tally was right, and I was at the crossroads of an identity crisis. And after being teased and rebuffed by the one guy who wasn't all that interested in my wiles, and feeling guilty over the boy who'd been first in line to break my heart, and then falling in the freakin' river, I could think of only one thing.

I hit the door on the most popular place on Main Street before Barbie could unfurl the welcome mat. My hairdresser, Barbie, was straightening up and waiting on the coffee to perk when I crashed through the door. She took a look at me in holey jeans and an off-the-shoulder sweatshirt reminiscent from the 80's which had "Quote Me" emblazoned across it. It'd seemed like a good idea at the time. I had on converse sneakers. My hair was in a ponytail. She frowned.

"Lilly Kay," she started, crooking a tiger orange tipped finger toward me. I started slowly toward her.

"I don't have an appointment," I said, almost apologetically.

"Yes," she affirmed. I pulled out my ponytail, and my hair puffed out in every direction.

"Barbie, what color is my real hair?"

She hesitated, looking me in the eye in the mirror. "Why?" she asked without moving. I broke our glance in the mirror.

"This," I gestured harriedly around the curly fuzz of my hair, "Is this me?" Barbie sighed and moved to a swivel chair at a nearby station. She sat down and then had second thoughts, holding up a finger at me and moving toward the back. She started over after offering me a mug. I wrapped my hands around it, the steam rising into my face, the heat of it defrosting my fingers.

"Lilly," she said evenly. "No one cares what color your hair is. Except maybe your mama. Because mama's are like that."

"Barbie," I said.

She interrupted me. "Your hair is a very dark blonde, a very light brown. Probably about a five, on the scale. When you were little it picked up highlights whenever you went outside. It was red and blonde and brown and a lot of other shades all mixed together.

Except for that one time when you put beer and lemon juice in it, and you turned it green," she smiled. I didn't. She sighed and took a sip from her mug.

"Lilly Kay, God knows you. We all know you. Whether your hair is pink, or green, or aubergine." I looked at myself in the mirror. She snapped her fingers at me.

"You hair looks good, girlfriend. Otherwise I'd have fixed it a long time ago. If *you* don't like it, we'll do something different. If you're trying to find yourself again, you're not gonna find her in a hairdo. If it's over a boy, either get your gun or unbutton a button or two on those fancy shirts." I cocked a smile her way with a sigh and another glance in the mirror.

"You're not gonna do my hair are you?" I asked her. She shook her head.

"Not without a forty-eight hour waiting period for you to process the implications." I rolled my eyes.

"I might be back," I told her.

"That's fine," she said with a nod. "In the meantime, pull a brush through it. Bless your heart." I left her with the still hot coffee, untouched. I still wasn't all that satisfied, apparently, so I made my way to my Mama's shop.

She met me at the door with another steaming mug, tea this time. I threw myself on a dark purple tufted settee.

"It's like I don't even know who I am," I all but whined to her. "Am I a little girl in cowboy boots and shiny tiara? Am I a fancy lawyer? Am I someone who goes around shooting people? Is my hair curly? Is it straight? Did I really almost marry someone like Van

Payton Ehlers the Third? After escaping the likes of someone like Cash David Stetson?" I paused and my mama didn't offer anything right away. She looked thoughtful. Then, slowly, and with great care and weight, she spoke.

"Yes," she said simply.

"Yes what?" I frowned.

"Yes," she said again, "You are all those things. You are the Lilly Pulitzer your Mama made you wear. You're the sequins your Daddy bought you. You're the jeans and t-shirts you wore to college. You're the designer dresses you thought you had to have. You're the pencil skirts and suit jackets. You're all those things because they don't matter." She frowned, ever so slightly, her lips pursing and her head cocking. "Your hair is curly though, please stop trying to make it straight. It kills me every time you take a straightener to it." I smiled ruefully at that, the automatic gesture of an oft-practice eye roll directed toward my mother. She went on.

"You are Lillian Katherine Atkins. You've been a force to be reckoned with from the moment you were born. You've always been set on right and the truth and justice. You are a girl who ran away when she got her heart broken. You're also the woman who came home when she figured out she needed to get whole."

"I knew it was bad, Mom and I stayed anyway. And then it bit me in the ass," I said, referencing Van, admitting out loud what I'd been toying with for a while.

"Or maybe God rescued you from a bad decision," Mama said.

"Are we talking about Van or Cash?" I asked reluctantly.

She shrugged her pert shoulders, "You pick,"

Once upon a time Cash had been a drug, and I'd been too young, too dumb to resist a relapse. But whatever he may or may not have done didn't require me to spend what I thought would have been the rest of my life trying to make it even.

"I thought Van would make it all better. Make Cash...," I trailed off.

"Come running? Disappear?" Mama asked, gently pointed. I didn't respond, my eyes locked on the crushed velvet. "What are you guilty of, exactly Lilly?" she offered the somewhat rhetorical question.

I wasn't sure of the answer. "Running away I guess? And using someone to try to hurt someone else..." That part came out clearer.

Mama nodded slowly, "Sweetheart, no one faults you for running away from Cash. It's a shame you had to go to another state, but you and Cash have never really been a good idea. Once upon a time maybe. But not after the subsequent times."

I didn't respond.

"You know," she went on, "People don't always understand it, but there's a strong difference between shame and guilt."

I was confused, and irritated because I *didn't* understand that.

"Guilt is that pit in your stomach when you realize you've done something wrong. It means you take responsibility for your actions and regret them. Shame is completely self-centered. Shame says *you're* wrong, not just that you've done something wrong. It paralyzes you, leaves you spinning in a vicious cycle of reliving the wrong. And it accepts no responsibility for your own choices."

"I've been feeling more than nauseous, lately," I admitted.

"Like you need to hide?" Mama asked.

I nodded, starting to understand. Realizing that I hadn't completely accepted that I had choices in my romantic love life. And that I didn't have to be the victim forever and ever.

"So I'm being self-centered?" I asked her, trying to sound sarcastic to alleviate the ache of that truth, already knowing the answer. Maybe needing my mama to say it to me.

"Lilly," she said softly, "If you had known at the time that you were trying to use Van to hurt Cash, or trying to use Van to replace him, or trying to use him to make yourself feel better, would you have done it?"

I looked at her, shocked and hurt. "Of course not," I said.

She nodded. "So you did the best you could at the time with what you had to work with?"

"I think so," I said.

"Sweetheart, don't cling to a bad decision just because you spent a lot of time making it."

"Am *I* toxic?" I asked, because it seemed the one thing all these relationships had in common was me. Mama looked at me hard, her blue eyes kind but steely.

"Your relationships were toxic. Cash. Van. It seemed like you lost yourself in both of them, in different ways. Going back for more, that's toxic. Acknowledging and removing yourself, that's growth. We raised you to have grit glossed with kindness, not get manipulated or run over. And running away has never fixed anything. Running away doesn't leave you with a lot of options. And even though you ran geographically, you were really just running emotionally. The only way to change anything is to turn and face it down. You see that, right?"

"I don't really have anywhere else to run," I said with a sarcastic little laugh.

"Then maybe you should stop," she suggested gently.

"Spencer Locke doesn't make me feel that good about myself either," I said petulantly, trying to change the subject a little, but meaning it. She didn't acknowledge my tactics, but didn't necessarily allow it, either.

"Well, maybe that's something to think about."

"Maybe," I said without any real strong commitment.

Mama is left-handed and all that that implies: romantic, artistic, and prone to delicate drama. But she could discern through crap like nobody's business and offer a well-timed zinger when most necessary.

"You, sweetheart, are a very worthy prize, crazy and all. And if Spencer Locke can't handle that, then so be it."

Chapter Thirty

I knew my mama was right, but it was like Spencer had said, sometimes believing the truth was easier said than done. I walked the short way back to my Jeep, parked in front of Barbie's, and climbed in. The sun had heated up the leather seats, and I relaxed into them for a minute, mulling over the men in my life, both wanted and unwanted.

I was sitting on Main Street, thinking about my conversation with Mama and the ideas of shame and guilt, when a black truck rumbled by. I looked up in thought, and my eyes followed it down the street. My adventure with Tally might have been a bad idea. Or not, because it now seemed there were two culprits to be on the lookout for, something all the men in charge of this investigation might not have found save for our jaunt. I'd chased down all the obvious avenues of my cattle-rustling investigation, and Jack Thomas was at the top of my list, but as far as I knew, there wasn't enough incriminating evidence to actually arrest him. The sold cattle had been hauled off without incident. So either Daddy's new lock had worked, or the sirens that followed Tally's call for someone to rescue me had served as a deterrent.

I hadn't told anyone but Fae about the incident at the stoplight. I wondered then about the three letters. If he thought I was tailing him, it would make sense for him to try to scare me enough to get me to back off. Or it would serve as a distraction, although Jack Thomas didn't seem like the kind of guy to take the time to mail threats. But you never knew. The charming inconsistencies of small towns are what make them go 'round.

I dug out my phone as I started the Jeep and punched in a familiar number.

"Hey," I said sweetly when she answered.

"Hey, Lil," Manda Kingsley answered. I pictured her at the dispatch office, headset on and coffee and Kahlua in hand, blonde hair pulled up and peachy complexion beaming.

"You busy?" I asked.

"Always," she answered, "What you need?"

"Can you run a plate for me?" I asked, heading out of town.

"Sure," she said, "Hold on, let me get a pen… Okay, what's the number?" she asked. I hesitated and rolled my eyes at myself.

"I actually don't have it yet," I told her slowly, "Just wanted to make sure you could do it."

"Sure," she said again, "You wanna call me back when you have it?"

"Yeah," I said, "I'll call you back in twenty."

"Sounds good," she said, "Should I tell you to be careful?" she asked.

I thought a beat, "Actually….," I drew out, "No."

Manda laughed shortly and we both hung up as I reached the edge of town, headed toward home. The only loose end of my theory on Jack Thomas was the weird, allegedly stolen, license plate. It might not matter, but it might be something. If the theory that Fae and I had about the plates being switched was true, it meant that the current plate on Missy's SUV would likely give a make and model on the black truck and that it belonged to Jack Thomas. We could at least get him hauled in for switching the plates, and see why the hell he'd done so. Which might lead to the cattle.

It was a long shot. A very long shot. But it was all I had. And a drive-by of our distant neighbors wasn't dangerous.

I avoided the turn off to our dirt road and headed up the hill to the one for the Spades'. I found the right one and turned off, dust blowing up behind me. Their house wasn't far off the road and Missy's white Yukon was parked clearly with the back end to the road. I slowed down and noted the tag, driving past and pulling out my phone, calling Manda back. She answered, and I rattled off the letters and numbers, turning the Jeep around as I waited for her to pull it up in the system.

"Missy Spade," she said.

"What?" I said, turning around at a wide bend in the road.

"It's registered to Missy Spade," she repeated.

"No, that can't be right," I told her. I knew the plate numbers weren't the same. I still remembered the first one.

"Well…," Manda drew out, trying to be helpful, "That's what's in the system. 2012 Chevy four by four, black, Missy Spade is listed as the owner."

"A black truck?" I asked, speeding up, "And Missy's listed as the owner?"

"Yep," Manda answered, not impatient, but I could feel her wondering what in the hell had all of sudden happened to my comprehension skills.

"Okay," I said shortly, "Thanks girl. Talk later," I said, hanging up before she could ask me anything.

I slowed down again as the gate to the Spade's came into place, and spotted it then, parked further away from the road than the white SUV. The black truck was parked sideways, and I couldn't see the back end, but it looked like the one I'd followed before.

Something caught my eye, and I glanced over to see Missy Spade waving me into the drive, dressed in bright pastels.

"Shit," I said, pausing, then finally turning to go in the gate. Missy didn't know that I knew what I knew, and at this point, I wasn't even sure *what* I knew. I pulled up to her and rolled my window down.

"Hey Missy," I said.

"Hey Lilly. I saw you driving by and coming back. You okay?" I cursed again inwardly, noting again the methods of the neighborhood watch committee.

"Fine," I said, "Just driving and thinking," I half-lied. It wasn't all that untrue.

She nodded knowingly, "You have had a time lately," she said with real sympathy. I *had* had a time lately. "You want to come in for tea?" she suggested, "Don't have anything but store bought cake; but it'll do in a pinch." I hesitated, not sure what I should do. The hair on the back of my neck was twitchy, but going to have tea with Missy would give me an opportunity to maybe see the back of the black truck and see if it was the same one. I wasn't interested in running into Missy's cranky husband, or eating her store bought cake, but I was here, and it was an opportunity. I smiled and nodded, grabbing my bag, which held my gun. Missy was nothing but sweet, and her husband was nothing but a choleric redneck, but I'd learned it was best to come prepared, like a Girl Scout, no matter what.

I followed her up the steps of the house, craning my neck as I walked behind her, trying to glimpse the back of the black truck to no avail. She turned back to me as she opened the screen door to the house, and I smiled at her as I stepped over the threshold in front of her.

The Spade homestead was ready for Better Homes and Gardens. More accurately, it was ready for Architectural Digest. I frowned at the décor: modern, plentiful, and even to my only slightly trained eye, very expensive. It was gold and silver with bright colors and sharp edges.

"Wow," I said to Missy, "It's gorgeous in here." I'd never been in their house and was surprised. Missy and Angus weren't poor by any means, but they weren't the Clarks or our outfit, and I wondered how they afforded this.

"Oh, thank you," Missy said with sugar, "I just love decorating. This is what they call 'mid-century modern with bohemian influences'," she informed me. I nodded as we stepped into the kitchen, equally modern and equally expensive. Mama had remodeled her kitchen a few years back. I'd negotiated the contracts so I knew how much it cost. Less than this one, I could tell.

I sat at the table as Missy gathered glasses and sliced the pound cake, watching her. She was dressed in designer, I noted. I hadn't really noticed it at the rodeo when I'd run into her, but she was well turned out, even more so than my sample sale wardrobe, I thought. I adopted a bright expression as she came to the marble-topped table.

We chitchatted and she kindly pried about Van and Cash, and even Spencer. We finally ran through the obvious topics, and the conversation turned around to the cattle rustling and my fall into the river.

"We were just worried sick," she said, "when we heard the airboats. My stomach always turns when I hear the airboat," she told me. I was surprised.

"You can hear it up here?" I asked, "I would think it was too far away."

She shook her head, "No, we hear them. So glad they found you safe," she told me, patting my hand.

Her husband walked into the kitchen at that moment, and I stiffened. She smiled cheerfully and popped up to greet him.

"You want some tea, darlin'?" she asked him. He grunted an answer, his eyes on me. I smiled weakly and gave him a thin wave.

"Something wrong?" he asked us both gruffly.

Missy waved her hands dismissively and smiled, "Lilly just needed a snack and some girl talk," she told him.

I nodded in agreement. "Yep. Thanks so much Miss Missy. I'll be seeing y'all," I said, moving toward the door to make my way out of the house. I waved at both of them and ran hard into someone else. I stumbled back and looked up in surprise into the clear blue eyes of none other than Jack Thomas. We frowned at each other in unison and then his eyes went behind me to Missy and Angus.

"Mr. Thomas," I acknowledged him with faux-sweetness, digging in my purse as I took a step back.

"Miss Atkins," he said, again pointing his revolver at my head.

I was prepared this time and raised my own at his before he could get off a round. I put on a hard-eyed squint, reminiscent of John Wayne, digging deep for some grit and gumption. We stood there, guns drawn, in the standoff for quite some time before I heard a click. I didn't dare turn my head, but Jack's eyes again went behind me. Quickly, I moved sideways, my gun still steady on Jack as I positioned myself to see Missy and Angus.

The click had been important. Because Missy now held level her own gun, small and snub-nosed. Angus was clutching the big cake knife beside her with a hard, beady look to his eyes. I sighed in relief. Until I realized Angus' eyes were trained on me and Missy's gun wasn't directed at Jack Thomas' head.

"Well, this is certainly messy," Missy said pleasantly. I didn't answer her, trying hard to work through in my head.

"I'm assuming y'all know each other?" I asked, trying to sound tough and casual.

"Jack's my cousin," Missy said. I looked at him closer, not seeing any resemblance. Missy sighed then, "Really, Lilly, if you hadn't been so unladylike about this whole thing and not inserted yourself into all this, we wouldn't be in this predicament." I stopped myself before I sucked in air, but narrowed my eyes at Missy. Angus still hadn't spoken. I faintly heard a car approaching, but no one moved, the need for the moment outweighing the need to know who was driving by. I hoped whoever it was would note my red Jeep parked in front.

"You?" I turned the question toward Missy, "*You* stole the cattle?"

She sniffed, offended, "Of course not. I'm not going to get my hands dirty with that." She waved her pink manicured fingers to emphasize her point. "Angus and Jack did the dirty work," she told me, "I took care of the rest."

"Shut up," Jack told her shortly.

She rolled her eyes at him, "Oh, what does it matter?" she asked, "We have to kill her anyway. Besides, Lilly," she said turning her eyes back on me, "I don't know why you took it so personally. It wasn't like it hurt y'all's pocketbook any. You can stand to lose a few."

I didn't acknowledge that she'd said she was going to kill me. I was only remembering the look in my Poppa's eyes and the burning indignation Daddy was still carrying around.

"So because you think we can stand to lose a few, that gives you the right to steal from us? We're your *neighbors*," I said strongly. She at least had the decency to look bothered by that. Something clicked in my mind. "My daddy ran up here to help you when your barns got vandalized," I turned to Angus, "And you stole from him?" He didn't answer me, only offering a rheumy look. "No one vandalized your barns, did they Angus?" He looked away. I heard another car engine and longed to take my chances and run screaming out of the kitchen toward it.

"No mind," Missy interrupted, "Let's get this over with," she nodded at Jack, who cocked his big trigger. I tried not to shudder. "Not here!" she screeched at him, "Don't kill her in my kitchen!"

"Have you been sending me letters?" I asked Angus, trying to ignore Missy and Jack. He frowned and opened his mouth to speak.

"Shut up, Angus!" Missy said crossly before he could say anything. She addressed Jack. "Let's take her car and drive her back out to the river and dump her. We can tie her up and weight her down. No one will find her for a while. And by the time they do, no one will be able to tell what happened." Jack nodded in agreement and uncocked his gun, jamming it in the back of his pants. He moved to grab my arm just as Spencer and Scotty filled the door of the kitchen. I didn't have any time to think. I reacted instead, pulling the trigger and catching Jack in the shoulder. Poppa has always told me to shoot to kill, but it was the best I could do with what I had to work with. It slowed Jack down, but he kept coming. Sheriff Clay, who'd entered behind Scotty, took him down effectively and professionally, even with his age and berth.

I heard a peppering of shots ring and felt the breeze of errant bullets rushing by. Missy was unloading her gun. I went down hard, hitting the Carrera tile, knocking my nose. I felt the warm sticky rush of blood and swiped it hard, seeing the bright red against the white and gray floor. Before it all faded to fuzzy darkness, I heard one stronger gunshot and silence engulfed the room and then me.

xxx

I opened my eyes blearily. Spencer Locke was swimming in front of me. He sat in front of me on Missy Spade's gilded coffee table. Someone had propped me up on her Hermes-orange couch and laid a blue fur blanket across my lap. The bright blue fur was matted with still-sticky orange. My blood. The room swayed.

"Don't puke," Spencer told me, pushing me back and gently laying something cold across my face. It felt like a bag of peas. I closed my eyes and took a breath through my mouth, willing the nausea to go away.

"Thanks," I said, sitting up and waving him away once it subsided. He was frowning at me. I tried to frown back but it hurt too much.

"It's broken," he said unnecessarily. I nodded.

"How'd you find me?" I asked him. He sighed and rubbed his jaw, where a slight prickling of stubble had been brave enough to sprout.

"Manda Kingsley to the rescue again," he told me. "She got worried after your weird phone call so she called Fae Lynn."

"Who called Scotty," I surmised.

"Who called me," he finished.

"Did you suspect the Spades?" I asked him, "Or do you just consider it normal to call out the cavalry every time someone is worried about me?"

He sighed, a bothered expression across his face instead of the slight smile I'd hoped to draw with my sarcasm. "You seem to need the cavalry more often than not," he said, but then shook his head. "Scotty had mentioned he thought Jack was related to Missy, but it wasn't until Fae told us about the truck and the SUV that we thought he might be running his enterprise out of here. We didn't suspect the Spades."

"What was the deal with the license plates?" I asked.

He laughed harshly without humor, "An accident. They're both in Missy's name and bought close together. They got switched when they were put on. Jack was driving their truck the day he spotted you tailing him."

"You know about that?" I said, wincing as I sat up straighter.

"Fae confessed," he said wryly. "*You* should have told me."

"I thought we were on a need-to-know basis?" I said teasingly, trying to ignore the pain in my face and the fact that I'd just shot someone. He didn't answer.

"I couldn't get them to tell me why," I told Spencer.

He gestured around the room, "I think it's pretty obvious why Missy stole," he said. I nodded in agreement. "Jack Thomas is a career con man. If he hadn't gotten caught here, he'd get caught somewhere else and maybe go to prison and then get out to run another con. Hopefully holding you at gunpoint and threatening to kill you will be enough to keep him there indefinitely."

"Why did Angus steal, then? He seemed almost sorry when I asked him." Spencer looked at me, then nodded at someone coming in the door.

"Because his wife wanted him to. With what little confessions we got from him, he was just trying to support the lifestyle she'd made herself accustomed to."

"A toxic relationship," I drew out slowly.

"Yes," Spencer said, his eyes on my face, "A textbook one." I averted my eyes.

"Did you shoot Missy?" I asked.

"Yes," he told me.

"Before she could shoot me?"

"Yes," he said.

"Is she alive?" I asked. He nodded. I lay my head back down.

"Thanks for rescuing me again," I told him honestly.

He gave out another short bark of humorless laughter, "I think you might be the death of me," he said. I lifted my head and smiled at him, blood on my lips and teeth, hair sticky with sweat and fear.

"But what a way to go," I said playfully, trying to be sexy amidst the seriousness of the crime scene.

"Yes," he said with a sigh. "What a way to go." He didn't sound all that enthusiastic about it. Spencer stood up to go answer someone waving at him. He looked back down at me as I saw Daddy and Poppa and Tally fill the door.

"You need an ambulance?" he asked.

I shook my head, "Not this time."

xxx

Poppa got to me first, his dusty brown boots eating up the floor in a careful way. He was shaking his head even as he inspected me. "We told you to leave this alone."

I didn't want to argue with him, but it was hard for me to point out the obvious. "I found the rustlers."

He nodded with a sigh, his eyes looking around the living room. "You did," he agreed.

"I never thought it would have been neighbors," I told him, "Kind of makes you want to reevaluate the neighborhood watch program, maybe get some more security cameras," I said with a little laugh, my nose throbbing. He turned back to me then, his eyes laser focused on mine.

"No," he said, "It does not." I tried to frown in confusion. "Lilly, home isn't always the safest place. Sometimes bad things, bad people find you at home. They can violate you and then violate your safe place. But you cannot spend your life expecting to be betrayed by people you decide to trust. You have to live your life the way God intends for you to. And God doesn't intend for us to live scared."

Poppa's eyes were on me. Mine had drifted to Spencer. He paused when he realized where I was looking and followed my gaze.

"I'm not going to stop trusting my neighbors just because some of them went bad. And you shouldn't cut yourself out of something good just because you've been hurt. He's nothing like those two boys," Poppa finished while he stood, patting me on the head. "You need to go get your nose set, it's broken." I tried not to smile. It hurt too much. To the rest of the world, the exchange would have been cold. Between me and my Poppa, it was pretty much gushing love. Papa, with his soft walk and big stick, was protective of me, but unabashedly proud of me, no matter that I'd openly defied him. He might not hug and slobber on me, but for an old leathery cowboy with a heart of gold, a pat was all that was necessary. And it wouldn't do for him to get excited about my injuries because that would only serve to upset me. Treating me evenly was a sure fire way to dispel any panic. Poppa is always calm, but fierce when necessary.

He walked away while I continued to look at Spencer. He was right. Spencer Locke was no Cash Stetson. Even not knowing him my whole life I knew that. Spencer Locke was definitely not Van Ehlers. That was quickly obvious. I wish it was as easy as Poppa seemed to imply, but with Spencer's now apparent hesitancy, I wasn't sure what to do next.

Daddy took Poppa's place, but didn't sit, blocking my view of Spencer.

"Your nose is broken," he told me, "Your mother's on her way to get you. You need to get it reset before it starts to heal that way." Daddy's tone was harsh and his big tanned fists were clenched. I sat up straighter and started to stand. He laid a forceful hand on my shoulder. I stayed seated. He finally sat on the coffee table beside me with a sigh. I couldn't quite meet his eyes, dark and seething, locked on me.

"I'm sorry," I finally said, looking up, expecting to see the anger shimmering off him like heat. I saw tears instead. I pulled back in confusion.

He clenched and unclenched his fists again and then pointed a finger at me angrily. "It's my job to keep you safe," he told me, "And I can't do my job if you won't let me."

"I'm a big girl, Daddy," I told him, "And I'm okay."

He smiled crookedly, the tears still in his eyes, but no longer angry, "That's what you told me when you were seven and you fell out of a tree trying to spy on one of the ranch hands." I tried a chagrined smile. He ran his big hand over his tired face and then the mirth was gone again. "I should have shot him."

I frowned, "Who? Jack? I shot him," I said.

He was shaking his head before I finished. "Cash. I should have shot him the first time you came home crying. And every time thereafter. And I probably should have run Van off after the first time you brought him home. But I didn't."

I was shaking my head then too. "I had to make my own mistakes and bad decisions, Daddy," I told him, meaning it, and realizing then what good can come out of bad if you actually acknowledge the pain and let it change you. And let God heal you. "I'm okay, Daddy," I told him again. "I didn't need you to save me."

Daddy, with his outwardly loud disposition, talked a mean game, but deep down, he was a jelly bean. While I'm sure the sight of his oldest daughter laid out on a couch with a bloody nose and the beginnings of a black eye were disturbing, anything contrary to the idea of me being fine wasn't something he was going to introduce. The cool, calm and collected aura of the men in my life while I was growing up had gone a long way during times of crisis. It was probably why I didn't rationally recognize a good crisis until it hit me in the face. I'd been raised fairly certain I could control them.

"You probably wouldn't have let me save you anyway," Daddy acknowledged with a shrug, leaning over to kiss my forehead awkwardly.

"Probably not."

Chapter Thirty-One

A week later, nose reset, swelling subsided and eyes black, I stood in my closet thinking about Angus and Missy and their toxic relationship, which of course led me back around to my own. The thing about betrayal is that it can be mind-numbing and debilitating. And even though you can go about your day shooting people, changing your clothes, solving crimes, and going to court, you find yourself in a vicious cycle of wondering what you did wrong, how it all happened and the dumbest philosophical question ever: "Why?"

All this leaves one with a strong inability to trust. Especially one's self.

I had been betrayed and let down over and over by Cash, then harshly and efficiently by Van. Always questioning myself, I'd made running away my go-to, thinking that would repair my heart and my ego.

I'd worked to be all tra-la-la about my life, but the truth was, I was carrying around a whole lot of shame. I'd participated. I'd picked. I hadn't been swept off my feet and held hostage by either one of them. I'd gone willingly. And I'd been feeling wrong ever since, almost paralyzed in a cycle of bad choices.

There had been plenty of nice guys willing to step up to sweep me off into the proverbial sunset, but I'd picked these two divas as the grounding points of my romantic history. Cash, I could tell you why. It all harked back to my sixteen-year-old self and that brief glimpse of sweet perfection that may never have existed. I'd been chasing that sunset ever since.

There had been no glimpse of good in Van's veneer, only the same male affectations that came from pretending to be a stud. And my own idea that his same differences would hurt Cash enough to make Cash come save me from my own choices, or make the grandiose image of Cash fade forever.

I knew that now. I was done being the victim in the story I had created. It hurt to admit that I'd been a co-author, but at least I could stop doing the same dumb shit. Going forward, I wouldn't make the same mistake a third time.

I was still standing in my closet when Tally found me, rifling through clothes and tossing things out onto my bed.

"Hey," she said batting away a pair of palazzo pants. I turned around, and she took in my face. "Oh Sister," she said, "*Now?*"

I could only nod as she wrapped her long arms around me, and we sank down to the sheepskin rug in an uncomfortable tangle of limbs. She had me in a veritable headlock while my head rested on her famous boobs. The sobs started then, hard and fast, and when I started shaking, she only squeezed me closer. The dam had broken. Tears I'd been storing up over Cash, tears I should have shed at the time for Van, tears for myself and my own misguided choices. I might have cried for an hour. Or three days.

Once I'd exhausted myself and soaked through Tally's shirt with salt water, I lifted my head wearily.

"You ruined my shirt," she told me calmly. "This is silk. You're going to have to buy me another one." I let out a short laugh followed by a hiccup. She added her own and then the exhausting tears were followed by hysterical giggles.

"Better?" she asked me finally.

I nodded resolutely. "Better," I said, meaning it.

"Finally," she drew out with a put-on drawl. "I was getting tired of you going through my closet."

"So many ways to be crazy, so little time," I told her with a bark of a laugh.

"Ever so true," she said.

"It did take a while," I acknowledged. "It probably would have taken longer if Van hadn't come back to town."

"Well, there's that, then," she said, tilting her head in agreement.

"I never realized how much Cash and Van really had in common," I told her, realizing then how much Cash and Van really *did* have in common, beyond the fake charm and all the requisite smarm. "I thought I was getting the complete opposite, but Van was the same song, different verse."

"Yeah," Tally said. "Cash is his own brand of dysfunction, but they do resemble each other at the core. And weakness," she went on, "is *not* becoming in a man."

"I think I'm ready for a man," I said slowly, meaning it, but not sure exactly how to go about taking care of that item.

"It's hard, you know, having Poppa and Daddy as the standard."

"For our behavior or as a future husband?" I laughed.

"Both," Tally said seriously. "You think maybe you unconsciously, maybe intentionally, missed the mark with both Cash and Van because you knew finding someone as loyal and honest and strong as the real men in your life was an almost impossible task?" she asked, echoing my earlier thoughts.

"Maybe," I said, "But for me, I think part of it was not being brave enough to choose one as loyal and strong and true as Daddy and Poppa. Because I was afraid I wouldn't live up to their expectations either."

"Because Cash acted like a dipshit and dragged your self-esteem through the mud?" Tally said plainly.

"Probably," I agreed.

"Damn, so much growth in so little time."

"When I finally get something, it usually falls into place fairly quickly. My comprehension is somewhat exponential," I said with irony.

"You can't change what you don't acknowledge," Tally mused.

"Consider it acknowledged."

"Well, thank God. Can we all move on with our lives now?"

"That's the plan," I agreed.

We stood and Tally took stock of my mess.

"You looking for a Jubilee outfit?" she asked. I nodded distractedly, shuffling clothes again. "Want help?" she asked. I turned back toward her and shook my head.

"I need to do this myself."

She nodded with a smile and went out as I shoved clothes down to one end of the rack. My mama was right. It didn't matter what I had on; I was me regardless. Bless my heart. I knew my breakthrough, while admirable, would require more work, perhaps choosing every day to live the breakthrough. But today, it was a start.

Trivial as it was, I wanted to get the outfit right. I wanted to make sure I felt like me at the Jubilee, a celebration of our family and how far we'd come. I stopped at the back of my closet, quickly pulling a piece off the hanger and making my way to the full-length mirror.

It would do. It would more than do. My eyes narrowed on my feet as I remembered a pair of leopard print Old Gringo booties I'd ordered and forgotten about. I pulled them out of the closet and eyed the dress again. It needed something.

I remembered then Jacque mentioning one of the hometown baseball studs had married a spicy little cutie from Miami who was doing gangbusters frosting inanimate objects. And that she'd jacked up some of Jacque's boots. I pulled out my phone to call Jacque, picking through all my jewelry as I waited.

"Yo," Jacque answered quickly.

"Hey," I said, "Do you have the number for that gal out of Tulsa who does the miracle work with the bling?"

"Hell yes," she responded. "I'll text you."

She hung up on me as I pulled out a pair of thick diamond studs.

If Spencer Locke couldn't make up his damn mind, I could at least give him something to miss. At the very least, I wouldn't be that easy to forget.

Chapter Thirty-Two

"I need caffeine," Jacque said, rolling out of her big cream Cadillac Escalade in a pair of leather leggings, orange booties with peep-toes, and an over-sized pumpkin colored sweater hanging off one shoulder. The troops had arrived. Mama had enlisted the girls, sans Fae, to help with the party. They'd pulled up bright and early that morning, ready to work.

I watched Char slide out of the front seat, skinny jeans and a gray wrap sweater. It was a boring look for Char. She'd made up for it with a necklace that would have made an Egyptian jealous, and a matching headdress-like headband. She had on harness mules in navy. Brandy was more or less subdued in her brown cords, tan boots that had been laser-cut like lace and a long, flowy tan top with amber colored rhinestones pasted on it. It was an intense outfit for her. I was impressed. Brandy taught school. Jacque sold real estate. Char spent money. This all worked out quite well for all of them. If anyone had attempted a crystal ball in high school, it would likely have heralded the same result.

"I need a shot," Char said at me, "It's freakin' early," she gave my arm a squeeze as she started up my mama's steps.

"Mama's got coffee," I said to Jacque as she started to unload her tote, which likely contained her own preferred tools over my mama's scissors, glue gun, wire cutters. "And Kahlua," I nodded at

Char's backside. Brandy scooched up close to me on her way to the porch.

"I'll just take a little of both," she said under her breath as Jacque rolled her eyes at me. "Just a drop," she emphasized. I nodded and slung my arm around her shoulders.

"Of course. Just a drop."

xxx

Day drinking aside, we were more than productive, even a few short. Fae Lynn was coming to the party, but she'd gotten out of working to stay home with the baby. We weren't judging her. Tally had some sort of restaurant emergency, and she'd grumped out the door. I would suspect there would be a For Sale sign in the window of the diner soon.

Mama had assigned us centerpieces, laying out all the flowers, containers and requisite accoutrements to put it all together. I'm not creative. I know it's required in the South for a gal to be able to bake a pie, put together a floral covered cornice board, and fill the house with home grown snapdragons all in an afternoon's work, but it just doesn't come naturally to me. My mama and Nonnie have made it look effortless my whole life. Like the men in my life, they are hard standards to live up to. Jacque excels in a lot of Southern areas, but she likes crap like decorating and gardening. Char can mix a mean cocktail and always has the right shade of red lipstick, and Brandy is perfectly behaved, irons her pajamas and is always volunteering, so the fact that she often burns her mama's meatloaf recipe is often overlooked. Fae Lynn is very choosy about which Southern belle rules she wants to follow, but she is a firm believer in being able to shoot straight and look good while doing it. The jury is still out on me, I think. The rules are drilled into my head. And it isn't that I don't *want* to follow them, but like I said, most of it just doesn't come naturally to me. Nonnie has called me a modern Southern belle, but I'm never really sure if she's being nice, placating me, or needling me.

Regardless, Mama really didn't care whether it was easy or not, the floral arrangements, so she put us to work. I knew Jacque would fix all our efforts, and then Mama would perfect it all to her satisfaction in the end. So it really didn't matter what we did. We were just mixing the concrete, not pouring. And Mama probably didn't trust us to do the smoothing anyway.

We were parked at one of the wooden picnic tables Mama had hauled into the barn for the celebration. The morning air was still crisp, but Nonnie had dragged in space heaters and the coffee helped. My black eyes had faded to purple. I was still bruised but not broken, and I'd thrown on designer sweats and tennis shoes to help. They'd gotten third hand information from Fae but I'd only had short text exchanges with the three of them since I'd survived my latest escape from death, so I gave them the whole story as we worked.

"Fae says we have to stop cussing," I informed them. Char dropped her scissors, Jacque rolled her eyes, and Brandy sighed in relief.

"What for?" Jacque asked.

"Because she wants Dixie to be a lady," I told her. She harrumphed annoyedly and shook her head.

"Whatever, she must have still been high. She cusses more than the rest of us."

"True," I admitted, and let it go.

"Did you know that Van of yours was staying at the Dancing Rabbit when he was here?" Jacque asked conversationally once I'd finished my tale, snipping the end off a pink begonia. I stopped my half-hearted fluffing of the yellow filler flowers that looked like weeds, in my opinion.

"Yes…," I drawled slowly. Jacque smiled and reached over to rearrange my arrangement. I looked at Brandy, who was averting her eyes and busying herself with pouring water into clear vases. "What did y'all do?" I asked suspiciously. Char was looking on with interest.

"Nothing," Jacque said defensively. I could see Brandy chewing the inside of her cheek, trying not to crack.

"What did you do?" I focused the question on Brandy only.

"Nothing," Jacque said forcefully, stepping protectively in front of Brandy.

"Y'all," I tried a shameful voice. Brandy cracked.

"Well, you know how my Aunt Lolly owns the Bed and Breakfast?" I nodded. Lolly Tines had been one of Nonnie's students. The Dancing Rabbit B&B was the same one Nonnie had strongly suggested to Van.

"Well, Aunt Lolly has been feeling kind of poor lately," Brandy explained. I nodded again. "So I've been helping her, cleaning and cooking some," Brandy went on. I looked at Jacque, who was regarding Brandy with an irritated expression. Char waved her hand at Brandy to indicate she should speed up the process. Brandy nodded.

"Well, I had a prayer meeting at lunch the other day, and I was afraid I wasn't going to get done, so I called Jacque to help me," Brandy smiled at Jacque sweetly. Because Jacqueline Denham was *such* a saint. "And well, we, uh. While he was in jail…Well, we uh, we…"

"We burned his clothes," Jacque filled in with a roll of her eyes. Char died laughing, flinging flowers and slinging water. Brandy started wringing her hands. I just looked at them. I would have hated to be Van last summer if the girls had been in Dallas and hadn't been given almost nine months to cool off. Good Lord.

"Y'all," I said again, without much force.

"*That*," Jacque said with a toss of her head and a turn back to her vase, "certainly got him to go away. The man is so vain, Lil, I don't know how you stood him. Even his underwear was designer."

"You even burned his underwear?" I wrinkled my nose. I suspected then that the beat-down and short stint in jail weren't what had gotten rid of Van. It was the fact that he might have had to wear Hanes.

Jacque rolled her eyes. "Lilly," she tilted her head toward me with a sardonic look. I shrugged. I was over trying to control the Posse or save Van from their wrath. The sonuvabitch had it coming, I guess. And right now, I wanted to forget he ever existed, party hearty, and pray that, indeed, my friends' disposal of a few of his favorite things was enough to make him head his ass back across the border and never come back. A girl could hope.

"Thank you," I told Jacque, meaning it.

"Your lilies are lopsided," Char pointed out with constructive criticism, shoving me out of the way to fix the arrangement herself.

I smiled. "Y'all want a drink? I could use a drink."

Chapter Thirty-Three

It was gorgeous. I don't think the best event planner in Dallas could have pulled this off. The barn was transformed into some sort of glitzy "rustic-chic" retreat. My mama and Nonnie have lots of talents, but their party-throwing skills are to die for.

Since the barn was new, it was basically an empty shell, before any stalls, work stations, or shelves had been put up. The twinkling glitter of a large disco ball bounced off the corrugated tin walls to dance between the oak wood beams and dirt floor. Mama had hauled in a dance floor in front of the stage where the band was tuning up, and she'd put down thick, Safiaveh rugs to keep shoes clean, but the dust only served to enhance the shimmer and shine on the less than glamorous beginnings of the building. Fresh white gardenias and ranunculus overflowed onto almost every surface, bound by lush greenery. Orange and pink buds dotted here and there, just for a little color, and yellow for filler. The flowers were arranged in silver pieces that belonged to my family, along with china, both chipped and not.

For western flair, Nonnie had pulled out cow skin, deerskin, rabbit skin, and sheep skin; strewn it about, stuck a floral arrangement on top with some heirloom piece and called it perfection. There were boots, belt buckles, and bolo ties. Hats, and pearls, and lady's books on the western frontier placed lovingly among the tables and seating areas. It looked like Glinda The Good Witch's prettier, sassier, cowgirl cousin had come in, waved her wand, breathed enchantment into the room and then quietly pleased, slipped out.

I hoped, one day, my wedding would turn out this good. To whomever. Wherever, whenever. It wasn't the *things*, per se, that brought life to the room; it was the spirit in which it was done. Lovingly, with great fun, with reverence to people's comfort, with thought to what guests might want or need. With a sense of love. And home.

Twinkle lights hung from the rafters and peeked in between plants. The smells of clean dust, fresh flowers, and shoe shine mixed with the food. Heavy apps, as mama called them were on a buffet and not passed, because that's snooty. Italian nachos, bourbon meatballs, a thick, soupy ceviche heavy with fat shrimp. Toast points already slathered with artichoke dip, pimiento cheese on waffles. Mini chicken fried steak and white gravy. And for color, and health, caprese salad on skewers, drizzled with balsamic vinegar. All ready for the full-size plates.

In addition to an open bar that included select beer, wine and champagne (because hard liquor makes people act the fool and any drink orders that don't match her menu is tacky to Mama), there was fresh iced tea and a lemonade laced with mint. A coffee bar lined the back of the room, waiting for the end of the evening. It lay next to the dessert table, built up with stacks of books underneath the Waterford tablecloths for depth. It held only one square pan of pecan cobbler. The rest of Brooks was bringing the rest. It's customary at certain parties in these parts, for revelers to come with their hands full of dessert. Mama hadn't wanted to adhere to this tradition. Mostly because she wanted to control the menu, but also because she didn't like the idea of any of her guests having to work to get to play. She was overruled by half the town, however, because they sniffed at the idea of her being offended, and wanted, mainly, to show off. The table would fill up, each option in someone's best pan, a name discreetly taped to the bottom.

In another corner, a local swing band was warming up, unrolling their thick oriental rug on the custom platform Mama had commissioned for a stage. I waved at Tim Dawson, and he waved his fiddle bow my direction. They played traditional swing music, but Tim, I knew, also had a thing for King George, so I knew there would be some newer classics in there. Next to the stage, a DJ set up his own equipment. Not mama's idea, but Tally had shoehorned her own opinion in, telling mama the crowd needed all kinds of dancing options and that the band would need breaks. Mama had acquiesced, only after giving the DJ a hand-selected, specially curated list.

Long picnic tables made of old barn wood were arranged in crooked rows like arrows and surrounded by comfortable seating arrangements with soft chairs and couches on the fringes. There were no place cards. Nonnie doesn't believe in telling people where to sit. According to her, just because it's fancy doesn't mean it's not rude.

It was flawless set up for a good time.

I'd settled on the perfect outfit. A black, off-the-shoulder, mixed media Tadashi Shoji that I'd bought on sale and on a whim in

Dallas. I'd never found the right opportunity to wear it. I'd pulled the tags off happily tonight. It had a hint of cleavage, hugged in just the right places, and the taffeta skirt swished with my hips. I'd topped it off with a heavy, antique turquoise necklace, which didn't match. But did somehow. My leopard-print Old Gringos were frosted with gold Swarovski crystals. I had a thick coral cuff on one wrist, and my expensive gold watch on the other, a big fat cocktail ring dancing on my right hand. And diamond studs in my ears. I'd also let my hair do its naturally crazy thing, and it stuck out curly at all angles. It was me. A little Tally. A little Char. A little Fae. A little my mama and Nonnie. But all me. I sighed deep and went to grab a minted lemonade, a swing in my step to match the fiddle warming up.

No one was there yet, hence the lone pie. I had managed to be the first one dressed and back after our day of work. No doubt Mama was polishing up herself. She wasn't going to be outdone or upstaged by her own décor.

I shouldn't have been surprised to see him there. He was never one to miss a party. Or adhere to the "fashionably late" adage. His black felt hat was tipped forward; his black pearl-snap sharply ironed. By his mama, I suspected. His belt buckle was big, and unearned, his jeans were snug in all the right places. His boots were black to match his hat and shirt, and, I suspected, his heart. He looked like he belonged on a bro-country stage singing cheating songs. I hadn't seen him since Quint Jackson had laid him out. There was still a rough welt on one cheek, but it only added to make him look more dangerously appealing.

I rolled my eyes as he started my way.

"Damn, Lil, you clean up nice," he told me with a flash of white and a crinkle of his nose, the twinkle of the lights bouncing off the sharp bridge of the nose, sunburned from being outside. "Even your nose looks better."

"You're awfully early," I said crankily without acknowledging the backhanded compliment, not even able to frown at him that hard, given my nose. It was caked in foundation and powder, and Tally's excellent hand had managed to cover up the deep black circles and yellowish, fading bruises.

He shrugged, "Thought there might be something last minute to do. Move a table or something."

"How benevolent of you," I said drolly.

"I needed a beer," he admitted. "Mom cleaned out the cabinets before I came out of rehab," he said. "She apparently thought a gambling addiction might extend to alcohol."

"Mightn't it?" I asked with a glance toward him. I didn't buy Cash having a gambling addiction. I thought he probably had an addictive personality, but as far as it controlling his life, I didn't think so. I thought he was just prone to the path of least resistance and the getting in over his head was something that happened because he couldn't control the situation with a flash of a smile and a tossed blanket of charm.

"And we didn't finish our conversation the other day, you know," he went on, referencing the one Dawg had interrupted outside the jail.

My relationship with Cash was simply a series of unfinished conversations. I didn't really know what to do about that. I'd tried shooting him. I'd tried punching him. I'd tried forgiving him. And it still seemed unfinished. Maybe we would never tell each other the truth. Maybe I'd never know how Cash really felt about anything. I felt fairly apathetic about that sad thought tonight, though.

"Does it matter?" I asked him. His blue eyes narrowed, not in irritation, but I couldn't tell if he was upset.

He didn't answer me before the DJ walked over and asked him if he could help him rearrange the speakers. Cash tipped his hat my way and headed to follow Grant Adams, leaving me standing there. I checked my watch, a gold vintage Raymond Weil with a deep scratch on the face that I'd found in a resale store in Dallas.

It was thirty minutes to show time. Mama and Daddy strode in arm and arm just then, decked in party regalia, Daddy in a white dress shirt and black blazer and new navy croc dress boots, Mama in an iridescent turquoise taffeta shirtdress and matching pumps, her jewelry bold and sharp. I smiled proudly.

Tally came next in what would be inappropriate on anyone else: a jade green feathery number with a slit high up on her thigh and the halter vee cut deep into her cleavage, a pair of blinking green boots on her feet and thick green snakeskin cuffs on both wrists and curly hair piled up to the Heavens.

Nonnie and Poppa slipped in the door dressed to the nines as Tally and I met each other's eyes across the room with a grin. Nonnie even had on pink cowboy boots and Poppa's were his dark gray custom ostrich quill. Fancy, but still serviceable in case of a disaster. Nonnie was waving at me insistently, so I started across the barn, ignoring that Cash was in the corner. I was focusing on what was important: my people and a damn good party.

"You look like yourself," Nonnie said, getting right to the point, "Finally."

I laughed, "Thanks."

"Did you see that pecan dessert?" Nonnie asked me, clutching my arm.

"Yes," I told her slowly, clutching her right back.

"I made that especially for that Spencer Locke. You make sure he gets the first piece," she instructed me. I smiled tightly and didn't object, not wanting to discuss the running debacle that was my lack of relationship with Spencer Locke. Nonnie moved off just as Fae and Scotty came in with the adorably mean Hazzard and a hot pink bundle. They looked tired and oh so content. Fae Lynn, while not yet back to her stick-thin frame, was back in her jewelry, so all was right in the world. I scooted over to inspect my namesake.

"Could her bow *be* any bigger?" I asked sarcastically.

"No," Scotty said shortly, but with evident pride, "She tried."

Fae Lynn elbowed him sharply and tried to lick and stick Hazzard's cowlick. "You know what they say: the bigger the bow, the better the mama."

I laughed. "Of course," I said, squeezing Fae.

"You look good," Fae said, nodding at Tally's makeup job.

"You too," I told her, adding another squeeze, kisses to Dixie Kay and Scotty, and a ruffling of Hazzard's hair.

I shook hands and kissed babies, receiving desserts as people started to pile in, dressed in their finery. I grabbed Annabelle in a tight squeeze, her flowery and expensive perfume dry and comforting like a cloud. Charlie harrumphed but nodded discreetly at me. Jacque and her husband Josh came in: Josh weighted down with two dessert carriers, Jacque's hands occupied with their two daughters. Brandy was flanked on both sides by Quint Jackson and Zach Charm, which wasn't all that odd, but interesting. They were with Jase and his wife Susie, everyone in their Saturday night best.

Char sidled up to me with her husband Aaron and nodded approvingly, "You go girl. It's nice to see Lilly's got her groove back," she told me, then moved away.

The crowd parted and Spencer Locke emerged from the split, a vision in a deep blue button up, dark jeans, and a shiny new pair of amber-colored cowboy boots. He caught me looking and strolled toward me, no limp or pinch of which to speak. Wardrobe had worked their magic. I hit him with a bright smile before he could speak, waving my hand toward the dessert table.

"So glad you came, make yourself at home. Nonnie made something pecan. Make sure you get some of that." Before he could catch me, I moved away, because I just couldn't deal.

An hour in, we were in full swing. Food, music, and drink enjoyed by all.

I'd taken a breath to tap my toe to the swing band's attempt at Luke Bryan's *Games*, much to Nonnie's displeasure. But it wasn't bad. Someone caught me by the elbow and pushed me onto the dance floor before I could protest. I turned around and fell in step with Jason North. Relieved, I frowned at him.

"Better make sure I don't step on your toe," I told him.

"I'll pay attention," he said with a wry tone. "You look nice," he said without a hint of anything but brotherly love in his tone, "Like yourself. Even with the black eyes."

I nodded as we stomped across the floor. "I found her," I said, "Again." I looked at Spencer across the room. "I think." Dawg followed my gaze.

"He's a good guy," he said without much inflection in his tone.

"Allegedly," I said.

"You don't believe me?" Dawg asked, seemingly offended.

"You don't know everything," I told him mulishly.

"My Mensa membership begs to differ," he said calmly.

"Whatever," I said, noticing how Dawg had shuffled us toward the side of the dance floor where Spencer was. The song wound down, and he shoved me toward Spencer, who'd stepped up.

He didn't ask. Parts of me wanted to take off for parts unknown, but I'd shined myself up for this event, and a big part of who I was *was* about never letting them see you sweat. I ignored my dampening pits and stepped into an awkward rhythm with Spencer when the fiddler left Luke behind and took up with George.

"Your nose looks better," he told me. I didn't answer. "How long are you planning on being mad at me?" he asked once we'd taken a few steps and turned in another direction.

"I'm not mad at you," I told him. Frustrated, hurt, all that. But not really mad.

"Okay," he said. I could tell he didn't believe me. I tried not to care.

"About the other night," he started.

"Let's not," I said, ignoring his look and waving at Brandy's Aunt Lolly.

"You are mad," he argued with me. My ears started to itch. I saw Cash blur by with Tally, and noticed the way Dawg had finessed me across the floor and the way Spencer was intentionally moving me in a deliberate, well-timed, and well-planned square. I stopped short when I noticed the way Spencer's eyes were on Cash. Sonuvabitch. The rest of the dancers kept spinning as I stalked out of the fray off the dance floor.

"Lilly," Spencer called after me. I whirled around in all my lawyerly, rhinestoned, gritty glory. I had meant to be sweet. I had meant to give him something to miss. I had miscalculated and not taken my own personality into account. I took both hands and slapped them on my expensively adorned hips.

"Stake a claim, dude. Pee on a tree, park your truck in my daddy's driveway, something. Or don't. I don't care. I do, actually," I said quickly, "But I'm not going to go all-in on caring until you decide to actually act as though you like me, and like you're not just annoyed with me." Now I was a little mad.

"I don't drive a truck." There was nothing cute or facetious about his tone and then he went on. "I've already been threatened by my aunt and uncle. My biggest competition is the guy I helped avoid jail for rehab. And I don't compete. And quite frankly, you scare the shit out of me worse than going undercover for the FBI in New Orleans. You have a death wish every time you walk out the door."

"There's no competition."

He shrugged. "I want to make damn sure you've decided you're done with Cash Stetson."

"Am. Was. A long time ago."

"We'll see," he said unconvinced.

"It's not a damn competition," I bristled, offended. "And I'm not some prize to be won. I resent that." He was shaking his head before I could finish. And then I tagged onto something else. The way he said it that *we'll see...*

"Are you testing me?" I backed away from him, shocked and disgusted. He didn't even have the good sense to look sorry. Or argue the outrageousness of that theory.

In that moment, I was tired. Tired of waiting to be picked. Tired of being tested. Tired of feeling like I came up short. Tired of feeling like I wasn't in control over my own destiny.

"You're a chickenshit," I told him, confidence in my words growing with each second, even though a small part of me sensed that this conclusion wasn't so obvious. "You do want me. Just like you said the first time. You're just too afraid to actually deal with me. Well guess what, Locke, that would be the hitch in the getalong on my last two relationships. I'd like to think I've learned something since then. Let's not make you the third in the trio of idiots. Forget it." I left him there and stomped away from him toward a tin bucket full of beer behind the bar. I ignored the bartender's offer to serve me. I ignored the Southern lady rule of never drinking from a bottle in public and twisted off the top with a relish. Cash Stetson chose that moment to interrupt me mid-swig.

"Dance?" he said, holding out his hand, bottle-free. I saw Spencer out of the corner of my eye, watching us. I wanted to flip him off, stick out my tongue, take Cash's hand and let him easily, choreographically, scoot me across the polished barn floor.

"No," I said, not looking at him. I felt him smile.

"It's true," he said, tilting his head toward the band when I looked up at him. He took the bottle from my hand discreetly and set it out of gossip's way.

"What?"

"You look good in love."

I shook my head. "Don't start, Cash," I told him, uninterested in his games. "He thinks you're the competition," I repeated the earlier absurdity.

"He's entitled to his opinion," he said.

"Shut up, Cash," I said.

"Am I?" he asked. I shot him a not-Zen look.

"No. You're not. Not anymore. Not for awhile."

"Hmm."

"He's testing me," I went on. "That's why you're at the ranch. Your little re-integration into society? That's a test for me."

He smiled.

"Hmm," he said again.

"Stop saying 'hmm'," I told him crankily. He reached back for my beer and took his own swig.

"Lilly. In rehab, I thought about being your friend for one hot minute. That's not really in my nature."

"I don't really want to be your friend, either," I told him peckishly.

"I know. But not in the same way that I don't want to be yours." I looked at him, confused but not. "Spencer's no idiot, Lil. It's not your test. It's mine."

"Listen Casanova, I'm not a competition," I burst out roughly, infuriated.

"Lil, isn't everything a competition?" he said, both of us still looking at Spencer.

I fell in love with Cash in the classic Taylor Swift way, both pre and pop crossover: because he knew the words to my favorite rap song. He'd been the first thing I'd really *wanted*, and I'd spent a lot of my time thinking, plotting and trying to figure out how to love him. All these years later, I didn't want him anymore. But I still couldn't figure him out. And it still threw me for a loop, no matter the long, tall drink of whiskey currently sucking the energy out of my airspace from all the way across the room.

I started to turn to look into Cash's eyes to try to find repentance. Some of the sorry. But then I thought it was likely in my best interest to take Tally's advice and leave that between him and God. I needed to forgive Cash to save myself. And that was that. He didn't have to be repentant because reconciliation wasn't possible. Somehow, all of a sudden, everything between me and Cash didn't matter.

"Let's talk about it," Cash said, raising the bottle and turning toward me with a strong look in his blue eyes.

"Let's not," I said evenly. "I don't love you anymore Cash," I told him. "I don't hate you. But I damn sure don't love you either." His eyes took on a cloudy look.

"I'm not sure what's worse," he said with a quick smile.

"Cash…," I said, wondering if I'd hurt his feelings.

"Save it, Lilly, just save it," he said shortly, cutting me off. I rolled my eyes.

"*I* am not up for grabs," I told him, jacking the beer bottle back and with my eyes narrowed on Spencer, swigging hard. "So keep your hands to yourself." I stalked off with a swish of my hair and several stomps of my boots.

Chapter Thirty-Four

I tried real hard for the next hour to avoid Spencer. And then, because I was trying to be a grown up, I went right up and poked him, opening my mouth to let him have it. He stopped me with a wave of his hand.

"I don't do tests," he said.

I shook my head. "I was wrong," I admitted, "Cash said you were testing him. Which is just as bad. But still…," I shrugged.

Spencer hit me with a look I was sure had been honed by nights out on the mean streets. "I don't do *tests*," he said with strong distaste, spitting out the last word. "If you'd be still long enough to listen, I would have told you, I don't do tests. However," he said, "I am not above using what I need in order to protect what I think is important."

I started to answer that I didn't have time for all his FBI psychobabble, and then it dawned on me. "You're using Cash?" I asked with a laugh. Spencer looked at me hard.

"I can't be everywhere all the time," he told me plainly.

"So you're using Cash to spy on me? Does he know?" I asked, not sure whether to be mad or relieved.

"Don't know, don't care," Spencer answered, his eyes never leaving my face. I saw then that Cash was as self-centered and dumb as ever, thinking Spencer was testing him. I ignored the fact that I'd thought the same thing. It was different. Somehow.

I cut my eyes at Daddy then.

"Is my father in on this?" I asked shortly. He looked like he didn't want to be the one to spill the beans, but he finally shrugged and nodded.

"It was his idea," he admitted.

Keep your friends close and your daughter's heartbreaker closer, I thought, then faced Spencer head on, leaving Daddy for later.

"So you want to protect me," I surmised, "But you can't decide if you really want me?" I said, irritated.

"I've decided," he said strongly, irritated himself, "I told you that the other night." I shook my head.

"Then why'd you say you couldn't in the barn?" I asked him.

"Because I'm tired of kissing you to shut you up. I'm tired of you kissing me when you're high. I'm tired of us kissing in the middle of a crisis. I told you I wasn't into 'kind of'. I want to kiss you in the middle of a Sunday afternoon because it's fun, not because it's a means to an end."

"Oh," I said slowly, looking at him. I started to tell him I understood. He didn't let me finish.

"I'm not going to play games with you Lilly, or hide the ball. I don't need to test you or Cash Stetson. But I meant what I said about you being ready."

I nodded then, ready to tell him I *was* ready; ready to let go of both shame and guilt; ready to be myself with him. Ready for a man.

And then the lying, cheating, sack-of-shit I'd once promised to marry walked in. With his current fiancée.

"Oh, you have *got* to be kidding me!?" I said, throwing my hands up in the air. "Just hold on a second," I told Spencer, holding up one finger and moving around him.

I wanted to turn around and run right out of the barn. But sometimes you gotta face yourself and the one who done you wrong. Only problem was, my freakin' gun was in my top drawer in my bedroom. I stomped over to Van, waving off Tally, feeling the surge at my back as partygoers filed behind me.

He was dressed in a pink gingham and paisley shirt, designer jeans and cowboy boots. They were Frye, which the girls allegedly hadn't found when they'd absconded with his clothes. I knew they'd come from Neiman's, and they'd never seen the inside of a chute, or the dirt of a field. And the closest he got to the cowboy scene was the Houston Rodeo Gala. He had on a new gray felt cowboy hat, so very out of place on his head… even more out of place than him being here in MY town, in MY barn, amidst MY people.

His cohort was next to him, easily and quickly recognizable as the big-haired, long-toothed fiancé I'd seen hugged close to him in the engagement announcement Tally had laid on my desk. She had high color on her sharp cheekbones and subtle highlights in her otherwise dark hair: rolled, coiffed and sprayed into pageant-appropriate submission. Miss Texas had perfected the art of Texas-size hair. Her legs were long, her limbs thin. She had on dark wide-leg slacks and heels, an oversized fur coat and thick chunks of diamonds everywhere visible, including her left ring finger. The fur coat was completely ridiculous given the weather. It made her look more out of place than she already did.

Her long, thin fingers were clutching Van's elbow. Her nails were pale pink, short and square with rounded edges. The gel manicure version of Essie's Ballet Slipper. Dallas Junior League nails. I curled my ragged cuticles into a fist.

"Would you care to explain, Van?" I said. Van looked tired and resigned. He shrugged, almost apologetically. Almost, but not quite. The new me smiled and stepped in front of Van.

"Hello," she said ingratiatingly, smiling at me equally as such, "I'm Valerie Marie. It's so nice to meet you. I've heard so much about you."

She said it sweetly. But even though I was no Miss Texas, I was no fool; I heard the dropped off 'bless your heart' even if she hadn't said it out loud.

"Can I help you?" I asked caustically. She fluttered fakely just a bit, but then leaned in real close and whispered conspiratorially to me.

"You know why we're here," she told me. "Just give it to me and we'll be on our way." I looked at Van's face. His eyes didn't meet mine. If they ever had.

I realized then what I was dealing with. Van, by upper crust Dallas standards, was a catch. He was shallow, well-groomed, and came with money and a family legacy. There had been shock and awe when I'd left him so close to the altar. It didn't matter that he'd cheated on me. In fact, the fact that *I* was surprised, surprised many. Van, it seemed, came from a long line of cheaters.

For a Miss Texas to seal the deal with an Ehlers, it would be worth it to overlook quite a lot. It would likely be more than worth it to ensure that her future was secure as the wife of a senator. A senator with no sordid secrets from his past threatening to pop out. The antique ring that had occupied my finger for quite some time winked under the disco ball and twinkle lights. My nose throbbed and my eye had started to twitch.

"I don't have it," I told her, feeling the growing crowd circling us. "I told Van that. Why he's still here, I don't know."

"I don't believe you," she said, looking between me and Van, her voice wavering and her hands shaking. Tally stepped up then, hair bigger, legs longer, dress custom.

"I am fixin' to whip you, Vannie. And her too," Tally gestured toward his new fiancée.

"Maybe we should just take her word and go, Valerie Marie," Van started with what I'm sure he thought was a calming gesture.

"Shut up," she screeched at him, not whispering to me now, desperation flooding her voice. He stiffened and frowned. Just then, the posse rode up. Tally was already close, Fae Lynn handed off Dixie and sidled up next to me. Jacque, of course, was packing, as she didn't own an outfit where her gun wouldn't fit. Brandy was wringing her hands, Char looked bored. Mama and Daddy stepped up. Daddy's expression was bland. Mama looked pissed. Val and Van were ruining the party.

Val was close to tears. She ignored everyone else and turned to me.

"Just give it to me! And we'll go!" I shook my head.

"I'm sorry." I sort of meant it. "I really don't have what you want."

"Yes you do! I know you do!" She flung a piece of paper my way excitedly. I reached down gingerly to pick up the crisp white stationery, a sharp tri-fold that had been crumpled in transit. I opened it slowly.

We know what you're doing. Stop.

"Let me see that," Nonnie said, stepping up and crowding in to grab the other side of the paper from me. The handwriting was dark and bold, and somewhat familiar. I turned to Tally who shrugged and shook her head. Tally's head turned to Fae Lynn. Fae Lynn did a palms-up gesture with her left hand, her mouth turned down. I looked at Brandy, who looked confused. Jacque looked complicit. Char was examining her manicure.

"Girls…," Nonnie drawled out without any disappointment in her tone.

"Y'all," I said to Char and Jacque. Neither one responded.

Valerie Marie was impatiently watching the exchange.

"What did you do?" I asked. Jacque shrugged. She finally dropped the gun by her side. Char shot her a dirty look and buffed her nails on her tuxedo pants, her foot in the stiletto bootie tapping impatiently. Char sighed then and crossed her arms over her ample chest.

"I actually found something," she admitted.

"We didn't want you to get your feelings hurt," Jacque explained. I glanced back at Van and Val, who was frowning with confusion. I turned back to Jacque.

"*We?*" I asked her remembering all the times she'd asked me why Van was here and I'd demurred.

She shrugged, "Char showed me after the bar fight."

"And you didn't say anything either?" I asked, touched, in a weird way.

She shrugged again, "Char and I were handling it for you."

I laughed and shook my head at her reasoning.

"What did you find?" I asked the two of them. Out of the corner of my eye, I saw Van's eyes widen and his face harden. Char got a disgusted look on her face.

"I found the tape," she said with a nod toward Van.

"Are you kidding me?" I said to her, "That's the only reason the gutless wonder was here."

"I know. I'm sorry," Char apologized. A new thing for her.

"We really did have the best intentions," Jacque said. Van started to step toward Char. At that, Jacque's gun finally came up, pointed straight at Van. He stopped with a surprised look, his hands coming up in surrender. He backed up, but the gun didn't go down. My mouth quirked up. I saw Scotty sigh next to Fae, who grinned. I felt Spencer's sigh audibly. Nonnie was standing in a Wonder

Woman pose beside me, deliberating, it seemed, on what her part in this should be.

"So give it back," Valerie Marie was back to making demands, her hands clutching at the fur at her neck, not at all concerned about the gun pointed at her future husband. Jacque and Char had mulish faces set. A slow thought started to occur.

"Why did you send her a letter?" I asked them, my eyes hard on Van's mother's newest project.

"She was sending them to you," Char said slowly.

"Why was she sending them to me?" I asked with a measured tone, my eyes then focused clearly on Van. "And how did you know it was her?"

"Are you fu… frickin' kidding me?" Fae Lynn said at Van. I moved past Jacque, my hand pushing her arm down slowly as I stepped up to the lying, cheating sack of dog shit who had once convinced me that Vera Wang was a better option than an unknown designer from Spain.

"Give me the gun," Tally said hotly. "I'll shoot him if no one else will."

"How long have you known your new fiancé, Van?" I asked. He hesitated. "How long?" I asked again, sharper this time, wishing I hadn't wasted my one get out of jail free card on the well-deserved shooting of Cash Stetson. Van didn't even have the decency to hang his head.

"Undergrad." I ground my teeth. Another huge mistake of mine for Spencer to witness. I found him looking on with an indecipherable expression on his face. I'd think about him later. I turned briefly to Char.

"And she's in the video?" I flung my hand in the general direction of Miss Texas. Char nodded with a grimace. I closed my eyes, remembering with quick clarity how supportive Van had been of any and all of my girl's weekends, trips home, business jaunts. He'd been cheating on me all along with a special kind of crazy. I was only surprised that she'd stood on the sidelines that long. Shocked that she hadn't taken to stalking me long before in an attempt to take the ring off my finger and slide it onto hers.

I looked at her. She was beautiful. Prettier than me in a classic, dark-haired, wide-eyed Texas way. Long, elegant, with a background that would make Van's mom quiver. I'd been a good idea to Van's family. I came from money, even if it was of the Oklahoma variety. I'd been schooled on Southern belle rules, I had a good education. I was smarter than their son, likely to produce athletic types, and appeared to be somewhat malleable to Mrs. Ehlers' whims. But I'd gone rogue.

In that instant, I felt so very sorry for Valerie Marie. I'd escaped. The blinders had been ripped off my eyes with only the aplomb that God can have. I'd had the good sense and strong foundation to run home and get stronger. Valerie Marie was still desperately trying to secure the crumbling façade of the castle she'd built on quicksand, and she didn't even know the stones were plastic. I turned to Valerie Marie.

"*Why* were you sending me letters again?" I asked.

"It seemed like a good idea," she said.

"What did you think they were going to accomplish?" I asked, actually curious.

"Scare you?" she said with a question.

"Into what?" I said with a more incredulous tone in my voice.

She shrugged, then, finally seeing the fallacy in her plan. I nodded.

"That is dumb, girlfriend," Tally told her, easing next to me. The crowd nodded in agreed unison.

"Well, okay then," I said with finality. I heard the buzz behind me, a questioning one.

"She's gonna shoot him, right?" I heard someone ask.

"Of course," a male voice replied, "She shot that Cash Stetson, and he didn't really do anything." I smiled at that. Van looked worried at my smile as I turned back to him, looking for something, some sort of chagrin, repentance, sorry. Nothing. I knew he wasn't sorry. Not in the slightest, as entitled, gutless wonders are wont not to be. I knew, like Cash, and me, it was between him and God. But still. It wouldn't hurt for me to make sure he left and never came back. I looked toward my parents: Mama gave me a soft nod and a sweet smile, the steely glint in her eye the only thing giving her away. Daddy's eyes were on Van, hard and locked. Poppa stood beside him, at the ready himself, just in case I needed them. I didn't. Not this time.

I tapped Jacque on the shoulder. She turned and handed me the gun. I pointed it at Van's crotch.

"Man, they really do throw the best parties," I heard a voice and another buzz of agreement.

"Ten to one she nails him in the nuts," I caught over my left shoulder. It sounded suspiciously like my Grandmother Gwen.

"I'll take those odds," someone else agreed.

"Me too," I heard Cash say over my right shoulder.

When I shot Cash, it was because I couldn't think of anything better to do. With Van, it seemed like the only thing to do. But I was so over it and ready to move on with my life that I knew I couldn't. However, if Van wasn't smart enough to get that, then that was his fault.

Valerie Marie, in all her pampered glory, looked stricken as her eyes traveled the length of where the gun was pointed. I had no intention of shooting him, and I was sure the safety was on, but she launched herself at me. I felt a scratch on my cheek, and she had a hold of my hair. I went on the offensive to get her the hell off of me. Her strength came from Pilates; mine came from mucking manure and inherited grit. We scrambled and danced, and a slight struggle ensued, the gun managed to go off with a pop. Valerie was so startled, she stopped attacking me and turned. I turned too as Spencer whipped her hands behind her back and sat her down like a sack of flour. Scotty moved over her to make sure she didn't get up. Spencer quickly relieved me of the gun, double-checking the safety and rolling his eyes toward me as he slid the gun into his back pocket.

I looked at Van, clutching his thigh and wailing.

"These jeans are designer," he said, pointing at me as blood started to ooze out of what appeared to be a flesh wound. I turned as

I felt a wave of nausea at the sight of the dark red stain. "Is there a doctor in the house?!" he wailed. "I need a doctor!"

I felt someone brush by me and pat me on the shoulder, the hand lingering a little too long.

"I'm a doctor," Cash said as he headed toward Van with a hurried set to his slim, hard back, and a grin that was too sly, too satisfied, and way too perfect.

I heard another wail as Cash reached him, but Van's fiancé didn't pause to ask if he was okay, she only twisted her head up at me.

"What about the tape?" she asked gratingly, trying to shake Spencer off as he hauled her to her feet. I realized how important the tape was for her. Politicians survived sex tape scandals; a former Miss Texas would not. I turned to Char, who looked pleased.

"I would suspect," Char started, "that it's waiting for you when you get home." Valerie Marie looked relieved. Van, who'd been in town a sight longer, looked nervous.

"You sent it to me?" Valerie Marie asked Char with a grateful color to her voice. Char looked her dead on as Jacque stepped up to stand beside her.

"Not exactly," Jacque said. Valerie Marie looked confused. Van let out a pained, guttural groan as Cash ripped his jeans apart. Valerie Marie looked at him with exasperation and wonder.

"Where is it?" she asked.

"Well," Char drawled with her darling Southern drawl, the sequins from her tuxedo jacket glinting brightly, her red lips perfectly lined and drawn into a clever, Cheshire-cat smile, "We didn't want it to fall into the wrong hands." Jacque nodded, a matching smile on her pumpkin-colored lips. "So we sent it to your mother," Char finished, pointing a blood-red nail at Van, drawing first blood.

I wanted to put my head in my hands. I also wanted to laugh. But I was Lilly Atkins. And these were my people. And they had saved me from myself. And God knew who I was anyway, He always chose me. No matter what I was wearing, or what I was doing. And even when I couldn't choose myself. So it was useless to try to pretend.

There were no more guns drawn. Valerie Marie looked like she was about to hyperventilate as Nonnie launched into a lecture on girl power, taking care of yourself, and trashy behavior. Van looked apprehensive as he watched Cash finish ruining his jeans by slicing through with a dirty pocketknife, the dough in his cheeks working furiously as he waffled between staying coherent and passing out. I watched Spencer make his way over to supervise.

The girls crowded around me, loud and buzzing, with a special charged relief. My parents stepped into the crush, and I felt my Mama's cool, dry hand on my shoulder. Daddy's comforting touch was the rough ruffling of my hair. I saw Poppa smile at me kindly before he went to go get Nonnie. I sighed deep, soaking in my own feeling of liberation.

It's tough, you know, this thing called growth. It can make life real hard when one tries to resist it. If you're the kind to run away from a problem, it will eventually catch up. Say, for example, if your first love breaks your heart and you can't stand to be in the same state so you head South. And then your fiancé cheats on you and you run back home without fully dealing with the betrayal, and blackmail him to make sure he leaves you alone. If one were the kind of person who might do that, it's a likely possibility that he'd eventually track you down, and in the midst of being slapped in the face with all the heartache you'd stuffed down, one might get real lost in the throes of an identity crisis.

Thankfully, thanks to my people, I found the right boots, found a gun, and found my groove again, even if it's not as Zen as I might think it needs to be. The crowd moved away from me as the adrenaline started to spread out and dissipate. My sister stood solidly beside me.

"You know," Tally said conspiratorially, leaning down and snaking her long, heavy arm around my neck as we stood watching Cash finish off Van, "it's like the late, great Flannery O'Connor said: if you squint real hard, you can take it all as blessing."

Indeed.

I kissed her cheek and squeezed out from underneath her.

"I'll be right back."

"You okay?"

I nodded with a smile, "I've got one more mess to make," I told her, moving away.

Before I lost my nerve.

Chapter Thirty-Five

Spencer had passed on Val and Van to a couple of deputies and Sheriff Clay to be disposed of in the back of Fae and Scotty's SUV, injuries notwithstanding. Not so easily rid of, Spencer stood tall and sturdy in the twinkling lights of the party.

Courage, according to John Wayne and Napoleon, is being scared shitless and getting back on your horse anyway. I have always been one to dust my ass off and climb back on, sequins and all. And I was done running, I knew that now. I was actually sorry I'd run in the first place. And I wasn't going to do it again.

I waited until Spencer had turned away from Scotty, and then ignoring the clean-up of the dishabille around me, I stepped toward him, crossing my arms and cocking my hip.

"How long?" I asked him emphatically. He smiled ever so slightly and barely lifted an eyebrow.

"Come again?" he said.

"How long would you wait?" I asked him again. He raised his head, indicating he understood, but didn't answer right away. That was fine, I had stuff to say.

"The thing is… it's not real fair. You met me at my worst. And it doesn't seem to be getting any better. And you're perfect. A few years ago," I went on, "we would have made total sense, but now… not so much."

"That so?" he asked, his expression neutral.

I nodded, probably a little too enthusiastically, "My hair's never fixed. I eat cake for breakfast. I wear cowboy boots with pencil skirts. I've also discovered I like the un-put together version of myself better than the uptight, perfect version," I went on honestly.

An unquestionably irritated expression crossed the expansion of Spencer's face. He ran a large, long-fingered hand through his shampoo commercial worthy hair.

"Look, Lilly, here's the deal. I'm probably always going to be hot. I've been genetically blessed since birth. I won several baby beauty contests as a child. There was a short chubby phase when I wore socks to bed and ate a lot of pickles. But the good looks and put together part have only gotten worse. So you should either get over that or count yourself lucky. But…." Here, he paused, his voice lowered, got sexier, if possible, "I sweat in court. A lot. When I'm nervous, my breath stinks. It smells like death. I've killed someone. I faked a learning disability in grade school to get out of public speaking. And that problem you have with not being able to talk yourself out of helping people? I have to talk myself into helping people. I'm the naturally selfish person you couldn't be if you tried. I'm not perfect, Lilly," he told me, "I'm human."

For once, instead of being blindsided by his good looks, and instead of allowing fear and the feeling of inadequacy to rule the day, I really looked at him. At the two scars, one on his upper lip, sharp and white in contrast to his full, sharp mouth. One above his eye, slicing through a dark, heavy eyebrow, not quite as severe, not as evenly healed. I took in his strong nose, his granite jaw and the features that weren't quite as symmetrical as they appeared on first glance. I really looked at him. At the sum of all his parts. They were perfect. That was true. There was no getting away from that. And his eyes were dark and assessing. Always. But they also held a weird hint of grey-blue and hinted at… kindness. And sometimes when he looked at me, if I looked real hard, they almost softened. The smile lines almost relaxed. Like he wanted to share something, a secret. Like I didn't completely annoy him. Like I wasn't some problem to deal with. It wasn't all that fair to judge him on his looks. Just because he was perfect looking, and perfectly-ironed didn't mean he wasn't *real*. No more than Tally's outside meant she was a vapid idiot.

"You're wrong, you know," he said, when I finally looked him in the eye again. I sighed. Sometimes he really needed to take a long walk off a short trailer bed.

"Of course I am," I sniffed drolly. "About what this time?"

"You are a prize. That's kind of the problem. You don't quite get it."

I frowned at him, faintly remembering my mama's earlier words.

His eyes took on a thoughtful cast, "Lilly, wouldn't it make life easier to spend time with someone who's seen you at what you consider your worst? Instead of trying to fit into the ideas those two buffoons have of you?"

My mouth dropped open. He had me there. I took a breath and grabbed the reins.

"Will you stop rescuing me?" I asked him.

"No," he said without quibble. "Will you stop needing to be rescued?" he asked.

I smiled a little at that, "Doubtful."

He shrugged with a smile, gesturing to indicate the obvious.

He stepped toward me, his eyes smoldering, and then went perfectly still, rock hard and unmoving. I started to move toward him. But then, because it was so fresh, and so tender, and so important, I didn't.

I held up my hand, "There's another issue of fairness," I told him. He didn't rock back, only curled and flexed his big hands.

"You're very concerned with fairness, aren't you?" he said teasingly. I gave him a look and added an eye roll. He simply offered a quick flash of white teeth.

I took a long pause.

"I don't want, um, *us*," I said hesitantly, "to be clouded by my other shadows. It feels cloudy, because well, now you know 'those other two buffoons'," I said, tilting my head at him. "And I'd want it to be fair to you. And it feels cloudy."

He smiled fully then, a shark's set of teeth. "You want me to throw Cash in jail?" he asked.

"You wouldn't do that," I told him, not in the mood to joke. And not really caring in that moment whether Cash was in jail or not. Spencer's eyes squinted in understanding. He nodded once, and then stepped closer to me, looking down at me, no humor in his expression.

"Life is cloudy, Lilly," he told me. "And yes, it's an interesting scenario to have gotten to know the boys who came before me in this way. And," he went on, "it seems to me that time and distance didn't really make that much of a difference in you moving on with your life."

He was right. But, struggles produce perseverance, and perseverance produces character, and character, hope. That's where I was today. Maybe, just maybe, I could let go of the shame I'd thought was guilt and get on with my life. But I wasn't all that happy about Spencer pointing out my shortcomings. So I started to argue with him.

He towered over me, smothering my protest with a wave of his hand.

"But," he said before I could interrupt him, sliding his big, hot hand to the back of my neck, pulling my hair as his fingers got tangled in it. He moved an inch closer, stepping on my toe. I didn't think to wince. I could feel his steamy breath puffing on my face and the electric heat from his body warming mine. "It's just a matter of *you* deciding," he went on, "All you have to do is decide, and I promise." he said, moving just a half an inch closer, until I could feel the outline of him on me. Knees, elbows, nose. "I *promise*," he said harder, "that I can make the sun shine."

I nodded, begging him to kiss me. Begging the moment to go on. Begging for me to keep my big mouth shut and not spoil the moment.

But y'all know me.

"I can't promise you I won't be a little crazy," I told him, leaning back slightly, honest to a fault, even at the worst moments. "It seems," I said painfully, "that I get a little crazy when I get scared."

He nodded, "I'm not asking *you* to promise me anything."

I took a breath, a smile starting.

"Yet," he finished. I opened my mouth in surprise, forming a response. Before I could, he answered by crushing his lips on mine, teeth clicking, noses mashing, his hand squeezing the back of my neck, yanking my head back as he pulled my hair. His sharp knee dug into my thigh, his bulky arm pinned one of mine to my side. It was an awkward position. Uncomfortable, uneasy. Interesting. I extracted one of my arms and slid it around his strong neck.

So there, under the spinning disco ball, in the middle of the crowd of my hometown, with my perfectly imperfect people looking on, I went ahead and broke down by breaking all the rules a good Southern girl should live by.

I made out with a Yankee.

In public.

Very enthusiastically if I do say so myself.

After all, y'all, a good man… they are ever so hard to find.

The End

(allegedly)

Acknowledgments

God. Dang, growth is hard. That Lilly, she learns the hard way. Me too. Thank you for always knowing we can get to the other side. And making it hard. Struggle, perseverance, character, hope. I try to remember.

Grant. You are the best kind of book fodder. No clouds in sight. Love you.

Rafe and Vara. Y'all are hope walking. You are my sunshine on a cloudy day. Love you ever so.

Mom. We did it again. Who'da thunk we would work so well together. You are literally the reason I'm beginning to get good. I'll never be able to thank you properly. I will try with jewelry.

Daddy. A standard as high as the heavens. I know it's the things you don't say that carry the most weight. Thanks for letting me fail in silence. And cheering loudly when I succeeded.

Nanny and Papa. A girl should be so lucky as to have such grandparents. You taught me to read, taught me to use a telephone, and taught me how to wear cowgirl boots. And were proud of me when I didn't even know to be proud of myself.

Nowlin. It's nice to have a cheerleading coach who knows you can do it. I know it's like polishing a rough diamond. Thanks for agreeing to put up with me. And being there along the way. Before the words ever came.

Girls. I used to laugh when I thought about us. Now I cry when I realized what gold good friends are. We've grown. And we ebb and flow. But y'all are the best. And I take comfort in knowing you exist. Because the world is a safer place with people who will tell you the truth and take care of business. Especially when one can't take care of it themselves. Kay, Peach, Bayly, Jennifer, Megan, Ashley, Huff, Heather Bear: who would have thought you'd start your modeling careers so late in life? #Posse4Lfye

Guys. I was blessed to have friends that were male. Boys that would tell you the truth when you didn't want to hear it. And step in and create chaos that I didn't even know about. I consider you all invaluable. I will always remember you all with love and the strong urge to punch some of you in the face. Just kidding. But really. Clint, Sam, Jackson, Justin, Matt, Joe, and the rest: Best Brothers I Never Knew I Needed.

Catie. Whoop, we did it again. I think you're an honorary Posse member. We're going to teach you how to shoot. I'm so glad we found each other. Friends for life.

Notar. Bless you and your splicing skills. You're the last person that touches this material before it gets sent into the world. Thank you for taking care of me.

Shake Shake. I'm gonna get the band back together. Because I'm running out of songs. And I believe in you. Thanks for the loan. And the flavor.

When God-Fearing Women Put On Boots

The MisAdventures of Miss Lilly

Volume Four

Chapter One

I didn't even know my last name.

The sun was excruciatingly bright against the painfully white ruched comforter. I squinted one eye and pushed back a stiff chunk of hair, an eternal curl that had been sprayed into submission the night before. My hand came away with a thick navy blue smudge. My extra-strength, guaranteed to stay, gel manicure was chipped, the ring finger on my right hand completely missing any polish on the nail. My head throbbed; my feet ached, and my own perfume was making me gag.

Just then, Spencer Locke walked across the room, shirtless; a pair of low slung, dark jeans hung on his hips, just below the indentions in his strong, swimming back. The jeans had a crease to make any cowboy proud. He propped himself against the doorway, easily crossing one foot over the other. I took a second to admire it all. The way his muscles rippled, carelessly, like he'd been born that way, and maintained the body just by being. No ripped, rough, 'roided look for this guy. His dark hair was pushed back from his face, still wet from an apparent shower, but it might as well have been styled by a Hollywood artist. There was a faint, reddish scruff on his cut-glass jaw, a slight sunburn on his strong, sharp nose, and an almost imperceptible bruise ringing his left eye. The bruise brought out the flecks of grey-blue in Spencer's otherwise milk chocolate eyes. I frowned at the bruise. Spencer was tall, dark, and handsome. He was Hollywood's version of a dreamboat, all packaged up with a big red bow. And now, he was barefoot, shirtless, and smiling at me like he actually might *like* me. Which was new.

I looked around the room quickly. It began to spin, so I laid my head back on the pillow and covered my eyes with my left hand, something solid knocking me in the nose. I sat back up, the events of the earlier evening coming back in snatches. Raining glitter, flowers, and sparkle lotion. I rubbed my arm, a glittery, gluey mess coming off on my palm. Flashes flitted through my mind. I ignored the throb of my temples and the burn in my stomach. I took a good long look at the best man I'd ever kissed.

"Are we married?" I asked him, looking down at my left hand. A snort filled the room. Spencer rubbed his chest and smiled.

"I'm offended you even have to ask," he told me with a casual sip of his mug, his eyes narrowing darkly and his nose wrinkling sexily. I lay back down. I knew my mama was gonna be so ashamed. But it seemed as though everything was going right in my world.

Finally.

Just then, a mass of dark auburn curls popped up out of the bed beside me. She struggled to open her bleary, true-blue eyes.

"Where the hell am I and just who the hell are you," she asked, somewhat facetiously. I didn't answer, my eyes having difficulty straying from Spencer's amused form. He wasn't prone to amusement, so this start to a morning was becoming more and more interesting.

Tally finally raised her hand to swipe her hair back, clumsily bringing mine with it, because, I finally noticed, that we were shackled together with a pair of handcuffs. We both struggled to focus. I turned back to Spencer,

"So," I said, hesitant for the answer, "We're *not* married?"

His chuckle was oh-so-sexy, and so out of place. Spencer was serious and most unchuckling. He smiled a slow, dangerous smile.

"I'll get you some coffee."

xxx

Six weeks earlier…

"Vegas. Duh." Char twirled a long, dark strand of hair around her gunmetal-tipped finger and inspected it for split ends. Jacque's face lit up and she nodded enthusiastically.

"Yeah, Vegas!" Jacque's grey eyes flashed conspiratorially. Brandy looked nervous, her plump bottom lip caught by her top teeth, the pink lipstick half-eaten. She replaced the lip with her thumbnail.

"I don't know, y'all," Brandy said slowly. "Maybe we should just do something low-key," she suggested. Jacque and Char regarded her with fond disdain.

"This isn't really about you," Char informed her. I laughed.

"It's her bachelorette party," I admonished. Char flitted her fingers.

"Details. The party's about us. The wedding can be about her," Char told me. I rolled my eyes.

"I'm pretty sure the wedding is about my mama," Brandy said with a resigned tone to her voice. I looked at her in sympathy.

"Word," I said, offering her a fist to bump.

Need more?

Want more?

Sign up to be a member of The Posse at www.kalanchapmanlloyd.com and receive BLAME IT ALL ON MY BOOTS, an exclusive reader novella, for free.

Blame It All On My Boots

All's fair in love and cowgirl boots…

Young Love. New Flames. Sweet Revenge.

When good girl Lilly Atkins meets bad boy Cash Stetson, everyone thinks they need a divine intervention.

Sophomore Lilly is intrigued when everyone's favorite player, Cash Stetson, has her in his sights. Everyone's telling her to turn and run, but when she glimpses something good underneath that dangerous charm, she just can't help herself.
Will he make a good girl go bad?

Senior Cash's reputation is state-wide, and not for his wide receiver skills. But something about little Miss Lilly Atkins and all her sweetness make him want to stake a claim.
Everyone knows that bad boys never go good.

Will Lilly and Cash stay hotter than a two dollar pistol? Or will they go down in flames?

About the Author

Kalan Chapman Lloyd is an attorney and author currently residing in Tulsa, Oklahoma. She enjoys big hair, Supreme Court Decisions on Intellectual Property, hats, the sound of construction and the feel of brand new sweatshirts. Kalan grew up in the small town Tahlequah, OK where she graduated from Tahlequah Senior High School. She attended Oklahoma State University and the University of Tulsa College of Law and has been a member of the Oklahoma Bar since 2008. She is a Junior League dropout.

Connect with Kalan on Facebook, Instagram and Twitter; or at www.kalanchapmanlloyd.com

Other books by

Kalan Chapman Lloyd

Volume One: Home Is Where Your Boots Are
Volume Two: These Boots Are Made for Butt-Kickin'
The Prologues: Blame It All On My Boots (exclusive reader novella)

Mo(u)rning Joy: a memoir

Made in the USA
Middletown, DE
30 September 2016